Donald Macdonald Kingsbury was born in San Francisco and now lives in Montreal where he teaches Mathematics at McGill University. He started writing in the 1950s and his first SF story was published by *Astounding Science Fiction* (now *Analog*). Two of his stories, *Shipwright* – which takes place in the same background universe as *Geta* – and *To Bring in the Steel*, have been collected in best-of-the-year anthologies, and *The Moon Goddess and the Son* was nominated for the Hugo Award for the best novella of 1979. Mr Kingsbury is working on a novel-length version of it, and also plans to write other novels set in the same universe as *Geta*.

DONALD KINGSBURY

Geta

PANTHER
Granada Publishing

Panther Books
Granada Publishing Ltd
8 Grafton Street, London W1X 3LA

Published by Panther Books 1984

A Panther UK Original
Published in the USA under the title *Courtship Rite*

Copyright © Donald Kingsbury 1982

ISBN 0–586–05932–6

Printed and bound in Great Britain by
Collins, Glasgow

Set in Times

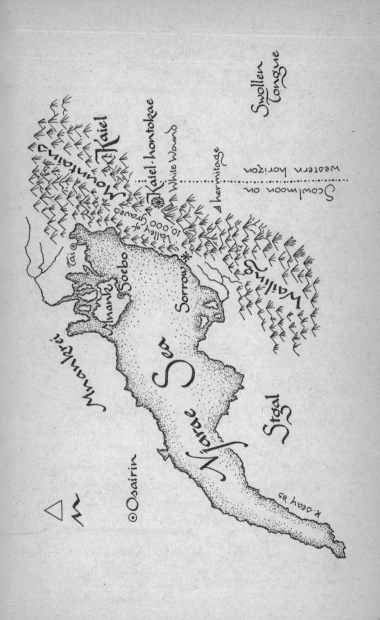

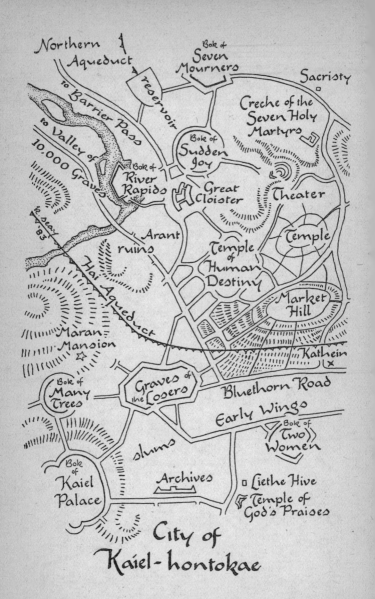

Northern Aqueduct

Bok of Seven Mourners

Sacristy

to Barrier Pass

to Valley of 10,000 Graves

reservoir

Creche of the Seven Holy Martyrs

Bok of Sudden Joy

Bok of River Rapids

Great Cloister

Theater

to Sorrel '83

Arant ruins

Hai Aqueduct

Temple

Temple of Human Destiny

Market Hill

Maran Mansion

Kathein

Bok of Many Trees

Graves of the Losers

Bluethorn Road

Early Wings

slums

Bok of Two Women

Bok of Kaiel Palace

Archives

Liethe Hive

Temple of God's Praises

City of
Kaiel-hontokae

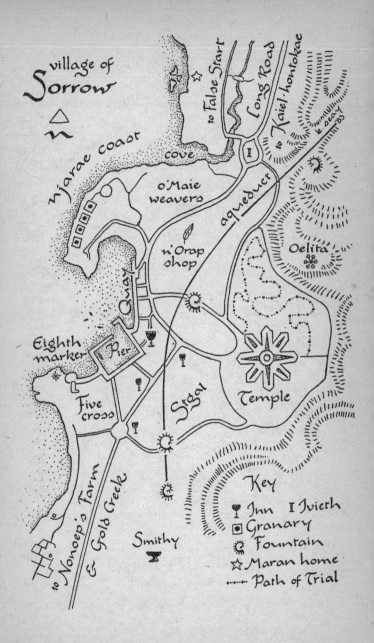

village of
Sorrow

▵
ᒍ

to False Start

Long Road

to Kaiel-hontokae

k. seay '83

n'jarae coast

cove

o'Maie
weavers

aqueduct

I

n'Orap
shop

Oelita

Quay

Eighth
marker

Pier

Srgal

Temple

Five
cross

to Nonoep's Farm

& Gold Creek

Smithy

Key

🍷 Inn   I Ivieth
◉ Granary
⚙ Fountain
☆ Maran home
---- Path of Trial

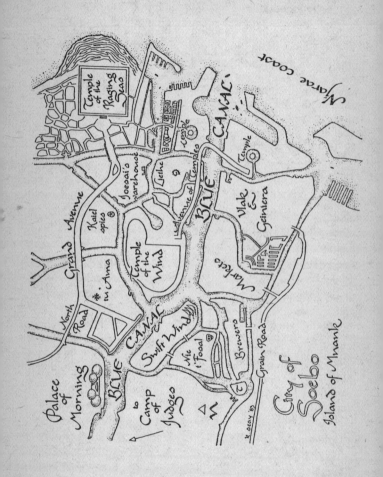

Temple of the Raging Sea

Temple

Joecoti's warehouse

Sethe

Avenue of Temples

Temple

Grand Avenue

Katel opici

Wak & Geiniera

tu Ama

Temple of the Wind

Market

North Road

BLUE CANAL

BLUE CANAL

BLUE CANAL

Swift Wind

Vic t' Tooal

Brewers

Grain Road

Palace of Morning

to Camp of Judges

Marae coast

City of Soebo
Island of Mhanh

1

In the deserts of the Swollen Tongue below the Wailing Mountains there lives an insect species which organizes other insects by mimicking their olfactory communication systems. The sense and control organs of the eight-legged kaiel are contained in an intricate design on their backs called hontokae. Priests of the human clan named Kaiel carve a stylized version of the hontokae into their skins so all will know they intend to command all.

Harar ram-Ivieth from his *Following God*

Prime Predictor Tae ran-Kaiel was long dead but he lived in the bellies of his aggressive progeny. Even the youngest of them had shared his flesh at a Funeral Feast still remembered in clan chant around the rowdy gaming tables of the Kaiel temples.

An old man, Tae had been skinned and then marinated and stuffed with insect-flavoured bread before his body was spit-roasted. In the evening of the first high day of the week called Skull in the years of the Mantis, when the coals of the spit fire were as dull as Getasun caught by a sandstorm, he was carved to the monotonous voice of chanting and served in a spiced sauce that had been salted by a spoonful of blood from each of his eighty-three sons and seventy daughters. All night long, the mourning Kaiel had pledged their loyalty in song and in speech and gift-giving and even, at the height of the celebration, with wry jokes about the toughness of his flesh.

The three brothers, Gaet, Hoemei, and Joesai had been among the sons of Tae ran-Kaiel who celebrated his Funeral. Boys then, wild comrades, they had felt more than camaraderie around the dull glow of the spit fire as the chanter, naked in the etched designs of his skin, carved up their father and sang the song of the Silent God of the Sky who waited for men strong enough to unify Geta.

That night they had been moved to take the vow of husbands, though they were only boys and knew no women they could share as wives. The drunken crowds, the drifting smoke mixed with incense, the emerging skeleton of the Prime Predictor fevered their souls. The three vowed to be husbands in a team that would bring honour to the Kaiel by carrying out the wishes of their father.

Since the Getan ideal was a balanced team, they decided that Hoemei should partake of his brains, Gaet should partake of his heart, and Joesai of his thighs. Thus they sealed their marriage as God passed overhead in the purpled sky.

'As God is my witness,' said Gaet, making the sign of loyalty.

'As God is my witness,' said Hoemei, his eyes on the moving God.

'As God is my witness,' said Joesai, watching their star-bright God pass among the stars.

A group of priests ambled through the crowd extolling Tae's virtues in pithy shouts, throwing their arms to the sky for emphasis. Was not Tae the greatest leader of the Kaiel? Had he not earned for his genes the right to host in many bodies? Who had more kalothi than Tae ran-Kaiel!

'They are drunk,' said Hoemei, fascinated.

'Do you think we could get a crack at the whisky barrel?' mused Gaet. Men's vows were oiled by drink.

'It is forbidden,' said Hoemei, reminding them that they were children.

'Wait till Aesoe makes his acceptance speech.' Joesai was grinning.

10

Some called Aesoe 'the Shadow' because of his continuous proximity to Tae. Now he was sitting on a whisky barrel, laughing with friends. He would be the new Prime Predictor, not because he was Tae's favourite, but because the predictions he had left in the Archives had proved more accurate than those of any other Kaiel.

Aesoe moved onto the stage. Even in those days he had loved to grip his audience with his booming oratory and waving arms. Joesai watched him, sometimes listening, sometimes sneaking towards the barrel.

'Since the epoch when God chose His Silence, priests have been isolating themselves from their people, and having lost contact, have been decimated when the underclans rebelled. New priest clans are legislated and are themselves overthrown. It was Tae who first analysed the true nature of this falling.'

Joesai stole an empty mug from a rapt listener who stood smiling at the thousandth retelling of the reason Tae had laid down his law of Voting Weight. Their new clan leader waited serenely, savouring the hush his words created before breaking it. 'Tae has decreed the rules by which we live and by which we have become strong.' He paused. 'Are we strong?'

'All power to the Kaiel!' the crowd roared in the deep voices of men and the higher voices of women and the enthusiastic voices of children.

Joesai sipped the last drop of whisky in the mug, then pretended he was paying attention to the stage. Aesoe blazed now like Getasun in storm. 'One: a Kaiel is to be allowed voting rights in the councils only in proportion to the size of his personal constituency.'

'All power to the Kaiel!' roared the massed clan in ritual.

'Two: the constituency of any Kaiel may consist only of loyal friends.'

'All power to the Kaiel!' Joesai was near the whisky

11

now, and planning his tactics. Stealing in a crowd, even when it was dark, required thought.

'Three: no Kaiel may belong to the constituency of another Kaiel.'

'All power to the Kaiel!' If he could nudge it, the spigot would drip.

'Four: no non-Kaiel may belong to more than one constituency.'

'All power to the Kaiel!'

'Five: no one shall be forced into a constituency by either fear or place of domicile.'

'All power to the Kaiel!' The mug was on the ground, filling up drip by drip. Joesai stood nearby, innocently.

'Six: the councils may challenge any Kaiel at any time to recite the names of the pledge members of his constituency and to describe in detail the concerns of each. Any person he cannot remember is stricken from his list.'

'All power to the Kaiel!'

Aesoe gestured a pause. In one bound he was off the stage and whacking Joesai viciously across the mouth. He tipped over the mug, and shut off the dripping spigot. Then he climbed back to the stage, grinning while the commotion died down. He paused for half a dozen heartbeats.

'Seven: a Kaiel who can summon no friends remains voteless and is required to remain childless or leave the clan.'

His audience was back in the mood, Joesai forgotten. 'All power to the Kaiel!'

'Your mouth is bleeding,' whispered Gaet.

'It is the soup pot for you,' whispered a frightened Hoemei.

Joesai just smiled with blood-stained teeth and produced a small wooden flask, half filled.

Gaet sniffed the heavy alcoholic fumes and shoved the flask under his coat.

'You stole it?' worried Hoemei.

'Couldn't resist,' grinned Joesai. 'The flask was just sitting there.'

Gaet tried to convince one of his sisters to take the first swig. She only smiled at him as if he were brave and foolish. After more joking the three brothers slipped away to the bushes and emptied the flask, spending the rest of the evening pretending they were sober.

That mischievous night had been long ago. They had left the creche, they had married twice more, they had made money and achieved a small fame. Though less brilliant than Hoemei who was favoured by the high councils, and less terrible than Joesai who was favoured by the Order of Hontokae, Gaet became the most powerful of the brothers in the lower councils with a voting weight of forty-three. He was the most suave, the most travelled, the subtle charmer of ladies; he smiled more than his mates and instantly befriended any human who served him. Now, fresh from an encounter with the aging Aesoe, Gaet felt surly, a scowl deepening the scars of his decorated face.

The stone mansion, bought by the three brothers with their first fortune, was on the slope of a hill overlooking the sacred catacombs that were called the Graves of the Losers. Beyond that, still only half built, the Kaiel Palace lay against the sky, a group of pink ovoids plumper than they were tall, as if stream-smoothed pebbles had been balanced on and around each other. The Palace glowed like molten iron at dawn while the huge furnace-coloured disc of Getasun rose to the east of it. To the left, larger even than the ovoids of the Palace, was the never-moving Scowlmoon, tangent to the mountainous horizon, full in its dark morning redness.

Gaet ignored it all, ignored his neighbours' villas. Furious, he even neglected to say hello to a passing Ivieth porter. He pushed through his gate, strode across the courtyard of his home, around the fountain pool, while his suprised two-wife Teenae scampered to follow him.

'Troubles on your soul! Give me troubles!'

'Where's Hoemei?'

'At the Palace. Joesai is home.'

'And one-wife?'

'Noe sleeps. What is it?'

'Aesoe has forbidden us to marry Kathein.'

Teenae stopped in shock, then turned away. 'I will wake and bring Noe!' She bypassed the stairs and leaped for a pole which extended from the courtyard wall, flipping herself up over the railing out of sight.

Gaet seated himself by the pool, having foreknowledge that one-wife would make him wait. Noe was not a woman to be hurried. He thought blackly of the orders Aesoe had given him, which were in direct conflict with his own plans. Images of a marriage feast passed before his eyes, the Call of the Bonds, the giving of the Five Gifts.

It did not suit him to relinquish Kathein in favour of a woman he did not know. It did not suit him, this idea of setting up residence along the coast. It did not suit him to leave the ever-fascinating struggles of the city of Kaiel-hontokae while he was still forging his family's Place.

Should he obey Aesoe and go to the coast to meet this heretical stranger and charm her and bring her home merely to gain the favour of Aesoe's Expansionists? Or should he send Joesai to kill her?

2

The God of the Sky gave us a harsh land because we are a rebellious Race. We wandered across the Swollen Tongue and He watched us. Ten Thousand died in the snow of the Wailing Mountains and He did not speak to us. We planted our crops by the Njarae Sea and He ignored us. West and east and south and north, deep were the graves carved into the merciless stone. Here are their names: the Graves of Grief, and the Graves of the Wailing Mountains, and the Graves of the Blind Eye, and the Graves of the Losers.

It is chanted that a Saviour will be born of she who spills her blood deep in the Graves of the Losers. We have founded Our City upon that hallowed catacomb. All power to the Kaiel! The city of Kaiel-hontokae shall give birth to the Saviour Who Speaks to God.

Prime Predictor Njai ben-Kaiel from her *Third Speech*

Hoemei Maran-Kaiel walked across the flagstones that led to the first huge ovoid of the Palace. He stopped to chat with Seipe, an old woman he often dealt with because he was spending large amounts of money and she was Watchman of the Coin and never believed in spending more than the Kaiel could collect in taxes. Even Aesoe could not shake her.

'I did not give you permission to put the rayvoice tower on Terrible Hill,' she chided.

Hoemei grinned. 'I put my own money into it and I'm charging toll.'

'I'll have to find a way to tax you.'

'I'm making sure that the tower has no profit. It has expenses,' he laughed.

She changed the subject to do business that would save her a runner. 'You are invited to my villa on the fourth high day of the Amorists' Constellation. Bring Teenae.'

'Teenae will be pleased,' said Hoemei affectionately.

'I know; that's why I want her there to help me. She's younger and quicker than I am. We will gossip while you haggle with your competitors.'

'Is someone after my share of the tax money again?'

'Your money? It's *my* money!' said Seipe with a great laugh, using the private possessive form as if the clan's coin were part of her own bones.

They held hands, each overlaid upon the other, as Getan friends did before they parted. 'God sees you,' he said.

His careful humouring of the Watchman done, Hoemei returned his feet to the flagstones and his thoughts to Aesoe. Aesoe was getting greedy. The power that the Prime Predictor smelled in the growing rayvoice network was as whisky to the nose of a drunkard. *How he drives us with his visions! He'll have more work for me.*

Hoemei wandered into the Palace maze within the main ovoid, distracted for a moment by the uncommon electric glow that still amazed even he who knew its magic and knew how it was fabricated in the basement workshops of Kaiel-hontokae. Aesoe saw an electrified Geta. That was foolishness. There was no end to the things Aesoe saw. These wild visions were afflicting even Hoemei's dreams.

'He's waiting for you,' said a friend who was passing.

Hoemei stopped him. 'What's his mood?'

'I think he just found a way into Seipe's vaults. Or else the woman of his dreams materialized from the steam of his morning tea.'

'He's in good spirits then?'

'A tug on his hair would lift off his head at the smile line.'

'Ah, then I'm not up for skinning.' That was a relief.

He paused at the entrance to Aesoe's lair, removing his shoes. When Aesoe did not notice him at the high doorway, he walked forward and seated himself upon the pillows, then looked straight at the Prime Predictor, waiting. Nothing would have induced Hoemei to interrupt the overpriest of the Kaiel clan. Old Aesoe sipped a drink, speaking to his scribe and to his personal o'Tghalie mathematician. He sipped again, brought out a map and put away some papers.

'I have already spoken to your brother Gaet.'

'One-brother has not yet seen me, sire.'

Aesoe shrugged. 'You know your family has been given the Valley of Ten Thousand Graves down to the sea.'

'Being the central route to the sea through the Wailing Mountains it will add to our wealth, but also to our burdens. Many have refused this gift.'

'. . . and will not rise to power within the Kaiel.'

'Which is why we accepted the gift, though it is not the Kaiel's land to give.'

Aesoe snorted at such pious morality. 'Do you know why this valley exists as an unconquered sliver in our side?'

'All Kaiel who settle there are murdered.'

'Have you speculated upon the nature of the murderers?'

'I deal in facts,' said Hoemei.

'Ah, but we who make policy can lose the game if we wait for facts. Speculate!'

'My guess would be the Mnankrei.'

'Why not the Stgal? The Stgal would have more to lose. It is their land.'

'The Stgal are cowards. They fear us. The Mnankrei covet the lands of the Stgal as we do. These sea priests have been known to advocate violence and their Storm Masters range up and down the Njarae unhindered in their billowing ships.'

17

Aesoe cleared his throat. 'Our spies tell us that a village called Sorrow was the scene of the murders.' He pointed out Sorrow on the map, a small harbour of the Njarae Sea. 'The Stgal have a great temple there. It is also a centre of heresy. Heretics, recruited from dozens of the underclans, tolerate their Stgal, finding priestly weakness useful. The Stgal tolerate them because they oppose us and oppose the Mnankrei.'

'It must be a new heresy.'

'Very new. But its basis has been latent in the region for some time. Priestly weakness generates heresy.'

'The heretics were the murderers?'

'Who will ever know? Perhaps. My spies tell me they are fearless. But so are the Mnankrei. And I would not turn my back on a man who smiles at me as the Stgal do.'

'You are telling me that we must stab with a three-pronged fork: destroy the heretics, destroy the Mnankrei, and destroy the Stgal.'

'Not at all. Your father Tae, who was my personal teacher, was a man of great wisdom. We conquer by making friends, not by destroying. If you are feared, you must fear. You maran-Kaiel were chosen for this mission because Gaet has a certain way with people and he never makes an enemy. He forgets though. Out of sight, out of mind. You're the administrator, the one who remembers to provide continuity.'

'Gaet never makes an enemy because he doesn't have to. He uses Joesai for all of his dirty work.'

'True. The making of friends often requires an open smile and a covert hand.'

'So the treacherous Stgal teach us,' said Hoemei ironically. 'But how do you make friends with a heretic who rejects all your values?'

Aesoe sipped from his goblet and laughed the great laugh so enjoyed by the Getan population. 'Heretics are

18

never as different as they seem. They are like genetic mutants. A mutant shares most of your genes. A heretic shares most of your ideas. Most mutations manufacture the wrong proteins. Most heresies are false. But then – we Kaiel are heretics.' And he laughed again.

'And how do you make friends with the Mnankrei and the Stgal?'

'Is it necessary when it is the heretics who control the hearts of the people?'

Hoemei became pensive. 'You are instructing us to weave together the common goals of Kaiel and heretic as the way to take over the Valley of Ten Thousand Graves?'

Aesoe laughed. 'My instructions are much simpler. You are to marry their women. Your family, for instance, is missing a three-wife.'

'We court Kathein pnota-Kaiel,' said Hoemei warily.

'No longer. I have given the orders. I have the votes. You are to marry Oelita the Clanless One who has single-handedly created this heresy.'

'And *she* knows of this?' asked Hoemei, his voice delaying while his thoughts raced.

'Of course not.'

'We are to take a Kaiel-killing heretic to our pillows?'

'It is to be so.'

'I don't like it.'

Aesoe flared at this rebellion. 'I have thirty families such as yours to deal with this week. Your personal problems are petty. *I* see the whole. I do what I must do for the clan. Without the clan you are destroyed. Therefore you will do what you must do. Some other day I'll argue.'

Hoemei felt his love for Kathein like a stab of warm pain passing down his spine. He thought of a time once spent with her in the garden, her black hair in his lap, while he chattered as if she had suddenly drilled an

19

artesian well into his unconscious with her gentle questions. *Ah, how loss makes us feel our love.* He stared at Aesoe, careful not to speak; for tears would have been an improper response to this order.

3

The Gathering of Ache marched into the Wailing Mountains to meet the challenge of the Arant. The Arant heresy proclaimed that the Race was created by machines in the caves of the Wailing Mountains. Arrogantly they stated that the God of the Sky was merely an inner moon – but they died by Judgment Feast while the God of the Sky orbited over the land He had found for the Race. And the Gathering created the Kaiel to guard the Wailing Mountains from falsehood.

The Clei scribe Saneef in *Memories of a Gathering*

Noe, one-wife of Gaet and Hoemei and Joesai, came out on the stone balcony of the inner courtyard only after dressing. She smiled down at Gaet. Teenae hurried up beside her, a full head shorter than her co-wife, to stare anxiously at Gaet with huge eyes that glowed beneath dark eyebrows.

Bathing his feet in the atrium's pool, Gaet looked up. Such beauty allowed him to dismiss his anger for a moment: Noe with her hair carefully braided into a helmet of excellence, Teenae with her hair shaved down the middle and flowing like liquid night upon her shoulders, Noe in a soft drape, her breasts scarred in a lazy honto-kae, Teenae in casual trousers stitched together out of hundreds of saloptera bellies and hung from a wide belt of the cured hide of her favourite grandfather, her breasts carved in the mathematical spirals that the o'Tghalie often sported.

Gaet was proud that *he* had found these worthy wives. He had even discovered Kathein, now to be denied them as three-wife. His brothers were shy with women, to their genes' disgrace.

Noe was a Kaiel – her mother the organizer of trading fleets on the Njarae Sea that tested the might of the Mnankrei, her father architect of the Kaiel Palace.

Teenae he had bought from the o'Tghalie clan when she was still breastless and pliable. He smiled. She had shown too great an interest in mathematical matters and the o'Tghalie men had rid themselves of her, for they brooked no competition from their women, a difficult convention when both sexes share the same genes. Teenae could do sums and products in her head as fast as you could give her numbers, though she had no training. She was a marvellous addition to their family councils – no one was better at uprooting the inconsistencies which crept into their group logic.

'Peace fights with your anger,' said Teenae, watching Gaet, 'and your anger laughs.' Her voice was gentle.

Gaet broke into a grin. 'How can my dark gloom survive the rising of Stgi and Toe?' The two brightest stars in the Getan sky belonged to the mythology of love and Gaet often used their names affectionately in reference to his two wives.

Joesai came to the balcony, towering beside his wives, his body scarred in intricate designs of unorthodox curve whose meaning lay outside of the conventional symbology. 'Ho. What is it?'

'Aesoe has denied us Kathein as three-wife!'

'Cause for anger! What compensation does Aesoe offer?'

'Little. He orders us to wed a coastal barbarian.'

'There are no Kaiel on the coast.'

'True.'

'What clan is she?'

'She is clanless.'

22

'Aesoe has gall! And why should her genes host in Kaiel bodies?'

'He vouches for her kalothi,' said Gaet.

'There are many ways of surviving! There are many kalothies! *Our* way of surviving is to organize. Answer my question: why should *her* genes be allowed to host in *Kaiel* bodies?' His body loomed above the railing.

'Aesoe is impressed because she has more than two hundred friends personally loyal to her.'

'Impossible!' snorted Joesai.

'. . . to one as ugly as you!'

Teenae smoothed the hand of her largest husband without looking at him. 'Is it true,' she asked of Gaet, 'that this barbarian commands loyalty so easily?'

'I have no reason to doubt Aesoe.'

'Then the order is logical,' said Teenae. 'The Council has deeded our family the Valley of Ten Thousand Graves all the way down to the Njarae Sea. But another clan jealous of the Kaiel rules there. A constituency of two hundred in that location would give us power. We cannot logically refuse this order.'

'You give up Kathein so easily?' prodded Noe.

Tears burst upon the smaller woman's cheeks and ran down along the ridges of her facial cicatrice. 'Not at all easily.' Teenae loved the Kathein she had never seen enough of. When a family was already five in number it was difficult to find a co-spouse who could love and be loved by them all. Some families never grew past five. Kathein could make Joesai laugh. She could make the taciturn Hoemei talk. She could dominate Gaet.

At first Teenae had been afraid of the powerful force that was Kathein and what she might do to the comfortable dynamics of their five. She had one of the greatest minds on all of Geta. And then one day Kathein had simply blocked out the brothers by piling furniture against the door and the three women had spent from noon to

23

noon together, hugging, talking about men, sharing secrets, and now Teenae's heart ached with longing when she thought of union with 'three-wife'.

'You're thinking,' said Joesai, returning the squeeze of her hand.

'I am thinking that the Kaiel have chosen the path of power and that the logic of power demands self-sacrifice.'

'Life does not always follow logical trails!' snapped Joesai. 'The bonds of loyalty take us *over* mountains, not around them!'

Teenae backed away a little from this fierce attack. She was the youngest and not yet sure that she belonged in this strange clan. She had been brought up to please men who built abstract models and who became upset if those models were found to conform to some reality. Now she was dealing with people who created reality.

'I love Kathein, too, but Aesoe has my respect as a man of formidable reason.'

'His path is not that logical, my little dark-eyed beetle,' said Gaet. 'This woman of the coast has many friends, true, but most of them are of low kalothi and will be eaten during the next famine. Some of them are noseless criminals and will be eaten *before* the next famine. She lives in our deeded land beside the Njarae, true, but that fact does not make her an asset – she is a fanatical heretic.'

'Aesoe knows this?' blurted Teenae.

'Yes, yes.'

'What is her heresy?' asked Joesai, intrigued.

'She's an atheist.'

'And what is the God of the Sky?'

'A moon like Scowlmoon, like the moons of Nika.'

'He doesn't look like a moon in my sky-eye. At a magnification of four He still looks like a brass button with a hint of filigree. Still, she's not far wrong. Is she aware that a moon can be God? What else does she believe? Did we come full blown out of machines in the Wailing

Mountains?' He winked. The brothers had been born from machines in the Wailing Mountains and those so brought to life spoke obliquely of their inhuman origin.

Gaet laughed. 'No. Worse than that. She proclaims we have insects for ancestors.'

'My God!' exclaimed Noe. 'She doesn't! She can't believe that!'

'Which insect?' asked Teenae.

'The maelot.'

'Logical. The maelot is the only four-legged insect with fleshy parts on the outside of its exoskeleton.'

'But a maelot is so small!' protested Noe.

'The largest insects are in the maelot class. The ones who have returned to the sea can be as large as your leg. Wrong amino acids, though. Wrong replication coding. Not logical. We are closer to the bee than to the maelot. We are even closer to wheat than to the maelot.'

'She has no place for God?' asked Joesai.

'None. She cites some impressive evidence for genetic drift and selective pressures, then supposes that the link between us and the maelot is missing because we evolved from a cannibal form of the maelot that ate its inferior offspring and so left no fossils.'

'Absurd biochemistry! Absurd history! We know the day and the sun-height of the day that the God of the Sky brought us here!' stormed the tallest brother.

'Not quite that precisely. Radioactive dating has its flaws.'

'I speak of the Chants. The Outpacing, verse 107, line 4.'

'Which version?' chided Gaet. He paused, ready to put the critical question to a vote. 'Who is in favour of continuing the courtship of Kathein?'

'I,' said Joesai.

The two women nodded.

'But can we disobey Aesoe?' asked Gaet, testing their

25

resolve. 'I suggest that I journey to the village called Sorrow and court Oelita.' He winked at Noe. 'I may bring back new ways of loving.'

Joesai grinned. 'You know too much already for the good of Hoemei and myself. I suggest that *I* slip into the village called Sorrow. I've been thinking that Aesoe cannot object if we court this coastal barbarian by Rite of Trial. She must earn her Place, and no Kaiel finds an easy Place.'

'He will not object to the Couth Rite.'

'I had in mind the Death Rite.'

'That would *not* please Aesoe. Premature death is a sacrilege if it does not take inferior genes with it.'

'If the Rite does not challenge her with Death how can it be a true test of her kalothi?'

'And if she lives? She may. Aesoe claims her kalothi is of the highest.'

'Ho! He hears that from the Stgal. Who takes seriously the kalothi rating of a village temple? *If* she lives, Gaet, she will be a worthy three-wife for us.'

'But could she love us after we have tried to kill her?' Gaet kept his game face, but his eyes betrayed mischief. 'Such mistrust might mar the harmony of our marriage.'

'That cannot be my problem. To survive she will have to kill me.'

'You will never be popular with women,' sighed Gaet.

'Some women love only the men they defeat.' Teenae's large eyes were sparkling. 'I love Joesai because I always beat him at kolgame.'

'Little larva!' He kissed the shaved streak across the top of her head. 'For that insult I'm taking you with me to the coast as my shield!'

'A shield you think I am! I would protect this Oelita against your zeal!'

'Ho. What is this? Already the heretic's kalothi shows itself to guard her? You both must host common barbarian genes. Good. Then with you by my side I will understand her!'

Teenae turned wildly to Gaet. 'He's not serious?'

'Yes. You must go with him. The Council has given us that land, but we must earn it, and neither you nor Joesai have yet mixed its dirt in the cuts of your feet.'

Noe grabbed her tallest husband by the biceps and forced him against the stone, lifting her face to speak to his. 'Even after Aesoe's *command*, you still think we will marry Kathein?' She was disturbed.

'Of course we'll marry Kathein!' snarled Joesai.

4

If Death is in front of you, he appears to be behind. A man who runs from Death, runs into the arms of Death. A man who faces Death turns his back on Death, and standing there, proud of his courage, is taken from the rear.

The nas-Veda Who Sits on Bees, Judge of Judges

Joesai's bulk overwhelmed the small stool in the archives of the Temple of Human Destiny while he copied out of the Kaiel Book of Death in the tiny, precise script of a man who has been a genetic surgeon since the time he learned to write. Reddish sunlight diffused from the curved mirrors around the window cut into the stone. At dusk he continued to work while the shadows deepened, but finally closed the books, unwilling to pen by glow-lamp. Evening found him wandering through the city, memorizing what he had copied, fleshing out the dryly recorded rituals with mental images of planned action.

Since Aesoe had disrupted their lives, orange Getasun had dawned fourteen times to the east of Kaiel-hontokae, marking seven high days and seven low days, waking them from seven sleeps. The Constellation of the Amorists had given way to the Constellation of the Ogre and Joesai's work was nearly done. He needed only one more boy to complete the team he was to take against the heretic – a mature boy, eager to please, a Kaiel, a brave and cunning youth, a boy who was not in a hurry, one who could play games with his opponents. Joesai already had his quota of girls.

At the Creche of the Seven Holy Martyrs he ate supper

28

from the Master's table above the machine-born children, watching them. They were used to him. He taught here and they thought nothing of his presence while they joked and reached for the steaming food, but he was weighing them against his needs, deciding which one he would reward with life by removing him from the creche as he had been taken as a youth. Only one in four survived the creche-culling and Joesai knew he was selecting an apprentice who, by being selected, would become one of the survivors.

The review narrowed down to Eiemeni. Yes. That shadow was fast and loyal and deadly. Joesai had heard it told that once Eiemeni had delivered a friend of his to death without tears. Joesai rose. 'Eiemeni!' he commanded, stilling the other youths. Eiemeni stood. 'Come forth.' Joesai had the table cleared and stood Eiemeni upon it, giving him a wooden bit for his mouth while he took out tools and carved an engimatic design upon the stoic's foreleg. In the morning Joesai brought the limping Eiemeni to the training camp outside Kaiel-hontokae and gave him to the group trainer, Raimin, to be integrated into the team. Another few days and they would move out.

Joesai spent the rest of the morning in the city working with miniature hammer at the table of goldsmith y'Faier. At Noe's suggestion her husband was to assume the guise of a wandering goldsmith, the kind of person who was liable to derive from mixed stock. No one would recognize him as Kaiel. He was a head taller than the ordinary member of his clan, as tall as the Ivieth who pulled the wagons, but too narrow to be of the Ivieth. His face was plain with a commonplace nose that fell straight from forehead to tip. His body decorations were of no recognizable pattern.

Teenae, it was decided, should not hide her identity. She could never pass for anything but o'Tghalie, but then, the o'Tghalie sold their women and it wouldn't be unusual for a goldsmith to have one as a follower. Certainly no one would suspect that she was Kaiel.

The family had temporarily split into two groups. Gaet and Hoemei tended to Teenae and slept with her. Noe spent these last low days with Joesai, impishly finding this an ideal time to teach manners to her 'cactus bush'. An unctuous goldsmith would know all the refinements of the coast. She taught him phrases until he rolled his eyes. She dressed him in robes, one of saffron yellow with embroidery that held metal and stones made by a tailor who was in her constituency, and she showed him how the girdle fastened and how to hold his skirts as he ascended stairs.

Laughing inside, because Noe liked nothing better than to tease an awkward man, she brought out one of her own coastal robes held together by complicated wrappings and gravely instructed him in how to undress her while at the same time praising her beauty.

'I'm a fighter,' he lamented, rebelling.

'But we are walking you to the coast to seduce a powerful woman, not to fight.' Noe nearly lost control of her face.

Later, on his knees, his mind rotted with sly flattery and his fingers sore from deft unwindings, he looked up imploringly and broke role for a moment. 'Goldsmiths do this?'

'Of course. They're very sensual. But much more gently and with far more conviction.' She slipped away from her husband. 'Here. I'll dress again and we'll start over.'

His imagination began to work on Joesai. One-wife stood against the window while the dusk sun, like a happy farmer unwilling to leave productive mountain fields, ploughed the textured furrows of her skin. Joesai saw the hontokae on her breasts sprouting profane tai berries, saw desert wheat springing from the whorls on her belly, and sacred corn from the fluted grooves along her legs. The

30

whole image was too powerful. In one passionate motion his hands surged to grasp her wrists so that he might kiss her, but though he pulled her body close, he could not find her dodging mouth or move her towards the pillows.

'No,' she laughed, 'not until you've learned your lesson!'

'How do they breed, those coastal barbarians, if they have to go through this to be loved!'

Passing by, Gaet heard the commotion, the outrage, the muffled kiss, the laughter, the struggle. Curiously he peered through the curtained doorway. 'Who needs help?'

Noe instantly accepted the alliance. 'Take this ruffian away.' But she managed her own escape. 'Do you think we'll ever make a goldsmith out of him? He never learns.'

'He learns when his life is on the line. His only skill is staying out of the stew pot.'

'I was doing some very acceptable filigree with y'Faier this morning,' grumbled Joesai. Y'Faier was a goldsmith of Hoemei's constituency, a man, Joesai claimed, who was suspiciously lacking in the legendary amorous talents, except, Noe teased, when he was alone with the ladies.

'Where is Teenae?' asked the dishevelled one-wife.

'With Hoemei.'

'Then you may stay with us tonight. You can teach him manners as well as I can, and I'm exhausted and need your tenderness.' She hugged Gaet with the kiss she had refused Joesai.

'God's Silence!' the big man roared. 'This manners business is madness, I should be out with Raimin training my men to run diversionary attack right now!'

Noe turned to him slowly. 'Down on your knees.'

Gaet was breaking into the great laugh. 'Down on your knees, boy!' He had an arm so gently around Noe's bare shoulders that his support felt like her own strength.

She slept between them that night, happy with her marriage, sad that Joesai would vanish for so long. She

31

held his hand while he slept. One day he would not come back to her. He would be dead – not like Gaet who never gambled with danger even in the temple games.

At the dawn of this, the third high day of Ogre, Joesai rose with dream-created plans in which he had cleverly resolved outstanding problems. Good. He kissed the sleeping Noe with a self-conscious tenderness and then kissed his old comrade of the deadly creche, but not so tenderly. Cheating Fate the Gaet, Sanan had called him; Sanan their brother who had not been able to cheat fate and who had gone to the dinner table and tanner. Joesai broke fast on corn bread and honey, solidifying his plans in his mind, then tip-toed into Hoemei's room where he whispered to a sleepy Teenae a list of provisions she would have to find that day while he gave his men their final briefing.

'Got that?'

'Ummm.' She rolled over and smiled, hugging the covers.

'Ho. You haven't got that. I'll write it down.'

'It's all right,' said Hoemei who seemed to be asleep but was awake. 'I'll remember for her.'

5

Should we doubt because God is silent? Feel the ground beneath your feet. There is the touch of God. He brought us here. Listen to the voice of a baby learning his first word. That is God speaking again the language He gave us. When we have stilled the cacophonous noise of doubt and quarrel, then we will hear Him speak.

Prime Predictor Njai ben-Kaiel from her *Eighth Speech*

The Constellation of the Ogre moved across the midnight zenith and was replaced by the Winner. Joesai sneaked himself through Kaiel-hontokae on the final day before the trek to the coast was to begin and, unannounced, appeared at Kathein's instrument shop. It was an old building of stone, converted from some purpose which had once required its own aqueduct. He had never been here before. The tedious craftsmanship of experimental fail-and-seek-again asked more patience of him than he was willing to give. The shop's primary purpose was to supply the priests with more and more accurate biological tools.

If you needed a device to promote cross-over in chromosomes you could have it built. If you wanted an organic machine to synthesize gene chains, someone would build it for you. If you wanted an implement to record from a neuron there were craftsmen who knew the fabrication ritual.

But, if you were like Joesai, and wanted a really large sky-eye for some theological investigation, forget it. Kathein had tried to fund the construction of a plate-sized lens for him but was refused the appropriation. She had wryly told her husband-to-be that she thought there was a fear in the Race of probing too deeply into the terrors of the World Above from whence God had rescued the Race. Joesai thought only that the obsession with biology was natural in an environment whose life forms would kill you whenever you failed to understand them.

'You shouldn't have come,' Kathein said when she found him in the arched doorway.

'The spittle of insects! You're quick with my child. I love you. In any event, I'm here! May Aesoe give his guests diarrhoea at his Feast of Ritual Suicide!'

She pulled him inside, obviously glad to see him. 'Getasun's flame will die before he finds himself at the bottom of the kalothi list!' Which was where she wanted him because only then would he be eligible for Ritual Suicide.

Joesai laughed at her venom. 'Don't be so sure. Someone will take his hide soon enough, may he roast slowly in an oven until he is too dry to eat!'

'We'll be caught here!'

'Ho! Find us a place where we can be alone!'

She hurried into one of the side rooms and closed the door. He found himself next to racks of bioluminous bulbs that cast an eerie pallor over bulky apparatus.

'It is for reading the crystal,' she said, touching the plastic casing of the Kaiel's most advanced instrument.

'You built it yourself?'

'Joesai! I built it with the help of thirty clans and all the gold of the Dry Bone Mine. I'm not even sure I know how it does what it does!'

'Was your hunch about the crystal right?'

'No,' she said sadly.

'It doesn't hold the frozen Voice of the God of the Sky?'

'Yes and no,' she said with puzzlement. 'Do you want to see some silvergraphs of His writings?'

34

'My nose in trade!'

She showed Joesai the single intact crystal, shaped like a small tile but transparent. When he reached out to touch it she pulled away. It looked like glass but it didn't refract like glass. The hand-size corroded machine which had originally read the crystals was nearby in its own protected case. An early Kaiel exploration had found it buried in the catacombs of the Graves of the Losers, holding this one crystal. For generations the discovery was a mystery known only to the Kaiel. Kathein was a student of the priest who had decoded the function of the machine.

To duplicate its function, Kathein's team had invented coherent light-beam generators and strange precision optical devices. She had made more advances in electron manipulation in the past 300 weeks than had been done since the electron was discovered. The resulting apparatus filled up half a room and sometimes even worked.

'You can't believe how hard it is to read from that crystal. There are about 4000 layers, alternately conducting and non-conducting. The conducting layers have elements in them that go opaque in the presence of electron flow. If the approach ritual doesn't please God He responds only with blackness but if our obsecrations are sufficiently servile only one layer is sensitized, There are 1600 pages to a layer. Even then different pages fade in and out and sometimes whole layers of pages overlay an area so that our vision is obscured. We can go for days without getting through to God and then suddenly a patch of forty pages will appear for long enough to be silver-graphed.'

'What do they say?'

Kathein showed him a silvergraph of a single page, one of the clearer ones. She lit an oil lamp to increase the room's brightness.

'The God of the Sky mutters,' he said, turning the page upside down and squinting at it.

'You can read it.'

'It's beetle talk. It looks like a beetle danced the maedi with ink on his feet – an eight legger.'

'No. You *can* read it.' She pointed with some excitement. 'That's the symbol for carbon and that's the symbol for hydrogen.'

'I'll be low listed! It's a genetic map. My God!'

'They're all plants, hundreds of them. *Sacred Plants*, Joesai. There's nothing there characteristic of the coding of profane biology.'

'My God!That means there are more than Eight Sacred Plants. What a strange thing for Him to tell us.'

'That's what I thought,' she said with deep puzzlement.

'Could He be telling us to make new Sacred Plants?'

'Joesai! We couldn't even make a wheat seed!'

'Maybe. We made my mother.'

'Your mother is half human, and the other half isn't there.'

'Don't you insult my mother. She has seventy-four artificial genes. How complicated can a wheat seed be?'

'God wouldn't ask us to do the impossible!'

'God could ask us to do anything. He could laugh at us. He could sulk for a hundred generations if it pleased Him.'

'Don't say that! If He hears you, I'll never get another picture out of that crystal!'

'Let me try talking with Him.'

'You won't get anything. I have to use all kinds of supplications to get the fineness that the reading requires.'

Kathein lit a small, quick-firing steam engine attached to a copper-wired wheel she called an electron pump. She waited for a short while until the steam pressure was up, and then waited again until the electron pressure stabilized. That done, she switched on and began to electrify one of the mysterious machines that was taller than Joesai. Banks of hand-made electron jars began to glow red from tiny internal filaments. 'We have to wait for them to soak up heat.' Then she inserted the crystal into the machine's mouth and made delicate adjustments with little wheels.

Time passed. The ritual reminded Joesai of a childhood toy called 'volcano' which required the player to roll five tiny balls up the slope of a miniature volcano, one at a time, holding each at the peak while the next climbed. Impossible but absorbing.

Finally they got one clear picture, another chain of genes. 'Are they all like that?'

'Yes.'

'I like your devotion to God, Kathein. It's an inspiration.'

She turned off the machine, and stopped the wheel of the electron pump, and doused the steam engine's fire. In the room, now quieter, she held him. 'What will we do? You inspire me, too, Joesai. When Gaet thinks big he thinks of the Valley of Ten Thousand Graves. When Hoemei thinks big he thinks of administering a united Geta. When you think big you want to face the God of the Sky.'

'Where do you think He came from?'

'A very dangerous place, if Geta is truly a refuge as the Chants say.'

He squeezed her. Then he ran a finger fondly but roughly along the lines of her facial cicatrice. 'You're the only person I can talk to about these things. I cherish you.'

'Oh you can talk to Teenae,' she said pushing him away, 'and you know it!'

'Only if I formulate my fantasies as mathematical problems.'

'That's good exercise for *your* mind!'

'And another reason I love you is because you make me laugh.'

37

'Did I tell you,' she added excitedly, 'that we just heard that a team of o'Tghalie from the north have completed a parallax measurement of the star Stgi and found it to be at least *one million* times as far away as the distance between Geta and Getasun! That's what you should be doing if they'd let you! Do you realize what that means? The universe could be so big that it would take a man's lifetime for light to cross from one end to the other. The God of the Sky could have come from anywhere!'

'We have to get to Him and talk to Him!'

'Can you express yourself in polynucleic acids?' Kathein laughed.

'You know about these things. How would we get to Him?'

'Energy, Joesai. More energy than you can possibly imagine.'

'We'll discuss it when I get back. I love you, Kathein. I'd murder to keep you.'

'Don't say that! Joesai! Be quiet! If you ever violate the Code once, *even once,* you'll be destroyed by the storm you will have created within yourself!'

'Ho! The Code was made by man. Different priest clans have different moralities. God stopped speaking to us to let us learn our own way.'

'Joesai, listen to me! I believe in tradition. It is there for a reason. It is the accumulation of more wisdom than one man can ever hope to master in one lifetime. I can't understand its purpose. You can't understand it. I have faith. Don't test it, Joesai! Please!'

'If this heretic has kalothi, she'll live. That's what kalothi means.'

'Fecal Fool! That is the justification for every sin that has ever been committed on Geta! You *know* that kalothi can be overwhelmed!'

He sighed. 'I promise you I'll be hard – but I'll break no rules.'

'Thank you.' She held him and cried. 'You're breaking one now by being here with me.'

'I'll go.' His face was wet.

'Be careful. Take care of Teenae. And watch out for that coastal witch!'

6

Men are the seeds from whom a new crop shall be grown. No
matter that the land is barren. No matter that the rains do not
come, or the irrigation ditches blow dust. No matter that famine
dries the skin to our bones. Men, like seed, are too precious to
be used as food.

Oelita the Gentle Heretic in *Sayings of a Rule Breaker*

The day was beautiful for herb-hunting. Getasun, as
usual, rose quickly through the sky, carrying its forge-
orange bulk out to sea where it would set beside the
stationary Scowlmoon before Oelita could reach home.
She kept to the ridges along the shore and whenever she
walked over a sandy crest, she stopped to drop her
packsack so that she could look down upon the sea she
loved. She saw a sleek Mnankrei trader blooming with
sails and a small fleet of local craft dredging for rope
fibres and iron-reed. Scowlmoon held steady two dia-
meters above the waves, half full, telling her that it was
noon.

The vegetation rose waist high, thick and spiny, taller
here than in the interior. She wore thick leggings to
protect herself from poisonous scatches. It was a striped
flower she hunted, good for stimulating babies who had
the sleeping sickness.

Her packsack was already bulging. Once across the
river bed, she planned to circle around to Nonoep's farm.
He was a renegade Stgal who lived alone, a marvellous
soul, and one of her favourite lovers. Having been trained
as a priest he knew a great deal of biochemistry and was

always willing to use his skill to extract from his boiling bottles any medicine she might need. Sometimes he gave her seeds for the farmers.

In return she would cook for him one of her special meals, or bake bread, and later enjoy love with him on his mat. He liked to hear her gossip about the village and he liked to argue with her about religion. He told her that she was the most sensual woman he knew. Whether his artful teasing was flattery or not, she enjoyed the soft warmth of the words.

Nonoep was a breeder of plants. He didn't breed varieties of the Sacred Eight but concentrated on wild plants. Many of the profane plants were known to yield edible fractions if they were crushed and dissolved and treated and filtered – but were often too expensive to treat. Nonoep grew different varieties and tested them for nourishment and poison content, and bred the varieties that were easiest to process.

When Getasun had floated three quarters of the way towards the sea's horizon Oelita came across a small hill farm hidden below a wind-sheltering ridge – Nolar clan for sure once she noticed how they cleared their land and built their hut. Spread below wasn't enough cultivated land for five, though there would be at least fifteen of them. She put down her packsack, securing it against children's fingers. The hut was tall – thick baked clay walls supporting a superstructure of woven rushes.

Oelita entered their home without being invited. The family was seated, pounding the stringy branches of a plant that provided fibres of cloth. She sat crosslegged with them and took a stone and began to pound her share of the fibres, emptying them into the vat for soaking. They stared at her shyly while she chatted.

The women were all pregnant and old of the poison. They lived barely long enough to reproduce themselves.

41

The family didn't clear enough land to raise an adequate crop of the Sacred Eight and insisted on eating too much of the palatable wild vegetation that surrounded their farm.

Oelita never tried to change these people's diet. Religion was too strong. They *knew* their diet killed them but the Nolar clan had an extraordinarily high kalothi rating only because of their high tolerance of the natural poisons of Geta. Without that they would be nothing – so they clung to the foods that killed them. All priest clans encouraged them and bought their women for breeding purposes. It disgusted Oelita.

In this region the Nolar clan had a peculiar social structure. They weren't content with normal group marriage. At puberty the children were either traded to another family or were ceremoniously married into their own family. *All* the male adults were co-husbands and *all* the female adults were co-wives. The eldest, and most poison-immune male, had first choice of the newly menstruating female. Inbreeding was thought to be desirable because it was quick to bring out lethal recessives. The children who died were eaten.

These Nolar chanted while they pounded, the old Chants of Knowledge as simple as a baby's mind. Oelita did not believe the myth that spoke of an Age of Innocence when only the children had kalothi – but certainly the oldest songs were childlike.

The Chants told how to clear the land and how to plant the Sacred Eight and how to breed for kalothi to keep the Race alive. Some were simply counting rituals. The most famous was a mnemonic that related the shapes of the alphabet's letters to their sounds. Some told of duty and honour. Some praised kalothi. The Outpacing Chant, so lengthy it was known in countless versions, told of the journey of the God of the Sky. Some Chants were as meaningless as the Chant to the Horse Piece of the chess game. Its monotonous inanity was good for pounding rocks against fibre.

'A Horse has feet, oh one, oh two, oh three, oh four; a Horse eats wheat, oh one, oh two, oh three, oh four; a Horse is meat, oh one, oh two, oh three, oh four; a Horse can snort, oh one, oh . . .'

Only after Oelita had smashed out enough fibre for a shirt and had made them laugh with her stories did she examine the children. Three out of four Nolar children died before puberty. One baby girl, who had forgotten how to walk from feebleness, was dying. Oelita tenderly breast fed the girl.

She kept her breasts full and productive. There was always a child to feed or a lover or a friend. It made her happy to be able to provide such a luxury. If she had no one to ease the ache she milked herself and made a delicate cheese.

Then she took a bag of medicinal food from her packsack and gave it to the mother with instructions for saving the life of the child. Someday she would come back to talk a disturbing form of religion.

One of the hovering children tugged on her arm. He had something special to show her. She had noticed how bright his eyes became whenever she spoke of the bugs her father collected. There out in the meagre wheat field the boy showed her some beetles, common underjaws, as if they were a great mystery.

'They're Horses?' he stated without conviction.

'Why would they be Horses?' she asked gently.

'They're eating wheat!'

Indeed they were. The underjaw was a very stupid beetle – being known on occasion to eat the wheat which killed it. She humoured the boy, remembering her own excitement at bringing common beetles to her father in the hope that somehow she might have found something unusual for his collection. But Oelita's trained eye nagged her. After a moment she realized what was wrong. Dozens of the underjaws were eating – and no dead beetles lay on the ground.

How peculiar.

She collected some to show Nonoep, rewarding the boy with a present, and thought no more of the matter. It was dawn again and she had to leave. She planned to make Nonoep's farm before low sunset so that her sleep would be in his arms, but suspected that she was too far. She walked and gathered, flooding her mind with ideas. When she rested she wrote up the resulting harvest of religious thoughts.

She had taught herself how to read and write – her father being illiterate, mostly because he was stubborn. But *he* had taught her how to think. He had been a brilliant man, devoted to the study of insects. His special fascination had been the eipa which spent its life in the sea and then metamorphosed into a form that flew inland where a variety of carnivorous plants ate it for its water and, in exchange, hàtchéd its eggs. The infants flew back to the sea and transformed into their sea shape. How he deduced these things was Oelita's introduction to logic.

Oelita had travelled far on foot with her father and knew the land from the sea to the desert. He had made the learning an adventure. She missed him. Strange that she was a vegetarian and spoke out fiercely against all forms of cannibalism but the moment the tower message came, recounting her father's death, she had driven herself mercilessly – running much of the way for three dawns and sleeping in the sling of a hired Ivieth the remainder – so that she could be at his Funeral Feast. She begrudged the others who ate of him, not knowing his strength and kindness and constant humour. She still carried dried and salted strips of his flesh that she only ate when she needed superhuman strength. She wore his hide as her best coat and it was his bone that was the handle of her knife.

44

Oelita wrote obsessively, never being without paper and ink. She often gave her disciples the task of copying what she had written as a form of burning her words into their minds. The Stgal she did not fear, but she was afraid that someday the Kaiel would come and put her on trial for heresy. She, being she, would not repent or recant. And they, being Kaiel, would eat her. Or if the Kaiel were slow to invade, might not the Mnankrei sea priests descend one week to seize the Priestdom of Stgal? They would cut her tongue out and chop off her hands.

She was afraid that her words would be forgotten. She wanted her letters and small books to be copied and sent everywhere so that it would never be possible for the priests to silence her by destroying them all. In her sleep-creepies she goaded people to copy faster. In her pleasant dreams she owned a printing press.

By sunset she hadn't reached Nonoep's farm and she was tired because she had been awake since two dawns past. She built a fire and heated soup and laid out her mat for sleep. The bloody sun died in Ritual Suicide, clotting to a deeper red as the stars, one by one, appeared, creating their celestial Temple. Sometimes she was lonely sleeping in the open at night. She missed being traditionally religious. Geta had such a rich mythology about the stars. She still wrote the old heroes into her stories.

Swiftly, the God of the Sky appeared and drifted overhead. In a trance she followed His flowing path until He dropped over the horizon. *Ah humans!* she sighed. When life was so harsh that a man lost all hope for himself, then he raised his eyes to a shining rock, worshipping it, just to find hope again, rather than looking to his own acts for hope and salvation.

7

To play kolgame is our sacred duty. How else can the Race remember to struggle for the total Union of Geta under the One Sky of God? How else can the Race remember that Union can only be achieved through relentless allegiance to the priest clans? How else can the Race remember that, to win, a man must break the rules, but that to break the rules is the worst risk a man can take?

From the Temple of Human Destiny's *Games Manual*

The oil lamp gasped to stay alive like an old bee buzzing its wings erratically along the ground. Teenae lay beside Joesai, watching him pass into sleep by this flicker. He looked so peacefully evil. So much she didn't know about him. He had been a professional provocateur, a veteran of many successful missions into non-Kaiel lands. Was it fair to launch him and fifteen of his chosen against one woman who had no warning of his coming?

Alien rocky slopes had been guiding them to the coast. She smiled her love for this man, feeling protected by his experience and by the agile massiveness of him. No desire to thwart him was in her breast but still, fresh with the warmth of his love in her loins, she began to formulate her own plans.

She was sure she was a better strategist, even given the handicap of no experience. Didn't she always beat him at kolgame? And not only could she beat Joesai, she could also beat Aesoe. What did those two know of human emotions? It should be possible to enlist the heretic woman as an ally without marrying her. Then Aesoe would have what he wanted and they could have Kathein, and nobody would have to die. Why couldn't non-mathematicians ever understand optimization?She kissed Joesai's nipple just the same.

Sleep did not come as she weighed plan against alternative plan. They were so close to Sorrow that she had little time. Eventually intense thinking made her sweaty and hungry and too nervous to lie still. She sneaked out of the tent, naked, to rummage through the supplies for hard-bread by the light of Scowlmoon, now nearly full because of the lateness of the night.

As they crawled down into the Valley of Ten Thousand Graves, the moon had been swallowed by the mountains, but had suddenly reappeared in the sky again, dominating it, higher than a Kaiel-hontokae. The river in front of them meandered to the coast, long ago eroding away all obstacles between here and the Njarae Sea.

Dull red moonglow shone on the shaved centreline of her skull, dyeing her cascading hair blacker than it really was, etching soft shadows into the carved designs that covered her body so that she seemed almost clothed while she stood there tearing the bread with her teeth. Fierce was her pleasure in the cold mountain breeze. The wind moaned the old song of the Wailing Mountains.

One of the Ivieth porters, as tall as Joesai but heavier and longer of leg, noticed her and rose from his pad. 'Is all well?'

Her teeth flashed. 'Hunger.'

'Soon we have warm starting broth. See, the eclipse has already begun.' He gestured at the moon. 'It is almost dawn. Go back to your man's flesh.'

She shrugged, smiling. The Ivieth were humble – except when they were being responsible for you on a journey. The roads they built and guarded were safe. 'I slept all last night in the palanquin.' That had been high

47

night when it was not the custom to sleep. '*You* return to your pad. *You* need the rest.'

'An Ivieth needs no rest.'

It was almost true. The Ivieth clan had been bred, by their own standards, to keep moving no matter what the barriers – mountains or heat or fatigue. It was not uncommon for an Ivieth to pull his wagon seven days and nights without sleep.

'A kolgame then, by the dark of the eclipse!' she challenged.

The rules of this game are known by every child, every clan. A kolgame begins with the creation of the board out of wooden pieces that fit together like a jig-saw puzzle with many solutions, the particular form being determined by the tossing of dice.

Then the territory is peopled by tenants and their Sacred Eight crops. The bees are distributed by chance and swarm when the crops are good. Each tenant belongs to a clan. The clan has its own moves and breeding ritual. Each move costs a vegetation piece which must be re-grown.

The game leads to frequent impasse conditions which can only be broken if a tenant violates the rules of his clan. To do so he loses kalothi. At the onset of each Culling Condition the tenant with the lowest kalothi is removed from the territory. A player must violate rules, but he must not do so often, and he must be careful about which rules he chooses to violate.

Strategically any clan may achieve domination over another clan or free itself from domination. A clan which is not the subject of control by any other clan is called a priest clan. The object of the game is to unite the board under the command of one priest clan.

Legend attributed the origin of kol to the need for an intelligence test to select those worthy enough to feed their brethren. In starvation times, where temple kalothi records were unavailable, kolgame tournaments were still held, losers donating their bodies for the survival of the others.

The dawn found Teenae crouched with her chin on one knee, in the shadow of the naked Ivieth, playing with such intensity that she scarcely noticed the waking of the camp, or the fires that heated the broth, or Joesai when he came up behind her, soaping the centreline of her scalp and shaving it so that she would be presentable for their entrance into Sorrow that day.

Teenae won. Yelping, she hugged the Ivieth warmly. If you wanted Teenae to hug you, you had to lose to her at kolgame. She was a sore loser. Joesai had her robes out and patiently dressed her, trying this and that for effect, aided by the good-hearted comments of the company. And so the expedition, which had been waiting, got under way.

The salty sea wind was breathtaking as it blew in from the ocean below the hills. She was awed. She had never seen the sea before. The village clustered small about one crooked inlet. Its magnificent temple seemed to be a she-magician who had shrunk the village spires and buildings into a doll city about herself. Teenae was pleased to ride into town beautifully robed in a decorated palanquin carried across the shoulders of a superbly muscled Ivieth couple, Joesai on foot beside her.

'Stay by me,' she whispered. She glanced around curiously for danger but found none, only seamen and merchants and Ivieth pulling wagons of farm produce.

The 'goldsmith' and his wife were elaborately welcomed at an inn overlooking the pier and provided rooms with a view of the village. The stone walls of their apartment were hung with old tapestries of men laughing at family Funeral Feasts. Once their belongings were hung away, the innkeeper personally bathed them in the scented waters of his public bath and insisted on serving them their

49

first meal in his kitchen. They ate well, for it was not a famine year – breads and brown sea rice and okra croquettes flavoured with profane spices. He brought them the most delicious honeyed bee crisps Teenae had ever tasted.

Fifteen of Joesai's band trickled in, one this day, two the next, some by land, some by sea, busying themselves learning about the village of Sorrow. A 'tailor' talked with tailors. A young 'Clei' woman took on writing contracts. A 'stone mason' asked after the new road work. A 'merchant' hurried through town looking for a house to rent. A 'sailor' gossiped among the import-export traders. The 'goldsmith' and his woman studied pencrafted copies of books by the Gentle Heretic, seeking contradictions in her reasoning by which she might be trapped. He sold gold and brought the gossip back to his wife.

Unobtrusive, but everywhere, was the Scar of the Heresy – a stem with its four wheat kernels each ending in a long fibre. A woman would have it tattooed between her breasts or it would be formed into the margin of a tailor's sign or be embroidered upon a tattered coat. Once Teenae saw a child carving it slowly into another child's arm, his lip tight in concentration. Its message was constant: do not eat those weaker than yourself, do not eat the malformed child, the noseless criminal, the cripple, the feeble minded, the wandering madman, the blind, the incompetent.

'It's always been that way,' Joesai grumbled. 'We're a generous people. We've always been willing to fatten the feeble minded – when the harvest is good.' He quoted a cynical proverb, 'A prosperous Getan will fill you with joy; in hard times, he will suck the joy from your marrow.'

'Why are we so harsh?' asked Teenae, moved by some of the things Oelita had written.

'It's a harsh world.'

'It's our duty to make it a less harsh world. We're *Kaiel*!'

'Yes, my little *o'Tghalie* imp!' He roared with laughter.

And then added as an afterthought, thinking of his childhood, 'Only the harsh survive.'

'This Oelita is not harsh. She is strong. She believes that teams working together can make harshness unnecessary through the power of cooperation.'

Joesai strode across the room to the tankard in dismissal. Ferment refilled his blown-glass cup. For a while he stared at the feasting mourners on the tapestry. A child, crouched in a corner, was gnawing the meat off his grandfather's ribs. A son had his hand on the buttocks of a red-cheeked young flirt. Two men in animated conversation were stuffing themselves with bread pie and sausage, discussing . . . philosophy? the price of bricks? Joesai peered through the liquid to the bottom of the green cup. 'God has gone to great lengths to tell us that there is *no* escape from harshness.' He turned to Teenae, almost savagely. 'Why did He bring us *here* if not to teach us that!'

'Maybe to teach us that no matter where we are, there is hope!'

'Hope. Ah, yes. Hope is the irresponsible heresy.'

'This woman will bring hope; even to you, Joesai.'

'Soon, then. My boy Eiemeni has found her.'

Teenae's breath froze. 'Is she dead?'

He laughed. 'Ho. The Death Rite does not start with death. And it does not always end with death. If it always ended with death, the Rite would be pointless.'

'What have you done to her?'

He shrugged. 'Nothing. We have not yet set the trap.'

8

Always expect the unexpected. But if you are sure that the sun will not rise because it has always risen, then expect the sun to rise. The day you have learned to trust your friend, expect betrayal without wavering from your trust. A wind waits beside every tent. Even your enemy may befriend you.

'I expected my son to love me,' said the father.

'I expected my crops to grow in this fertile ground,' said the farmer.

'I expected happiness,' said the puzzled maiden.

Look behind that bush for it is not a bush. Contradictions do not perplex the logician. They arise because there are more rules to an open game than can be known. Even God expected man to be good.

Dobu of the kembri, Arimasie ban-Itraiel in *Sight*

Oelita watched the glassblower. Lazily the glass flowed and grew on the end of his pipe. Suddenly he would attack it and pull or whack the slick mass to the shape he wanted. He peered into the blazing kiln and readjusted the band around his wet forehead. In three days he had nearly replenished Nonoep's store of glassware and was ready to move on.

She was pumping him for gossip about the local temples so while he worked he told her of the young boy who had been carried in an iron-reed basket to Remiss to have his nose cut off. He recounted the tribulations of the wives of one Mirandie who supplied the lead oxide for his clear glass. 'But the Stgal!' she insisted. 'You must have timely stories of the Stgal! You work for them!'

The man laughed as sweat rolled down the valleys of his

scars. 'The Stgal do not talk to glassblowers! They plot behind brass doors. Now if *I* heard a tale, it would be a lie put out to titillate the masses.'

'I would hear their lies then, knowing the truth by printing the lie in white ink on black paper!'

He shrugged at her analogy and countered with his own. 'Getasun seen through green glass is black.'

She mussed his hair affectionately. 'Give me just one of their lies! Please.'

He grinned. 'Yono has cuckolded her husbands by filling her bottle in the whisky cellar of Neimeri.'

'That's *her* lie,' sulked Oelita.

Mirth roared out of the glassblower. 'No. That's a *Stgal* lie. Yono's husbands have been refusing to pay their taxes and are now being slandered by Stgal Ropan who needs the money for a new wing of his temple.' The glassblower banked his kiln fire. 'Soon I'm off to Kaiel-hontokae. I'll bring you back better gossip!'

'Kaiel-hontokae is far!'

'So I dirty my feet. The better to learn new ways.'

'Come.' She took the man's bicep with both hands. 'You're finished here. I'll take you down for a bath!'

'I'm seduced by your gentle fingers but my enthusiasm is tempered by the knowledge that I will have to endure a long lecture on religion with the bath!'

'I'll clean behind the ears of your soul. They're filthy.'

At the pool, which Nonoep maintained above his fields for irrigation, they stripped on the dock beside the great treadwheel that lifted water by a climber's effort. They dunked their clothes, pounding them clean.

The glassblower dived into the pond and when he emerged Oelita pulled him up on the planks and began to soap him as she tried out new thoughts she was having on the important differences between human will and human strength. Finally he threw her off the dock to shut her up

53

and jumped in after her for the double purpose of rinsing himself and keeping her head underwater.

She escaped onto the treadwheel and they chased each other with frenzied futility, lifting great buckets of well water that splashed into the pool. With the help of two small boys, working at the Nonoep farm to earn coin for pilgrimage to Sorrow's Temple, she was laid out on the dock where they gently massaged and soaped her. The glassblower, still in a mood for revenge, delivered a merciless lecture on the art of optical glass making.

'So! I thought I heard merriment!' Nonoep had appeared through the brambles on the rise above his pond. 'I'm a proud father today. I have a wonder to show you, Oelita.'

'I'm all soapy!'

'Rinse her off.'

Oelita's companions grabbed her by the feet and arms and pitched her into the water. She emerged, spluttering. 'My clothes are wet. I can't come. I'm naked and I'll get scratched!'

'You can have my shoulders.'

'I'll get dirty again, you stinking old farmer!'

'It is our fate to get dirty again.'

The small woman rode high on the shoulders of her lonepriest lover over the rise, down into the east field. 'You'd make a great Ivieth,' she said, enjoying the jog.

'I may join them someday to see the world.'

'Where are you taking me?'

'Remember the first day we met?'

'How could I forget such an overpowering event? You were sitting on a barrel of wheat and dribbling honey from your bread into your beard while pontificating about the stubbornness of profane botany.'

'About hair-weed in particular.'

The nodules of the hair-weed were relatively free of the poisons – however, because of their smallness, were

54

hardly worth the pickings. To his frustration Nonoep had tried raising hair-weed with larger nodules and, in that grain store in Sorrow, had been complaining about his failures. Oelita then barged into the conversation with a detailed explanation of the symbiosis between hair-weed and certain insects. It had been a revelation to Nonoep, and he had courteously invited her to come and stay at his experimental farm whenever it pleased her and was rather surprised when she hung around and followed him on the long trek home and took him as one of her lovers that very sunset.

'That's my latest patch over there,' he said.

Gentle with her body, he set Oelita down beside some of his cultivated hair-weed, new in its vigorous growth. Stooping, he showed her the gorged nodules along the stem.

'Ah,' she said, her eyes bright. 'You found the right kind of burrowers!'

'No. That proved to be impossible. I *bred* them.'

'Your ways have changed since you met me!'

'Perhaps,' he said, lifting her up again to ride on his shoulders while he headed down toward the buildings, 'but I'm just as lecherous as ever.'

'And you're still willing to eat meat,' she reprimanded, pulling his ears.

'Have I had so much as a morsel since I met you?'

'There hasn't been a famine since you met me!'

He seemed to sag under more than her weight. 'There will be another one soon.'

'You can't be serious!' She tried peering over his head to see his face. 'The wheat crop is spectacular this year!'

'Have you forgotten the deviant underjaws you brought me? The first batch of eggs have hatched. They *do* eat wheat and aren't affected. I was amazed. The local underjaws that I collected die on the same diet.'

'Will the deviants multiply?'

'Yes.'

They reached the house. 'What can we do?'

He was puzzled by something that fitted nowhere in his priestly knowledge. 'An underjaw doesn't have the enzymes to digest wheat. I need advice. I'm going to send some eggs to Kaiel-hontokae with my glassblower.'

'You wouldn't!' Oelita beat on his head and jumped down. 'I don't want to deal with the Kaiel!' She was enraged at the mention of that name.

He laughed and followed her through the curtains. 'They are the best geneticists within walking distance. Or on Geta.'

'They breed babies to eat! You can buy meat in the markets at Kaiel-hontokae! *You* cope with the underjaws! *You* know genetics. *You* are Stgal!'

'I'm a farmer. The Kaiel are the magicians.'

Furious, she disappeared into their room and began packing. When he saw that she was going to leave, he argued. She fought back. In the middle of his careful defence, she left for the kitchen to assemble provisions. When she reappeared he was somewhat subdued and put his arm around her.

'Don't touch me!'

She dressed in leggings, swung the full packsack onto her back, and marched out towards the pool to pick up her wet clothes. Nonoep followed her, smoking in angry defence of himself like a huffing steam machine on wheels. She had assumed the tactic of not replying, so he alternately invented arguments for her and answered them. Unreached, she stuffed her wet clothes into the packsack and headed towards the northern trail that branched up to Sorrow. By now, sulking at her intransigence, he walked silently behind her.

On the edge of his land, Oelita turned. 'You insist on dealing with the Kaiel?'

'There is no other way!'

56

She wheeled and left him.

He watched her little figure disappear through the brush, loving her. *Damn fool woman!* he thought.

And she listened to hear if he was still following. When she was sure that he was not, tears came to her eyes and she stomped on at the quick pace of the agitated, flinging branches out of her way and ignoring the vegetable claws that tried to rip her boots and clothing.

Anger is quickly burned in active legs. By afternoon she was only thoughtful. Her frustration again flared briefly when, hungry and ready to eat, she remembered that she had left her packed food pouch sitting on Nonoep's kitchen table. Her stomach cursed her. No matter. There was no way she could recoup that loss. She resigned herself to scrounging for edible roots and building a fire to roast them. The effort took more time than her plans allowed and she was not ready to move again until the stars were out.

She endured an additional wait for the crescent of Scowlmoon to grow thick enough to illuminate the landscape. Then, thoroughly rested but still famished, she set an impulsive course towards Gold Creek. That meander would make an easy night journey to the sea from where she could work her way along the beaches to Sorrow. It was not her usual route and she was not quite sure where she was until she crossed the old gold camp. The sluice runs had created dozens of tailing fans of sand that had not yet succumbed to the crawl of life. She perked up her ears. Yes, she could hear the low rumble of the sea through the gorge.

The path narrowed. She listened to the gurgling call of a river maelot enticing his female and was caught for a brief moment in a swarm of gliding issen whose finger-long wings imprisoned the moonglow in their veins. The trail narrowed still more and disappeared in a landslide, so she edged down into the water and began to wade. The water was low and sluggish and offered her little resistance. There was no reason to look for a better path until she saw two rocks ahead transmogrify into shapes of men.

Travellers, she thought gratefully. *They'll lend me food.* But instinctively she peered back and around her for an escape route should that prove necessary – and found two other silent men moving in on her from behind.

9

If one man says whore and another hears hoar, of what use is it?
Speech, no matter how eloquent, is not communication. If one
man draws a star and another sees a cross, of what use is it?
Pictures, even if they contain colour, even if they move, are not
communication. If a man caresses a woman and the woman feels
the blade of a knife, of what use is it? Touch, no matter how
deeply felt, is not communication. For a communication to
happen, the construct in one mind must be duplicated by another
mind.

Foeti pno-Kaiel, creche teacher of the maran-Kaiel

Traditionally Getan messages were carried by travellers
and, if speed was essential, by Ivieth runners or by the
flags and lights of the towers. Over difficult terrain some
of the modern towers were connected by wire. But
fantastic change was upon the land.

Kaiel neurophysiologists, curious about the electric
field of the brain, had hit upon a trail that took them to
mechanically induced electromagnetic radiation. Effects
barely measurable by beetle-leg jerking first led to organized experiment and then to increasingly sophisticated
instrumentation. Suddenly the Kaiel leadership found
itself with the beginnings of a message network several
orders of magnitude swifter than the network of every
rival.

Hoemei was a member of the team assessing the most
rapid way to exploit what they all knew would be a temporary advantage. He spent days at the communications
command centre in the Palace among the shelves of coils
and electron jars puzzling over transcripts of rayvoice calls.

His main centre of interest was the Njarae coastline, listening for echoes of his brother.

Hoemei's electromagnetic eye took in the whole of the immense Njarae Sea. His agents were established at fourteen key points. Over the weeks as he attempted to shadow Joesai, using that problem to feel out the potential of this machine, he became increasingly fascinated by what he was seeing with his new toy. Joesai remained invisible – but the view!

He found himself watching game players who thought they were hidden. They had no reason to suspect that their huge board had been connected by spies in instant communication. *The Mnankrei were poising themselves for a lethal strike against the Stgal.* In his notes it all came together.

Even Aesoe would be hard-pressed to believe their boldness because such a plan broke too many rules. And Joesai: innocently Joesai had entered the focal centre of their game, unaware of the fury rising distantly at sea.

Hoemei stood at a circular window of the Kaiel Palace, his back to the electrons that leaped across hot wires through net to dock, his mind flickering with images of far places superimposed upon the images of his city. Kaiel-hontokae had been built on the ruins of the Arant to guard against the return of heresy but, instead, had been possessed by questions which led to newer heresies.

Truly the Palace has magic eyes, he thought. Would those eyes deliver the power to rule the world they saw? Before he descended from this high room he spoke to each member of his staff so that they all tasted his joy in their competence. Hoemei wandered home through the walled maze of the city, deep in his own mental maze.

Kaiel-hontokae had roving streets, paved in stone, which turned upon themselves or stopped abruptly in stairs or reached a dead-end at the gate of some wall-building. The wall-buildings were enormous three-storied structures that completely enclosed areas where commercial activity was taboo. Each such palisade had its own name. There was the Bok of the Fountain of Two Women, the Bok of the Kaiel Palace, the Bok of Seven Mourners, the Bok of Sudden Joy, the Bok of Many Trees, the Bok of the River Rapids.

His feet found a path home while his mind tested the passageways that power could open to a priest, leading him to light or to lightless labyrinths. These thoughts meandered along twists and turns until they returned to Noe where they were content to rest in comfort upon the shifting images created by his memories of an enigmatic woman.

I will need Noe's counsel, he thought. She knew the Mnankrei better than any other member of his family.

Hoemei had been enjoying his days alone with Noe in the stone mansion on the hill. Gaet was away. Joesai and Teenae were far away. Their absence gave him time to explore this woman whom he had never understood, who was never in a hurry to be understood, who alone of the women he knew relished power.

Noe possessed more useless skills than he had ever known existed – patter that pleased but meant nothing, sailplane gliding, flower arranging, rock reading, staig poetry, dream analysis. She had learned her sexuality as a temple courtesan honouring men who were preparing themselves for Ritual Suicide. She indulged herself outrageously in things like the body sculpture that had given her those delicate folds of skin along her ribcage which Joesai teasingly referred to as her 'handles'. There was no end to it.

When Gaet first brought her home to their bed, Hoemei had thought of Noe as a scatterbrain. But she had her own direction. If she indulged in luxury, she was also a master of such stoic arts as cross-desert hiking,

61

Was it style she craved? Her only consistency was style. Even hardship was raw material for her style.

He shook his head. There was a gulf between them. He was the disciplined product of the creches where a child demonstrated his abilities quickly or was sent to the abattoir. Hoemei had never been given a second chance nor had he needed one. Noe was a pampered child of riches.

How alien they remained. When he entered the courtyard of the mansion she was placing a bowl of profane flowers called blooded-teeth. An excited bee had found the bouquet. Lovers were said to forget all quarrels near this aroma. Hoemei was touched. The gesture could only have been meant for him. She smiled. 'My love.' And hurried on her way to the kitchen without kissing him.

He lingered near the flowers, fragile white petals with red rims, guarded by a stem of poisoned spikes. He sniffed, then followed Noe's scent, faintly grinning. She was like a flower, herself.

She fixed him an appetizer of baby-liver pâté on crunch bread. That was so like her. She always had delicacies around regardless of the expense. 'I discharged all of our due-debts today,' she chatted.

'You can slaughter a whole day that way.'

'But I arranged it so that I visited half my constituency while I did the money rounds,' she said smugly.

'What did they have to say?'

'The usual problems. We'll have to find a means to get more water up to the Kalkenie. And you?'

'How would you kill an underjaw beetle?'

She laughed. 'Step on it.'

'Millions of them. You know about such things. I don't.'

'Why?'

'I'm about to make a fateful prediction and some policy decisions to be registered and witnessed for the Kaiel

Archives. The outcome will drastically affect my kalothi rating one way or another. My unconceived children will live or die by this decision.'

She looked at him sharply. 'Gaet and Joesai and Teenae should be here!'

'No. The decision has to be made tonight. And you are the perfect person to advise me. You know the rituals of genetic modification.'

'Only what Joesai has taught me.'

'But you are good at it. And your mother ran trading fleets against the Mnankrei. You have a feel for those wind riders.'

'They dominate through trade.'

'Exactly.'

He took her by the wrist and pulled her into the study where he rolled out a map on the table, weighing down the corners with carved ancestral skulls from Noe's and Teenae's families. The largest of Geta's eleven landbound seas, the Njarae Sea, extended along a northeastern diagonal one-fourth of the way around Geta, fat to the north, narrow to the south like a poised club. Sorrow hugged the western shore formed by the Wailing Mountains. The Mnankrei islands lay to the north but the Mnankrei priests had generations ago spread from the islands to the northern plain. Hoemei moved his finger down from the Stgal mountain reaches, far south into the Stgal Plain, a distance covered by bad roads and controlled by six loosely confederated Stgal clans.

'There's famine here.'

'I heard it was a good crop.'

'It was. Plagues of underjaws are eating the wheat.'

'But they die when they attack the Sacred Food!'

'These don't.'

'Oh my God!' The idea was terrifying. It was a disorienting event, like God falling from His Sky. 'A mutation?' She couldn't imagine a mutation that drastic.

'No. I've had my men on it. We've been in constant contact via rayvoice. They haven't got the equipment they need but one of my women is of the creches and she's a brilliant microbiologist. You wouldn't believe the short-cuts and sidestepping she can do. The underjaws are manufacturing some human enzymes. And other such strangenesses.'

'They are carrying human genes?'

'Exactly.'

'Now *that* is a Violation of the Rules,' she said, awed by someone's audacity.

'Could it be done? That's what I want to know.'

Noe retreated into a deep scan of her knowledge. 'We made your mother.'

'Yes, but she's human in her way. I didn't think it was possible for sacred and profane cells to operate together.'

'I could think of ways. It would be difficult.'

'Then it is the Mnankrei who have unleashed this plague.'

'Not the Mnankrei I know.'

'Look. The rayvoice has given me an immense vista.' He swept his hand up the map. 'The port watchers are sending us data on every Mnankrei ship movement. Relief ships loaded with grain left the islands for Stgal Plain harbours *before the plague even started*. And now they are departing for the northern ports. A grain ship set sail for Sorrow even today. It is like carrying honey to a beehive. The harvest is due.'

She picked up the skull of her great-grandfather, carved in swastikas and leaves. 'What would you say, Pietri?' He said nothing. 'Pietri died in defiance of the Mnankrei, so goes the family story. It was a famine. The Mnankrei offered food in exchange for control. My great-grand-father offered his body at the Temple to keep the Mnank-rei away.' She smiled ruefully. 'I think he was skinny. The Mnankrei came anyway. They came during famine. Food

64

for control. Always, always, always. My grandfather wedded himself to the sea as a free merchant to take their hand from his wrist. That's where the seamen on my mother's side of the family come from.'

'Food for control,' said Hoemei darkly, 'and now famine to create the need for food.'

'I can't believe that of them. How could they face God?'

'We have to believe it of them. They are moving in to take over the land *we* have been granted by the Council. Our children's heritage. We'll be disgraced.'

'Joesai is there.'

'It's bad. Joesai will make it worse. It was a mistake to send him. We're going to need this Oelita woman. Her position will be weak when the famine comes. It is easy to tolerate a Godless heresy when the crops are good but the day the famine hits, they'll spit-roast the lot of them. Teenae can temper Joesai, maybe.'

'If you think Joesai shouldn't be there taking care of our interests, go yourself!' Noe flared.

'With Kaiel killing ogres lurking behind the bushes? No thank you. I intend to be a feast for my great-grandchildren. I respect people able to kill Kaiel with impunity. I show my respect by staying away.'

'You're a coward!'

He laughed the great laugh. 'Sometimes.' Then his shoulders sank in dejection. 'Have you seen Kathein?'

'She won't speak to me.' Noe's voice was pain. 'I saw her today and it was as if I had absently walked into a wall.'

'Come eat with me. We've forgotten all about the meal I was making!' Her eyes flirted with him while she retreated from the study.

Noe was like a magician, he thought, changing a knife into a flower right before your eyes. And she always got him. Out of nowhere came this desire to bed her and forget the decisions he had to make. He watched her cook for a while, wondering what delicacy he would prepare for her when it was his turn. He couldn't resist the lushness of her hips. He felt compelled to go over and hug her.

'Away from me, you insect!' she teased. 'This is a very serious evening. I'm thinking how the Mnankrei would justify the creation of famines.' She turned her head and brushed his cheek sensuously before walking away with the soup. 'You know what they say: "A Mnankrei always has meat on his table."' That was a reference to the sea clan's practice of continuous Culling. The more common Getan belief was that meat was a famine food.

Hoemei grinned. 'The version I heard was, "A *Kaiel* always has meat on his table."' The creches kept Kaiel-hontokae supplied with meat, a custom found nowhere else on Geta.

'That's not the same,' she said petulantly. 'Babies are only bodies.'

'You have a delicious body.'

'I don't think you want my advice. Your blood has all gone to gorge your loins. I won't say another word!'

'Yes, I want your advice,' he said, kissing her on the cheekbone.

'Well,' she went on, totally ignoring the kiss, 'if I sent a man of low kalothi to the temple for Ritual Suicide when the silos were full, you'd call that murder – but the Mnankrei would only call it Culling. So why shouldn't they create a famine? It would only be another form of Culling to them.'

'A clan that thinks such thoughts is damned to a Gathering.'

'Drink your soup.'

'Make love to me.'

'Aw, it's your favourite soup.'

'Now.'

'Finish your soup first.'

He took her on the patio under the stars with a driving

desire that noticed she was somewhere else but that couldn't stop to find out where. Her fingers absently caressed him, affectionately enough . . .

In the afterglow he stared at the face beneath her twining braids that he was never able to understand. Her head lay tilted, eyes fixed on some star but she wasn't there. Musician fingers found a groove in one of his decorative scars and plucked it as if tuning an instrument, but she wasn't there, either.

Finally she turned to him with a languorous smile. 'I see how to kill your underjaws.' She moved a fingernail from the hontokae on her breast to his belly where she stabbed – and laughed.

10

The Death Rite shall be invoked only in the case of heresy and shall consist of never more than seven trials, for would not an endless trial become persecution? Though each trial conjures a more subtle death, each death, even to the seventh, shall leave open an escape that can be perceived by an adept of the common wisdom, for is not the common wisdom a memory of the Race's escape from Death? And is it not the common wisdom we are protecting when we challenge a heretic?

From *The Kaiel Book of Ritual*

Oelita was bleeding to death tied into the iron-reed basket by thongs through the centre of her wrists, bobbing in a small cove, half drowning every time a large wave broke over her head. When she wasn't struggling to breathe, the agony in her wrists throbbed with a heartbeat still in panic.

It wasn't an actively threatening trap. If she kept her legs stretched out, she could stay afloat with her head above water indefinitely – except that blood loss would gradually weaken her. She had to act *now*. Yet there was nothing she could do! She could move her legs but, if she worked them forward, her head dipped back into the water and she began to drown. Worse, she could sense that if she pulled her feet up too far the trap would flip over and she would be held face underwater with no chance of righting the structure.

She tried to think, but the only thoughts that came were the useless 'what if' thoughts of a mind that has given up the present as hopeless. What if she had moved faster when she first spotted the men? She had attacked two of them before the other two had a chance to close in, She had been fast enough to knock one down and swing a rock lethally towards the other's skull, but he had been miraculously evasive, and there had been no time for a second swing.

Water sloshed over her face. She kicked dreamily. What if she had dumped her packsack sooner? What if she had climbed the bank and forced them to come after her?

No use. The bobbing lulled her. She tried to be furious. *How stupid to allow myself to be angered by Nonoep. What if I'd been reasonable?*

A wave poured into her nose and brought her coughing back to the present. But there was only twisted rock and iron-reed trap and pain. *The Mnankrei,* she thought. The Mnankrei would use the sea to initiate their Death Rite. But the pain was too great for thinking. She sank far back into the past, squatting with her father in the sand beside a loan gnarled tree that squatted too, watching four executioner ants keeping an armoured beetle at bay, patiently waiting for the beetle to weaken.

'I'm going to help him,' she had said. Now, in her mind, she picked up a straw to joust at the executioners.

'No, no,' the voice of her father was saying. 'Watch him get away by himself. You won't have help when you're caught in a trap like that.'

'God will help me!' the child replied, defiantly.

'You'd better bet your sweet meat He will do no such thing.'

Oelita jerked. Her father was dead. She had to fight the trap. *How does a Mnankrei think?* She rode the sea. She was a boat. She was a sea captain. There had to be a way out. A Death Rite Trial was always a formal puzzle. She could pull her legs up and drown. But maybe she was only meant to think she would drown? Maybe the trap would fall apart once it had capsized?

69

Oelita was gripped by an irrational desire to try that sudden manoeuvre – what other choice did she have? – and if she drowned, what did it matter; certainly she was going to die if she did nothing. But a keen analytical mind did not allow her body impulsive gestures. She began to build the iron-reed trap in her mind, the way a master weaver would build it, imagining the pieces she could not see. If it were to fall apart, how would that come about? The question gave her a picture. She saw the two pieces, and then she saw the trick. If she merely flipped over, she would drown. But if she could move one of the reeds beside her foot up over the fork that had been cutting her ankle, then when she flipped, the cage would break.

She prodded with her toes and craned her neck. She cursed her toes for not being fingers and gave up and watched a turbulent stream of red blood from her wrist drift away in the green water. She tried again. The reed caught against the fork – and slipped off. Again, desperately, she manipulated her toes and this time, while the reed held, she flipped, her lungs full.

Fright kept her eyes open to see the murky bottom rotate into view, almost touching the fine seaweed that released a darting eight legger and – *nothing's happening I'll die here* – but the trap slowly came apart under the shifting of weights and she staggered onto the pebble beach, nude, dragging the trap by the thongs through her wrists, unaware of the pain, until she sank to her knees, crying, wondering only how to rid herself of the thongs. Death no longer mattered; what had been a minor nuisance now reached her conscious mind with full priority . . . pain . . . pain. Blood began to paint her palms, merging with the sea wetness, to run down a finger or two.

She saw it then, the tiny ceremonial table holding a bronze knife whose handle was worked in the stylized wave design of the Mnankrei and set with stone fragments of blue and white, an ironic gift from someone who knew what she would need if she got this far. The knife she used with unwilling fingers to sever the thongs. Her attempts to bind the wounds failed – her fingers were too useless – and so she merely wrapped around her waist those thin pieces of leather that had been stripped from the back of some poor man of low kalothi, using them to hold the knife against her kidneys.

Oelita found her packsack upstream with her clothes neatly folded on top of it. So they expected her to live. That implied future terrors of a fiendishness that would grow more complicated with every new trial. She dressed in a rage, favouring her fingers, flinging defiance at the bushes which now held phantoms.

To flee or to dare? She chose audacity partly because she knew the rules never condoned a second trial on the same day. She returned to the iron-clad trap and built a bonfire with it on a rocky prominence facing the ocean. Let the Mnankrei see where she was

'Ho!' came a voice from the night.

It sounded like the call of the chief priest of the clan of darkness. She looked for the voice but saw only a horde of hidden ghouls ready to attack. Slowly she reached for the knife. Her hand could only hold it loosely. 'If you come closer I will kill you!'

'And why should I cause such fear?' the slightly foreign voice boomed.

'I'm hardly afraid of you!' Her arms were trembling. 'It is just that I'm in a particularly foul mood!'

'Did the ship that left a while ago leave you behind?'

'You saw a ship?'

'A small one.'

'They are no friends of mine! And who are you?'

'Joesai the Goldsmith. I've been looking over the gold diggings.'

'They are worked out.'

'Ho! You think that! I've already panned a spoonful of

71

dust. I've found a source. Washing is not the only way to find gold. There is tunnelling and there are no tunnels here.'

'Come into the light of my fire.'

Joesai walked down a slope and out of the underbrush. He had been farther away than she had guessed. He stopped, well out of range of her knife, a tall man, bigger than most who were not Ivieth. That softened Oelita. He could not have been one of her attackers. They were all a head shorter than he. Nor was he Mnankrei.

'You are injured,' he observed.

'A minor injury,' she replied defiantly.

'You could not use that knife.'

'My feet are deadly.'

'Are the wounds fresh?'

'Bleeding and painful.'

'Let me examine them. I'm a surgeon, better than most.' He did not move forward.

She looked at the smiling man. She knew he would go if she ordered him away. 'Can you dress stabs? I can show you how. My own fingers are too swollen and weak.'

'I promise better than that.' He came forward and asked her to sit while he examined her wrists. 'Let me take care of it now. I'm a master. The scar will blend with your cicatrice when I've finished.' He took out tools before she gave permission. 'These are no ordinary wounds,' he pronounced.

'No.' She cringed as he began his work.

'You have enemies,' he said and his finger sent fire through her arm.

'All those who are loved fiercely have enemies.'

'You must be the Gentle Heretic.'

'Some call me that.'

'Cause for astonishment! My two-wife is a student of yours. She is not a great intellect. From overhearing her, I have concluded that your teachings make weak sense.'

Oelita laughed. 'You may not be a flatterer, but you have a kind way. Kindness is what I preach.'

'I am ruthless when it suits me. Can you walk? We'll do better at my camp. I have food. You need not use your hands and I'll serve you a feast.'

'You adopt my enemies very easily.'

'Should a big man like me fear men who would attack a defenceless woman? I'll walk you back to Sorrow. Perhaps you would grant two-wife an interview?'

'No. The Mnankrei Death Rite is upon me and I need hide. The ground has ears. No one should know my whereabouts.'

'Then I will show you where to contact her, and you may arrange a meeting whenever and however it suits you.'

They walked back up the stream, wading most of the way near the edge, jumping along rocks and boulders where the water was shallow. He showed her the outcropping that had borne gold, and where a tunnel should be carved. 'Overlooked riches,' he said. 'Some don't have an eye that sees underground.'

'You trust me to know this?'

He laughed with amused force. 'Hasn't two-wife told me to trust the Gentle Heretic in all ways? But I do not need trust. I care not who digs the gold, as long as I am the one who buys it.'

Joesai's camp was only a tent big enough to crowd two men. He built a fire and busied himself preparing cake and potatoes and a sauce he frequently insisted that she taste and judge. He was so oblivious of danger that she relaxed. Getasun rose, rouging the eastern hills, before the meal's aroma was on the air from the bubbling pots. They ate with the full orb of Scowlmoon hanging over the thick-leaved brush trees to the west. When they stood up, they could see under the moon a faint horizon of purplish sea. He fed her and teased her as if she were a child.

'I'm beginning to see the source of your innocent philosophy. Now open your mouth like a good girl and have some potato.'

'Do your penetrating eyes also see my heart of gold?'

'There is no heart of gold in your bosom. I see a heart of flesh that pumps blood to your blushing cheeks.'

'Why do you take me as such an innocent?' She was curious. She had many lovers, old, young, high kalothi, and low kalothi. She thought it showed in the carelessly dishevelled air she wore.

'The things you write about. Weren't you the one who said we were a world of children who had never grown up after the poisons had claimed our parents?'

'I was only making a parable on that old myth! People understand myths!'

'It's what you want us to believe – that you are the only adult.' He tossed a stone into the fire to make sparks. 'I'm a living breathing adult, dead neither of the poisons nor of famine; for children look no farther than yourself.'

She had been opening her garment unobtrusively. She stopped, anger rising to lash at his incredible insult. She laughed instead, the great laugh. 'Grandfather, I think it is your bedtime.'

They were tired and ready for rest. It took manoeuvring for the tent to accept them both. She held him to her bosom, surprised that he merely took the warmth of her with his own arm without trying to take more of what she was willing to give. His presence made her feel safe, for the moment, from the Mnankrei. The panic was gone and somehow the pain in her wrists seemed less. Already she was able to plan how to hide and how to attack. Then they slept.

11

It is a fast bee who escapes the fei flower. Thus the magenta fei country breeds swift bees who have mastered a quick sip.

Proverb of the og'Sieth

Benjie was what the clans called a dobu; in his case, a dobu of machine design. But he was more than a creator of machines; he was a dobu, class eight, and the og'Sieth clan recognized nothing higher than the eighth level. He had the beginning of wrinkles and the easy manner of one who has already made his mistakes.

Within the workshed he held up a thumb-sized slug, fresh from his lathe. Gaet watched Benjie mask the small steel part with wax, readying it for etching.

'This is the first of five etchings.' said the dobu.

He was building a small power supply for the Great Cloister of Kaiel-hontokae. Gesturing for Gaet to follow, he walked across the shed. His apprentice was seated at a desk, working within a spot of sunlight brought in by mirrors. Her eyes and fingers concentrated on a polishing operation.

The girl wore the og'Sieth headband of the unmarried, pinned at her forehead by the brass token of the apprentice. When Benjie was sure of her competence as a machinist, duty would require him to gift her with child in a public temple ceremony and, once the baby was born, release her for marriage. Such were the clan obligations of an eighth-class og'Sieth dobu.

He took the part from his apprentice and held it in the

75

sunbeam for Gaet. 'She is almost finished, this piece needing only the furnace to diffuse hardener into its surface.'

Gaet was more interested in the girl than in steam engines. He smiled at her and she turned away.

Benjie spoke out approvingly. 'My little one does excellent work; I'll have to find a husband for her soon.'

'It's none of your business!' she flashed. 'I'm going to marry Mair and Solovan.'

Benjie laughed. 'Mair is her best girlfriend. The women are growing more stubborn by the week in imposing their will upon our world's chaos.' He paused and his look was that of a man who likes to tickle small children. 'To the best of my knowledge, Mair and Solovan are not yet married.'

'But they *will* be. They're friends! And Mair promised to introduce me to Solovan at the celebration tonight!'

'If you flirt as well as you polish, I suspect their fate is ordained unless poor Solovan has more wits than I've noticed.'

Her shyness gone, the apprentice smiled at Gaet. 'You see why I don't get any work done with this *flatterer* around all the time, talking nonsense in my ear and stopping me to show whatever I do to all the passing visitors because my work is prettier than his work.'

The two men passed from the shed to the hillside trail. 'If you've been wondering at my visit, I've come to inspect my holdings,' explained the priest.

'Ah. You're our new landowner?' asked the under-clansman.

'From here to the sea.'

Benjie laughed. Gaet knew enough not to interrupt, and the chuckling continued until they reached the road. Benjie was a member of Gaet's constituency and they often laughed together. 'So,' said Benjie finally, 'the priests fight again. This ownership of land which possesses

76

the priests has always puzzled me. Once you own land, you are not free. You cannot walk beyond the boundary you have set yourself without inviting a fight. You must stay up past the time when any honest clansman is asleep, drawing your maps and colouring them.' He stopped Gaet and pointed out a swarm of bees who had taken up a new home in the rocks beside a cluster of carnivorous fei bushes. 'The bees are free. They can go anywhere. Why should they care who owns the land? An og'Sieth is free. I can be anywhere my will chooses and know my clan will receive me.'

'Someone has to worry about the sewage,' Gaet grumbled.

'You always have a *problem* when you come to see me,' said Benjie. 'What is it this time?'

'The sea is too far away. Haulage is the problem. Nothing to discuss while we are sober. The mind is too practical when it is sober.'

'Come to our party tonight. That will remedy your sobriety!'

'I was thinking along the lines of a mechanical Ivieth, a machine that could run day and night harnessed to a wagon, faster than any man can run.'

Benjie began to laugh again. 'Wait until you are drunk! Wait!' He held out his palms in a stopping gesture while he choked on his laughter. 'Not now!'

Gaet made no further mention of his wild schemes. He bought a keg of mead for the party and helped his friends set up the tables and bring in the food to the village's small common yard. He forgot his troubles. He wasn't a man who stayed worried when the whisky was out.

He spent his time listening to those he thought might make useful additions to his constituency, but lost interest in all political matters when he cornered an old og'Sieth woman who had worked metal as far away as the distant Sea of Tears. Like almost every Getan, he was curious about faraway places. The conversation was interrupted by a faint call.

'Gaet maran-Kaiel! Gaet maran-Kaiel . . .' The voice was resonant enough to echo off the hills and carry along the vales up to the mines and down into the worksheds of the og'Sieth buildings that surrounded the tunnellings. It was an Ivieth runner paging Gaet, probably with a message which had been relayed through the local rayvoice atop Redstone Hill.

He left his conversation to intercept the runner. *More work,* he thought in resignation. It would be from Hoemei. Hoemei always had work for the family and Gaet knew why they all responded instantly to his call no matter how harassing or trivial the assignment. Long ago they had learned to trust his intuition. The brothers' bond of unshakable loyalty went back to the creches where quick teamwork was the only road to survival. Their women had absorbed the same loyalty by an osmosis of experience that passes between people who love each other.

The message handed to Gaet by the only slightly winded runner was sparse but detailed enough to make Hoemei's conclusions convincing. It ended on the usual personal note. A kiss from Noe through the fabric of space for his nose. And a worried sentence to mention that there was no news from Joesei or Teenae.

'Bad message? May I carry a reply?'

'God's Streak, no need for such a hurry. I'll be spending time on my answer.'

'I will wait here.' An Ivieth would wait in one spot forever if it was asked of him.

'No, no. Come,' Gaet said to the man who towered over him. 'I'm inviting you to a revel. When you are drunk enough you can sing for us. What songs do you know?'

The runner grinned. His clan were travellers and they

78

all knew songs of far mysteries. Their tales bound the culture of the planet together. The man's grin said that he could sing anything, and would do so for a drink.

Gaet escorted him down into the central yard where the party was buzzing like a hive that had located new flowers. They approached the young woman who was in charge of the buckets and bottles. She was slightly woozy from fumes and from sampling her different concoctions. 'Give my friend a drink,' said Gaet with the camaraderie of a politician who was always willing to add someone new to his constituency. 'Whisky with a mead chaser. He has a lot of waiting to do while I collect my thoughts.'

She pushed a drink into the tall Ivieth's hand and held on for a moment to keep from toppling. She looked up. 'You have a good view of the party. Do you see my number three around? He's the one with the lines radiating away from his mouth.'

In the meantime, Gaet had walked off across the flagstones with his arms around two wives of Benjie who, his women were boasting, could build steam engines so tiny they crawled through the eye of a needle towing a thread. The triplet found their dobu at the food tables, his mouth full of a red potato salad that had been delicately bittered with profane fruit.

'Benjie, suddenly I have a job for you.'

'Don't give them both to me at once,' he said, admiring his wives.

'Make me a steam engine as big as a silo, say with forty wheels to roll on.'

'Forty wheels! This morning you wanted from me a mechanical man! How will we fire this giant silo, with your ego?'

'I just got a rayvoice briefing from my brother.' The drink was making it difficult for him to think. 'A famine is moving up the coast. There will be refugees. He wants me to begin setting up relief stations so they won't all die in the mountain passes. I thought we might carry food to them instead.'

Benjie had some spice cake and spoke through stuffed mouth. 'They won't starve. The Mnankrei have wheat to sell. The days of the big famines are over.'

Gaet was weighing all the political consequences, running a rapid simulation of alternative futures through his mind. 'That's what I'm afraid of. They'll sell their wheat and you know the price. The Mnankrei are expanding too fast. Craftwise they can't begin to match our resources, and yet they are making boots out of us. It is the ships. We can't keep up with their ships!'

A loud voice, somehow attached to perceptive ears, guffawed from across the courtyard. 'Ever seen a Mnankrei sailing in our desert?' His laugh was drunkenly slurred. 'They're going to put wheels on their boats. Sail 'em right up on the beaches.' His laugh went out of control. 'Soon they'll be chasing our asses right across the Itraiel Plain.' The tears were rolling down his cheeks helplessly and all those around him were laughing in resonance. 'Ever been chased by a boat across the Itraiel?'

Benjie joined in the game of chewing on Gaet's leg. 'I think it is just that the Mnankrei are more intelligent than the Kaiel.'

'You think it takes brains to stick a wet finger in the breeze?'

'Ya, but Gaet, they *have* to be smarter. They are the fastest Cullers on Geta. They mow their wheat before it is blade high.'

'Only one out of five go to their temples,' answered Gaet aggressively. 'That's no record. I come from the creche. Don't talk to me about Culling.'

'I can't say as I see how that puts you ahead of the Mnankrei,' Benjie continued to tease. 'It depends upon what you Cull for. How come they let an oaf like you get through? A silo with forty wheels!'

'They couldn't resist my smile.'

'See what I mean?'

Gaet's mind was permuting the conversation. 'All right, Benjie, what about sailboats on wheels? Why not?'

Benjie looked him in the eyes.

'I said, "Sailboats on wheels."'

'Silence of God, I do believe you're serious!'

'Of course I'm serious!'

'No, no, Gaet old friend. You run the world.' Benjie pointed with exaggerated emphasis at the priest. 'Let me build the machines.' And he pounded himself on the chest. The drunken dance had begun.

Gaet backtracked along his mental maze knowing he was onto something important. He sensed it. His mind had that wild flavour. 'Why not a silo-sized steam engine driving wheels? I've seen your little models with wheels. I've seen your power engines in the Cloister!'

'Sure, sure, I can build you a big one. We just built a monster for the Palace to run one of those electric pumps.' He was saying yes, but the tone of his voice was saying no.

'How long will it take?'

'Gaet, that's not the point. Cris, come here.' He nodded to a wise old o'Tghalie who was drinking quietly by himself. 'Gaet, I know what you want. Let's postulate a land-based haulage fleet that can move as much freight at the same speed and over the same distance as the Mnankrei wind fleet. Tell him, Cris. We've gone over this backwards and forwards for a couple of thousand sunrises now.'

Cris generated the relevant numbers from his strange o'Tghalie brain. He showed how fast the desert vegetation would be stripped to fuel the engines and to reduce the iron oxide for the iron roads – and how fast it would grow back and how much labour it would take to collect the fuels.

Benjie summed up the argument: 'You want to preside

81

over a nation gone to sand, go ahead. God's Streak, we could do *anything* if we had the wood!'

Gaet paused. A Kaiel who made decisions had to register at the Palace what he thought would be the consequences of those decisions both in the short term and the long term. To be proved wrong by time meant that his genes would be purged from the liquid nitrogen sperm banks of the Kaiel creches.

'But there *must* be ways to move as fast across the land as a Mnankrei ship flies across the sea!'

'There are – and they all gobble fire.'

'I'm not so sure. Think about it. It is said that God moves without effort and He circles the whole of Geta seven times for every sunrise.'

'Have your creches breed Ivieth for gods, then,' said Benjie drunkenly.

Gaet went to bed earlier than he had intended so that he might begin immediately the work Hoemei had thrust upon him. It was chilling to think of losing the coast to the Mnankrei. Failure on the family's first assignment from Aesoe would be fatal. There were too many other families in line. The five of them would find themselves administering the Kalamani desert. Better to end up as soup and ceremonial vests. He needed to talk to Joesai. But Joesai was not a rayvoice man. Curse the distance. He dreamed about the mythical wings of God.

Artists had visualized the wings of God as if they were the great laced lifting fans of the hoiela, the one insect that could soar halfway around the globe before it died. How the hoiela sparkled on the breezes! The fine tough fabric of the wings was so iridescently beautiful that it was prized by women to sew into their sexual finery. God's wings, myth said, were even more beautiful but so fragile that they did not float on air but took lift only from the purest blackness, a black so black that even light was eaten without a trace.

82

In the morning, wild and elated screams were interlaced with Gaet's dreams. They were happy screams but blood-curdling enough to send all the beetles within a day's walk scuttling for their burrows. *Ah, the revel is still alive,* he thought, waking up. The boisterous merrymaking continued while he washed his face and shaved – until his curiosity was tickled enough for him to peek down over the courtyard.

Five grown men and eight children were chasing a contraption about the flagstones that was circling this way and that in mad escape manned by a frantic og'Sieth youth whose feet were pumping up and down but never touching the ground. The 'wagon' he was propelling was hardly a wagon. It had only three wheels, two large ones in front and a small 'rudder' wheel in the rear. The wheels were so insubstantial that there seemed to be no supporting structure between axle and rim. Even the wagon framework was missing, being replaced by what appeared to be light steel tubing.

Later Gaet examined the machine after it had broken down and been removed to a thatch-roofed shed for extensive rethinking and redesign. The argument of the evening, evidently, had continued to evolve after he went to bed and since it was a party of craftsmen, not all of them articulate, they had settled the matter by building what their drunken imaginations had conceived. Only drunks would start by postulating an unfuelled, massless wagon that could keep up with the wind. And only a tribe of sloshed og'Sieth would try to build one during a festival. They were still sleeping under the shed's tables.

Gaet smiled like a child who has just seen the insides of his first clock. He took a morning walk beneath the mountains to breathe in some of the possibilities. His trained Kaiel mind blocked out new futures. Which to make real? He saw, for one, the breaking of a stalemate.

No priest clan of the sea had ever been able to dominate

Geta because the eleven seas were isolated from each other by the land; neither had any landlocked priest clan been able to dominate because land passage was so slow. Now he saw fleets of these three-wheeled ships, pumped by strong Ivieth, racing over mountain and across prairie with the speed of a flung stone. It was a heady image for a politician. Imagine what it might do for tax collection!

Gaet sought out his Ivieth friend to discuss his vision over rolls and tea. The powerful giant only smiled as if the wire-wagon was a mere toy. 'Running with the ease of walking is a thrill, but the roads are too rough for such flimsy spider work. It will break every thousand man-lengths! Men are stronger than steel.' And he grinned. He had been bred to outlast steel.

A sober Gaet returned to the shops for still another viewpoint. Benjie lay in stupor but a fresh crew of og'Sieth were at work. They laughed at the idea of men being stronger than steel, and though they did not back up their laughter with convincing words, one rash youth whacked Gaet across the chest with a hammer to illustrate their feeling.

They had little time for Gaet, chattering as they were about the drive rods and gears which jammed repeatedly, brainstorming alternative mass-conserving designs. They could not talk long without hammering or boring or chiselling metal on the lathe, and the talk remained cryptic – phrases about tempered wire and torque and crushing strength. None of the failures seemed to upset these people. They were already calling the massless wagon a skrei-wheel after the twelve tenuous long legs of the rock skittering skrei, as if their device was worthy of a permanent name.

12

A human who is consistently fair to his friends will find unexpected allies among his adversaries who will plant his kalothi beyond the bounds of its formal territory. A human who degrades his enemies in word and deed will also be seen to scorn and beat the wife he loves, insult his comrades, cheat his parents, commit treason against his clan, and listen to flattery with a warm feeling in his heart. Do not trust the man who is ruthless with your enemies for he will make a poor friend.

> The lonepriest Rimi-rasi to the Gathering That Honoured God

'What did you do to her!' Teenae raged.

'I'm pleased not to have been there for the attack. She nearly killed Eiemeni.'

Teenae was impatient with such chit-chat. *'Is she alive?'*

'For a person as tough as her, death comes slowly. She's fast, too. Her surprise lasted a mere half wink. She's a deadly killer.'

'She's all gentleness!'

'I'm glad *I* didn't make the mistake of believing she is what she writes when I planned the ambush. I learned respect. She's quite capable of killing a whole Kaiel family with her bare hands.'

'You did not answer my question!'

'Whether she is alive?' Joesai mused.

'Yes.'

'I thought to be cleverly misleading and use the Mnankrei Death Rite opener. We fastened her to an iron-reed basket through her wrist and floated her in a cove.'

'What a horrible way to die,' said Teenae acidly. 'You

85

don't dare bleed to death so you drown yourself. She died?' Teenae felt helpless.

'The Mnankrei prescribe seven ways to escape from the first trap, each more difficult to perceive but each easier than the last. She could hardly have failed.'

'She's alive?'

Joesai laughed and lay down against the pillows, facing the bay. 'I escorted her home. I have an ironical sense of humour. It pleases me to know the enemy from the start.'

'Then she's alive. Thank God. Tell me where she is!'

'Even knowing where she is would be cheating. I let her vanish.'

'You'll hunt her down again?'

'The next time there will be six ways for her to escape.'

'You'll kill her in the end.'

'She'll go at least to the fifth level, that hurricane. I like her.'

Teenae took a wrap, a crocheted lace of marching and flying insects, and left the inn for a walk along the stone quay of the harbour so that she might be away from Joesai. The wind from the sea this day was cold and she held the wrap tightly to her body, while the brisk air flapped her black hair and froze the shaved centreline of her scalp.

The Joesai of Sorrow was different from the husband she knew in Kaiel-hontokae and she was not pleased. Her anger came, she thought, from the frightening coolness with which he faced someone else's death, but she was not aware of how much of her rage derived from the mere fact that he was winning the game to which she had secretly challenged him. Real life walked on more legs than a kolgame. Joesai had the experience while she had only wisdom. It was intolerable.

She stopped at a fisherman's stall along the quay and bargained with an old grandmother for five swimmers. These swimmers were eight-legged armoured creatures as big as a man's fist. They were tasty but also more trouble than they were worth. They could not be cooked in their shells because then the poisons diffused throughout the body of the meat; they had to be cracked and carefully dissected. Only the brain and gills were edible, perhaps two fingers' worth of morsel, a modest mouthful. The remaining muscular flesh might safely be eaten if it was carefully sealed with a special bacterium and left to rot until it reeked. There were recipes to disguise or boil out the oily ripeness. Some people preferred such dishes to human flesh. Teenae did not.

She wandered far beyond the quay, slogging through the sand, puzzling out Joesai's mental process. Such an analysis was difficult because he did not reason with logic. Sometimes she doubted that he reasoned at all. He was tradition-bound to a fault, though never imprisoned by a tradition that did not suit him. He acted out old formulas, not as if he believed in them, but in a kind of jovially absent-minded way, as if being traditional saved his mind the bother of thinking while it was occupied elsewhere at more important tasks.

He had his men and she had none; that was the problem. He had the eyes of a bee, and she had merely two. To win, she must first establish a balance. Was she here alone to flatter Joesai or to counterbalance his weight with her own vitality? She needed mass. She needed allies.

Up ahead a dancing child played with a decaying length of sea vine, snapping it like a whip. To avoid the soft beach, Teenae was now walking along the border between the endless battle of sea and continent that had pounded out a lifeless curve of wet black sand. The attacking foam seized her hurried feet and the counterattacking sand left behind heel-deep pools of water.

'Hi,' said the boy, whacking the surf with his vine. Its rotten stalk broke. Because Oelita was on her mind, she scrutinized the four wheat kernels on the boy's back – the Scar of the Heresy. The first underlay of the design, she noted, had been executed by a traditional craftsman of the n'Orap clan. There were few so skilled in Kaiel-hontokae. When the boy reached his full growth the final delicate details of the cicatrice would be cut in or embossed and coloured. 'You got some swimmers,' he said to her. 'Yeech. I throw them back when I catch one of those.'

'Do you lay traps, or do you dive?' she asked.

'I mostly bait, but I'm a good diver.'

'Who decorated you? I notice that your scars were all done by the same artist. He's very good.'

'My two-father. You should see my mothers! He is not yet finished with my body.'

She thought about a man who would commit his son to a heresy in a way that could not be erased. He was a believer. Joesai would not have approved. Since a child he had been adamant that no one's symbol should ever be carved into his body. The designs he wore were meaningless. And so Teenae conceived her plan for telling Joesai of her opposition to his actions.

'I have some work for your two-father. Would he be home?'

The boy's family lived on one of the crooked dead-end streets at the bottom of the hill below Sorrow's Temple, a street wealthy enough to afford paving. Its houses and shops were a motley mixture of yellow and red brick, of field stone and mortar, of cut stone and elegant arches, all with slanting slate roofs and tiny windows. Stairways disappeared into common courtyards or to second floors or meandered up the hill to the next street.

Three children were carefully daring footholds in the stones of the aqueduct that passed overhead to feed the eight public fountains from which the townfolk drew their water. Other children pestered shoppers to carry their bags for a coin. An Ivieth couple, the female far taller

88

than her mate, pushed a smelly sewer wagon as they made their rounds to collect fertilizer for the fields. Coming in the opposite direction a father and his daughter hurried past the wagon, laden with water tanks on their backs, bringing in the evening supply from the nearest fountain.

At the shop entrance Teenae removed her sandals and washed her feet in the small footbath. Watching her intently was a little girl with naked skin as smooth as freshly bleached fine paper, who, upon deciding that the visitor was safe, ran over to her half brother and climbed to his shoulders for a ride. From that perch, arrogant but silent, she looked Teenae straight in the eyes and simultaneously steered her brother by the ears. Down the hall another girl, older, hauled a jug of water upstairs, smiling broadly at Teenae when their eyes touched.

A sloe-eyed woman with elaborate spirals radiating from her eyes greeted them in a shop filled with imported fabrics, tapestries, rugs, fine porcelain, brass kitchen utensils, even clocks from Kaiel-hontokai. The family obviously dealt in luxury imports.

'I have never seen such fine porcelain!' exclaimed Teenae.

'This is only our display room. It would please me to show you the ceramic collection down below. We have more from the o'ca kilns than we can show here. A new shipment has hardly been unpacked.'

'This is o'ca?' Teenae was impressed by their enterprise in importing from such a distance.

'She's here to see Zeilar,' said the boy.

'Ah. You are interested in the skins. We have a small but superior stock. My husband Zeilar only collects them as art so that he shall remain inspired by the masterpieces of others. He saves the best of the leather that passes through the hands of my husband Meikam.'

She led Teenae upstairs and then up another flight on an almost vertical wooden ladder to a large room that was

89

the only room on the third floor. It was spacious and better lighted than the apartments below. Zeilar sat upon several of the larger pillows that littered the floor, reading a handwritten book beside a window three times as tall as any other in the building. Through the window the peaked roofs of the village thrust upward to obscure the sea. The hides of perhaps a dozen men hung about the room as partitions or in place of tapestries. Surfacing the low table that dominated the whole space was a quilt of leather designs and behind this table stood a multijointed mirror, man high, with almost golden reflectivity, which was built to give one an image of oneself from many viewpoints.

Zeilar set his book aside and she saw that his face was carved in an abstract symmetry that would make the effort to decode his current expression an almost impossible task. 'Look around,' he said comfortably.

The most enormous hide was perhaps the strangest for it carried unconventionally representational scenes of mountains and cities and ships connected by a wild looping of roads. 'Do you know the stories of these men?' she asked.

'Harar ram-Ivieth,' Zeilar replied. 'He was an accomplished songwriter and one of the few men ever to have rounded Geta on foot. I never met him for he died before I was born but many Ivieth know his stories and more than once an Ivieth has passed through Sorrow called to Harar's Pilgrimage. I have a copy of his book, *Following God.*'

The smaller hide of a woman attracted Teenae's attention when she recognized its delicate workmanship. That's what she wanted. The cuts, the fine work, the control of the scar-tissue texture, the embossing, and the final tattooing were unbelievable.

'Not for sale,' said Zeilar noting her interest. 'She's my oldest niece. I had her skin to work with since she was a child and she inspired me, the saucy wench. She was drowned by the Njarae. I'm not sure she wasn't murdered. Her death left a knife in my heart.'

90

'I'm not here for leather.' Teenae dismissed the notion, saddened that a woman had lost her life to the sea in the fullness of her youth. She smiled at the artist. 'It's for me.'

Was it consternation or joy that crossed his indecipherable face? 'Ah yes.' But the voice carried pleasure. 'What design do you wish? Choose any one that catches your spirit or I can give you an original sketch. The work cannot all be done in one day, you understand. Many healings are required to control the texture.'

'I wish some form of the four wheat kernels.'

His motions froze. 'You are a convert to the teachings of our Oelita?'

'Yes,' she lied with her gentlest voice.

The son appeared up the ladder again with tea, followed by his naked sister. The tea was poured into shallow o'ca bowls.

'Do you wish this sacrament done now or with friends?'

'Now. You are my friends for you follow Oelita.'

'Son, hurry and fetch a maita leaf from my satchel to freshen our guest's tea.' He turned to Teenae. 'I prescribe only a mild narcotic since awareness of the pain brings faster healing. Fast healing gives an aura to the new tissue, a fineness of texture and colour.'

'I have never used a narcotic, maita or otherwise. It is not logical to fear pain. It is only logical to fear the damage that generates pain. The symbol is not its referent. So the o'Tghalie teach.' She went to the mirror and disrobed. An infinity of golden Teenaes formed ranks in that geometric never world. 'My lower back is smooth,' she said.

The boy re-emerged from the trapdoor with the large maita leaf, followed by an eruption of sisters and another brother. For these young ones it was an event to watch the master work his magic with brush and knife and flesh. Each child made his presence unobtrusive. None let their eyes stray from Teenae.

91

Zeilar swabbed and cleaned her back with alcohol and then began to sketch on the skin over her kidneys while she stood inside the mirrors and watched this new flattery take shape upon her crowded body. Sometimes he erased and began again. Sometimes her eyes wandered to the hides of these other humans who had all once stood naked like herself in a shop like this. The children stared.

Teenae's logical mind was relishing the ironies all about her. She never really understood the way in which the non-o'Tghalie staggered blindly past, and over, the contradictions of their private worlds. They neither saw nor felt nor heard the storm. Zeilar worked in a room that was a showplace of cannibal feasting, creating the symbol of a philosophy that denied cannibalism upon the back of a woman who would one day be eaten. She smiled. Artists had a way of living with the cross-purposes that flowed through the soul of the Race.

Teenae wondered why she was here, why she was doing this. As yet the design was only ink. But it was not Oelita's dietary laws that attracted her; it was the woman's gentleness. Teenae had lived in a stern family that had not let her grow up to practise mathematics, and now she was part of a clan inexorably bent upon planetary conquest. Gentleness attracted her.

Slowly the essence of maita leaf saturated the tea. The boy brought it for her to drink, lifting the bowl to her lips. She sipped. For a moment the artist paused, then brushed on some finishing lines. He stood back for her approval and she saw a hundred golden Teenaes with their backs to her and their heads turned. All of them nodded.

The design had been modified to flow with the form of the prior cicatrices; the wheat stem was bent, as if caught by the wind while ripening on the round hills of her buttocks. Zeilar was satisfied; she was satisfied. He paraded her before his children who clapped, too, and began to josh each other for positions around the table, not so

92

quiet as they had been. The master went for his tools and Teenae took her place on the table, stomach down, face resting in her arms, smiling at the littlest girl, winking.

'Is Oelita as warm as she sounds?'

He brought Teenae rods to hold in her fists and a strip of hardwood on a finger-high stand so that she might bite or leave it, as she wished. 'Our Oelita has a golden kalothi. You and your husband are the ones who know gold. Life beats her in hammer strokes but she never breaks. A little bit of her is enough to gild everything with lustre.' He selected a knife, and adjusted a mirror to get a better light from the window. 'Are you ready?'

'So many people seem to worship her.'

'Oh yes,' said the artist making his first cut.

Teenae gasped and clamped her teeth on the hardwood, breathing with deep breaths as the knife opened up more lines of blood. 'Wait! God, wait!'

He indulged her but used the time to expose the design again by washing away the blood with a light solution of numbing maita tea. 'I'll be trimming next. The pain will be intermittent but sharp.'

'Has she been here long? Did you notice her as a child?

'This will hurt.' Snip. 'She came and went with her father.' Snip, snip. 'Those times when he brought her to the village she would run far ahead of him.' Stab, snip, stab. 'I remember the time when she crawled upstairs and sat down to supper with us.' Slice, snip, stab. 'She chattered our ears off. How's it going?'

'Just get it over with!'

He laughed. 'We can't hurry or I'll slip. I'm going to cauterize some points and put a mashed beetle salve on other spots. That gives a different texturing effect. The salve will sting worse than the fire.'

Teenae's body was trembling. 'All right.' She breathed deeply to stay out of shock, smelling her own flesh burning from the hot needle.

''S all right,' said the naked little sister crawling over to pat her on the head.

'Was Oelita a temple-goer?'

'Oh, she was at our temple all the time!' He began to cut again and Teenae's body shuddered once. His male voice dominated her senses, flooding over the pain like maita. *Concentrate on the voice.* The voice droned in and out as if the speaker were not in one place. 'She competed in everything. She raced.' An endless scream traced its path down to the hump of Teenae's buttocks. 'Oelita played chess. Her eyes were the quickest, her hand the fastest. She'd spend days with a puzzle. She's the village kolgame master, though you'd never know it . . .'

Teenae took her teeth off the hardwood strip long enough to interrupt. 'I love kolgame!'

'. . . because no matter whom she plays, she only wins half the time!' Zeilar's hand sought a new knife and that brief moment of relief was spring and summer and autumn. 'Nobody ever earned a higher kalothi rating in this village.' The new knife began the quick manoeuvrings again. 'She does not need to be merciful,' he said proudly, 'but she is.'

'Wait! I have to wait!'

'We are almost done. I think it will be beautiful.' Tenderly he mopped up the blood and applied more stinging beetle mash.

'When did she become a lonepriest?'

'Doesn't wisdom come on us in hard times? Life was full for her. She had a great father, may he still nourish us, and all the friends a human could hope for. She could have married into a great clan. She could have had any clan, except perhaps your o'Tghalie.'

'Our men would have loved her!' Teenae laughed.

'Are you ready yet? Shall we continue?'

'Yes, but keep talking. The knife is bearable when you talk and I can concentrate on your voice.'

'She could have joined a Stgal family!' The knife began again with a torturing zigzag walk. 'Even the Kaiel would have had her, I'm sure of it. The Kaiel! She was beautiful. No woman ever took more care in decorating her body! But it was not to be.' The knife paused while he shrugged.

'She took a lover. A great traveller. He came overland from the Aramap Sea. Imagine that. The Aramap Sea. Handsome. Powerful kalothi. She was young then. Very young, and wished to prove to the world her worth as a bride by bearing the most beautiful children in the village. She had twins, both of them genetic cripples, nothing wrong in their minds – they were both alert and intelligent children like their mother – but crippled in the legs. You know the disease, Ainokie's curse. She's a carrier and never would have known had she picked another lover.'

'She didn't eat them at birth?' asked Teenae, so appalled that for a moment her pain vanished.

'No. She has a gentle soul. She raised and protected them but would not marry. They had kalothi. She always said that. They had kalothi. But the famine came.' The thought seemed to disturb him and he began to carve the kernels of the wheat in silence.

Teenae cried in gasps, 'Go on with your story. Don't stop!'

'It was a bad famine here; I don't know how it was where you came from. The Culling began. First the criminals. The famine gnawed at our bellies. The low in kalothi went to the temple to give us life. Even the old went to the temple to give the young life – that's how bad it was. One out of every ten became part of the living. We were decimated. The village shared Oelita's children. That was when she stopped Chanting to the God of the Sky, our rock of superstition, and when she began to show us a better way.'

How cruel to keep monsters alive in the name of mercy, thought Teenae through her pain.

The artwork continued. The story continued. Teenae ceased to be aware of either. She endured the pain. She struggled to stay conscious. She breathed deeply. She tried to crush the rods in her fists. She left teethmarks on the hardwood bit. Sometimes she screamed through clenched teeth. She could not stop the tearless sobs. Somewhere in her mind she thanked the God in the Sky that she was a woman now, a full-grown woman because there was no more blankness upon her body. The littlest girl, who had all of this still to experience, kept patting her head compassionately and when it was over, she was there, directly in front of Teenae, smiling.

Zeilar swabbed the wounds gently and bandaged them. Two of his wives came up the ladder. They had been preparing Teenae's swimmers. They fed her the raw brains and gills. Pain sharpened the taste buds, they said, and now was the time for delicacies. The remains of the swimmers they had packed to rot in little jars so that the meat would be ripe in a week.

'You're spoiling me,' she said when the women began to sponge the sweat from her face and body.

'We welcome you to our bond,' said the younger woman.

Teenae had saved her most important question until exactly the logical moment. 'Will I ever get to meet her?'

'Yes,' said one-wife.

'Of course,' said three-wife.

'She is in hiding now,' said Zeilar, 'because the Mnankrei have challenged her by Death Rite.'

'I'd heard a rumour like that. It frightened me.'

'Her wondrous kalothi will protect her and so they cannot win, but still she must be careful. You will meet her.'

'Why can't people just leave each other alone!' Teenae spoke with adamant anger against Joesai, though it seemed that her anger was directed against the sea priests.

'Oh, but she welcomes the challenge. When the Mnankrei lose they will owe her a Great Favour.'

Yes, you will owe her a Great Favour. Teenae savoured the coming victory over Joesai. Logic was better than tradition.

13

When the land is full of strife, the mother of the Saviour – knowing that she is the mother of the One Who Speaks to God – shall spill her blood deep in the Graves of the Losers and the child who is born upon the stones, breathing the incense of kaiel with his first cries, shall rise from that mournful place suckled by his mother's certainty.

From the *Chant of the Prophetic Wanders*

Hoemei had left a message and she had not replied. To meet him was forbidden by clan edict. Even to speak to him was forbidden. Why did he persist? Those maran-Kaiel were shamelessly bold! Did they not fear Aesoe? Was their love so small they would endanger her?

Yet how could she just forget them. She folded her arms crossly above a belly so large that it indicated a baby near term. Life was grief and anguish. Was a refusal morally correct? She had not refused Joesai. It had overwhelmed her with surprise the way Joesai had approached her after the interdiction, pushing through the social barricades so casually. Love that strong was difficult to resist. Since then duty and fear had hardened her. Being forewarned by Joesai's behaviour and no longer surprised, she had refused when Hoemei had first tried to see her. She had been cold, she had ignored him – and yet in his shy way he persisted. Her loneliness was weakening her resolve.

She wanted to see Hoemei. She desperately wanted news of Joesai – and Teenae, too. *I will not see him!* But what could Aesoe do if she spoke to him for a moment?

Suppose the meeting was carefully clandestine, how could he even find out about it? The thought frightened her. Kathein was afraid of Aesoe.

I'm not brave. Her mind paused. *I'm weak!* she added furiously. It was their boldness that had attracted her to the maran-Kaiel when they had decided to court her. She was conventional. She stayed on the roads and only wondered about shortcuts. Gaet and his cavalier way with all that was sacred had fascinated her from the day they met. How did he *survive*? When he had brought her home she had expected a conservative family to balance his impulsiveness, but the whole family had turned out to be equally free of what seemed to Kathein to be the irreducible constraints. They were freer than Kathein had ever wanted to be.

She knew she talked boldly. She had a witty line. She knew she was charming, But there had never been boldness in her actions. At first Hoemei's shyness seemed like tradition personified but when she coaxed from the man his deepest feelings, he was a catacomb of heresy. No safety there. Joesai talked of concepts so comfortably worn that they had the feel of a temple touchstone. He had seemed like a safe person. Then he had taken her and made love to her one day without so much as a token gesture to the rituals, a presumption so surprising she had been unable to find a way to say no. The whole family frightened her but their reckless ways had been a heady experience that had infused her personal life with the same thrill she got from physics.

And yet how like her life that they had been taken away. Here she was ready to bear her first child and there was no family to share her joy. She missed Joesai. If only she could cry out her grief with Noe. But now she was more afraid of them than she had been on that first wondrous evening.

Aesoe was watching.

She did not want to be another sweetmeat at the maran funeral. Yet how she loved to dive into the depths of Hoemei's wariness and break surface having flushed a smile he had been hiding. How she loved to relax his worried frown. How she could use his smile right now!

There were friends who would be glad to celebrate the birth with her, and who would take care of her, but she wanted her family, and if she couldn't have them she was going to bear the baby alone. The first contraction hit her, almost too faint to notice. The baby jerked. *I'm all alone,* she thought and closed and opened a hidden switch that triggered a chime in the servant's quarters. It was a silly foible of hers. A rope and bell was just as adequate and didn't need a fussy electron source.

Yar appeared in the stone archway. 'You belled?' She stood awkwardly, a youth from the creches who was not yet accustomed to the strangeness of her good fortune. She lived with a boy whom Kathein had picked for her. They were lovers and the nucleus of a new family and they served Kathein while they studied physics.

'What could we do to make my hair beautiful?'

'You've decided to see him?' asked Yar excitedly, though she was more interested in the lectures on lightning and momentum that always went with the hairdressing.

'No. It's for myself. If Hoemei comes it will be your duty to send him away.'

'I'd be so awed I wouldn't be an obstacle at all!'

'You could tell him how wicked he was.'

Yar giggled. 'I could hold out my skinny arms to block the way. I'd rather bake sweetworm cookies. How shall I do your hair?'

With a toss of her head, Kathein strode to the mirror and sat down but, suddenly gasping, clutched the arm of her chair.

'Mistress!' cried Yar.

'It's all right. The labour is beginning. It will go away.'

'Lie down.'

'No. My hair is important,' she said stubbornly, as if ordering the world to follow the morning's written plan.

But the contractions did not go away. Their intensity persisted, building for many hundreds of rapid heartbeats before fading. 'They're gone,' said Kathein. 'We'll do my hair now.'

'They're not gone. I've seen the machines at the creches give birth. I'll get the midwife. You go to bed.'

'No.'

'Please,' said Yar, tugging at her mistress.

Kathein considered. She sighed. So it had come. Now there was no way she could receive Hoemei, bless the God of the Sky for this interference. She took herself slowly down to the kitchen, waddling, Yar helping her on the stairs. 'Get Reimone. Send him for a palanquin. Have the Ivieth bring it up the Bluethorn. I'll meet them on the road.'

'You should stay here! The midwife can come here!'

'Child,' she said with annoyance, 'I'm having the baby alone! Now do as I say.'

Yar looked at her, appalled, then rushed away. Kathein collected a sack of water, some food, some flannel swaddling, matches and a torch with refills, a knife, twine, some yellow chalk and the incense of kaiel bellies. She rolled them in a mat, which she placed inside a harness that hung from her forehead. Yar followed her, carrying the load until they met Reimone returning with the Ivieth bearers. 'Speak to no one of this,' she cautioned from the window of the palanquin. The vehicle bobbed slightly as the Ivieth adjusted their load. With her finger, she made the circle that was the sign of God while Yar and Reimone returned the sign.

'May God be overhead at the first cry of the birth!' said

101

Yar as her mistress disappeared down the road in a light that was already dusk.

When the two Ivieth porters arrived at their destination, Geta's brightest stars, Stgi and Toe, were rising and Kathein, gripping the poles of her decorated chair, had completed another series of contractions. Bioluminous globes glowed in the windows of the unbroken ring of buildings that surrounded the sacred hill. In some windows, lamps flickered. Trembling, she wasn't sure she could walk, but her body, inured to obedience, followed her will. She rose from the chair and lifted the strap of her burden to her forehead and dismissed the huge Ivieth bearers with a coin.

Only when Kathein was alone again did she find strength to approach the pointed arch that was a gateway through the wall of houses circling the hill. Once she had passed through the perimeter there was no light and no life save for the stars and the odd flying glowsting. The City of Kaiel-hontokae had abruptly disappeared.

She was unafraid. She knew the catacombs of the Graves of the Losers by heart and did not quail at their evil reputation. In some way they were her life's work for the sacred instrument that occupied her obsessively had been found sealed into these walls with the crystal that she had always believed somehow held the secret of the Voice of God.

There were four oval entrances to the catacombs themselves, and one jagged hole where a tunnel roof had collapsed. Clumsily she made her way to the black opening that the Chants had named the Mouth of the Southern Death. She needed a torch and had to lay down her burden to pull it out. The effort precipitated the return of labour. She paused, kneeling on the ground, her legs spread apart, keening her lonely cries, begging the child to wait.

God rose over the wall to the south while she moaned,

102

and she watched Him between gasps, the sight of Him streaking across His Sky stirring her with the awe that Getans have always felt in the presence of their God. Her contractions became more prolonged, relinquishing only as He set in the west beside the dark but thinly crescented Scowlmoon.

Kathein lit her torch. She had to hurry. She forced her cumbersome body down through the macabre tunnels. No older architectural structure was known. Kathein herself thought of this maze of passages, not as a work of man, but as a work of God at a time when God still spoke to man. She knew that the caverns had been carved by a knife of heat hotter than any fire her best potters had been able to duplicate. A finger-thick scar tissue of solidified melt lined the walls. There was excellent evidence that rock had been gasified.

The Chants spoke of riches here, of metal coffins, and fine machines, but looters had long since stripped away whatever the rooms had held. Later clans had etched designs upon the walls and built crude chapels. Long before written history a children's temple had existed on the lowest level, sorting kalothi and supplying a local village with meat and bone and leather and perhaps sacred relics. No place was farther from modern man; no place was closer to God. Here the Race had failed and here the Race would rise again.

So it had been prophesied.

Eventually Kathein could bear the pain no longer and selected an arched room at a level one stairwell higher than the low dungeon she had hoped to reach. Dank water seeped from cracks in the stone. She laid out her mat upon the floor. The torch flickered, relit, and died. She screamed her long breaths in the darkness in tune with the contractions until she had taken the child from herself, holding him, Joesai's child.

Fingers crept along the floor, patting for the knife. She

103

cut the umbilical cord in the dark. Still in the dark, she thanked the sky-spark that was God and held the bloody infant to her breast, warming his fury, while she recovered her strength. Only following the afterbirth did her unsteady hands light another torch. Monsters carved into the walls balefully bared flickering fangs at madonna and child. Over the torch she heated kaiel bellies for their incense. The prophecy said that kaiel incense would greet the Saviour Who Speaks To God when he was born in the Graves of the Losers.

Carefully she swaddled the baby in soft long strips of flannel until he was soothed. *Like God, I've brought you from an easy world to a harsh one.* He was so tiny. She cried a little. This was the only gift she had left that she could offer her beloved Joesai – to make him father of the Saviour. When she walked back into the light she was proud and her weakness did not overwhelm her.

14

Do not force upon others your forbearance towards the weak but do speak bravely. There will be times when braveness is stylish and there will be times when only the brave will dare braveness.

Oelita the Gentle Heretic in *Sayings of a Rule Breaker*

Men were outside, guarding the modest house that stood on the highlands overlooking Sorrow's Temple in an area of difficult streets and stairways and cobblestoned back alleys. Apparently there was no front entrance and so the boy took Teenae to Oelita via the back, down stone stairs to a room that faced the sea through leaded windowpanes of bubbly green glass. The shy guide did not know how to make introductions; he just stood by awkwardly. Oelita was standing. Her eyes met Teenae with such open clarity that Teenae feared she knew everything and that this was a trap. Those wounded wrists!

'Where did you get such a beautiful gown?' she blurted to hide her fear.

'A friend. The oz'Numae weave them in one piece. My friend tells me that the oz'Numae are a small clan who live on the islands of the Drowned Hope Sea.'

'Then it indeed comes from far! Where Scowlmoon is on the *eastern* horizon! A long overland trip!'

'You are a stranger to Sorrow,' said Oelita. 'You've come from afar yourself.'

'Who on Geta is a stranger to sorrow? Really, you're not a stranger to me. I read your *Sayings of a Rule Breaker* long ago,' she lied.

'Zeilar gom-n'Orap tells me you wish to publish a small edition of that book.'

Ah, thought Teenae listening to the eagerness of her voice. *I've chosen the right snare.* She reached into a pocket and brought out a fine book on kolgame strategy printed in Kaiel-hontokae. Bait. 'This is an example of our craftsmanship.'

'Beautiful,' said Oelita enviously, turning the pages, fingering the needlework of the binding. There was no paper like this among the Stgal, nor was the printing here as crisp.

'It would please me,' continued Teenae, 'if you would care to look over my handwritten copy of your manuscript for mistakes. In your growing wisdom you may even wish to incorporate alterations.'

'I've been thinking on this matter all night, ever since Zeilar carried the good news of your interest to my attention. But we'll discuss business later when we know each other better.'

A little girl sneaked into the room and crawled under the table as if children should be heard and not seen. She spoke in a sing-song voice. 'Toeimi walks to False Start at dawn. He wishes to know if there is anything you want him to bring back.'

Oelita went to her knees, smiling. 'There's a little shop that carries root-spice just below the stalls of the tinkers. There's no root-spice in Sorrow.' She glanced at her wrists. 'It will help the healing. That's all, my wee bug.' The girl waited impatiently while she received an affectionate head rub, and then crawled out from under the table and ran off. Oelita turned back to Teenae. 'Are you in the mood for a game?'

'Kolgame?'

The holy woman smiled. 'I'm a kolgame master. You'll have a hard time. Perhaps chess?'

'Kolgame.'

Teenae watched the game for clues to Oelita's character from the moment they threw dice to assemble the many-shaped blocks of the game's territory. A pattern emerged. The heretic seemed to take over territory only to stabilize her food supply so that the Culling condition would occur less frequently. Teenae countered by occupying key command centres. Surprisingly, Oelita shared the burden of the inevitable impasse conditions among her tenants, making it difficult to eat them. This was an unorthodox defence and astonishingly well played. Oelita could see *very* far into the future – but it was always better to load your weaknesses onto one tenant and grant suicide. Oelita could have won had she been willing to sacrifice more often but she would cede control rather than lose a tenant and so Teenae's o'Tghalie mind ruthlessly annihilated her by playing on that one weakness.

And Teenae knew then that the Kaiel could conquer her. Threaten someone's life and Oelita would be set against herself. She was neither willing to kill to save a life nor willing to stand aside while that life was taken. Such contradictions, intensely analysed, were always at the fulcrum of Teenae's shattering attack.

Oelita's weakness reminded Teenae of the teachings of the kembri-Itraiel. Those who are not willing to kill make tempting victims and thus have chosen endless conflict, while those who *are* willing and able to kill may always *choose* a peaceful life. Whosoever values his life becomes enmeshed in the game of saving his life.

Teenae's own thoughts were more mathematical in nature. A strategist might seek to minimize death, but the attempt to *eliminate* death invited such a misplacement of resources that the only result must be a higher than minimal death rate. Especially if you were playing against Teenae.

'You are a merciless soul,' said Oelita, conceding defeat with a smile.

'Only when I play kol. Otherwise I'm very tender-hearted.'

'Will you stay for dinner?'

Teenae laughed with pleasure. 'I shall be delighted to share your time and bread.'

'Could I send a runner out to find your husband? I'm really quite obliged to him for the help he gave me.'

Teenae was suddenly alert. 'Joesai cannot. He's such a man of business. His time is planned dawns ahead. He's such a wretched man to live with.' Her eyes were twinkling. 'I'd die of boredom without my other husbands.'

'I found him very kind.'

Oelita cooked the dinner over a small ember fire in the central stove of her room. She chatted happily with her new friend about the outside world and books. Teenae noticed that every mention of the Kaiel made her wary.

'You've been to Kaiel-hontokae, have you?' Teenae asked, probing.

'I wouldn't dare. The Kaiel priests would attack me for heresy. I wouldn't enjoy the game and they wouldn't get their coin's weight; I'd make a tough Judgment Feast.'

'They're not like that!'

'They're so sure they are right, so sure of their destiny!'

'But a person who is sure he is right feels no need to persecute,' said Teenae gently. 'It is only those who are *not* sure that they are right who have a need to harass heretics.'

'So you think it would be safe?'

'Kaiel-hontokae is the one city on all of Geta where there is no fear of dissent.'

'But they are bloodthirsty! They eat children! It's revolting. I want nothing to do with them!'

'The Stgal ate your children and you have courage enough to preach to them,' said Teenae logically.

Oelita winced as if she had been stabbed. 'Pouring oil on yourself and striking a flint to illuminate the darkness of a strange city is a futile gesture.'

108

'I know Kaiel-hontokae. I would guarantee your safety.'

'I should go,' Oelita thought pensively. She was recalling how much trouble her foolish rage against the Kaiel at Nonoep's farm had already cost her. 'You've probably heard that the Mnankrei are after my life. But,' she added angrily, 'I should stay and fight, too. I'm afraid.'

'Let me tell you something else. You have influence here. The Kaiel are hungry for influence in this region as you well know. They would bargain with you.'

'What could they offer me? Would they stop their butchering of helpless babies?' she asked bitterly.

'They could offer you time, protection. How long will the Stgal last? It's a changing world. Your books have made friends in Kaiel-hontokae.'

'I'll sleep on it. You'll tell me more about your mysterious city. We hear only the wildest rumours.'

The smell of the food attracted curious children from the neighbourhood. Once inside they played with Teenae and crawled all over Oelita. She finally shooed them away but at the door was greeted by a noseless man who had chosen that moment to return one of her pamphlets. The two women talked with him for a while, debating theological points, and then he left.

'You're so at ease with criminals.'

'He's harmless!' exclaimed Oelita impatiently. 'He stole a loaf of bread from the first harvest after the last famine. A loaf of bread! Have you ever seen a dangerous criminal? The dangerous ones get to make their Contribution-to-the-Race in a hurry!'

'He loves you. You give him hope,' Teenae retreated.

'He needs hope, poor boy. Will you have broth with your meal? It's profane but harmless. I'm careful that way.'

'A small cup.'

Idly the discussion came back to printing Oelita's

manuscripts. She was eager and trying not to show it. There were other books she considered more important than *Sayings*. She left her cooking to fetch her newest work from a messy pile and in her excitement to show Teenae the pages she almost toppled her insect boxes with a brisk swing of her arm.

'It's such a clutter here. I've just moved in and I have less space.'

'You have quite an insect collection.'

'My father's.'

Teenae examined the fine dissection kit and microscope that had been used to draw and classify the insects. It sat beside a rock collection.

'Is this glass?' Teenae was so startled by one of the stones that she forgot the manuscript in her hands.

'It's too hard for glass! And it is the wrong crystalline shape for a diamond. I don't think a diamond ever grows that large.'

'Where did you get it?'

'I collected stones as a child. That one I found while swimming. It was just there in the sea overgrown with weed and I took it.'

'The sea?'

'My father taught me to swim. It's not dangerous.'

'Joesai says such crystals contain the Frozen Voice of God.'

'If we put it on the fire will God come out by the hearth and tell us stories?' chided Oelita.

'He talks about genes,' said Teenae defensively.

'Like a priest when he's drunk on whisky?'

'I've never seen it happen.'

Oelita laughed. 'But you've *heard* about it. Do you think that rock in the sky ever spoke to anyone?'

I'm sure of it. 'I don't know,' said Teenae to avoid controversy. She did not know what to do with the manuscript that Oelita had suddenly forgotten.

'We're such a superstitious people!' the Gentle Heretic raved. 'There is a rational explanation for everything. We could chant that God brought the insects – but you can trace how they changed to meet challenge until they fill every niche where life can exist. My father found life in the driest desert! He found, embedded in stones, the shells of insects that don't even exist today. Do you know how long it would take for that kind of stone to form from clay soft enough to trap an insect? Eons! And the Chants say that the Race just appeared here in a puff of smoke at noon practically yesterday!'

'There are no human fossils.'

'We make soup out of bones!' exclaimed Oelita, setting a meal before her guest, beside her newest manuscript.

'*My* family *collects* bones.'

'We'll find human fossils. You'll see. No one has ever looked! And they haven't looked because they haven't dared! And we *have* found bone tools.'

'Recent ones.'

'Teenae! We've only been a tool-making insect recently. There weren't many of us before. It's been a rapid evolution.'

'Because we *ate* the less intelligent ones.' Teenae had wanted to bring up this contradiction in Oelita's philosophy. Oelita condemned cannibalism while claiming that the vitality of the Race derived from cannibalism.

'Yes,' came the defiant answer, 'because we *ate* the less intelligent ones! People always get me wrong. They say I don't believe we should follow the path of kalothi. I believe in kalothi! It created us out of insects and it is our destiny. We haven't stopped evolving and I don't want us to stop evolving. But we don't have to *eat* each other to evolve! There are other ways. *I* can think of other ways.'

A long pause ensued while a thoughtful Teenae nourished herself. 'What ways would you suggest?'

'If we women got together and only had our children by

111

men of great kalothi, that would be one way. Those of us, like me, who have defective genes can decide not to breed. That's another way.'

They argued while they ate, but Teenae never tried to win. Oelita's ignorance in too many fields was too appalling to make it worthwhile to argue logically. There *was* a God. That fact was so obvious with the proper background. Without the proper background one could only have faith. Oelita had neither knowledge nor faith. She was an ignorant, unsophisticated, self-educated country girl. Teenae liked her but was rather horrified at the thought of being married to her. Aesoe was a mad dreamer. When she had Oelita in Kaiel-hontokae she would convince Aesoe that there was a better way than marriage.

Oh Kathein, I love you so!

The sun was long gone before the two women were talked out. They cleaned up from the meal. Teenae read part of the new manuscript. She accepted a small gift from Oelita and gave one in return, exacting with it the promise that they would meet again for supper.

'Soon!'

'Soon,' smiled Oelita.

Crashing waves raised by the wind brought salt spray all across the village. The blackness was full, for Scowlmoon was dark at sunset. Only the starlight illuminated her pathway home. She was going to relish her triumph over Joesai. She had begun the first steps in a real negotiation and she felt elated!

Fingers took her from behind over the mouth, muffling her protests while two other men clamped vice-like grips upon her fiercely struggling body.

15

In his lifetime a man will pace over all the stones in the river, the large ones and the small ones, the flat ones and the slimy ones. The stone he misperceives will kill him. The merciless man does not see mercy and so when he needs mercy his feet cannot find it. The man too proud to show his mistakes makes a fool of himself missing his jump. The man who lives in dangerous waters and leaps nimbly from suspicion to suspicion will be unable to cross the river because he will not trust the solid stones.

> Foeti pno-Kaiel, creche teacher of the maran-Kaiel

Joesai was worried, yet not ready to worry seriously. He had Teenae's note and he was angry at her for slipping out of his protection in the town where two Kaiel families had been murdered; but she hadn't promised to be back before dawn, and Getasun was only one diameter above the horizon. Noe, bless her, would not have gone without consulting everybody, but Teenae was Teenae. She liked secrets. Five of his men watched for her quietly.

Damn! I'll spank her bare wheatcakes when I catch her. Restless, he left the inn and paced up the long quay. *If they've hurt her I'll hang their screaming skinless bodies for the bees to hive on.*

He turned and saw Eiemeni approaching along the granite with Oelita and four of her fierce men. The way of their walk was foreboding. They were in a hurry. Her robes flapped in the sea breeze.

It was going to be the news about his wife. In a flash he suspected that Oelita had met his deception with a deadly counter-deception. *I'll kill her if Teenae is in danger!*

113

When Oelita was close enough so that he could see her face he knew his conjecture was right. 'Teenae!' he hissed as he quenched his anger and poised himself with a tempered soul, ready for anything, emotionless.

'The Mnankrei have your wife! It's my fault!' Her voice was stricken.

Of course he did not believe her. She had taken his headstrong child bride and was now paying off Joesai in the coin of some grisly joke. 'Explain yourself.'

'Your wife left my place and four thugs took her. Two of my guards, who had been following her for protection, tried to interfere. The thugs left one unconscious. The other followed to spy.' A tall, deeply scarred man bowed. Oelita went on breathlessly, 'I don't know why they took her. Perhaps they thought she was me.'

'The ones who challenged you with a Death Rite?' he asked without letting his face show a flicker of disbelief.

'The Mnankrei? Yes. I don't understand them,' she said.

Now there was a bluff for a temple's game table! 'Where is she now?' *What is your price?*

'On their ship. It arrived yesterday, warning of famine to the south.'

Joesai nodded to Eiemeni and his man left on the run. Oelita's face was compassion. He did not know what to say. She seemed to be able to lie as well as he lied. He dared not openly voice his suspicion of her for fear of walking into a trap Oelita had set for him. His respect for her deviousness increased enormously. Not content to organize a defence against attack, she was returning the attack ruthlessly. It had never happened to him before. 'I love that woman,' he said darkly, locking his eyes with the heretic. 'Whosoever harms her, I shall destroy.'

Oelita touched his arm. Her treacherous sympathy enraged him.

'Why was she with you?' he asked.

114

'We were discussing a publication scheme I've had in mind for a while. We hardly talked about it. We played kol and chatted about gentleness and the reasons why people should not destroy each other. Your wife thought she might be able to help me get a book of mine printed.'

So that's how you reached her, he thought in an aside to Teenae. He cursed himself. All the time he had spent with Oelita escorting her back to Sorrow along the coast, she had known who he was and was plumbing him for weaknesses, preparing her counter-offensive. She had the audacity to flaunt herself in front of him now. But there was nothing he could do but pretend innocence while she pretended innocence. 'I want her back,' he said.

'They're still here.'

'Who?'

'The Mnankrei.' She pointed impatiently. 'Their ship.'

He had to grant her a chagrined smile. She constructed her story well. A Mnankrei freighter was indeed at anchor far out in the bay, its sail furled. He did not believe for a moment that Teenae was aboard. 'What do you suppose *they* want of her?' he said with muted sarcasm. 'Ransom?'

She stared at the ship with hatred. 'What do you suppose they want of *me*? I will get her back for you. I have a score to even with them.'

'That sounds brutal coming from the mouth of the Gentle Heretic.'

She smiled briefly and tweaked his nose. 'There are ways to even scores without being brutal, my chitin-hearted man. Watch me! I am not powerless. They think to use your wife to trap me. I will trap them!'

Eiemeni trotted back along the quay. 'She is held in yonder ship. It is confirmed.' Eiemeni had his eyes fixed on Joesai.

For the first time Joesai looked out at the ship with alarm. He braked his alarm. Best not to rush too fast, he thought. Eiemeni was not old enough to be aware of the intricate turnings which a trap might take. A magician could convince you that his head was full of pebbles.

Joesai explored different theories. If Oelita had an alliance with the Mnankrei then the deception of the Mnankrei Death Rite would have been transparent from the beginning. But if there was such an alliance then Oelita was truly dangerous and rescuing Teenae would pose grave risk and might not even be possible. *I will be forced to negotiate with Oelita.*

She left, promising to be back. Joesai gathered the key strategists of his group at the inn for a game council, awaiting further intelligence. Rumour spoke of Mnankrei priests at the temple offering the Stgal to bring in wheat if that should prove necessary. Finally one of Joesai's scouts returned with a grin. He had boarded the Mnankrei ship as a 'port inspector' and indeed caught a glimpse of Teenae below decks while pretending to check harbour regulations. She was naked and manacled.

That was all Joesai needed to know. 'We'll sink the ship,' he said. *When I get Teenae back, I'll keep her in irons myself,* he thought gruffly, not meaning it. Then he called a planning session.

16

The purple Njarae is the breeder of our ability. Does she not drown the careless sailor?

Proverb of the Mnankrei

Sea priest Tonpa, Storm Master, sat in his carved swivel chair, long hair braided into his beard, his face scarred with the flying-storm-wave design, examining Teenae, who stood naked, ankles manacled, wrists manacled in brass chain, holding her head high, guarded by two erect seamen. He felt fatherly amusement for the tiny girl but was quite willing to hide that in order to properly terrify her.

Tonpa could see in the quivering of her mouth that she was not taking her humiliation well. Probably she was being silent to hide her near-tearful state. These Kaiel, who watered down their stock with the genes of the underclans, were all bluff. As the saying went, they were the kind who could only play games on a steady table.

'We arrived here,' he said severely, 'after having run a storm to bring in relief supplies to the south. This port is an out-of-the-way call on our return, but we think of it as our sacred obligation to warn of the plague that brings famine to the Stgal communities below, for it must come here as the wheat ripens. And what do we find? Lies. Slander against the Mnankrei. It is not to be tolerated.'

He waited for her reply. She did not reply but stood rigidly stiff, her expression slightly disgusted as if the ship-smell of ripe sea creatures and salt offended her mountain nose.

'We hear of this act perpetrated against one of the most respected women of this community. True, she is a heretic. True she speaks falsehood and foolishness, but she does not lie. So who is the source of these lies? The innocent folk who live here are willing to listen to lies about the Mnankrei just as they are willing to listen to lies about the Kaiel, so they look no farther for truth. But we *are* the Mnankrei and so we look for the source of these vicious lies. Of course we suspect the Kaiel.

'Are not the Kaiel known for their devious lies and their arrogance? The kaiel insect spreads false scent so it can control. The priest insects who have usurped this name spread calumny for the same purpose. But the salt spray that clears the nose gives us immunity from such ensnarement.

'Was it hard to find you? It took a day. You stand on *my* deck against your will, shaved of your dignity, in fetters. We also have spies. Our spies are more brilliant than your spies. Haven't we Culled for intelligence week by week while you baby-eaters wait for famine to tell you when to Cull?' He paused and cleaned his fingernails with the point of his knife. 'A Kaiel posing as an o'Tghalie. True Kaiel deception. Futile. The wind that fills our sails does not need feet. Speak! Defend yourself or confess!'

To abate the adrenalin terror, the manacled woman clenched her fists and breathed heavily, breasts rising and falling with her chest, but she would not reply.

Tonpa flipped his knife and it sank into the deck, vibrating. One of the seamen recovered the thin weapon, returning it with a bow. The Storm Master never took his eyes off Teenae. He accepted a mug of warm broth from a boy who emerged up a ladder and still he did not unlock his nude victim from the brig of his gaze. He grew impatient.

'This woman you wish dead, whom you have so cowardly attacked in the name of the Mnankrei, is coming

118

aboard ship. *You* know she is in no danger here. But because of your lies, she was difficult to persuade. I have had to offer hostages. You will have to face her.' He watched Teenae flinch and laughed the great laugh. 'She does not know the truth.' He watched Teenae shrink. 'I do.' He watched Teenae turn her head away ever so slightly. She was breaking. 'I give you a choice. You may face her and keep silent and make your Contribution through Ritual Suicide to the larder of this ship which has sacrificed so much to bring food to those threatened with starvation, or you may speak with honour the truth and escape with only your nose being cut from your face for the crime of slander. Speak!'

Teenae was glaring at him with a hatred that had overwhelmed her fear – for the moment. Tonpa shrugged, deliberately feigning indifference. 'It's been a long voyage. Be stubborn. The men will not object to the taste of fresh meat.' He watched her eyes dart between her two guards. They were grinning. Her hatred crumbled to fear and he had her.

'I will speak the truth to Oelita – but not for my life,' she said with loathing.

'Because you are honourable, of course.' He couldn't resist that last whiplash. A gesture told the guards to take her away.

Tonpa followed her down to the lower deck but his ever-alert eyes caught the stare of one of his sailors as the prisoner was escorted past him. Arap was a big boy, bigger than Tonpa, and useful in a storm for his untiring ferocity. He was young, very young; he had no more than fuzz for a beard but he was precocious with the women, a jolly soul who could convince a matron twice his age that she was young again, and never failed to try.

'What a waste!' he sighed to his master, his hand gesturing in open grip as if he would take heaven by her round buttocks.

'Nothing is to be wasted,' replied Tonpa to provoke Arap. 'Every finger of her is lean meat.'

'Storm Master, sir! How c'd you? A comely girl like that-un? Leave me the appetizer. You c'n have the steak.'

'She'd scratch your eyes out!'

'Not me, sir!'

'Follow me,' said Tonpa abruptly.

Arap whitened. 'Sir, if I've offended you . . .'

'You have not offended me.' The Mnankrei priest brought Arap of the lesser clans into his luxurious cabin and set him down in the velvet seat by the desk, amused at the boy's discomfort. Clan code did not permit a seaman to enter the Storm Master's cabin and Arap had never been here before. He did not want to sit in the velvet seat but he obeyed orders. The room impressed him.

'Shall I give the wench into your hands?' Tonpa teased.

Arap was sweating. 'We c'd all have a go at her, sir. Perhaps I c'd train her not to fight too hard.' The sailor was growing appalled at his position. It was a trap and whatever he said was coming out wrong. A horrible suspicion was dawning. Their master was known to lead by the ear. 'Sir, you're not liable to assign me to butcher her? Really, sir, I lack skill in such art.'

'You think of me in harsh terms, Arap.'

'No, sir.'

'I know exactly what you say about me below decks!'

Arap mentally began to ready himself for keel-hauling. 'Them's only jokes, sir,' he said helplessly.

'I'm assigning you to guard duty on this Teenae. The first watch you will only smile at her and do her silent favours of the smallest kind. Other seamen will discuss recipes with her in a somewhat bawdy way. When she is sufficiently terrorized, you will become very tender with her. Appear infatuated to the extent that you are willing to risk your life for her. Tell her your jokes about me; the one about how I bail a boat will do nicely,' he added wryly.

Arap was near to fainting.

'See that she knows you consider me to be a monster. Tell her our plans, exactly as they have been told to you.'

'But, sir . . .'

'Then help her escape.'

'We're to leave the wind have those legs?'

'I didn't say you couldn't collect whatever gratitude she might offer. But don't use force or I'll give you fifty lashes. Wet your oar gently if you wet it at all.'

'Sir, I've b'n set with the party to row ashore and burn the silos.'

'I know.'

'I'm to spill *that* in her ear?'

'That's what I said.'

'And I'm to take my way with her?'

'If you're clever. I doubt that you are. In any event she is to escape.'

The illumination of day and then night passed dimly over the only nearby porthole. Smells in the dark cubicle where Teenae was chained sifted through the air and she could hardly see the man-boy who brought her food. He was the only one who had been kind to her when the cook and his assistants were down making ribald jokes in very bad taste. She didn't want to eat now but if only she could get those chains unlocked for a few minutes! 'Please, if you take the chains off I can eat.'

He would not do that, but he sat down beside her and fed her the gruel carefully. 'Don't be afraid of old Lace Beard. He never does much more'n keel-haul a man. Can't stomach killin' even if it means a good meal. 'Course the men've b'n complainin' 'bout the food and sometimes he gotta keep the peace. I'd be suspectin' the worst he'd do is make you ship's whore and then you'd be lucky 'cause I'd take care of you.'

She backed away as far as the chains would let her.

'For you, I'd even dunk a bath.' He offered the food

121

again. 'Don't make such a face! We don't get better'n this ourselves. Don't to worry. He's goin' to let you go.'

'Without my nose!' she sobbed.

'It's a pretty nose. Maybe he'll let me keep it for a souvenir.'

Teenae spat gruel at him but became infected by the great laugh as he had wanted her to.

'What'd he say to you?' asked the boy who was taller than she. 'A mean wind he is. He struts 'round on deck and makes pious sayin's at us like as if we don't've enough with settin' and riggin'.'

'He told me the Kaiel are rotten liars and Mnankrei are saints,' she laughed.

Arap glanced over his shoulder furtively. 'Us underclan folk get to see the rope-deck. Saints. I'll tell you. Do my soul a favour for the poor folk of Sorrow. You're gettin' off the ship and you c'n warn 'em. Next midnight we're to shore and burnin' the granary on the peninsula, so's we can tack 'round and sell' em wheat. That's what we're here for. Keel-haul the Stgal. Old Lace Bear can't kill a tender meal like you, but he c'n starve a thousand without sheddin' a tear.'

She started to comment, and he slammed a hand over her mouth. 'You want 'em to serve me for soup? Now how 'bout a little kiss 'fore I go?' He put his arm around her.

'Don't you touch me.'

'What a silly pout for a chained-up girl to say.' He kissed her and it was the kiss of a large boy who had been too long away from home and was hungry to be tender to a woman. Death didn't seem so close when somebody kissed you like that.

'When is Oelita coming aboard?' asked Teenae.

'It's all set for after sunup.'

'And when is Tonpa going to chop off my nose?'

'Soon as the woman leaves.'

'Why don't you take off my manacles?'

122

'You're thinkin' escape,' he grinned.

'I'm thinking about my nose!'

'I'd be skinned alive and rolled in salt, was I to unfetter you.'

'You could always run away with me.'

A pale beam from Scowlmoon reflected off the brig wall, so faintly illuminating her legs that the scarified design of them was invisible, leaving only the shape of legs like those of a young child. He felt his lust rouse. He could do what he wanted and there would be no painful consequences. Slowly his hand touched her thighs, caressing them, moving slowly down to the manacles, knowing that she would not stop him while he was close to doing what she wanted him to do. She remained silent. Excited fingers worked with the locks around her ankles. 'I sh'dn't be doin' this,' he said hollowly.

'The wrists, too,' she replied.

'No,' he said.

He put his arm around her as gently as he could and with all the care his hand knew, caressed her body. She sent him neither resisting signals nor encouraging signals. The total power of his situation annoyed him. Having that much power was never any fun. He wanted her to like him. Slowly he won her body, while he restlessly suppressed the surf of his own desire. Once, with a barely perceptible motion, she snuggled up to him. Triumph welled in the sailor. It was going to be worthwhile.

'You smell funny,' she said clinically.

Ashamed, he remembered he hadn't bathed. He moved away.

'Don't go away,' she said, alarmed.

But he left in panic and found another part of the ship where he could wash himself in salt water. He scrubbed the important parts of him until they were red. Then he came back with some old blankets so that she could have

a pillow and found her struggling with the hand manacles. She was crying.

'You came back,' she said petulantly.

'I got blankets to make you more comfy.' And he put
the blankets on the deck and moulded her into them and
tried to take her, but she kept her legs closed.

'How can I hold you if you don't take off these damn
hand manacles!' There was a thread of anger in her voice.

He hurried to unlock them, and she held him and they
manoeuvred for a less awkward position and he held her
tightly while his lust commanded him because he was
afraid that she might run away too soon. 'You're a pretty
woman. I c'd go for you. You're the prettiest I've ever
had.' He kept talking to her to try to make her feel loved
the way women liked, and the more passively she took his
thrusts the more talkative he became. For a while he was
swallowed up in his own pleasure but after the release
came and he found this sweating woman in his arms, lying
with her head tilted, her mind somewhere else, he grew
affectionately worried. 'What're you thinkin' 'bout,
babe?'

'About my nose,' she said quietly.

She listened carefully as he told her how to escape. She
had to wait until he was off watch. Then she had to count
the next guard's pacing. When he had passed the fourth
time she was to count to fifty and then throw off her still
unlocked shackles and push open the porthole, which
Arap would have unlocked, and then jump into the sea
and swim ashore.

The time came. She counted to fifty by the thumping of
her heart and made for the tiny hole in the side of the ship
and slithered out, hanging for a moment by her fingertips
before she dropped feet first into the moonlit bay. She had
never swum before in water over her head, nor in
anything bigger than a river pool. It did not matter. She
was ready to fly if she had to.

The salt water closed around her head and she bobbed to the surface, hearing cries from the upper deck. Her plunge had been seen. For one heartbeat she felt what it must have been like for her husbands to grow up in their creche, outwitting the death trials. Terror and hope. Then her o'Tghalie mind took over. This is what she had been bred for. This was a problem. Without even knowing how she did it, her body created a powerful swimming stroke that pulled her through the water at minimal energy cost.

17

The carnivorous nota-aemini will never attack one of its own kind and so that innocent and delicious beetle known as the false nota-aemini has prudently disguised itself to resemble its enemy. Yet life is too restless to allow a solution to exist for long. The narkie, a much smaller prey of the nota-aemini, now has a subspecies which imitates the harmless symbiotes of the false nota-aemini – but in order to survive this new home, where none of the narkie's natural foodstuffs exist, it has developed a taste for its host's brains.

Rial the Wanderer, as dictated to his daughter Oelita

Gaet rode the fifth model of the gossamer skrei-wheel through Kaiel-hontokae, attracting stares and a wake of children who followed him for blocks on end with their high excited laughter. The tri-wheel had independent suspension for its two front wheels and nine gears in a compact gearbox plus a rudder wheel larger than on earlier models. The frame had been extended and was capable of carrying freight.

Sometimes Gaet had to lift it over obstacles, but it was well suited to the mountain roads maintained by the Ivieth. It was not the latest model. The best creators of the local og'Sieth clan were already working on a stripped-down bi-wheel for rapid personal transport which had no suspension and was evidently capable of maintaining a vertical balance by gyroscopic action similar to the forces that balanced a top. Progress was being delayed by a problem with the new lightweight gears which should have worked well but in practice had an unfortunate tendency to jam and even snap.

The journey through the city reminded him of nothing so much as the shoulder-hitching he'd done on the backs of Ivieth runners as a child, except that on a straight stretch of the main road he could reach a terrifying speed that was faster than any man could run. He had been told by Benjie, the og'Sieth's local craftsmaster, to give his skrei-wheel a rough workout since much more information about its wear modes was necessary before they dared put the device into production. It wouldn't do to have fifty of them that all needed the same replacement part every week.

The buildings rushed by and the children couldn't keep up and he kept to the streets between the hills of the city. He was thinking, as he took the cobblestone bumps, that if such vehicles became as common as footwear a man might not have to spend so much of his time away from his wives.

Ah, wives! There was his motive for hurrying! He was going to be glad to see Noe again. With Teenae away and Kathein interdicted and so much to do, Hoemei and he had been reduced to near-celibacy.

Gaet left his skrei-wheel unattended outside the walls of the Great Cloister of Kaiel-hontokae. In a city where even the petty criminals were eaten and used for leather, theft might happen but it was no great preoccupation of the populace. The Great Cloister curved halfway around the base of a small hill, a formidable stone building. It was a Kaiel sanctum and the root of their technology. None but the true Kaiel walked within. After kneeling in the sacrarium and offering a prayer to the God of the Sky, Gaet headed straight for Noe's cell. A faint odour of solvents was in the air. His walk took him past an ancient stained-glass window and rows of stone pillars. He had to climb stairs and walk through one wing of the building to get to yet a third wing.

On tiptoes he entered Noe's room, which was fully

equipped because she, as did many Getans, maintained several residences. She was asleep on large yellow and blue dyed pillows that took the shape of her body. He thought that perhaps he would not wake her, perhaps he would just delight in being with her for a few moments and then leave. Hoemei had mentioned how short of sleep she was.

'Hello,' she said lazily.

'I didn't mean to wake you.'

She motioned with her body for him to come to her. 'My nap is over. I need your shaft to wake me up.' Slowly she began to undress him while he lay with her, but she gave up and let him finish, and then pulled him under the blankets.

'Mmmmm . . . you're cool,' she said deliciously.

'You're warm. I feel like a loaf of bread being baked.'

'Mmmmm . . .' She went back to sleep but a corner of her brain that stayed awake persisted in arousing him and they made love, she less and less passively, until she cried convulsively and sat up, hugging herself with her arms.

'What are you doing in the city? I thought you were in the mountains?'

'I'm chasing ball bearings,' Gaet laughed.

'Hoemei said you were making wagons. I didn't believe him. He said they were light enough for two men to lift.'

'I can lift one myself. They're fast. We are going to have fifty of them built, maybe seventy, in time for the coastal famine. But only if I can find the craftsmen to provide those damn ball bearings.'

She giggled. 'Only Hoemei could get you to do trade clan labour.'

'Only Hoemei could get you to work at all,' he retorted.

'I must say dallying in the temple beats administering the labours of fifty juveniles fresh from the creches. The Cloister is a human pressure cooker! There is so much to do!'

128

'Getting anywhere?'

'You can bet your coins we are! I have them working in ten parallel teams. They are terrified of me. They think I'm going to make soup out of them if they don't overachieve. Guess who saved us weeks of work?'

'I brought you some honeycakes in case you were awake.'

'Is that all you ever think of? Making me fat so you'll have more to hold? You never listen to me.'

'All right, who saved us weeks of work?'

She munched on her honeycake. 'Our betrothed.'

'Kathein?'

'No. Oelita. We were requisitioning samples of the wheat-eating underjaw and before we got the order out, they arrived by way of an itinerant glassblower. Oelita seems to be an observant woman. She collected some a while ago and gave them to a renegade Stgal priest who breeds detoxified profane vegetation. He was worldly enough to send them to the Cloister here. Oelita also had written out an amazingly detailed description of the underjaw life cycle.'

'Do they contain human genes like Hoemei maintains?'

'They certainly do. It is an unbelievable crime. It's Judgment Feast for the Mnankrei. We'll have to break the whole clan to a lesser status, maybe destroy it.'

'You'll wear Scowlman's crescent for a necklace before you see that happen. It's impossible. They tried it with the Arant and we're here.'

Her eyes blazed. 'We're Kaiel – not Arant!'

He laughed. 'I see you believe our forged history.'

'They let too many of you atheists out of the creches!' Noe was above all an aristocratic patriot.

Gaet did not bother to remind her that the creche had been essentially an Arant idea or that the God-made ectogenetic machines on which the Arant heresy arose had probably existed and been destroyed during the terrible crusade. Instead he changed the subject. 'I figure Sorrow can hold out for one reason against the Mnankrei. They have enough reserves for that. If the underjaw is still an abomination by then, the Stgal are doomed.'

She grinned smugly. 'We already have the underjaw control ritual. It is not yet God smooth, but it will be.'

'That's fast work!'

'I'm a fast woman,' she flirted. 'Why do you think you fell in love with me after one heartbeat?'

'You mean it wasn't your family money?'

'Don't you remember? It was right after I offered you that purple drink,' she teased, licking the honey from her fingers. 'Extract of slave pituitaries.'

'That's what you plan for the beetles, to spike their drinks?'

'We need only to synthesize three artificial genes.'

'For what purpose?'

'The underjaw carries up to a hundred tiny symbiotes in its cervical carapace which are its only source of the alalaise it needs to power its wings during migration flight. When underjaws overgraze, the population begins to die. A dead underjaw triggers the sexual phase of the symbiote whose larvae thrive on the corpse. In their winged phase they find living underjaws and as the underjaws become symbiote-saturated, a migration begins. We've found a way to use the human protein in the deviant underjaw to trigger the sexual phase of the symbiote while the under-jaw is still alive so that it is eaten alive. The larvae mature and find other underjaws. If the new underjaw is of the Mnankrei-synthesized variety, then the sexual phase begins again instantly. If not, the symbiote establishes a normal relationship.'

'Clever. Who thought of it?'

'Me, you oaf!' She cuffed him. 'When I was reading Oelita's description of the life cycle. Get dressed. I'll show you.'

'I just got undressed!'

The labyrinth of the Cloister contained perhaps one-third of the entire Kaiel wealth. There were the tapestries and the windows and the gold foil and silver inlay, of course, but that was for show. The major investment was an intricately crafted biochemical apparatus, dust-free and sterile rooms, electron eyes, silver-graphing techniques that could capture the image of a protein string on boron-anate plastics. There were rooms where genetically truncated and modified microlife cells fabricated difficult chemicals. Priest-changed zi-ants performed much of the necessary micro-manipulation and sensing. Within this labyrinth the ancestor of Gaet's host mother had been synthesized from human and artificial genes. Even among the priest clans where breeding and biochemistry was a familiar art, the Kaiel were known as magicians.

While Noe took a nap with her head on the desk top, Gaet curiously examined relevant silvergraphs and pondered over hundreds of variations of hypothetical genetic chains that had been inserted in the fast-breeding sym-biotes and tested. It was not his field of expertise but he read the group's work well enough. In the Getan language the same word was used for 'priest' or 'leader' or 'biologist'. Nobody survived the creches who was not a fine biochemist.

'Hey, this one seems to work!'

She woke up and looked to see the source of his enthusiasm. She smiled proudly. 'It's sluggish but my children are optimizing it.'

'You're still sleepy.'

'I need the mountain winds in my face.'

'How about a run on my skrei-wheel?'

'Is it dangerous?'

It was dangerous so she loved it, clinging to Gaet's back, flying faster than men could run. The ground rushed under her eyes like that peak-risk moment when a sail-plane comes in for a landing, but there was no jolt or collapse of wings – the earth kept slipping past in endless orgasm.

18

Note how the large maelot is captured by a true sea master. We do not deck this creature with the first haul. The maelot is strong and the line is fragile. Let the four-legger escape until it has lost all hope. Then it is weaker than the line.

Mnankrei Time Wizard e'Nop
of the Temple of Raging Seas

Storm Master Tonpa was waiting in a skiff behind his ship when the cry came. He could have overtaken her easily but he did not. He kept his oarsmen far enough behind her so that she had hope, but moved them fast enough in pursuit so that her desperate hope would exhaust her.

When he finally took her, Teenae raked him with her claws and his crewmen had to tie her feet while he held her. They fastened the line so that she was hauled behind the boat. Face down. She had to struggle frantically for air. Tonpa gave careful visual attention to the vigour of these splashings. If they ceased it would mean she was drowning and would need revival.

The skiff slapped safely over the waves to the mother ship. There Teenae was reeled aboard by her bound feet, recklessly swung against the hull by the cavalier sailors, and left to hang by the ankles until Tonpa himself had climbed aboard in his own good time.

The sea priest did not bother to speak to her. He ignored his clawed face. Callously he supervised his men while they lashed her into the painful four-quarter rigging, as if her limbs were the four corners of a sail replacing the furled fore-topsail. Up there her husband would be sure to see her at dawn, upside down, silhouetted, perhaps even rosily outlined.

Arap was also lashed to the rigging, but right side up, and lower down. Tonpa told Arap that pleasure set better in the memory when it was framed by pain. And then he laughed. 'How else do I convince her to convince her husband that what you told her was whole truth?'

As an extra precaution he moved his ship out of the bay, silently and without running lights, to foil whatever rescue efforts her husband might attempt. There would be no need for a rescue. At dawn they would be back and what was left of her would be returned to her man.

At the fading of the stars, when Getasun was only peeking at the Njarae from behind the mountains, two rough seamen lowered Teenae and slopped salt water on her crumpled body to revive her. They towelled her down, joking cruelly. A taciturn sailor shaved the strip at the top of her head. They fed her. All the while she said nothing. For a long time she was kept below deck, and then they took her up, unclothed, to face Oelita. She would rather have died on the mast. Not only was Oelita there, but many of the townspeople she knew as well. Oelita, in disbelief, made her say what she had to say over and over again. That was a special torture.

Finally Oelita turned to Tonpa and asked with a precise electric force, 'Is she speaking under duress? Are you forcing her to say this?'

'Do you imagine that people only speak Falsehood under duress? Yes, she is speaking under duress. Can you imagine this Truth to be pleasant for her? She speaks Truth under penalty of death.'

'She seems to be ill-treated.'

'I have been under no obligation to treat her well.'

'What will happen to her?'

'She loses her nose for slandering the Mnankrei and then we give her to you to do as you please.'

134

'You will not harm her in any way or I will slander the Mnankrei in ways you cannot imagine!'

The sea priest chuckled. 'Ah, the Gentle Heretic who forgave her worst enemy. Flowers for the criminal. So be it.' He bowed. 'We've been wronged, but yours is the graver wrong.'

'May I speak to her alone to see that she is not speaking what torture has commanded her to speak?'

'Of course.'

On the deck away from everyone, Oelita placed a shawl around Teenae's shoulders to protect her from the sea chill. 'Why? Tell me why?'

Teenae shook her head.

'Why!' Oelita insisted with a storm's force.

'We were proposing to you,' she said in the tiniest of sounds while looking at the deck.

'You were what?' Lack of understanding made Oelita's voice antagonistic.

'Proposing marriage.'

Oelita stared.

Teenae was in a state of shock. 'Our marriage is incomplete. We need another.'

Finally the calm wonder with which one treats the truly insane mellowed the Heretic of Sorrow. 'Is that a Kaiel custom, to murder the bride?' she asked as if she was asking about the weather.

'If you survive, you're worthy.'

'And you think I would be willing to present my grall after such a courtship?' The grall was the bride's gift, a layering of sacred and profane foods.

Teenae hung her head.

'Was this the way *you* were courted?'

'No,' said Teenae with a wistful absence. Her mind hardly functioned. 'My husbands took me to the mountains. They sang songs. I was only a little girl. I didn't even have any breasts. They were kind.' She was crying. 'Don't

135

you see? They didn't want you! They were ordered to marry you! We wanted another.' She sobbed. 'It's too complicated. Joesai was the wrong man to send but they had to send him because all the Kaiel they've sent have been murdered and he's a violent man who is at home with murder and I was supposed to mute him and I didn't.' Teenae spoke more but nothing that was comprehensible.

The older woman led the young one back to the Storm Master's stateroom. 'We'll go now,' she said, defying any of the Mnankrei to stop her. They let her go, her arm around Teenae's shoulders, having gotten what they wanted – witnesses to tell of Kaiel deceit and weakness.

Among a quiet group on the quay, Oelita reunified Joesai with his wife. 'Take care of her.'

'Thank you for this favour,' he intoned stiffly.

'Am I glad to see you,' muttered Teenae, hiding her nakedness in her husband's chest.

'I brought her back without killing anyone.' Oelita was defiant.

Joesai laughed because he was so happy to have Teenae in his arms again. The laugh blazed as a forge does while it melts steel. 'But imagine the violence that has been done to my pride.' His fingers combed Teenae's long hair. 'To soothe that fire I'll have to kill them all.'

'It is wrong to kill,' Oelita said.

'No,' he said.

'I have contempt for the traps you have laid for me, and the deception with which you have laid them. Both of you!'

'The next time we shall take more care to win your respect,' he replied ironically.

'So! You're not going to leave me alone!'

'You read me that easily?'

'Yes! You are Kaiel! You are a creature of ritual. Ritual; that's the plague of Geta.' She sounded frightened. 'I'll survive you!'

He was grinning like a skull. 'I don't recommend that. Then you'll have to marry me.'

His arrogance possessed Oelita with a stormy mixture of rage and fear. 'I'll poison the grall!' she said, not knowing what she was saying.

Joesai couldn't contain his laughter. With Teenae back, his fear was gone. 'It's wrong to kill,' he chided. All this time he was appraising the hostile crowd. He gestured his group into a defensive formation and they moved out.

Kaiel men surrounded Teenae, fast-pacing along the quay from the angry mob. Far across the bay, the Mnankrei ship was blending darkly into the waves. Only now, as Teenae was beginning to be aware that she was alive and even safe, did she have time for rage.

'That shipleech Tonpa, may his scars turn to pus! I'll never forgive him. Never.' She felt her nose. It was still there. 'Kill him for me, Joesai. You can do it. I want a new pair of boots!'

Joesai's mind was more on immediate survival. 'First your feet will have to acquire a new set of calluses. Second you will have to row to the moon. Third . . .'

She was in no mood to be joshed. 'Kill him for me tonight while my hatred is hot enough for me to enjoy it!'

Joesai laughed. 'He's just lucky he didn't make the mistake of beating you at a game of kol!'

'You'll have your chance to kill him at lownode!'

'How?'

'Cut his throat at lownode!'

'And what happens at midnight's halfmoon?' he asked cautiously.

'A Mnankrei party is going to come ashore and burn down the peninsula granary.'

19

The wheel of Strength has four spokes – loyalty to Self, loyalty to Family, loyalty to Clan, loyalty to Race.

It has been said that Self is the first loyalty, for if the Self is not whole can we build a Family? can we build a Clan? can we build a Race? But I say to you a selfish human is a one-spoke wheel soon broken, a fool trying to move the boulders of Mount Nae by himself.

It has been said that Family is the first loyalty, for if the women and children are not protected can there be men? But I say to you a Family of selfless humans, who stand against their Clan while exploiting the Race for the sake of their children, will not roll far.

It has been said that loyalty to Clan is the first loyalty, for is it not the Clan which moves mountains and brings its terrible force against evil? But I say to you a Clan dominated by loyalty to itself will destroy its families and perish.

It has been said that loyalty to Race is the first loyalty, for without genetic purity can we hope to meet the Danger? But I say to you the Race is heartless without its Clans and Families and Selves.

The Wheel of Strength has four spokes – each equally weighted and balanced or there is no strength at all.

Prime Predictor Tae ran-Kaiel
at his first Festival of the Bee

Kathein had never met Aesoe before. She did not know what he looked like, for whenever they had been within sight of each other – and once she had been as close as an arm's reach – he had been gazing at her and she had dared not return the gaze. She could feel his fascination deep in her loins as a face can feel the sun that eyes must turn from. She did not know what to make of this summons to his country residence.

Two Ivieth from his personal livery came for her with a richly cushioned palanquin. A wet nurse met them at the carved doors to take the baby. Another woman led her to a hot tub where a male and female servant bathed her and anointed her with perfumes upon her ears and nipples before dressing her in soft robes resplendent enough for an audience with the Prime Predictor.

Kathein could not even look at him now as she made her entrance into his grandroom. It was with relief that she knelt in formal bow to touch her head upon the stone-cold floor of smooth granite. Music was playing – gentle strings, a reed. She had watched the musicians briefly with eyes that were avoiding his. The afterimage of these delicate women stayed with her.

They were of the Liethe, small beauties shrouded in fabric woven from the soft wings of the hoiela, blending unobtrusively into the tapestries of the room. Aesoe valued them for their rarity. Who knew where they bred? Perhaps on some forested island of the Drowned Hope Sea? Gossip had Liethe appearing from and disappearing into the islanded ocean.

They sold themselves for gold if the buyer was a priest, but they were not slaves. A Liethe would leave her master but another always came and took her place. Aesoe's three had the same face and body. Rumour spoke of parthenogenesis. Rumour also spoke of varied physical types. Somebody far across the Itraiel Plain had once confided to a friend of Kathein that they garrotted their sons. Veiled daughters came and vanished. It was said aloud that any man who was served by a Liethe became all-powerful. It was whispered that any man who kept one became a slave of the Liethe. Whatever their powers, they played enchanting music.

An iron-strong hand lifted Kathein's chin. 'I've wondered about the colour of your eyes. I've only seen the length of the lashes.' She saw a man's face wrinkled with laughter, his shirt opened to a foam of white hair. He was an old man but he had all the grace of a blacksmith in full swing. He was Prime Predictor because the prophesies he had registered in the Archives as a youth had been more accurate than the vision of any other Kaiel. That was how the Kaiel elected their leader. He would be Prime Predictor until he died or retired or was ousted by a man who had proved a clearer vision.

Aesoe awed Kathein. She, whose greatest skill was the making of predictions in the simple world of light and stone and bouncing atom, could not even approach his ability to see and control the future. Half of a prophet's strength was his ability to monitor a prediction and *make* it come true. Aesoe was one of her gods. The God of the Sky was a comforting protector. Aesoe she feared.

He took her hand. 'I've done you a grievous harm,' he said, 'but I have no regrets.'

'I am too close to my sadness to understand.'

'Sadness is a disease of youth.'

'You're never sad?'

'Never.'

'I'm sad.'

'The maran-Kaiel family is expendable. You are not. That is the whole of it.'

'How can you say that about them! They're wonderful people! I know. I've loved them!'

'Hoemei I would hate to lose. The sun may rise on the day he becomes Prime Predictor. I could manage to say pleasantries at Gaet's funeral without gagging. And there is nothing I can do for Joesai. An impatient eater falls into the soup pot, goes the proverb. To lose Noe would cause a scandal in those circles where scandals are most quickly forgotten.'

'And my beloved Teenae?'

'I don't know if I am fond of Teenae or not. I've never slept with her.'

140

'You're callous!'

'I'm generous. I'm giving them Oelita. They can make use of that opportunity and be gloriously successful. Or they can fail. I see no alternative way of reaching the coast this generation. Yes, we have other mature families. But which of them is so impetuously foolhardy as the maran? You I dare not endanger. If our population was twice as large as it is, and twice as bright, I might ask you.'

'Then I can bargain.'

He smiled. 'As long as it has to do with physics and not love.'

'There's a machine I want built.'

He laughed. 'A mere machine? I had intended to give you far more than that. How about leading your own clan?'

Was he jibing her? That was her greatest dream. As a child she had drawn her own clan cicatrice and even now wore it between her breasts. It was an impossible dream, but to hear *Aesoe* offer it made her heart pound, even if he was only cruelly jesting. 'That is not yours to give,' she said with formal rebuff. Only a Gathering could create a new clan. As the Gathering of Ache had created the Kaiel.

'In the history of the clans, which clan was founded without a Gathering?'

'There is no such clan.'

'The Liethe.'

She searched her mind and found nothing, only tale and mystery and fear. 'There must have been a Gathering.'

'No. One woman created the Liethe. And so it shall be again. You can have whomever you want, up to a hundred bodies – from the craft clans, from the creches, from the Kaiel. As long as they are good at physics. If I have to divorce them from their families, you shall have them! You are to create the traditions and the breeding rules. Your assignment is to duplicate your own peculiar mental

141

bent – and perfect it if you can. I have predicted that the Kaiel shall win all of Geta if it is possible to true-breed your abilities. That is why I cannot risk your affair with the maran-Kaiel who perhaps are lovable but who are not worthy of you.'

He must be demented. Was this how senility suddenly attacked? She stared at him in amazement. 'You cannot . . .'

'I can! I am a Gathering of One! I am doing it!'

Kathein dropped to her knees again – weakly – and touched her head to the floor. 'The honour is too much.'

Quickly he knelt beside her and took her bowed head in strong hands that had held many women. 'How pleasant to see you no longer sad! I think you are liking my gift. Perhaps we will have time to share our mutual interests on the pillows?' He was chuckling. His grin was so wide that he had difficulty kissing her.

She was totally confused. 'Is that why you've brought me here and offered me my soul's desire with a plan that must defy all of Geta, because you lust for me?' There was sting in her voice.

He lifted her to her feet, undisturbed by the anger. 'It is uncanny to be the Prime Predictor. I see Kaiel power born through your womb – the vision is clear – but who knows if that is a future I see because I'm a prophet or because my lust for you drives me to create it? Who knows? Not I.' He was amused.

Kathein fled from him. 'Take me to my room,' she demanded of his servant. Her lone backward glance showed her one of the Liethe women moving to Aesoe's side. Safely in the room, she barricaded the furnishings against the massive door and lay on the bed sobbing out her love for Joesai and tender Gaet and shy Hoemei and Teenae whose kiss was as soft as the hoiela wing and Noe who loved her. It was hopeless. She would never touch them again, never kiss their scars. The most powerful man

142

on Geta had seen her body and desired it. She sobbed and sobbed and sobbed and when there were no more tears . . .

Thump.

A jerk of her head brought her facing the sound. The window had been taken from its casing. He was hunched there in the frame, grinning like a carnivorous ei-mantis ready to spring.

'You!'

'You don't think a simple barricade would stop me?' he said, climbing down into the room.

'I'll refuse you! I'll dig my claws into you!'

'No you won't.' He was laughing. 'I wouldn't be here if you were going to say no. It is a prediction I would put in the Archives.'

She pushed him away and turned her head while he kissed her cheeks and eyes and slipped about her neck some golden lace that held a foggy gem set by Liethe hands.

'You don't love me,' she wailed.

'Of course I love you. You're the finest woman I've desired all week.'

20

The fei flower that traps the pregnant geich female savours but briefly the eggs of the ferocious geich larvae waiting within her abdomen.

Proverb of the Stgal

Their base of operations had been shifted from inn to ship. Below deck Joesai quizzed his wife in depth with the sceptical thoroughness of a professional. Eiemeni, who was an expert in the Bnaen technique for cueing memory recall, helped him with questions. It did not seem probable that Teenae was right. Why should the Mnankrei risk burning a Stgal granary while they were negotiating to supply the Stgal with grain?

Teenae grew impatient. 'You play the doubting fool when you could be sharpening your knife. We must warn the townspeople and lead an ambush. We'll be heroes and make up for the stupid way you treated Oelita, the cruel way you treated your *betrothed*.'

'At the present moment we couldn't get away with accusing the Mnankrei of washing their bums in sea water. Maybe next week.'

Teenae was calmer now. 'I told you exactly how they are going to attack and when. That is what is important; not what people believe!'

'You told us what *Arap* told you,' said Eiemeni.

'You're still angry and want sudden vengeance,' said Joesai.

'Of course I want vengeance!' Teenae raged.

'Vengeance is a waiting game for one who can control his passion.'

Sensing a stone wall, the tiny woman changed tactics. 'That's why I have chosen *you* as my instrument!' She took his arm as if she needed his protection, grinning all the while. 'I'm just an overemotional woman and would spoil everything.' She paused. 'That's why you have to look out for me,' she added petulantly.

'Ho!' he said, feeling her tease and trying to edge her back towards reason. 'It is not *logical* for them to burn a granary now. It would make people suddenly forget how virtuous they are.'

'They could blame it on us,' she suggested wickedly.

Such a sobering thought prompted him to take her story seriously. He sent her away and four of his counsellors analysed the tale she had been told aboard the Mnankrei freighter. In the end they decided that it was probably the invention of a boy trying to impress a beautiful woman but to be on the safe side they had to assume it was true.

Joesai left a small crew in his ship and sneaked the rest of his men out onto the peninsula within striking distance of the granary. He deployed them efficiently. None of his watchers were in sight, but they could maintain patrols that kept the coast impenetrable. Any small waterborne vessel that might attempt to beach itself could be captured within a matter of heartbeats.

Scowlmoon, fixed in the sky, overlaid six times as much of heaven as did Getasun. At sunset it was darkly huge but as the night progressed and the crescent expanded from its evening sliver, the moon began to cast considerable illumination. On the moonless side of Geta a surprise manoeuvre under cover of night might have been possible – but not there. By halfmoon Joesai was ready to believe that it was already too bright for an attack. Either sea priest Tonpa had changed his mind or the boy was a mischievous liar.

Joesai glanced at the granary and for no particular reason was staring right at it when the orange roiling balls of flame erupted. The flames had soared to four man-heights before he heard the explosion. Firebombs! His first impulse was to run towards the fire – until the horror of their situation struck his imagination. The bombs had long been in place! Probably they had been set off by fireproof *Kaiel* clockwork.

He had been keel-hauled twice in one day!

There would be no Mnankrei about. But Joesai and his band were close to the fire and they would be blamed because there was no way to sneak back to the village without being seen. Thus it was emergency. They were heartbeats away from their lynching!

'Ho!' He was rising as he yelled. 'Avalanche formation! Run!' The piercing cry from his caller's pipes echoed his order.

The only thing they had going for them in their dash was that, though they might meet angry people on their way, none of these people would know how to fight or attack. Such were the children of the Stgal. And so nothing stopped Joesai's wedge until it reached a growing crowd on the stone wharf where their small ship had judiciously retired to a moat's distance. The ugly crowd half retreated as the wedge appeared but one braver group penetrated the Kaiel ranks – and were quickly catapulted into the water. The crowd moved back while Joesai lunged to protect his wife.

'Teenae!'

But Teenae was already falling with two stab wounds, crumpling, then pitching forward crazily. Raging, Joesai and five men slashed the crowd back while simultaneously their ship docked, first inflowing two men bearing the dying Teenae, then the other Kaiel in exact formation, and finally the rear guard, bumping the quay only once before casting off. With one reach of his massive hand

Joesai retrieved the knifeman from the sea by his hair, tossed him to a subordinate, and returned to Teenae.

Eiemeni was tending her on the deck.

'Back off, you meat-dresser. I'm the surgeon.' Joesai had had hours of meticulous practice on rejected babies of the creche before they were sent to the abattoir. 'I need a cloth!'

One was produced instantly from some back. On Geta there was no need to sterilize for routine surgery. Sacred bodies killed profane bacteria just as sacred wheat killed the beetles who tried to eat it.

'I'm dying,' came a feeble voice.

'Yeah, yeah. The pieces need to be sewed together. How can you kill an o'Tghalie body?' he said gruffly. 'They make them out of chromium-nickel-iron. God knows from where they get the gene combinations. They locate them with some kind of damn mathematical juggling. They don't tell us how they do it. It's a damn clan secret.'

'I'm weak.'

'That's because you need a transfusion. As soon as I can plug Otaam into you, you'll get it.'

'Dearest Joesai, even if you lose at kol every time you play, I'm glad . . . to have you around.'

'Shut up.'

Otaam, who had her blood type, had spliced into her. He did not move while she slept. Joesai stood guard until Scowlmoon was full and the eclipse came and passed. No ships attacked them. He promised himself that he would someday bring her those leather boots etched with the flying-storm-wave cicatrice of the Mnankrei. Silly, how he was willing to do anything for this strong-headed and rather foolish woman.

21

Whether you be saint or fiend, those you touch, through time
and persistence, will eventually be successful in doing to you
what you have so casually done to them.

Dobu of the kembri, Arimasie ban-Itraiel in *Rewards*

Teenae awoke at dawn, Blood-red Getasun bathed her
from its perch above the mountains with hands that
rippled redly over the bay. She examined the pain of her
wounds with her mind. 'I would drink blood for my
strength,' she said, meaning the blood of her assailant.

Joesai was brooding out across the bay and was not
aware that she had finally roused from her delirious sleep.
He did not hear her faint voice.

She rolled her head towards him and raised her voice. 'I
would drink blood for my strength!' she repeated angrily.

'Is that wise?' counselled Joesai, still deep in his reverie.
'He is one of Oelita's people. She showed us mercy. I am
in her debt. We can return mercy. Tae ran-Kaiel once said
that you can only hold a land where you have three times
as many friends as enemies.'

'I do not forgive a man who tries to kill me. I have
contempt for a man who tries to kill me and is captured. I
wish to see his generous offering to the Race so that the
Race may be purified.'

'Revenge should wait until your pain has healed.'

'No.'

Joesai shrugged. 'It will be dangerous to bring him on
deck and to give him a knife he might throw at you.'

'The obvious continually eludes you,' she said impatiently. 'Strap the knife to a mat so that it cannot be thrown. Leave one arm of my assailant free to rub his wrist against the blade.'

And so they carried her to the youth bound upon an iron-reed frame. Joesai, in his role as priest, invoked the ceremony in the expected musical monotone. His bearing changed. He spoke for the Race.

'We did not have kalothi. We died of the Unknown Danger.' The pain of the Race was in his voice. Then his voice became resonant until it challenged even the sea. 'And God in His mercy took pity and carried us from the Unknown Place across His Sky so that we might find kalothi. We wept when He gave us Geta. We moaned when He cast us out. But God's Heart was stone to our tears. Only in a harsh place beneath His Sky might we find kalothi. And only with kalothi shall we dare to laugh our laugh in the face of the Unknown Danger.'

Joesai brought out the priest's Black Hand and White Hand, each with special scars, each carved from wood and mounted on short rods. He held them above his head so that he became long-armed. 'Two Hands build kalothi.' With a vibrating sound that was half formal laughter, half formal grief, he meshed the wooden fingers together. 'Life is the Test. Death is the Change. Life gives us the Strength. Death takes from us the Weakness. For the Race to find kalothi the Foot of Life follows the Road of Death.' The small ship heaved upon the waves. No land, no sea on Geta was immune from this ritual.

Joesai's voice was implacable. 'All of us contribute to God's Purpose. All of us help distil the racial kalothi. Some of us are here to give Life. Some of us are here to give Death. Of these the greatest honour is to contribute Death for we all love Life.' He paused for only a moment but in that moment spliced irony into his monotone. His gaze was upon the youth. 'It is with awe that I accept the offering of your defective genes.'

'It is against the Code to kill,' said the youth serenely.

'Oelita's code, not mine!' snarled Teenae with such a thrust of hatred that her wounds stabbed her again.

'It is against the *Kaiel* Code to kill,' he sneered.

Joesai silenced Teenae with a piercing glance before she could reply a second time and returned his eyes to the youth. The Black Hand and the White Hand slightly askew, he answered in a voice that was more vengeful than priestly, 'Of course. And we shall not kill. We are only here to *receive* your offering.'

'I have no offering for you.'

Joesai continued the ritual, unperturbed by such blasphemy, bringing forth from his robe certain sensual delights which were the Receiver's obligation to the Giver. They were simple delights, for this was only a ship, not a temple. There was pure water, the touch of smooth glass, a shave, the taste of a berry. Each was refused.

Then came the time for the Cutting of the Wrists. But the youth defiantly held his fist away from the knife. Joesai placed the blood bowl. His men began the Chant of the Blood Flow, harmonizing like a giant heart in vigorous pulse, a heart whose beat began to slow and fade until it drifted away in silence. The youth laughed, proving he was still alive, but no man noticed because to them he was already dead.

Carefully, as if the Cutting of the Wrists had indeed been performed, as one would if he were planning to tan and shape and sew a fine leather coat from the hide of a corpse, Joesai began to skin the boy, unmindful of the surprised and then terrified screams that carried across the water and into the hills of Sorrow. The skinning was hardly begun before the boy's pain and fear took his wrist against the knife that had been bound into the mat. He cried out for mercy, for the skinning to stop until he had had time to die, but Joesai did not stop.

The butchering went quickly. No part was wasted. The

150

meat was salted or hung in strips to dry, glands were set aside for medicines, tendon and gut preserved, the bones went into a soup. A bowl of blood was presented to Teenae as her due.

Eiemeni, who had come to admire Oelita, expressed his regret as he washed the blood from his body in the sea with Joesai beside the wooden bulk of their ship. Joesai was unmoved as he sudsed his hair. 'He chose to approach Teenae by *my* rules while he expected *Oelita's* rules to protect him from reproach. Oelita lives by her rules and is protected by them. For her I have sympathy.'

They showed Teenae the hide as they stretched it for drying. She fingered the especially well-cut wheat stem cicatrice of the heresy. It would make a fine design on a leather binding for her copy of Oelita's book.

Oelita!

A thought startled her, causing her pain because her whole body reacted. 'Joesai! I forgot! In all the excitement I forgot to tell you that Oelita owns a Frozen Voice of God!'

22

I was impressed by the style in which you faced the Mnankrei
Tonpa while being true to the code you have forged for yourself.
You gamed with Death and won. How could I not count that as
the Second Trial of seven? You have earned my respect.
Someday, if you live long enough, perhaps I shall earn yours.

Joesai maran-Kaiel to Oelita of the Gentle Heresy

Oelita crumpled the note that had been penned in high
script on fine blue paper and delivered anonymously. She
threw it across the room at the four advisors she had
convened for a council. 'Manyar!' she raged, 'the Mnankrei and the Kaiel are crushing us like a nut between the
arms of a nutcracker! We have to fight! It is too soon!'

'It is always too soon,' said Manyar, pulling his robes
closer to his body.

'And you, Eisanti, is that all you have to contribute,
bland homilies that serve no further purpose than to keep
the high day conversation sparkling? The Mnankrei offer
us food while the Kaiel improve the road through the
mountains. The famine isn't even here yet and the beetles
are already laying their eggs to feast off our death. The
famine will come and then it will go, but will we ever rid
ourselves of the Mnankrei priests who will take our men
and women daily to that slaughterhouse in the Temple?
Will we ever rid ourselves of the Kaiel priests who salivate
after our tender children? We must resist them!'

Eisanti played nervously with his bracelets. 'We will
have to compromise until we are in a stronger position.
Manyar is right; we cannot take an unyielding stand as

152

yet. The tree bends until it is thick enough to resist the wind.'

'*Tomorrow* the Stgal are calling for the first of the Ritual Suicides. We *have* food! We don't know how much of the new crop the underjaws will devour! We don't know how much food we can buy. We don't know that it will be impossible to rely on our other sacred sources!'

Old Neri interrupted. 'O'Tghalie Sameese has calculated that there will be less death if the Stgal begin now.'

Oelita flared. 'Of what use are the numbers the o'Tghalie manipulate? If you have measured the breadth of your field wrong it does not matter that you have the length correct for you will not be able to calculate your acreage!'

'Perhaps she is right,' said Taimon from the back of the room. 'Perhaps the Stgal find this the opportune time to eliminate their opposition. Who will be able to say that they move with wrong motives?'

'It is our weakness,' said Manyar, cleaning his nails, 'that we attract the low in kalothi.'

'That is our strength,' retorted Oelita.

In the end, as she always did, she made her own decision. She waited until her council had dispersed inconclusively. Her fists were clenched. It was a shock to her to discover that because they all had high kalothi they weren't motivated enough to oppose the priests. But how could she form a council of the low in kalothi? She'd have to do all the thinking and she'd be constantly handling mistakes like that fool attempt to meet the Kaiel threat by murdering Teenae. *I suppose it was always thus,* she thought bitterly, *a society stays stable by preying on those least able to defend themselves.*

Her final decision was impulsive. She walked out into the town of Sorrow with only two bodyguards down where the old buildings began, and pulled together a fearful crowd of those who had the most to lose, melding them into a group

153

large enough so that they might find courage in each other while she led this mob towards the Temple.

All the Village of Sorrow above the waterfront was temple grounds. The Path of Trial wandered tortuously about the Temple itself and up over the hill above the Temple, twisting between the garden settings, each of its obstacles crafted to challenge the swiftness and strength and flexibility of some part of the body. Here the Stgal tested the physical kalothi of those who came under their jurisdiction. The Temple itself, built like a crescendo in this serpentine garden, began as a modest star that grew until the points of the star became halls dedicated to the Eight Sacred Foods and, continuing inward, transformed themselves into massive stone buttresses that rose majestically to support the tower that held at its pinnacle the rooms of Ritual Suicide. Nothing in Sorrow was taller than that tower. Whether the village was obscured by hill or haze, the tower could still be seen. Ships used it as a beacon. Of all the glories of the Stgal, the Temple of Sorrow was their greatest.

Inside the tower the gaming rooms spiralled around a shaft of air, seemingly supported by the light that laced through the coloured glasses of the tall, narrow windows. There a Getan might play kol and chess and games that could not be won without sharp eyesight or steady hand or creative mind or colour sense or ability to leap the obvious. Unobtrusively the Stgal priests kept score so that one's kalothi rating could be updated, while supporting the Temple by collecting coin for food and drink and the company of male or female courtesans.

Getans were addicted to games, and they flocked to their temples to meet and laugh and compete. Outside the temple they might gamble for money or favours; inside the temple the games were free. There a Getan was gambling with his life and loving it.

To the imposing Temple at Sorrow, Oelita brought her

154

motley group of losers who were not even sure that they had a right to life, much less sure that they had the ability to fight for it and win. Nearing the immense facade of this place where they had been defeated so often, some of the bawdy spirit that Oelita had infused in them began to vaporize. Here was the focus of their lost self-esteem. One man tripped and another made a loud joke about his friend's clumsiness. Oelita posted them in front of the main portal with instructions to be vocal about their protest but when she was gone they hung back and took on the nature of a crumbling wall of bricks that busy people pass without a glance.

Oelita was welcomed into the inner sanctum of the Temple as an honoured guest by the highest of the Stgal priests. They had been expecting her and received her with outward warmth. She was given cushions and drink and encouraged to talk. She spoke eloquently of opposition to both the Mnankrei and the Kaiel, and urged restraint in calling a condition of famine. There were other ways. There were other foods. Vaguely she had some of Nonoep's profane triumphs in mind. Oelita built her strategy on an appeal to Stgal vanity – they were as good as the Mnankrei and as good as the Kaiel, and cleverness could defeat their opponents.

The Stgal listened, drew her out, laughed with her, and finally, without explanation, had guards take her up to a room high in the tower. It was said of the Stgal that they would feast you with great camaraderie, waiting until the dessert to poison you. She could see her people down below. No one dispersed them, even noticed them. She shouted to them through the bars, but she was too high. No one heard. Till dusk she watched, and with the setting of the sun they just melted away.

Her tower room was more than comfortable. Here the kalothi-weak were pampered to honour the sacrifice they were to make for the Race. The Lowest on the List spent his last night with everything a Getan valued – clear water for the throat and incense for the nose and tastes for the tongue from the stamen of the hug flower and the chanting of a choir of friends and a mate to please the body. Here was gold to feel and the finest cloth to lie upon. Still, the window was barred with iron. From this window, they said, no more exalting sight ever met a human's eyes than that last transit of the God of the Sky across the stars.

She couldn't believe she was here. Was it a mirage, that fervent group of people she had commanded? They were ghosts. She was alone. Was it illusion to think that words would ever raise people to action? *The first crisis, and my words collapse like a sand city cut down by a single wave.* Was that loyalty? What made men stick together in good and in bad? *I thought I knew.*

She was trying to understand why she was here. It was against the rules. She had the highest kalothi rating in all of Sorrow. And then she laughed through the bars at the night sky. The rules were to be broken, as every kol master knew – if you could have the consequences of the broken rule. And what was her death to them? She would slash her wrists and die. *I'll have no choice.* No one would care. Life would go on as if she never was.

She found herself staring through the bars vacantly, thoughtlessly, waiting, waiting for God. And when God passed overhead, she laughed and cried. God was a stone. When you were brought up among a whole people who believed in God the Person, some of His Morality remained a part of your soul. God the Stone had no morality. Even knowing that, she had never really felt it before. She was here because there was no morality. God was a stone. That's all there had ever been.

And Oelita wept.

23

A man who never makes mistakes has long since ceased to do anything new. A man who is always making mistakes is a doomed man with swollen ambitions. But he who judiciously salts success with mistake is the rapid learner.

O'Tghalie Reeho'na in *The Mathematics of Learning*

The small ship and its one-masted companion were anchored near an ancient breakwater that was smashed by wave action. Someone had tried basing a small fleet here long ago and had given up, defeated by a rocky coast, harbourless and inhospitable to ships. Joesai chose this refuge only because of an o'Tghalie clanhome in the mountains near the sea. Teenae had been carried on a stretcher up through the foggy woods and left with relatives to recuperate.

The sweet moments he spent with Teenae soothed his brooding turmoil. Restlessly he wandered through the woods, once finding a red flower of an intricate design he had never seen before, bringing it back to Teenae knowing that his little gift would please her. His anguish was forgotten.

'It is like a little temple,' she said and smiled at him.

'I was up on the peak looking to see if our ships were still there.'

'In this mild weather you expect them to blow away?'

'I expect the Mnankrei to sweep down upon us.'

'We'll run away together. We can fly before the wind faster than they can. Haven't I had experience as a sail?' she teased, laughing and taking his hand.

The o'Tghalie observatory fascinated Joesai, for he had always been interested in the stars. He often brought a bottle and a load of bread along the trail at dusk to spend the night there with one of Teenae's uncles who told stories about that imp's stubborn youth. 'You can see why they sold her!' And he'd roar with laughter.

This uncle was not a very conventional man. He had a love of instruments, which was unusual among the o'Tghalie. He was the renegade who had taught Teenae things she shouldn't have known. O'Tghalie brains were peculiar in that if they did not learn to perform complicated additions and multiplications in their heads as a child, they never learned to do these operations well. Thus o'Tghalie women, denied school as young girls, became servants rather than mathematicians.

Joesai was awed when he watched 'uncle' o'Tghalie take measurements and transform the numbers by elaborate computation during a mere pause and holding of the breath. But uncle was not a man who rested happy with mysteries, and one cloudy night he showed Joesai how to 'throw the bones', a system he had devised so that a non-mathematician might calculate with reasonable accuracy. It was based on the weird principle that multiplications could magically be transformed into additions and back again. Joesai was so delighted by this trick that one morning he brought the bones with him and set them up behind Teenae's head so that she wouldn't see what he was doing. He had her give him multiplications to perform which he was able to do correctly, to her amazement.

Joesai learned some facts about astronomy that he had never known before. Once he was speculating with Teenae's uncle about a philosophical point Oelita had made in a pamphlet. God behaved like a stone. Joesai was convinced that, since God wasn't a stone, there should be some way of pointing up the difference.

Uncle brightened perceptibly and dragged Joesai down

to the library to pore over soiled books of calculations. God's orbit was indeed predictable to a high degree of accuracy, but there had been two anomalies. The orbit had changed twice with no known cause since it had been under observation. No other celestial objects ever did that.

Joesai remembered Oelita's crystal and what Teenae had said about it. He was sure that it was only a piece of glass, but what if it really was one of Kathein's crystals? The enigma of the Silent God was the most fascinating of Geta's puzzles and it might well be worth a major effort to look into this piece of the riddle. He hadn't thought about Oelita for a while. He had been preoccupied with the astonishing revelation of Mnankrei intentions the night of the silo firebombing. He was now planning a probe into northern waters. But perhaps while the men took the ship north, he could make a quick return expedition to the south and find out more about that crystal.

He rounded up two little o'Tghalie girls who were pestering their mothers at the paper mill and took them out so that they might show him the source of the mill's clay. That became a pleasant high day spent moulding clay models of the houses around Oelita's residence from memory and telling tales to his wide-eyed companions.

Oelita's house, he recalled, was perched on a hill with an easily defended back and no access to the front at all, or so it seemed – except to a man like Joesai, to whom the scaling of sheer stone walls was a minor climbing trick that required only a hammer and iron-reed spikes, He could station two spies with flags on two select rooftops and break in with a very low probability of discovery. Teenae he had already quizzed in detail about the interior. She knew exactly where the crystal was kept. The foray into Sorrow should be a quick in-and-out affair. After his disasters there, he wasn't really willing to linger.

Simultaneously he planned a cautious reconnaissance

up north while his two tiny o'Tghalie counsellors climbed his shoulders and pulled at his ears and hair with clay-slick hands.

'I'll feed you to the Mnankrei,' he said nasally as one of the girls pinched his nose and held on.

'I'll stew you in ca-ca!' retorted the girl while the other giggled.

Joesai rose to his full height and tucked the girls under his arms. 'Off to the sea we go.'

'Why the sea? I'm hungry.'

'The sea is where the cannibal sea priests are! *They're* hungry!'

The girls began to squeal and wriggle, but he got them to the rocky ledge where swimmers went, tossed them into the water and gave them a bath, so he wouldn't have to return them to their mothers full of clay. 'Let me show you my little sailboat.'

He had acquired a swift three-man vessel for the trip south, and so the larger ship would go north under the command of Raimin. Later they would reunite for a more daring raid against the Mnankrei. Joesai was anxious to bring back to Teenae her pair of boots but was wary of pitting his sailing skills against those of a seasoned Mnankrei priest. He watched the naked girls play in the tiny vessel. He was not yet sure of a strategy. Sinking wheat-laden boats headed south was appealing, but such a tactic was a double-bladed dagger since it meant starvation for those who did not receive the wheat. Judgmental errors of that magnitude tended to annoy Aesoe. How would Aesoe think? He would steal the wheat and reship it. Joesai laughed.

'Come along,' he said to his two clean girls.

'Catch us!'

A sudden storm nearly wrecked his too-small vessel on its way to Sorrow, delaying them a full day and smashing three of Eiemeni's ribs. A much-sobered Joesai debarked for his brief mission. He wore a faint make-up that emphasized unnatural lines in his facial cicatrice so that recognition would be more difficult, but there was little chance of discovery in their covert route to Oelita's residence. Strangely they found only one man guarding her place, at the rear. Breaking in via the frontal wall was easier than expected.

A quick search showed that much rearrangement had occurred since Teenae had been here. The crystal was gone. Nor was there time for a destructive search. Joesai had no intention of alerting the outside guard, and so when his flagmen signalled the all clear, he retreated down the wall leaving his iron-reed spikes in place.

The three men regrouped in the street, moving not as fast as they might have because of Eiemeni's ribs. Storm-winds were still lashing them but they preferred the miserable weather because the clouds and rain and fog shrouded them and gave them an excuse to hide their faces behind wraps. Few villagers were abroad.

'We'll have to find out where she is.'

'That'll be days. We aren't equipped.'

'She's probably not in town or her place would be better guarded.'

'I'll find out.' Joesai was thinking of several inns where he might pick up some information but one with a small wheat stalk carved into its door struck him as ideal. He reconnoitred the streets for the best escape paths, and entered, dripping, holding his cloak close about him. He ordered a hot mead and when it came spoke casually to the barkeep. 'Any more news of Oelita?'

'She's still in the tower.' The voice caught. It was upset.

Joesai allowed himself a quick sip of mead while he digested that. The Stgal had picked her up. They would kill her. Incredible. 'A rough place to be,' he muttered.

By the time he was out on the street again, he had decided what they would do. He looked at Rae and

Eiemeni. 'Rae, you're the strongest. Get back to that God's bane of a boat of ours and bring the spy's-eye. Eiemeni, I want you to lay out a path from the Temple tower that just fades into the town. Take your time. Learn every stone. I'll have to go to the Temple for some information. We'll meet at Five Cross, or if that gets too prickly, the Eighth Marker at the waterfront. I'll try to get back by the third highnode of God. If I'm not, wait for highnode of the next Orbit.'

The Temple was lightly attended. Joesai had his choice of courtesans. He picked a small girl he knew was new to town, a pretty Nolar girl, probably a runaway. He asked for a quiet game of kol in one of the more expensive booths. Privacy was important after that silo-bombing fiasco. The girl played a creditable game. She was eager to please and he began a conversation with her, slowly.

Part of him was not comfortable trying to charm information out of such a lovely youth, but another part of him was long used to inducing people to tell him what he wanted to know. The secret was to start them talking about what interested them, then get their speech level up to a chatter and listen.

This girl was fascinated by the Temple. It was the most beautiful place she had ever worked, so he got her to talk about it. It wasn't long before she touched the topic of the fabulous tower rooms. She knew he wouldn't be touchy on the subject because she could sense instinctively his kalothi level, and the luxury of working with Ritual Suicides intrigued her.

'There's going to be some consoling for you to do up there,' he said to keep her on the topic.

'A poor woman is in the north room already. I hear her crying every night. Why are they keeping her so long?'

'Have you served her?'

'Oh no. The north room is not mine. I'm new and that's the finest room. If I stay here long enough, maybe. I'd like that. If I please enough men maybe they'll let me.' She smiled ravishingly, and he could feel her embarrassment.

He let her please him. She started with a hot bath that did wonders for knotted muscles that had been through a howling night of near death on the sea. It was the best thing he could do before the coming ordeal. He paid his petite courtesan well so that there would be no lingering doubt in her mind about her ability to please.

He knew most of Oelita's people by rote memory and picked from his mental files the man he wanted, a burly ironsmith who was as gentle as he was big. When Joesai entered his smithy, the man was at work, his forge fire challenging the cracks of its prison walls.

'You!' The man raised a red hot rod but Joesai knew he was harmless.

'I need your help.'

'My help!' the man choked.

Joesai had chosen to reach this man through a judicious mixture of falsehood, truth, and bamboozlement. 'Ho! you believe every lie the Stgal tell?' He knew the Stgal were well known for their oily versions of the truth. 'Why do you think I would harm the gentle Oelita? Would you? Ho!' he emphasized, moving right to the point, 'it is the Stgal who have her in their prison, is that not so?'

'You tried to kill her!'

'Are you sure?' He lied by indirection. 'It is the Stgal who wish her dead. Isn't that self-evident now? And if the Stgal had tried to kill her, wouldn't it be like them to direct the blame elsewhere? If there is a famine now, cannot they clean their streets of the infestation of heretics? Who knows who caused the silo fire? Who has better access to it than the Stgal?'

'Your woman confessed!'

'After being raped and abused and hung from a ship's mast all night! Do you call that a confession?'

The ironsmith returned his rod to the fire. 'You were

163

seen at the site of the silo burning.' He waited with his hand on the rod.

'And why should I have been so clumsy!' snarled Joesai, releasing his emotions now that he was certain they would not betray the truth. 'Would I do a thing like that in broad sight? For what gain? The Kaiel have wheat and cannot sell it to you because of the mountains. Recall that when the silo was bombed, the Mnankrei were negotiating with your Stgal to sell you wheat! Perhaps those two infamous clans plotted this together? By so doing the Stgal could rid themselves of your like, hoping to betray the Mnankrei later. The Mnankrei would see such a deal as an opening to betray the Stgal and so gain dominion over the coast. My wife overheard the Mnankrei scheming to burn your silo and we scoffed at her but prudently deployed ourselves to prevent such an atrocity, failing in a way that made us look both guilty and foolish.' He did not wait for a reply. 'Do you wish your Oelita out of the tower? I'll bring her out.'

The smith's eyes were narrow with suspicion. 'Why?'

'To clear my name,' he lied. 'I have not enjoyed the way the Stgal have made a fool of me.'

'No one can escape from the tower.'

'Give me iron spikes and a rhomboid jack. Do you have that? I need nothing else.'

The smith's mother appeared at the inner doorway, rag in hand, a feeble woman, half blind, half deaf, a candidate for the tower in times of famine. 'Who is he? Why do you shout?'

'I will let you follow me,' implored Joesai, striding now more boldly towards the fire. 'You will see for yourself that your Oelita remains safe. Her friends can help. If I'm lying and I remain here and she remains in the tower, how can I harm her? If I'm telling the truth, how can I harm her if I carry her down while all of you watch my every movement?'

'What's he babbling about?' croaked the old woman hysterically.

'Old mother. The man needs a jack.' He returned his attention to Joesai. 'Of what use is a jack?'

'And spikes. I'll look at all the jacks you can find, and pick the best one.' He turned to the hag and spoke slowly and with directed volume, for she was evidently hard of hearing. 'And you, kind woman, if you've some hot soup, I have a long climb up the outside of the tower, and soup would do me good. Your son and I are going to rescue our beloved Oelita!'

The woman beamed, understanding at last.

Totally in control, Joesai approached the furnace and picked up a glowing rod with a pair of tongs he appropriated. 'I'll need spikes that fit between the stones of the tower. This is too thick. I'll show you.' He began to hammer the metal until it was the shape he wanted. 'Like this! Can we make them?'

'No one has ever climbed the tower without a scaffold,' said the ironsmith, taking the spike and quenching it.

Joesai grinned. His cloak was steaming and his diagrammed face had already begun to sweat. 'Ho! That's why we'll get away with the preposterous feat of stealing our heretic away from the Stgal!'

24

A secret shared is no longer a secret.

Saying of the Liethe

The caravan of a hundred and twenty men stretched along the Itraiel desert. Behind them lay the mountain range called The Pile of Bones and, to their left, the implacable Swollen Tongue. Here the land was flat or gently rolling, but greener, though the vegetation was never more than waist high.

Three massive Ivieth clansmen pulled the wagon in which she rode. There had been four but one had died. That meant meat for a day. The woman who bore the outward name Humility, yet who was driven by a more lethal inward name, had enjoyed the stringy toughness of roast Ivieth but was less pleased with the walking that became necessary to alleviate the load on the remaining three porters. Without a full team, the passengers often had to push the wagon themselves when the road was rough.

Tonight they were making camp on a rise where the Ivieth kept a murky well but maintained no permanent settlement. She ran to exercise her limbs, dancing even, for she was a dancer and the suppleness of her body gave her great delight. When she skipped too far from the caravan road a giant Ivieth trundled after her. The Ivieth herded their passengers with care.

'Wanderlust is not wise,' his voice boomed reproachfully.

'Look!' She held up a spray of blue flowers whose tips deepened to purple. 'Have you ever seen anything so gay?' She shook off her hood and put the sprig in her hair, defying the giant to be angry with her.

'It is not wise to touch what you do not know.' He checked her leggings to see that she was properly protected for a walk in the desert.

'These innocent little blue flowers?' Humility grinned up at him and slipped her slim fingers around the elbow of her self-appointed protector. His elbow brushed her shoulder. She let him lead her back through the brush to safety, elated by her uncommon discovery.

In the blue flower lurked a poison rare enough that it was unrecorded in the literature. The petals, when sundried and then leached in alcohol, yielded a sweet essence so powerful that drops of it could kill a man. It numbed like one whisky too many, filling the body with a rosy warmth, a pleasant drunken stupor, and then the heart stopped. Assassin's Delight was the only name by which she knew the flower.

Her own name was recorded as se-Tufi'87 but she was addressed as the se-Tufi Who Walks in Humility. Like every Liethe woman Humility wore her line signature in scar. The se-Tufi were signed by seven nodules running from the base of each eye to the jawline like a string of jewels, and a bracelet of nodules on the upper left arm. She was not adorned with the sign for 87 because every Liethe of a line expected to be used interchangeably with her sisters. Unlike the bodies of normal women, Liethe were uncut except for the line signature. Humility also carried a secret name which she had taken, as was the custom, on the night when she had seduced her first priest – a white-haired priest of Saie, now dead. The name locked in her breast was Queen of Life-before-Death and that was how she thought of herself.

After pressing her precious flower, Humility used her

brass mirror to retouch the facial makeup she wore to disguise her almost scarless features under appropriate artistry. It was taboo for a Liethe to reveal her clan while travelling. She ate rations of biscuit and honey and mash standing up against the wheel of her wagon, and then wandered ahead to spend the last of the evening by the fire of the Ivieth, her cowl over her head against the sudden cold.

She loved the Ivieth songs. It was the musician in her. How they sang about Scowlmoon! She could not imagine what it was like to have a moon in the sky since she had lived all of her life on the far side of the planet. As if it were a slowly rising cookie in the sky's oven, the moon nudged above the horizon, day by day a little higher. It was exciting.

The giants laughed so. They enjoyed their songs so. How could she resist snitching a small harp and singing to them one of her own ballads? Liethe Code would not permit her to sing a Liethe song. Liethe music was for the priests. She threw her melodiously high voice farther than the reach of the fire.

On the Mountain Kaemenek
A wildish road claws steep incline
Where I take rest
To overlook the Drowned Hope.

Gusts of fury lashing by,
And drifting clouds maraud the sky.
I hold my cloak
Above a Sea of Drowned Hope.

Swift the blooded circle-sun
Quick quenches all its daytime heat
And boils the Sea
To reddened rush of Drowned Hope.

I'll not see this sight again,
Nor ever come this way again,
But I'll take rest
In song of spume at Drowned Hope.

They arrived in Kaiel-hontokae by night. She hardly noticed the approach, so intent was her interest in the moon. For a week the moon had dominated the horizon, growing. Now it was fully risen. All through each day it waned until by sunset there remained but a thin sickle arcing above the distant mountain line. The sickle reversed to become a bowl during the blazing yellow-reds of Getasun's retreat and then began to fatten as the wagons squeaked westward into a purpling night. Scowlmoon! The moonless world of her youth had vanished!

She left the wagon and walked towards this moon, hypnotized. Even the stars dimmed in its glory! It lit the land! She had a shadow at night, a pale extension of herself that disappeared down the road! Great Scowlmoon brought music to her feet and song to her heart. What a night for loving in a landscape erotic with the soft red pallor of sinister death.

Finally she begged one of the Ivieth to let her ride on his shoulders. She was scarcely a burden for him. She was such a small thing, clinging to his hair, her legs crossed upon his chest. That was her perch when she first saw Kaiel-hontokae by moonlight, the ghost form of the aqueducts, the shadowed symmetry of the buildings.

Ho! she thought as they mounted the crest of a hill and glimpsed distantly the cadaverous ovoids of the Palace celebrated in song but never seen, *mine enemy who will be my lover!* Skilfully she lifted her feet to the Ivieth's shoulders and rose in perfect balance with her arms outstretched. The Ivieth reached a hand to steady her. She kicked it aside. Slowly she doubled over, and made a half twist, and then a head stand, her hair buried in his, her feet toed to the zenith, so that she might view a Palace turned upside down.

The cell she was assigned in the Liethe hive at Kaiel-hontokae had been built within the buhrstone walls of an old whisky cellar. There was floor for a sleeping mat and upright space for simple wooden furniture – but no tapestries, no luxuries at all. She woke early, prayed, and, to clear away the mood-residue of dreams, assumed the mental attitude of White Mind while placing her body successively in the Three Positions.

Then, unhurriedly, to work. She allocated a sun-height of time to her memory drills, today a review of two songs and the mnemonic key to her genetic file.

A face sneaked into her room, giggled and retreated. Humility leapt up, barefooted, still bare-breasted, and peered down the hallway. 'Hey!'

The face reappeared, cloaked in hair robe and also with bare feet. A face with bare feet. *Her* face with bare feet. She giggled. Humility's clone sister smiled in reply. 'The se-Tufi Who Cocks Her Ear,' said the woman, cocking her ear in formal introduction.

'The se-Tufi Who Walks in Humility,' came the formal response coupled with the flat hand and the drop of the eyelid gesture that was universally associated with humility. The Liethe of the same genetic line used these quick signals to recognize each other.

'Would you like to break fast? Come.'

The kitchen was austere, but there were bins of flour and potatoes and ample jars of ground bees and spices. 'I'd like pancakes and honey.'

They began to mix the batter and gossip as if they had always known each other. 'Have you heard the fame of Aesoe? You're my replacement. I'm pregnant by him. This time it is a girl.' She meant: this time it did not have to be aborted. 'The old crone is sending me to hivehome to have the baby. I've never travelled so far. I was born in Oiena. You've travelled.' Cocked Ear would already have exchanged data with other se-Tufi sisters about Humility and have it accessible in her genetic performance files even though they had never met. 'What's it like to walk so far? I get to cross the Njarae by ship!'

'I saw the moon last night!' Humility was rapturous.

'Is *that* all that happens when you travel! I'm afraid of rape. Were you ever raped?'

Humility slid out of her chair and, before she had turned around, began a forward thrust that took her into the air as a rotating ball which uncoiled, feet first, to hit the far wall with a devastating thump. She fell back into a cartwheel and landed gracefully where she had begun, on her feet. 'You should see the look of surprise on a man's face when you smack him in the chest that way!' She went back to the pancakes.

'Where did you learn such ferocity?'

Humility only smiled. The training had been part of her assassin's course. 'Ugh. Travelling is mostly getting out and pushing your own wagon when the Ivieth die on you. That was the most interesting day of my last trip. I've never been to an Ivieth funeral before. You're lucky you get to sail across the Njarae, I've read so many poems about the Njarae that I get hoiela wings fluttering in my brain just thinking about it. Imagine the ocean at night with Scowlmoon in the sky and the sails out and one of those munchy Mnankrei with his smelly arm around you on deck, tucking you under his armpit. I swoon.'

Cocked Ear curled her nose.

Humility was instantly aware of the hostility. She was surprised. The Liethe had been Mnankrei allies for centuries. It was widely believed among the Liethe that the Mnankrei would rule all of Geta come the Union. Liethe who had served Mnankrei lovers were proud of it. Humility had once strangled a wandering priest who carried messages against the Mnankrei. 'The Mnankrei have kalothi,' she said.

'The Mnankrei are evil!'

'Beetle piss.' Humility took a mouthful of pancake. 'You've been living in Kaiel-hontokae too long. It's time you were moving on.'

171

'The Kaiel have a magic ear in the Palace that can listen to the Mnankrei talking *right now*! What those sailors are doing frightens me.'

'Who's telling you about magic ears?'

'Aesoe!'

'The Kaiel are vowed enemies of our Mnankrei! Do you believe everything a fat old priest tells you? They love pulling off girls' legs and eating them right up to your brains!'

Cocked Ear smiled a little laugh that made the beads of scars down her cheek part like a curtain. 'I know he does. He laughs afterwards too. He had this poor Kaiel woman over the other day and while she was piling the furniture up against her door, he was coming through the window! Thank our God for Mind Control. I had to go into White Mind to keep a bland face. Aesoe is such an adorable baby. I worry that he's going to have a heart attack.'

Humility was choking on her pancake, wide-eyed. 'You're in love with him!'

'I am not!'

'It's just that he's a good bum kisser?' Humility teased.

'I'll miss him,' Cocked Ear admitted. 'I hope his daughter grows into the greatest line the Liethe have ever known! He adores us. He really does!'

'Recksh,' she gurgled. 'And I have to sleep with this man?'

'All the time knowing that he thinks you are me while you're cooing at him!' the sister retaliated.

'God's Streak, this is going to take some getting used to.'

'Our old crone is only going to give you three high days to assemble your act.'

Humility's eyes widened. 'So soon?'

'She's going to work you down to soup stock!'

'Don't we ever wear out?' The hive mother, Humility knew, was of the same se-Tufi line as they were. She was the notorious se-Tufi Who Finds Pebbles.

'No, we don't wear out, we just get bitchier.'

Humility thought about that. The hive mother had lived five of Humility's lives. That was a lot of bitchiness. 'Why the hurry?'

'The se-Tufi Who Sings at Night has been filling out Aesoe's threesome this week but she is to be sent south. That leaves only four of you for three roles. I'll be here for a while as a back-up, but not for long.'

'What kind of a kalothi-zero is this Aesoe? His ego is so big he needs *three* mistresses and for ten thousand sunrises he never notices that they are playing a shell game with him and he never notices that they aren't aging? This is the man who overlords the Kaiel? This is the man who has delusions of grandeur that cover the whole land? The Mnankrei will skin him alive!'

'He likes to sleep with his head pillowed on your breasts. And he snores.' Cocked Ear was enjoying herself.

'I'm going to love this! Women have killed men for less!'

'And when he calls you Honeybee, your reflex action is to snuggle up and suck at his ear lobe.'

Another woman entered the kitchen, taller than a se-Tufi, fuller of hip and more sultry of face, wearing a signature of eight nodules on her forehead. The jawline was almost familiar. She made the sign of the berry, hurriedly, and headed for the pancake batter, but when Humility returned the sign of humility, she stopped and broke into a smile.

'I don't know you!'

They introduced themselves formally. She belonged to a daughter line of the se-Tufi which was not yet established over the full age range, having been founded only half a lifetime ago with the melding of se-Tufi and be-Mami ova. Such a line, like most Liethe lines, had no father.

Three introductions later, as the kitchen filled up, the

crone appeared in the doorway looking straight at Humility, the first really older version of herself Humility had ever met. It was a shock. She was *old*. Humility knew well the map of her own line. This woman would be close to death – but her mind would still be strong, her ways demanding, and her energy relentless if economical.

'Your drill begins now,' said the crone mother severely.

'Yes old one.' Humility was on her feet and bowing. She did not finish her pancakes.

25

If one is wary of an enemy bringing gifts, can there ever be the union of mankind under God's One Sky?

> The lonepriest Rimi-rasi to the
> Gathering that Honoured God

The squeak woke Oelita to a sudden sitting position. Panic located the intermittent noise at the window. Then she saw the screw between the bars, happily turning and pausing in an erratic fashion, pulling together two heavy nuts that were, in turn, pushing a rigid framework against the bars, bending them and in the process slowly extracting them from their stone base. It was fascinating because no one could be out there. She watched for a while. The screw turned and paused, turned, grunted, protested, paused again. A bar broke loose and the machine sagged. Instantly she grabbed the rhomboid shape and pondered for a moment how to reset it between the remaining bars. She would have to rewind the screw until the machine was thin again. 'Shall I reset it?' she asked the sky, bewildered.

'Ho,' came a voice on the wind, 'that would save me a nasty trip. Any guards?'

'They're asleep.'

'Is the bent bar free?'

'I think I can work it free.'

'Don't drop it outside . . . make a racket to wake God!'

'Where are you?'

'I'm the beetle on the windowsill.'

For thumping heartbeats she said no more, but just

reset the screw and removed the loosened bars. The screw was being worked by a metal rod from above. Finally she could stick her head out and look down below, far below, at the Temple's base. The height was sickening. Normally it wouldn't have bothered her. 'Are you coming inside to help me?' she asked weakly.

'No. You're coming outside to help yourself.'

'I'll never get down!'

'All you need to do is crawl out the window and gravity will take it from there.'

'I hate your sense of humour!'

'Ho! I thought this was a good time for levity.'

She had no choice. Her heart was racing and she began to crawl out the window, clawing for a grip that found only smooth stone. When she saw the man above her, she froze in terror. It was Joesai, the Kaiel murderer. The wind that was trying to blow her away and her own expectations had changed the voice.

'Ready for Trial Three?' He was grinning in supernatural stance on a ledge above her, a ledge half a footprint in breadth.

'I'm going back inside.'

'There's a door in that room, and it is Death's door. Your choice.'

She was so paralysed that she couldn't even return. 'You'll kill me!'

'No,' he grinned. 'Won't have to.'

She took the harness he lowered to her, made from the hide of some unfortunate pauper. It fitted around her waist and under her crotch. Iron rings were sturdily woven into the belt. He showed her how the ropes attached and how to walk down the wall with her weight being held by a piton, but mostly the wind took his words and she had to reason out the process. He let her lower herself while he backed her up and then he lowered himself while she backed him up. Once he screamed because she was doing

176

something wrong but it was too late and a piton gave way and all the security of the rope was gone. She fell. Terror. But the second rope went taut and she was slammed against the stone. She never even paused. She just secured herself and called up the signal. 'Ready! Go!' He dropped and secured himself. 'Ready! Go!' he shouted down at her. When they reached a ledge on the first large buttress the terror came back again and she had to fight it off before she could move on.

'In Trial Four you have to climb *up.*' He laughed the great laugh while they shared this ledge built for one and a half.

'Why don't you just push me off!' she replied savagely.

'Kiss me or I will.'

She was clinging to him, but not out of love.

'We have to go,' he said.

'I can't.'

He waited patiently. He waited longer than he wanted to wait. 'You've shown at least half of the courage you need to get down.'

'If this is a Trial in a Death Rite, you shouldn't be helping me.'

'I'm not. I'm not carrying you on my back, am I?'

They reached the roof. He lowered the ropes and harness to a strategically placed lackey after being given the all clear signal. Then they jumped. The waiting small crowd had robes for them and they faded into the town. Joesai indicated a gaming tavern up a side street. 'Ho! I have thirst after such a climb!'

'No,' Oelita protested, pulling at his robe. She didn't want to risk it.

'You really think the Stgal cowards will come after you now?'

'They were going to murder me!'

'Never. They were merely working on a ruling to give you special permission to contribute your known Ainokie gene to the Great Chromosome Sink.' Joesai laughed, picked her up and carried her into the tavern, continuing the conversation by whispering into her ear.'And you pissed on them by waving your kalothi while they sat in ponderous debate. They'll have their heads tucked up their arseholes tonight!'

He set her down on the tile floor while their companions swarmed up the stairs behind them, then made a flourish to the startled customers. 'May I present the Gentle Heretic!' And he took her arms roughly, and, stripping the sleeves from them, held her arms up, wrists out, unslashed wrists, in the universal gesture of high kalothi. The barkeep was weeping. Both drinkers and gamers cheered, raising their mugs. An old man went to his knees on the floor. Joesai bought the house a round of mead, courtesy of Aesoe's coin vaults.

She was sitting at her table with fingers around her mead when Joesai brought her a handful of spiced wheat sticks to help along her thirst. 'I don't understand you,' she said. 'I don't understand your morals. I don't understand your beliefs, even your loyalties. Why do you do what you do? Is it possible that we might stop your little game and start something simple? Perhaps a friendly bout of chess?'

'I always lose at chess.'

'I noticed. You're a fool for a set-up – that move where your opponent threatens a piece and you rush up to protect it, and two moves later you have lost your defender.'

Joesai clanked her mead mug with his and smiled wryly. 'Then you know I didn't burn the silo?'

'I wasn't sure. I told you I didn't understand you.'

'Life is a race to outwit Death.'

'No it isn't. Life is peace if you create that peace.' She looked him in the eyes and saw the transit of a dark moon across a green and alien planet. 'Peace?' she implored.

He laughed. 'Till tomorrow!'

When they took her home, Joesai's two men comman-ded a patrol of men who checked out every intersection and alley and doorway before they moved forward. He told her there was no danger but he wanted to be thorough. He offered to lead her out of Sorrow to some strongpoint she could hold.

It was while they were waiting for patrol feedback at a corner that Oelita got impatient and peered around Joesai up the street, touching him, her hands holding one of his arms. She wondered then if she could seduce him. She had always been honest with her favours, not promising what she could not give, and had found that genuine affection with a little physical spice bonded men to her and often changed them. Why not keep him with her for a few days?

Where will I go? She could go to Nonoep's farm. It was the logical place from which to mastermind a defence against the Mnankrei. Nonoep knew how to extract safe food from all kinds of profane vegetation. They could defeat the Mnankrei that way. But he was Stgal and, for all his rebellious nature, carried their fatal trait of help-lessness in the face of large projects.

In a dire emergency Nonoep could probably provide food for ten people, but town-scale production would frustrate and defeat him. He was Stgal, dreamy, amoral, self-centred, finicky about detail to a point where he lost track of deadlines and schedules. He would make a huge batch of jam and forget to have pots to put it in. She laughed, remembering.

Perhaps if Joesai were with her, organization of volume profane food production might be possible. She could keep him close to her. Surely a man could not harm a woman who pleased him. She wondered how Nonoep would receive another man. He was not the domestic type. But she had made love to the glassblower and he had not minded.

Of course Joesai had his woman. Teenae had hinted that there was place for another. She was recovering from her wounds somewhere and he would go back to her. *I liked Teenae. Teenae liked me.* Perhaps together? Teenae, she knew, would relish humiliating the Mnankrei. Such a ruthless game of kol she played!

Whatever was done, had to be done soon. Once the sea priests came with their wheat and their administrators, it would all be over. It frightened her to be trusting the Kaiel. They were just as violent as the Mnankrei. They coveted this land just as much. What was the difference between Teenae being hung from the mast of a ship, and the way Joesai had fixed her in an iron-reed basket to drown? *But I can reach Joesai,* she thought. *I'll reach him tonight.*

When her convoy arrived home she simply ignored the pandemonium of the neighbours finding her safe and the refusal of her guards to leave her. She showed Joesai the incredible view through pale green windows at the front of the house overlooking the Temple. Her house was built on the high ground above the town. 'I love it up here but I chose this building for its safety.'

'You're almost at the height of the tower.'

'My tower of Life and their tower of Death.'

'Teenae enjoyed it up here.'

'She told you?'

'Yes.'

'Is she well?'

'She's chattering again. She was telling me about your insect collection and that little crystal you have.'

'I remember that the crystal impressed her. She called it a Voice of God. You Kaiel are such superstitious people.'

'I find it superstitious to think of God as a rock. And dangerous. Could I see the crystal? It is probably just very nice glass.'

Oelita was indignant. 'It is *not* glass!' She went and

180

brought it. 'The place was such a mess when Teenae was here. I'd just moved and didn't know how to use my space yet.'

Joesai took the crystal reverently and she could see his excitement. 'It *is* a Frozen Voice of God.'

'What does that mean to you?'

They were interrupted by the entrance of the ironsmith who had made the pitons for the tower climb. Joesai greeted him warmly and set down the crystal and took Oelita over to tell her what a great help he had been. 'I can't believe you're safe,' said the huge man, moved almost to tears. Their eyes locked fondly. When she looked around again, Joesai was gone and so was the crystal.

There was no way he could have passed through to the rear of the house. He had to be on the balcony. Outside she noticed the iron-reed spikes running down her front wall, but only because she had just mastered the descent of the tower facing and walls no longer seemed like barriers to her.

She wheeled around, returning to the house, 'That man!' She was furious. 'Thief! God's bane! He's a liar!' she stormed. 'Maiel! Herzain! He's taken my crystal! Can we catch him! It's a nothing crystal, but I found it and I want it back!'

One of her friends came forward. He was of the iron-reed dredgers. 'No need to chase them. I know where their boat is beached. It's the most likely place for them to go.'

'I want my crystal back! Can you get it for me?'

'There's only three of them.'

'But I don't want them hurt! I forbid that!'

Suddenly she decided that she couldn't rely on any of them. There was that stupid incident of the stabbing of Teenae. Would they never learn! 'I'll go with you.' She brought out a blow dart, a weapon not known in Sorrow

181

but given to her when everyone thought she needed protection. Oelita had liked the weapon because it was effective and harmless. The darts carried distillate from the fur of the dreaded ei-cactus. Actually the ei-cactus was harmless – if its fur penetrated through the skin a man was knocked down within four heartbeats but the paralysis was only temporary. The danger was in being alone and falling into a clump with one's skin exposed to the fur and dying of starvation or exposure, conscious but too helpless to move a muscle.

They set up an ambush and nobody came. Oelita was ready to give up. Her temper had subsided and she was becoming more aware of her own danger and her own necessity to leave Sorrow when suddenly the three of them appeared, feeling quite safe. She felled the youth with the broken ribs immediately. One of her men grabbed Joesai and she took out both him and her own man. The third man she pricked while he was being held by the iron-reed dredger and the ironsmith.

She recovered the crystal and had the three Kaiel tied up before they revived. They remained conscious. It amused her to bind them with a puzzle knot that could only be undone by the victim who had time, patience, and perception. She ordered their boat repaired. The storm had damaged it extensively and the sail was ripped. When she saw Joesai painfully flexing his fingers, she sat down beside him, unmindful of the gravel beach that cut into her knees.

'That's Trial Four of the Death Rite! Do you understand?'

He muttered an unintelligible reply through a reluctant tongue.

'If I attack men who are as dangerous as you, I risk my life. That counts! That's Trial Four!'

She cried. She was afraid of death. She was afraid for her people. For a while she walked along the beach in

182

despair. How could she go to her friend Nonoep, who had run from responsibility? She thought of her beloved followers. Was there one among them who could lead? No. They were not priests. They weren't bred to lead. Why was it that if one sought to escape the tyranny of the priests one had only the priests to turn to?

Wisdom matured in crisis. She felt ignorant. She had made it a policy not to deal with the priests. She had scorned the Kaiel and loathed the Mnankrei, but were they not part of humankind with their own special skills? *I should have preached to them. I should have won them over.* Now it was too late. *I have been afraid of them.* She wove visions of heretical trial. She remembered the slaughter of the Arant and the new clan of Kaiel sitting in Judgment Feast. It was a horrible vision.

Oelita ran along the beach and then became afraid that she had gone too far from her friends and turned back. She cut across the sea to make the trip shorter. Ah, water and tradition had much in common. If you fought it, stamped it to death with your feet, as she stamped and slapped it now in her hurry, the brine/tradition merely splashed aside and when you were gone, flowed back as if you never were.

Her people up ahead were dutifully repairing Joesai's sail.

Like the squall that brings the rain, sudden hope lashed over her desert despair. Joesai had made her less afraid of trial. *I'll be brave.* She trembled as she had when the men closed in on her at Gold Creek and as she had when she actually made the decision to crawl down the outside of that tower wall. *I'll go to Kaiel-hontokae.* She could use the crystal as hostage for her safety.

26

A Liethe is beautiful, for the clan propagates only beautiful bodies. That is not enough to captivate a priest. A body needs grace. Grace can only be achieved by discipline. Discipline can only be found in an ascetic place.

A Liethe is clever, for the clan only propagates clever bodies. That is not enough to bewitch a priest. Cleverness needs form. Form can only be achieved by discipline. Discipline can only be found in an ascetic place.

She who comes from an ascetic place can relish pleasure, for what can give more contrast to pleasure than denial? She who comes from an ascetic place can wield power, for discipline has made her the master of those pleasures sought by power.

From the Liethe *Veil of Chants*

In a bare room, the se-Tufi who was recognized by the way she cocked her ear, stood in the role of teacher, facing her sister se-Tufi. Both had assumed the erect Resting Power Position. They were interacting through the catalyst called the Nine Tier Matrix of Understanding to transfer to Humility the essential knowledge of Aesoe's previous concubines.

Many se-Tufi had served Aesoe but he was aware of only three Liethe – Honey, Cairnem, and Sieen – personae created, unknown to him, out of his deepest woman fantasies by the Kaiel-hontokae hive. It amused the crones that he was blissfully proud to be able to distinguish between three identical women just by the way they thought and moved.

Humility was learning, first, the persona of Honey.
Action Mode:

Cocked Ear uttered some warbling sounds, then broke the Resting Power Position to set her body into a pensive stance. With her left hand she pulled and slightly twisted a strand of hair. She returned to The Position and gave Humility the Go signal. Humility had been listening and watching. She broke Position and exactly duplicated Cocked Ear's motions. Only Honey, of the three, played with her hair when she was pensive.

Thought Mode:

Humility recited, one by one, the cues from the mnemonic list called the Attributes of the Male, while Cocked Ear answered from her store of knowledge about Aesoe. Humility paused briefly while she memorized the answer before producing the next cue. It was more important to know Aesoe's mind than Honey's since Honey was only a figment of Aesoe's erotic imagination.

'Vanity,' said Humility.

'He believes that he knows all. Thus everything he does not know can be used as a mask. We hide behind the image of the woman he expects to see,' replied Cocked Ear.

Humility attached a mask image to the cue. She cleared her mind. 'Vanity; consequences.'

'Since he is the only one who knows all, he must tolerate mistakes from others. Making a mistake with him transforms him into a teacher.'

Humility recorded a mental picture of an all-knowing teacher impaled upon a (mi)*stake*. 'Vanity; control handle.'

'Since he knows all, he must be teaching Truth, therefore he cannot tolerate disobedience which is deviation from the Truth. He can be controlled by the subliminal threat of disobedience which freezes him in his Teacher Aspect.'

The drills of the Nine Tier Matrix went on for sun-heights, alternating between Action Mode and Thought

Mode. Other se-Tufi who had been with Aesoe took over when Cocked Ear tired, but Humility was not allowed to show fatigue. It was like learning an intricately choreographed dance so that, should a dancer be replaced, the audience would never notice. The gruelling workout exhausted her, a sacrifice to Liethe perfectionism.

Action Mode:

The gestures and behaviours that clued Aesoe to the Honey persona were words and sentences constructed out of a lexicon of behaviour that the Liethe had invented to facilitate mimicry and role change. The lexicon was complex enough to allow rich combinations, yet simple enough to learn quickly. Each motion of the lexicon had a verbal symbol so that an accurate mimic could be communicated through the haunting song of a warbling language.

The se-Tufis who drilled Humility sang at her, sang their corrections, and she sang back at them. At higher levels of the Action Mode one sister would mimic Aesoe in exaggerations of dance, and Humility would reply, with comic abandon, in a whole sentence of Honey's body talk. Exaggeration quickened learning. Behaviours as cues were only as effective as they were different from other behaviours.

Thought Mode:

Honey, Humility learned, was sweet and scatterbrained and submissive sexually. She was conjured from the faery substance of an Aesoe fantasy woman who was totally loyal to him but was so desirable to other men that she might serve as a delicious reward, when he wished it, for those who were loyal to him. She was the easiest of the roles to play, allowing forgetfulness and demanding little more than radiant charm and careful attention to the needs of the men important to Aesoe.

If hurt, Honey expressed resentment by a slight slowness, followed by a sudden gush of affectionate forgiveness. She forgave everything. She was never jealous. She was quick to serve, anticipative, restless, shifting and changing in the way she dressed or sang or put her fine meals together.

Honey was an adventurous lover, reflecting Aesoe's uncommon curiosity. When Aesoe wished to show her off to his intimates, she became exhibitionistic, willing, but when he mediated she was unobtrusive. She spent her time alone practising her dance and music and singing. Very occasionally she wrote her own songs and might shyly perform them for Aesoe if he wanted to hear them enough to be sufficiently persuasive. She was that way because he enjoyed persuading people. Honey could not tolerate a finger playing in her bellybutton. She was that way because he enjoyed having simple teases. Yes, an easy role.

'And what is Cairnem like?' Humility asked during a break for tea and rolls.

'Cooler. Aesoe thinks of her as the greatest artist so we conspire always to focus on Cairnem's performance. When Aesoe wants to sleep with her, he pretends disinterest. She enjoys sex only as the aggressor – when she is taking a man away from something that is important to him. She is rigid and only makes love in the over-position. She cries and loses control at orgasm. She is the planner of Aesoe's household, the one who gets things done.'

'Where did she come from?'

'We created her out of his fantasy need to be with a competent woman.'

'And Sieen?'

'Sieen is the most difficult role. She requires intellectual continuity. You will not be allowed to be Sieen for many weeks. The crone mother will brief you on her and run you through your basic drills. Sieen is Aesoe's confidante. He tries out policy on her, explores ideas with her before he takes them to the Council. She is almost dull in public and merely competent while serving other men. Only with

187

Aesoe does her mind erupt and her face catch fire and her body warm to the sensual.' Cocked Ear brightened, remembering being Sieen. 'She's no role. It's like sailplane soaring – with the ground expanding and no updraught. God! when you are Sieen, you're alive. Then you know you're Liethe! That's where we learn about Kaiel policy before it is made and where *we* make Kaiel policy!'

'With a little help from the old crone,' Humility added cynically.

'You will be master of Kaiel policy before you are ready to be Sieen.'

'Who decides who gets the roles? What if two of us wish to be Sieen the same night?'

'Whim. If there is a dispute we throw dice. But not while Aesoe is looking!'

After dinner six of the girls were singing or playing to relax – but the crone mother did not let Humility relax. When the ancient one was through instructing the orn-Gazi Who Cries for Berries, that pleasant girl appeared and, trying out the ways of seduction she had just learned, gently informed Humility that the respected hag wished to see her.

The old woman sat in her luxurious room on a huge round pillow that she used as a bed. Two beeswax candles burned on her silver inlaid desk. Behind her was a rich tapestry celebrating the pleasure of laughter. Beside her was a small pantry of pale wood. Stoicism was for the young. In the midst of this splendour, Humility was not sure whether she should remain standing or take a cushion.

The crone mother was the oldest se-Tufi she had ever met, surely near death, but it would not be her mind that would fail her, it would be her heart. The se-Tufi had been the longest lived of the Liethe lines until recently and they lived twenty per cent longer than the average Getan who died of old age. Some day the se-Tufi would be replaced by a sister line that had their ability and a better blood pump. The Code allowed no less. No line could hope for immortality.

It was macabre to be confronting herself at the end of her life, as if her travels across the Pile of Bones and the Itraiel Plain had taken her on a journey in time to meet herself as she would become. No word passed between them. Finally the crone mother rose, and Humility ached to help her stand on those legs, but one did not help a crone mother unless asked. The woman took her by the arm, on the band of signature, and carefully brought her to cushions near the candles. Her gesture said that discipline deserved pleasure. She poured liqueur into two tiny goblets, carefully, for her hand trembled. Then sighing, she sat down again, offering the second delicate sipper with a smile that carved her face into finer lines than any artist could have wrought.

Humility was tired. She wanted her mat and her cell, she craved the hardness of the floor and sleep, but the unspoken moments gave her time to work the White Mind. The day vanished. Her body relaxed. In the whiteness appeared her urgently central concern and she spoke first.

'The Kaiel and Liethe are traditional enemies.'

The old woman smiled mysteriously. 'You are anxious to go to work?'

'What is my assignment to be?'

'My child, your first assignment is patience. Think no farther than the five pleasure points of Aesoe's penis.'

Humility was somewhat offended. 'I am no novice to stand while Geta turns.'

'So I have heard. Your reputation is that you act with consummate skill. But do you know why you do what you do? Be sure in your own mind that it is right. Only you will bear the consequences. Whatever the Liethe do in secret, in public they side with the law of the land they live in.'

'I need only to be competent. I take orders from whose wiser than myself.'

The old woman sighed. 'Tell me, why are the Kaiel and the Liethe enemies?'

The Queen of Life-before-Death had nothing to say. The enmity was an understood.

'You see, you are Action Without Thought. Aesoe does not even know we are traditional enemies. He thinks of us as mere women for hire and a bargain at the price. He is more fond of us than some men are of their wives. Vengeance is only in the Liethe soul.'

'The Kaiel are mass murderers.'

The se-Tufi crone sipped her drink, and trembling, set it down, emotion shaking her frail body. 'Yes? That is something which touches you?' She spoke her question searchingly, as if she did not understand what Humility was talking about.

'The Judgment Feast of the Arant,' said Humility warily.

'That was ages ago. I believe I am correct when I state that there was no Kaiel clan at the time.'

'The rubble under our feet is Arant! This whole city is built on the bones of the slaughtered Arant! Dig down! You'll find their cellars. You'll find the treasures they hid before they were wiped from the face of Geta! The Kaiel clan was founded so that the Arant would never rise again! The Kaiel was given Arant territory and Arant coin and they took it, thus they have the blood of the Arant in their bellies!'

'I see,' said the old woman as if she were blind. 'Why does that concern the Liethe? We seek only two things: beauty and the power that beauty brings.'

'Have we not avoided Kaiel-hontokae like the poison? It is part of our tradition! It has always been important. Why did you bring a Liethe hive here? I assumed it was to attack.' Of course it was to attack – the hag was leading her on.

190

'You speak of the Arant rubble beneath our feet. Do you know the old Arant name for this city?'

Humility spent some time accessing an unused part of her mental files. 'D'go-Vanieta.'

'What does it mean?'

'Nothing.'

'Repeat d'go-Vanieta. Keep hammering the word with repeats until you break off the rust of the old speech. Change the inflection.'

Suddenly Humility was giggling.

'Ah,' smiled the old woman, 'you have it!'

'God's Vagina?'

'Now recall the passage in the innkeeper's memoirs when Liethe was confronted by the sailor who brought her to the island of Vas.'

'She said she came from the Vagina of God. But she was only teasing the sailor!'

'I doubt it.'

'You think she was Arant?'

'I feel she was born here, yes. But Arant? No. I've been doing research at the various Kaiel libraries. People are willing to tell their inmost secrets to an old woman with smile wrinkles who is about to die.'

'*I* would not tell you my secrets!'

'And *I* would not tell you what I am about to tell you but that you are se-Tufi like me and I know you and have foreknowledge of what you shall become. I do not wish to die with my most unpopular opinions unshared.' She paused, wheezing before she spoke again. 'I believe Liethe was a servant. I believe she was ugly and unloved by men.'

'Mother!'

The crone was enjoying her minor heresy so much that she took another tiny glass of pale liqueur. 'I believe she was an ignorant servant who worked in Arant basements doing routine cloning work, day after day.'

'The Arant never knew how to clone! Only the Liethe know cloning!'

'We have no information about the Arant except what their enemies said, and their enemies all agreed that they were great biologists. In point of fact the Kaiel know how to clone; they have always known how to clone but make minor use of the technique.'

'Where did you find this out?'

'Here in Kaiel-hontokae. You don't think all I do is suckle young girls!'

'The songs speak of Liethe as the most beautiful of all the Liethe.'

'The songs would. She left no writing, she left no research, and she was abysmally ignorant of genetics. She had no husbands. She spent her time cloning herself and it was not she, but three daughters of her clones who codified our ways. She left us with a page of comment that is single-mindedly obsessed with beauty and power. Think! Who would have a goal to be beautiful and to use her beauty to dominate the most powerful men?'

'A Liethe!'

'That is not the right answer, child. It is an easy riddle.'

'I don't know the answer.' Humility was slightly antagonistic.

'Consider an ugly woman without charm who is ignored by men. Might not she have a raging desire to create the kind of beauty and image that would dominate the men all women desire?'

'I'm *not* ugly and I *do* dominate men!' Humility was defiant.

The old woman smiled, recalling herself in her prime. 'And you do *not* have the *goal* to be beautiful and dominating. You *are* beautiful and dominating. Perhaps you dream about living longer than any se-Tufi has lived. Perhaps you dream of finding the man who can father a daughter who will found a great line with a better heart

192

than your own. Perhaps you look for the ultimate poison. In ways your beauty may have fostered counter-goals. Sometimes you will seek ways to be *ugly* so that when you travel you will not be molested. One's goals only reflect what one does not have.'

'I came here to kill Kaiel.'

The crone mother nodded. 'So did I. And I found the most vigorous priest clan on all of Geta. They may break the stalemate. They have a magic ear which can go anywhere on the planet in a single heartbeat. They have delicate instrumentation beyond belief. Did you know that a Kaiel can transplant a single chromosome from an ovum with a success rate of one in a hundred? They even do genetic surgery on the chromosome while it is out of the cell with viruses they grow in beetles. Do you know what that means for us? We could forge sister lines that differ by a single chromosome!'

'Do you think *the Kaiel* will be the instrument of God's will to unite Geta?' This was a somewhat horrifying thought for Humility.

'No, my child. They came on the scene far too late. God's command has already been carried out.' The smile of wrinkles was there again. 'Which clan is represented in every major city on Geta? Which clan has achieved access to all policy decisions and is present when they are made?'

'Mother!'

The hag cackled. 'How easy it is to rule when you sneak into power as a man's possession. We're not a priest clan. Who would have suspected us? Who would have opposed us? What can seem more harmless than a woman for hire who does everything she is told to do?'

'But dear crone, we just lay them! We flatter them, and play them off against each other and, seeming to obey, make them give us what we want . . .' Her eyes widened.

'Go on.'

'But that's not ruling a planet! There has to be policy. We'd have to be making momentous decisions!'

'Like which priest clan shall win Geta?'

Humility scoffed. 'We aren't going to do that! We're going to side with the winners. We're going to ride to power in their beds!'

'And what of the Timalie? that clan of priests who abhor mistresses? Would you allow them to win?'

Humility burst into the great laugh. 'They haven't got a chance!' She stared at herself as she would be five of her lifetimes from now. 'Mother, I think you are serious!'

'Of course I am serious! But don't think I am impressed with our power. We did all this without knowing we were doing it. Our relative strength is great on the planet as compared with any priest clan, but it is as if we commanded a bee's brain in a human body. What could be more pitiful than a human whose brain takes all day to send a message to his hand? Rule and hand go together. We may be stronger than anyone else, even the Mnankrei, but we are weak. We must use our position, build on it, or in a single generation all could be lost.'

Humility scanned over her ambition and pride. In a sudden flash, it seemed trivial, bloated. 'Will I ever be humble?' she cried out.

The old woman took the young girl and brought her down on the bed, holding her head against a dried bosom and caressing the flowing hair of youth. 'Not if you grow up like me, you won't.' She paused. 'You have beautiful hair but it's dry from your trip. We have superior hair tonics here in Kaiel-hontokae. I'll buy some for you.'

Humility was sleepy. She struggled to get up, to wake up, to get back to her cell where she could sleep.

'No, no. Stay here. Your journey was enough asceticism for a purification. A night with me in this little room won't spoil Aesoe's Palace for you.'

'Why did you bring me to Kaiel-hontokae?'

'I need an assassin. I'm too old for that kind of job.'

But Humility was asleep.

27

There is a saying that in the western regions of the Kalamani Desert only a stone has kalothi.

Dobu of the kembri, Arimasie ban-Itraiel in *Triumphs*

Reading over his old predictions, ineradicably and forever a part of the Archives, Hoemei was appalled by his naivety. Aesoe had taught him like Tae had taught Aesoe, and he had imitated his master, not always grasping the direction of Aesoe's vision. Now suddenly he was seeing with a new clarity.

The rayvoice project had been a shock. Aesoe believed in a Geta where authority was centralized in Kaiel-hontokae. For such a structure to be viable, rapid communication to and from the city was a necessity. Yet Hoemei had established only forty-five rayvoice stations, fourteen along the Njarae coastline, and the information flow was already unmanageable. He was now sure Aesoe had miscalculated the complexity level of a centralized government by orders of magnitude.

Hoemei's visions came erratically, in dreams, perhaps suddenly in the middle of a conversation, often in full colour. Sometimes as he sat over his papers by candle-light, well past his bedtime, he heard Getans from many futures discussing trivial problems of their day. He saw strange machines whose purpose half-baffled him.

Once when he had been reading an aerodynamic report that related flyer skill to flyer size, prepared by sailplane enthusiasts and o'Tghalie, he was washed with the image of a clan of tiny sky people who could stay aloft almost indefinitely on their man-made wings. Another time he saw a rayvoice that carried a flickering picture. He saw a man standing beside a great wheeled vehicle worrying about a problem ten weeks' march away as if it were his own.

When he disciplined his strange vision to peer into the specific future which would use Aesoe's map of a united world, he saw, sluggish as the armoured ice worms of the far south, a huge social creature ridden by vast clans that moved rivers of information with little real effect. The images disturbed Hoemei because Aesoe's cause had been his world, too, his avowed goal.

An o'Tghalie friend calculated for him that a reasonably nimble central government, with modest responsibilities, might require hundreds of times as many decision makers as there were citizens. Hoemei had been astonished. Prediction, it seemed, was treacherous when one embraced the fuzzy pictures that lay beyond the range of one's myopic eyes.

He used an increasingly focused vision to sift through centrally governed futures, sometimes a dozen alternative Getas a day, each of which had been founded on different organizing principles. The clogged snarl of their cultures finally drove him to find wider worldscapes. He often stared into space, unaware of the room he was in, or of the people he was with, as if he were of unsound mind. From those visionary travels along the bewildering branches of far tomorrows he brought back a simple conclusion.

Too much *local* authority leads a region's priests to maximize local benefits sub-optimally at the expense of distant peoples. Such cases represent the situation where essential information sources remain far from the deliberation and execution points and so tend to be unused.

Central authority, which theoretically maximizes benefits for the whole by gathering and using *all* information,

197

in practice quickly becomes so choked that wisdom breaks down, again leading to far less than optimal solutions. Carrying information from any large area to a central location, and there correlating it, takes longer than the useful life of the information. Data degrades as it travels, or it doesn't arrive in time, or it gets lost in the incoming flood and is never used.

Between the local/central extremes Hoemei saw many balanced worlds. Slowly he began to formulate his 'short-path' theory of government that forever changed Getan history. There was a way to construct the decision nodes of a network so that the most optimal decision path tended to cause the atrophy of less economical ones. Nodes had to be connected in such a way that there were *no* unique paths to the top of the hierarchy. A man maintained his power within the system only by being on the most effective decision route through the multiple pathways leading to a solution.

Hoemei had much help from his o'Tghalie staff in formulating his notion of an ideal government. His basic model derived from the information flow theory which described an evolving biological ecology.

Not all of Hoemei's efforts were serious. One evening he had a free-wheeling discussion with Noe about a world run by manifold governments, each layer's fate being subject to kalothi ratings and Ritual Suicide obligations. Noe brought out a bottle of whisky. Before the bottle was finished, their imaginations were buying choice cuts of their least-liked agencies at the local butcher shop and concocting recipes to disguise the foul taste.

The amount of work Hoemei was learning to handle in one day was extraordinary. He was researching the consequences of different styles of governing, managing the rayvoice project, planning a famine relief programme for the coast, monitoring the production of skrei-wheels, and designing a strategy to foil the Mnankrei, plus responsibilities on the new aqueduct design, and a small genetics hypothesis he was pursuing. However, he had his limits. He could falter and he did.

A clerk of the Clei, that indispensable underclan, entered the inner sanctum of Hoemei's office where he was never to be disturbed and bowed deeper than usual because of the gravity of the interruption. 'Yes?' Hoemei was curt, even though he knew that no one would enter here without having considered the urgency of his cause.

'We have just received a rayvoice message concerning Joesai.'

'Is he all right? And news of Teenae?'

'The information was relayed by our Soebo station, maran.' He spoke that half-formal form of address with another bow, reluctant to go on. 'The message lacks completeness,' he was trying to soften the blow, 'but it is unpleasant. Here is the transcript.'

Hoemei scanned the paper in great leaps. A Kaiel ship had been captured by the Mnankrei and brought to the port of Soebo. The identity of those manning the ship was not available but it was a number consistent with the party Joesai had taken to Sorrow.

'What in the Firestream of Getasun is he doing there!' Hoemei's fear exploded as anger. 'He's supposed to be in Sorrow playing dandiman!'

'Joesai is an unusual priest, maran. He may have disliked the role of dandiman and taken it upon himself to investigate odours drifting from the north.'

Hoemei slumped. 'That's my brother.' *Oh my God, and they will have Teenae, too.* The report did not say they were dead, but a clan willing to starve thousands for political advantage would not be a kind captor. With a will he quenched himself – hot iron to steel. Death. Life had always been thus. A Getan protected himself with a large family so the loss would never be as great. But two at once!

He remembered the naked child, Joesai, saving him in his first Trial of Strength at the creche when he had been too young to really understand the danger. He had always been of small stature and unable to repay Joesai in kind, but many were the times he had anticipated Joesai's troubles and thus prevented them – Joesai whose flashes of energy were too quick for sound judgment. Everyone had always said that this brother of theirs courted death, that his rashness lacked kalothi. Hoemei had expected him to die and had long ago prepared his stomach for that event, but not, it seems, prepared it well.

My brother! screamed his grief. Hoemei remembered Gaet laughing in the creche after the particularly harrowing Trial of the Knife and Puzzle. 'When Joesai falls into the soup he makes a boat with the noodles.' How they laughed together as Death shaved their eyebrows!

While the man of Clei stood watch over the increasing shock of his respected priest, reluctant to leave until his maran seemed less shaken, a remembrance came to Hoemei of Teenae in the early morning of their wedding feast, he frozen by the door, his mind anxious for his child bride so vigorously taken by three young husbands who, affectionate as they might feel, had shown no real control over their lust. For a long time he stared at her, his guilt imagining her dead, desperate for signs of life in the wan pre-dawn moonlight.

Her head lay against the pillow where they had left her, her nose in sharp profile, like sculptor's wax, her body sprawled, one leg up, hand clutching his gift of lace nightdress above her hips so that her navel was shadowed. She was too young for a woman's hips and showed but the barest signs of the high breasts she was later to carry. And she was so still Hoemei had hated Joesai for those overwhelming thrusts while they took her virginity; she was as still as death, her kalothi leached by pale Scowl-moon.

Then, it seemed, she breathed. Such relief. He went closer to watch her, to hold his fingers below her nose to feel the truth of her breath. Her head turned and her eyes opened serenely. 'Um,' she said, remembering. 'What was that all about? Am I really married now?' She pulled Hoemei to the pillows with her, curling around him, already asleep again. He left his hand cupped to her child's breast, feeling the breathing, happy.

I need her, he thought now, unable to weep.

Dismissing the worried clerk, he paced about his office, the careful draft of his speculations about different governmental structures left in mid-sentence. Then he walked up through the ovoid levels of the Palace to the communications room and took command of the rayvoice and tried to reach Gaet who was in the hills supervising the laying of the new skrei-wheel road to Sorrow. Gaet could not be found. He left an anguished message to be relayed on foot by some Ivieth runner.

On the way home, he slogged for centuries through a berserkly giant kolgame in the city streets of Kaiel-hontokae laid out by cruel players, a wooden piece moved for some obscure strategic advantage. Noe *knew* when she saw his face. He never told her; he just cried. She refused to believe that Joesai and Teenae were dead; she questioned him and held out hope, barring her own shock, but Hoemei was sure and he bawled.

Noe would not cry. She *did* have a beloved co-wife with whom she could share her men, and little Teenae was *not* dead and Noe would not cry for nothing as long as she could force all her emotion into comforting Hoemei. Yet when her man slept, the tears burst forth, silently, rolling down the cicatrice designs of her cheeks like a flood upon ploughed ground.

28

During the time of Arant glory it was the Arant who said that
suffering leads to greatness of spirit. The Kaiel think otherwise.
It is greatness that leads to suffering – for who can understand a
great man? and does not the lonepriest live the agony of holding
worlds which cannot be shared?

Tae ran-Kaiel at the funeral of Rimi-rasi

The mountain inn was tucked into the branch of a gorge
high among the peaks that had taken an unseasonable
snow cover. Like all inns of the Long Road, it was run by
the Ivieth. Old porters, who could no longer bear the
burdens of the road, brought wood for the fire and kept
the soup hot and cared for travellers who might seek
shelter, as well as tending the healthy Ivieth who passed
through with pack and wagon.

Young children abounded, bigger and broader-
shouldered than they should have been, unruly with each
other, racing through the halls of the inn, but unreser-
vedly polite with the inn's clientele. Their half-grown
siblings were already out on the roads to carry the
burden that clan kalothi demanded. Before puberty an
Ivieth hauled his load or was walked to death and eaten.

Oelita sat in a corner alone but as close to the fire as she
could get and still be inconspicuous. She was subdued.
Ordinarily she would be sitting at a table with the Ivieth or
would have intruded upon travellers to make new friends
and joke away the tiredness of feet. But this was already
Kaiel territory. The fear had grown as the rolling hills had
given way to rocky slope and twisting trail and heights that

awed her while chilling winds played with her body like the bush she had seen caught and tossed into a ravine.

She had sent the crystal ahead by trusted messenger and it would be safe – but still she was afraid.

One of the little Ivieth boys rushed up with a cloth and over-eagerly wiped her table. Then he noticed her bowl and sniffed at the broth that was no longer steaming. 'I'll get you some more,' he said before whisking it away, tiptoeing with a careful eye on the bowl's rim, remembering that he had already slopped some on the floor and had had to mop it up.

He was the same age as her boys had been when they were taken to the Temple of Sorrow.

Presently a white-haired woman, who was stooped and old but still far taller than Oelita, brought in a new bowl of hot soup followed by her angry grandson who was displeased that his grandmother did not see fit to trust him to carry it. 'He's being such a help, busy as we are with all the road building. I've scarce seen such a crowd!'

As she spoke three other men entered the door and pulled it closed behind them against the tugging wind. One Oelita recognized as clan Mueth from the brilliant headdress of fibres woven into his hair. One was a far clan she did not know. The third stood shorter but carried himself with such authority that she knew him to be of the formidable Kaiel.

'Gaet!' said a man at the far end of the room, raising his mug. The Kaiel returned the gesture but went to another table and was lost in animated talk. Three Ivieth children, obviously well known to him, rushed forward and began to climb all over his back to remove his outer garments. For a moment Oelita glanced up and saw the grandmother standing transfixed, smiling in the Kaiel's direction, waiting, as if she expected to be noticed shortly. He ignored her, making his rounds, a joke here, a backslap there, a fistclasp at another table, a hair ruffling for a child.

203

'Gaet!' said the old woman impatiently.

Finally, he turned to her, warmly. 'You think I'm hungry, eh? You *know* I'm hungry. I could eat the bark off a tree! What's in the soup?'

'Gaet, you sit yourself with this young traveller who's braving the mountains without escort – it's the only table we have free – and I'll work up something to fill you.'

The man sat down. His shirt was open and Oelita could see the hontokae carved into his chest. She wanted to run, she wanted to be among her friends on the coast, yet he was smiling at her easily enough. She faced him with her back to the wall and smiled the soft smile she used to seduce men.

'How's the broth this low day?' he asked to make conversation.

'Very good.'

'You're far from the coast.'

'How else am I to reach Kaiel-hontokae?' she asked gently.

'It is a long journey. You must have deep purpose to send you such a distance.'

'I do. I hope to plead for the lives of my people. Perhaps in doing so I shall speak against your beliefs. You must have equally deep purpose. We are as far from Kaiel-hontokae as we are from the coast.'

'The improvement of the road through the mountains has been a recent concern of mine. But truly I am this far west for one reason only.' He grinned. 'I've come at breakneck pace since I heard a rumour that a certain beautiful woman passes through the mountains unescorted. It seems to me that she courts unnecessary danger.'

Oelita startled. He knew her then! He had been sent. He was here for the crystal. He was one of Joesai's men. *No, I cannot use him. I shall fly from him!* 'Would a Kaiel escort give me safety?' she asked ironically.

'Ah, then you have met Joesai!' he exclaimed, slapping the table.

204

Her heart began to pound at the mention of this name. Here was a game she did not understand. 'I want no Kaiel escort. I value my life.'

'There are disparate factions among the Kaiel. Is that not the case among all priest clans? I represent the faction of the Prime Predictor who very much wishes you alive.'

'Who is Joesai?'

The man called Gaet laughed at her intensity. 'Joesai might perhaps be called a lonepriest. He has strong loves and his own ideas of the way things should be. He survives best when he is a long way from the reach of orders generated by men he disagrees with.' He sobered. 'I don't believe you have anything to fear from Joesai. We have reason to believe that his group was captured near Soebo.'

'The Mnankrei have him?' Oelita was incredulous.

'We know only that the Mnankrei took his ship and fifteen of his band. He may have been killed.'

'You lie!' she said hotly. 'He and two of his men were with me in Sorrow too short a while ago. I've travelled at night afraid that he was at my back.' She watched a profound look of reaction cross Gaet's face. What was it? Astonishment? Hope? Relief? Such a response made her afraid again. This stranger was no enemy of Joesai.

'Was he with a woman when you saw him last?'

Ah, I cannot trust this man. He loves Teenae. 'She was stabbed. They took her up the coast somewhere to recover. Wherever Joesai might be, *she* is not in Soebo.'

'Thank our God.'

'Joesai sent you?'

'Hardly. We've had no word from him. Hoemei of Aesoe's staff bid me escort you safely into Kaiel-hontokae. Hoemei is purveyor of the relief programme to the coast. We have sketchy information that a famine approaches. What say you?'

'The underjaw ravages the land. The Mnankrei burn our stores. We need help.'

205

'It is fortunate that we have met.'

'The price you will ask for your help is too high.'

Gaet laughed a short burst and trailed off into silence. He began to turn his soupbowl with extended fingers, staring at it. She noticed that he only had nine digits. A little finger had been amputated. Over the soup, the aromatic vapours rose and dissipated like thoughts forming and unforming. 'This pottery – pleasant design, eh?' he began. 'I like the mix of cavorting moon-children who chase each other as if the chase was all. Do you like it?'

'I've never seen such shape before or such pure subdued colour.'

'A fine glaze. The pieces chip easily. It's not stoneware. These pots are common in Kaiel-hontokae, perhaps not so common on the coast. They are fired in a small mountain village and I mention it only because of a Kaiel bargain made long ago that created the markets. Did we ever need the pottery? Hardly. The village was suffering and this was the way out. Did we strike a hard bargain? No. We could have. We had and have the power. But we Kaiel see the future with almost the clarity of dreams. A hard bargain struck while we have advantage leads always to strife in the future, always, always, always. We make bargains in hard times, yes, for that is our skill, to mute misfortune, to merge leg and arm and head and heart and liver and anus into harmonious marriage, but we do not consciously forge bargains that have no use when times are better.'

'You will offer us food for rule – just like the Mnankrei,' she said bitterly.

He shook his head. 'We cannot even offer you food in the weight that can be shipped from the Mnankrei islands. The mountains and the distance are great obstacles, but we offer you sounder rule. It is not the Kaiel who blended human gene with underjaw body so that children will not have the wheat that has been nourished by the sweat of their parents.'

'They did that? That, too?'

'Someone did.'

'You found human genes in the underjaws Nonoep sent to Kaiel-hontokae?'

'Yes.'

'That's criminal! That's horrible!'

'It is power gone awry as power will. When a priest needs power more than he needs to be a craftsman of human destiny, such things happen.'

She saw the burning silo at Sorrow, saw the arrogant sea priest Tonpa clearly by its light. Yet were the Kaiel more honest?

Annoyingly, he went on to disparage others in the hope of making his own kind look good. 'The Stgal have failed you. You should be rich and you are poor. You have more wealth in your land than Kaiel-hontokae. Sorrow should have fleets of ships to match the Mnankrei but it is a minor maritime centre. Does Soebo have a better harbour than Sorrow?'

She had had enough of his sly boasting. 'And you will bring your creches with you and fill our meat markets!'

His answer was easy, glib, as if he had spoken it a thousand times before. 'Only the Kaiel have creches. It is the way we breed for leadership. We do not interfere with the breeding rules of any other clan. In times of famine the clan groups who have sworn us allegiance accept our will. They are free to move and swear their blood to a better priest clan.'

'When I see the blood in the temples, I think we might do without the priest clans!'

Gaet shrugged. 'It has been tried. And those who tried it did not survive their famines.'

She had a moment's memory of her children, carrying them to the sea in her packsack because their legs were useless. Bright eyes they had, watching a nest of sand beetles. She felt tears. Her hand took Gaet's. 'Do not quarrel with me.'

'Your interests are mine,' he said comfortingly, reading her thoughts.

'How will you possibly get wheat through these mountains? I was not awed by them when they were only words to me and a hazy jag along the horizon – but here I am and I'm awed.'

'Come.' He kept her hand and led her outside into the wind that howled along the gorge. Her skirts flapped. He endured the cold, shivering. The world seemed dreadful and dark with Scowlmoon eclipsed by the mountain peaks.

'We'll freeze out here!'

Gaet brought her body closer to his own, manoeuvring her around to the back where the wind clawed less, sheltered as the spot was by a craggy wall of rock. They came to a filigree machine with three fine wheels partly buried in the drifting snow. 'A new device. It looks fragile but it amplifies the power of an Ivieth enormously. It can't carry more than a one-man wagon but it moves much faster. We're rebuilding the roads to take them. Wheat can move west in such vehicles which can then return people eastward to famine camps in the foothills above Kaiel-hontokae.'

She saw the swift Mnankrei ships and the good harbour at Sorrow, and at the same time she saw the Wailing Mountains and the treacherous trail through the Valley of Ten Thousand Graves. Was he aware of how absurd his challenge appeared – a frail vehicle against this frightful terrain? 'Let's go back inside.'

'You don't seem impressed?'

'How could I be?'

'Neither am I,' Gaet said, subdued by her coolness. 'It's the best we can do.'

She invited him to her tiny room and he built a fire for

her, then rummaged about finding a quilt to warm her back. It was a lesson to her. All the Kaiel were different. This one was not violent like Joesai. He had an easy compassion. 'I must ask you one more question.'

Gaet nodded while feeding another bush trunk to the blaze.

'Were you sent here to get the crystal from me? I do not have it with me.' There was defiance in her voice.

He looked up at her, the flickering light playing over the scars of his face. The face revealed nothing, no surprise, no alertness. He was merely waiting for her to go on. He had not understood what she said, and so perhaps it was true that he had not been in contact with Joesai.

'The crystal that Joesai called A Voice of God,' she explained.

'You have one of those? Yes, that would catch Joesai's fancy. I know little of such things.'

She was disappointed. Gaet did not react at all as Joesai had. His disinterest frightened her. She was staking her safety on the value of that crystal to the Kaiel, for whatever superstitious reason they might want it. 'It is of no value to you? I thought I might exchange it for wheat.' That had seemed like a good idea once. Now it sounded foolish.

'I'll introduce you to a woman who will be extremely interested.'

'You're still insisting on escorting me?' She did not feel so safe now.

'I must. This is Kaiel territory. You have no choice.'

'I have been challenged by the Kaiel to a Death Rite. I wish that ridiculous game to be cancelled. I wish protection from such nonsense.'

'Joesai?'

'I'm afraid of him. I feel haunted by him, as if he is following me through the mountains.'

'Lovely woman, I will protect you from him.'

209

Impulsively she began to search Gaet for knives. He only laughed and squatted by the fire, letting her touch him.

'Is this Death Rite a personal obligation of Joesai, or is it a clan obligation?'

'Once he has initiated it, the Death Rite becomes a clan obligation.'

'I'm going back to Sorrow.'

'No need. There are many ways these things can go.'

'Yes,' she flared. 'You could kill me tonight. I have no reason to trust you.'

'How many of the Seven Trials have you survived?'

'He has said three. I count four. And I'm frightened.'

Gaet was amused. 'Aesoe seems to have been correct about your kalothi.'

'I'm just a woman. I can die. Living is itself a Death Rite and no one survives!'

He pondered. 'I'll tell you what we can do. It will fit each of the criteria. We won't return via the road. We'll knife through the mountains, over the White Wound. That will be Trial Five.'

'You think so little of your own traditions that you mock them!' she snarled scornfully, backing away from him to the pillows where she wrapped herself in the quilt.

Gaet reproached Oelita with a hurt look. 'The White Wound is no mockery. That mountain still kills.'

Horror gripped her. He was serious! 'A moment ago you promised to *protect* me!' She had walked with the spectre of the Death Rite at her back, hurrying, furtively watching over her shoulder – suddenly to glance forward and into the eyes of the Fiend himself! He was roasting his hands there beside the fire between her and the door.

'I *will* protect you. There is nothing in the Death Rite that requires you to face an ordeal alone. Is it not true that a person who cannot have help is low in kalothi?'

'They say you Kaiel are born of machines. It's true! It's true! You're a machine! Just like Joesai!' she raged.

'The climb over the White Wound is an exalting experience. Why should one face death and find horror and pain when one has the choice of facing a beautiful death?'

These Kaiel! The way they lived with the Death Fiend! Morbid people! 'I want peace! I want peace! I've always wanted peace!' she raged against her pillow until she was sobbing. 'I want to be left alone by you priests! Leave me!'

And he was beside her, stroking her hair. 'It is never that easy.'

Gaet became Oelita's lover in the wilderness during the ascent up the ragged slope of the White Wound's north face. The danger wore her out and his tenderness revitalized her. She did not understand why she had come to trust him, or why it was becoming important to her to impress him with her strength, or why she was beginning to love him.

At the top of the peak, windblown, cold, barren, she huddled with Gaet, amazed by the most incredible sight of her life, mountain shapes, blue and purple below her and a vast plain in front of her, yellowish to the horizon. She could even see the smudge that was Kaiel-hontokae. They were so high that the moon was no longer hidden. The sun rose in reds of glory. Here, man was nothing.

29

The Mnankrei priests claim that since the past is known and fixed, so must the future be fixed – for is it not true that the genetic pattern knows the unfolding of the adult? No matter what crime is committed the Mnankrei invoke the historical necessity of the event – for, if the past is fixed and the future is fixed, how could what is happening be otherwise? A priestly crime becomes justified as an inevitable stage in the development of the genotype towards its final destiny. This is arrogance.

The Mnankrei tells us that after long study of their doctrine, a Mnankrei priest, in trance, can see the images of this fixed future revealed to him. This is false.

Every backwards transfer of information through time destabilizes the future. The mere act of observing the future changes it. Not even God can violate the first Law of Clairvoyance.

If we had a torch to illuminate the darkness of the future, as Getasun illuminates dark Scowlmoon, what we would see would not be what will happen.

Some events, like the motion of the planets, have great temporal inertia. Who can change the heavenly motions? We look at them and come to believe in determinism.

Some events, like a burning house, have little temporal inertia. A man who sees his house burning tomorrow can, today, snuff out the candle that would have set the fire.

Future events with great temporal inertia are like the lake waters at the bottom of a valley. Future events with little temporal inertia are like the precariously teetering stone on a mountain's ridge that will fall and bounce down the mountainside in any direction a climber chooses to push it.

The future seen is not the future that will be – because it was seen. Learn this law well, Kaiel child, use it, and you may become the Prime Predictor.

Foeti pno-Kaiel, creche teacher of the maran-Kaiel

Hoemei left the communications room and aimlessly wandered about the golden and alabaster luxury of the

Palace. No additional word from Soebo. Not a word about Joesai or Teenae for days now. Somehow he needed a confirmation of their deaths so that he could quiet this restless need to do something. Noe was threatening to march for the northern coast and gather a fleet from her mother's allies and take it to Soebo. Such a path seemed to invite disaster. Hoemei saw only burning ships and Mnankrei crowds in elated Judgment Feast of hapless Kaiel sailors who were not sailors.

He wandered until he felt some hunger pangs at the smell of food wafting from the great dining room which kept twenty cooks busy. It was a room where Kaiel met and where Kaiel decided. They were a clan that enjoyed eating while they worked.

In the hall, Aesoe hailed him from the great wooden table where only the most powerful dared sit.

He was with Kathein. The shock hit Hoemei.

To avoid them his eyes shifted to the small Liethe woman. Aesoe's Liethe were as cold as a northern river dammed behind spills of ice until they smiled at you in a way that made you feel as if you had just met the love of your life. Hoemei had shunned these women like poison, though that was dificult to do because Aesoe was a great socializer and liked to share them as if they were some fine liqueur to bestow upon his closest friends – but for a price. Hoemei had never liked the price: total loyalty to Aesoe.

The Liethe's blue and flecked eyes were watching him boldly. Once he had disliked these women as ostentatious examples of Aesoe's power but he had lost his dislike the first time one of the Liethe – he could never tell them apart – had served him tea and flattered him outrageously. He never tired of watching them dance, as they often did at Aesoe's parties. Some said they were very intelligent, but graceful as they might be they were far too servile for Hoemei's taste. This one was serving both Aesoe and Kathein – and she ate with them as if she were their equal.

Kathein and Aesoe.

He felt bitter. He would have avoided Aesoe now, but he was with Kathein. The temptation was irresistible. She had not spoken to him since Aesoe had made his command. Now she would have to speak to him.

He went to the table. She pretended to be in animated conversation with the Prime Predictor and only when Hoemei arrived did she look up and nod. He nodded back. They said nothing.

'Kathein was telling me of an interesting communications trick she has between her toes. She wants to bounce long heat waves off the moon.'

'Devious mirror magic,' said Hoemei with frigid politeness.

'No, no,' Kathein said stiffly. 'It is just like the rayvoice only the waves are shorter, more difficult to generate. We're working on it.'

The Liethe woman radiated at Hoemei's side, glancing at him, offering him a choice of pastes for the hard crackers. It gave him a good excuse to ignore Kathein. The moment he smiled at this strange unmarked creature she spoke. 'The baked spei is wonderful right now if you're hungry. That's what you're smelling. I'll bring you some.' She waited.

'Honey, a jug of mead, too,' said Aesoe.

She touched Hoemei lightly with her fingertips, then withdrew. 'He didn't ask if *you* wanted mead. They have juices today.'

'Mead is fine.'

When he looked back at Kathein she was searching him anxiously. 'Have you heard from Joesai and Teenae?' she asked formally.

'No reason to think they aren't dead.' His bluntness was deliberately cruel.

214

Kathein shrank into herself. 'I told him to be careful.'

'There was never any hope for Joesai,' said Aesoe solemnly.

Hoemei could not answer. Tears were brimming in his eyes, more because he had been cruel to Kathein than for Joesai. It took him a while to regain control of himself. Aesoe made no further comment. Kathein was hard put to suppress her suddenly unleashed upset.

'So tell me about bouncing voices off the moon. What will the far side of Geta do for conversation? I suppose you're not speaking to them, too?' He hated his sarcasm as soon as he had spoken it.

Honey returned with the food, and Hoemei used her attention as an excuse to say nothing while Kathein chattered inanely about technical matters. All this time the Liethe woman never lifted her eyes from Hoemei and, finally, when he had finished eating she spoke to Aesoe. 'He is leaden with grief, Aesoe prime Kaiel. If it pleases you I shall take care of him.'

'No! Let me talk to him. I'll go with him,' said a stricken Kathein.

'You will stay here,' said Aesoe.

Hoemei left them abruptly, but he was followed by the flowing Liethe. That annoyed him. 'I didn't ask for your presence.'

'But I asked for yours.' The se-Tufi Who Walks in Humility spoke softly. 'I've noticed you. I've wanted to be alone with you for years,' she lied. Then, with gentle authority, 'To your room, creche child, before you fall apart.'

He was mystified when she uttered the words 'creche child' in that light tinkle of her voice, waves of grief touched him and he had to fight to keep phantom losses at bay. In his room she lit a single candle. Her presence recalled his childhood dream fantasies of women. Some such women had leaned over him that terrible Night of the

215

Crooked Trial so long ago. She turned to him and he did not know the name of the year.

'It is not all right that they are dead, is it?' she asked, putting no qualifier on who was dead.

He saw creche mates dead, and funerals, and the dissection tables at the creche, and Sanan, his brave brother, dying in the desert when he was a boy. Hoemei wept. Only when he calmed would she speak, and then only to probe some horror, or to lift a black corpse from some sewer, or to make him weep again.

He talked about his family, first incoherently and then with calm passion, and then he had to laugh. He was remembering what a poor sport Teenae was when she lost at kolgame. Somewhere in all this Humility moved away so that when he finally noticed her again, he found her sitting serenely on a cushion with her elbows on the floor, looking at him, listening solemnly.

'Tell me,' he said with genuine liking for this creature, 'why does a man get the impression when you make eye contact with him, that he has just met the love of his life?'

'Because he can't have me,' she teased.

'Don't you ever feel that you've met the love of your life?'

'Why should I? I can have any man I want. How's my sad man right now?' She was smiling directly into his eyes.

'I think I'm all right. I've been brooding for days in an abyss. You'd better get back to Aesoe. Thanks.'

'I'm staying. Aesoe thinks you need a vacation from your work. So do I.'

'Which of the three are you? I always get you mixed up. Aesoe claims he can tell the difference.'

'I'm the frivolous one. I'm easy to arouse, curious. I'm curious about you. Aesoe doesn't think I'm intelligent, but I'm much smarter than he thinks I am. I just need someone like you to bring it out in me. Do you want to do something frivolous?'

'You're bringing out the shyness in me.'

She slipped over so she could hold his leg. 'I'm shy, too. Men don't know that about bold women. They think that just because we boldly go into a man's quarters where no woman has ever dared go before, that we aren't scared to death.'

'I sincerely don't think you are frightened of anything.'

'Oh yes I am. I'm scared of what you're going to do when I sing a lullaby in your ear.' Gracefully she rose, slipping fingers into his hair, her body touching his, her mouth next to his cheeks. She sang in almost a whisper:

> If beetles chirp
> And babies hear
> Can the wind a-knocking go?
> Walking feet
> And tickled chin
> A baby's smile will know

She kissed his ear. 'I'm full of nonsense. You have funny ears. Did you know that Aesoe says you have a magic ear and can hear anything anywhere on the planet? Is that so? Is this a little magic ear I'm kissing?'

'Almost.'

'Aesoe says it's all secret.'

Hoemei laughed. 'He thinks of strategic advantage. I don't think secrecy is a big help. My own prediction is that the Kaiel will be much more powerful once the secret is out and all can build a magic ear.'

'Only the Kaiel can do that.'

'No. It's easy. It takes pieces of wire and bits of glass all hooked up in a magical way that anyone can learn, no more. I'll show you.'

'Can you really talk to faraway places?' Humility was impressed.

'Sure.'

'To Soebo?'

'Especially to Soebo.'

'You don't really know what happened to Joesai and Teenae, do you? They might still be alive. I could find out if I could talk to Soebo. Aesoe won't let me so we'd have to do it in secret. Can you keep a secret?'

'You have contacts in Soebo?' Hoemei was suddenly keenly interested.

'Of course. There are Liethe hives everywhere. We've been concubines for the Mnankrei since long before I was born. We get to ride in their biggest ships. Their women don't like us but we are used to that. So we know everything that happens in Soebo except what the women are gossiping about.'

Hoemei smuggled her into the communications room and placed a call to his Soebo spy group. After he had made contact he put the round earvoices over Humility's head and she listened open-mouthed to the crackling speech. When she talked, the earvoice answered her! She instructed her voice friend in the details of a cryptic code with which he could contact the Liethe hive. She told him that it would be enough to get him the information he wanted. Soebo promised to call back in a day or two.

Humility was very curious about the electron demons that danced in the soft red glow of the sealed jars. She was appalled by the complexity of the strange machines and poked about in them until she received a shock that made her jerk away in surprise. 'You said I could make one of those,' she pouted. 'It doesn't like me. It kicked me! And I was just petting it!'

30

One man alone is like a cripple bound to his pillows, ennobled/ humbled by the daily discipline of conquering trivial detail, even the lacing of boots a major challenge. When does the One achieve more?

Two may live serenely, with occasional storms of high happiness, if the weather and the times are with them, and chance smiles on them, and Death does not halve them. The man of such a union must take vows of poverty; his one woman will never be rich as his dreams. The woman of such a union must learn to cherish weaknesses and lacks; her one man will have to work too hard to be the best of lovers. When expectations are small, and life benevolent, a Two works well enough.

Three restlessly seeks another mate like water seeks the sea, but a triumvirate is the freest of all marriages from conflict. A chair with three legs does not wobble.

Four is the threshold of emotional wisdom. Only masters of the four phases of love and the four nodes of loyalty can juggle a marriage of four without losing a ball. The Four is a game for the players of the game of love who have won.

Five, like Three, is sensually unstable but transmutes more opulently in the harmonies of its shiftings. The Five is an energy amplifier of great power based on loyalty, love, experience, communication, and flexibility. Mates of a Five are adepts at conflict resolution. It is said that a clan is in safe hands whose leader has achieved a five.

Six is the marriage of completion. The children of the Sixes shall inherit the stars for the symbol of six is the star.

Version of the Marriage Troth
from the *Kaiel Book of Ritual*

Relays of Ivieth kept the palanquin moving at a run. Gaet remained awake on this last lap of their journey, though Oelita dozed beside him. He held her and let her sleep against his shoulder. The White Wound was left behind them and they were back on the staggering road, sometimes passing one of the strange skrei-wheels. It was over his shoulder, after a jolt, that she first opened her eyes and saw Kaiel-hontokae spread across the rolling hills. The city seemed enormous to her if only because of the size of the aqueducts that marched towards its distant roofs.

When they arrived, Oelita thought she should be happy, but she became sick with fear in the maze of buildings, broad streets, stairways, and alleys that turned her around so badly she was dizzy. It did not even smell like sea-perfumed Sorrow, this slight tang of urine and decay. The fear was worse than before. She trusted Gaet, yes, but all about her the Kaiel were swarming like the tiny halieth fliers that rose from their acres of burrows during mating day. In all her life she had never imagined such a city! There were many clans she did not recognize, angular faces, costumes, types.

Their palanquin passed a market of stalls larger than the market at Sorrow and still the city went on. Palaces, temples, apartments, hovels, hives, factories, stalls, mansions, parks. Gaet stopped their hurry once to indulge her, telling the Ivieth to wait. The inside of the building he showed her was full of printing presses spewing out pages. A boy passed with a cartload of books for the bindery. It made her feel lost. She would be lost in all that printed chatter and no one would ever hear her voice. Once she glanced around and Gaet was gone. She panicked but he appeared again almost immediately with two cups.

'A little juice for us. We deserve it.'

She sipped while they continued. The hill of mansions which held Gaet's home on one of its winding streets amazed her. She had not realized he was rich. Strange emotions were overtaking her. She felt like bowing at his feet – and she never grovelled before anyone! With effort she kept her head erect. It did not suit her image of herself to be so awed by splendour. He took her by an arm through the massive wooden door into the inner patio. She had never seen such luxury outside of a temple. It could almost be a place of Ritual Suicide.

He cocked an ear. 'I think we have this mausoleum to ourselves.' Then he raised his voice. A great warble came out of his mouth that would have carried across a mountain valley. He cocked his ear again. 'Even the servants are out. Well, let me offer you Greetings.'

'I'm most honoured to be your guest.' She bowed and smiled at him.

They heard footsteps. 'Gaet! You brought her!'

'My one-wife Noe,' he announced, 'taking her time as usual.'

Oelita bowed stiffly.

'So you are the one who has been causing us so much excitement.'

'Isn't she a feast for an empty stomach?' he extolled.

'One-husband has a vulgar sense of humour,' answered Noe warmly.

'Hoemei must come home tonight if we can reach him.'

Noe's eyes twinkled. 'We may never see him again. He has been caught by one of Aesoe's Liethe.'

'God's Leer!' roared Gaet. 'Hoemei? You can't be right! Is he sexing her?'

'He's been suggesting some very strange positions to me in our recent lovemaking.'

'I'll have to go over to the Palace and fetch him after our bath.' Gaet was laughing. 'Rescue him is more like it.'

'Who are these Liethe?' asked Oelita. 'I've seen them following our Stgal at five paces, but I know nothing about them.'

'The Stgal they *would* follow at five paces. Anything to please a priest.' Noe's voice held veiled contempt for a woman who would try to please a man who would require her to walk behind him. 'For *our* men they dance naked.'

'Only when we least expect it,' insisted Gaet defensively. 'The last time I was at an Aesoe party they danced the Sunset for us and I don't think we got to see a thumbnail's flash of skin!'

'But you looked!' teased Noe. She turned to Oelita and explained. 'The Liethe Sunset dance begins with the dancers in pale blue. They change costumes on stage, with a magician's cleverness, so that you are never fast enough with the eye to see how they do it. The costumes go from sky blue to yellows, to oranges and brilliant streaming reds, and then fade to purple and finally spangled black. The men, of course, jockey for position to steal what glimpses of flesh there are. If all he saw' – she poked her husband with an elbow – 'was a thumbnail-sized patch of breast or thigh, poor Gaet got the worst of the jockeying.'

'One of these days,' said Gaet darkly, 'I'm going to sell you to the Liethe.'

'No you won't! You love me too much. Besides they wouldn't buy me. The Liethe bodies are undecorated.'

'They might need you for leather and soup.'

'The Liethe don't scar their bodies?' Oelita was scandalized. 'And they show themselves to men like that?'

'It is a wicked city, my little coastal barbarian.' He turned to Noe. 'Do we have hot water?'

'Come with me. You're both filthy.'

The bath house was already steaming. Oelita marvelled that pipes brought the hot water to the raised stone tub. Gaet was smiling broadly. 'I'm relaxed already,' he said dipping his finger into the water while Noe began to pull off his boots.

It was almost frightening for Oelita to undress in such luxury – as if this were to be the final bath. The room was entirely done in tiles of earthy browns with a rough texture that promised safety even with soap underfoot. The pipes were burnished bronze. There was a huge carved kaiel to hold the towels, its hontokae inlaid in gold. Oelita, trembling, began to disrobe.

But she stopped in embarrassment when Gaet signalled covertly that she was breaking ritual. *These Kaiel!* she thought furiously. *Do their rituals never end!* She was ashamed that she was ashamed, that she did not know the ritual. Noe had not noticed her mistake.

'Guests do not undress themselves,' whispered Gaet, coming to help her with gentle hands.

'You have fine artists on the coast,' Noe said, admiring the lines which enhanced the womanliness of Oelita's body.

Noe had shampoos ready, and perfumes, and delicate soaps made from rare beetle oils, and sponges of a scrubby texture so delightful that Oelita vowed she was going to abduct one. Noe took great familiarities with her husband's body and when he tried to sass her she stuffed soap in his mouth so that his laughter prduced a shower of bubbles. Oelita felt put out, cut off, watching them. Noe was his wife, for sure, but she, Oelita, was his lover!

She did not care what the rituals were! She took a sponge and began to wash Gaet herself. He was hers, too! Noe took no offence but transferred her attentions to Oelita. The washing was a casual caress, an easy intimacy. Noe even kissed her lightly on the back of the neck. It was a strange feeling. She felt shared.

She had thought once of marrying a man. She had had many lovers, more than she could remember, but her relationships were all one to one, as if she had somehow never left her adolescence. *I'm too much of a loner.* She was enjoying being shared. It made her feel part of everything. For too long she had struggled in her outside world, even though the struggle had been rewarding.

She was almost not scrubbing him now. She was touching him with her fingers. She smiled at him the smile she used to seduce men and then looked out the corner of her eyes to see if Noe watched. Noe was watching, and Noe smiled at her glance in a way that seemed to say: don't we have a nice man? For the first time in her life Oelita smiled at a woman with the smile she used to seduce men, and felt confusion. Noe responded by washing her face. *I wonder who he'll sleep with tonight, me or her?*

'It took you all long enough to get here!' said Hoemei coming through the threshold. He picked up a sponge. 'I can see these women are being too gentle.' And he began to scrub his brother. 'Let's see if we can get some of the stink off you. Silence of God, where have you been!'

'We went over the White Wound. A roundabout way to boil potato soup.'

'You what? You let him take you there?' Hoemei stared at Oelita in astonishment. 'The last time we went over the White Wound there were ten of us who set out and only seven of us who came back. That ordeal by climbing terrified me to the roots of my hair. Of the seven of us, only Joesai has ever dared go back.'

'We were babies then. I got the itch.'

'Do you know Joesai?' Oelita asked warily.

'Same creche.' Hoemei laughed. 'He's been giving you trouble?'

'Yes!'

'I just got a report on him today. From Soebo.'

Noe froze. 'Go on!' She breathed once, heavily. 'He's dead?'

'He's not in Soebo.'

'And Teenae?' Noe was anxious.

'Not a word.'

'You love them don't you?' said Oelita accusingly. 'He's your friend!'

'Sometimes,' said Noe, wryly.

'Sometimes,' said Hoemei, laughing.

'Hardly ever,' said Gaet with a straight face.

They were making fun of her! She didn't like private jokes when her life was at stake! She made waves in the tub and tried to step out, but Noe and Gaet held her while Hoemei poured a jug of rinse water over her head.

Then he brought a thick towel and began to wrap and pat her dripping body. 'We have much to talk about,' he said. 'I've been charged with organizing coastal relief.'

'Gaet told me. I didn't want to meet you with my hair stringy like this.'

'I'll remember to revise my first impressions tomorrow. May I keep this impression in a special place?' He let the towel fall off her shoulders so that he could see her.

'I can dry myself!' she answered, clutching at the towel. 'You're being very bold with your hands and your eyes.'

'Something that's come over me lately.'

'The sweet flatteries of a Liethe to swell your manly ego?' suggested Oelita coyly.

'God's Teeth, you're as bad a tease as Noe!'

Noe returned with fresh clothes. For Gaet she carried an aery robe, embossed with vines, for Oelita a shimmeringly silken garment, white. 'This is a favourite of Gaet's. Come. I'll take you upstairs. I have everything a woman needs.'

'Meet us in my room,' said Hoemei. 'It's the cleanest. Gaet and I will put together a snack.'

Amidst green bottles of oil and boxes of perfume sticks and piles of stitching for a quilt, Noe did Oelita's hair and dressed her. 'How can I wear this?' exclaimed Oelita. She adored the ruffles, but the gown was split up the sides, all the way, and split down the back and the front, all the way. It hid nothing. She would have felt more comfortable had she been nude.

'I've worn it in the street,' said Noe.

'You didn't!'

'At night,' Noe admitted, grinning.

'If I'm going to wear this, you have to wear something provocative too.'

'No. I'm too lazy to change. And it's too late. The food is ready.'

Oelita hesitated. 'Noe, tell me. Am I in danger here?'

'For your life? No. For your soul? Yes.'

'If I ever offend you, tell me first before you act, please.'

'I'm known to be blunt.'

'Am I intruding on you? I mean with Gaet?'

'Little barbarian, we're looking for a new woman. We had one but these things sometimes are poured into a cracked cup. You're very welcome to share whatever I have as long as you feel the same with me.' She kissed Oelita on the cheek and took her hand.

And so the evening went, with a wild game of kol that had the men screeching and Noe laughing at Oelita's unorthodox play. No one could understand why she was beating them. Gaet sat beside her on the pillows, affectionately caressing her from time to time through the convenient slits. She accused him of trying to throw her play. They talked about art in the city, and Noe promised to take her to the Chanting for which Kaiel-hontokae was famous. When the candles were near to burning out, Noe began to undo a few of the clasps that held Oelita's garment together so that Gaet could fondle her more easily.

So, she's going to give him to me tonight. Oelita wanted him. He was the only security she had against a rising panic. She had to have him, so knowing she was going to get him relaxed her, and her erotic warmth began to grow. But Noe took Gaet with her and they said goodnight at the door, leaving Oelita half undressed on Hoemei's bed.

'We could go to your room,' he said ambiguously, implying both that he was willing to abide by her rules and that he desired to be with her.

She trembled. She did not want to be alone and she did not want to stay with a stranger. She tried to read the soul of Gaet's co-husband, searching his face.

'You're welcome to stay,' he said.

'For a little while. You have a cosy room.'

'It's strange to meet you,' he said.

'I'm all disarrayed,' she replied. Hoemei was handsome in the candlelight. Was he being shy now? He had been so bold earlier. *I should do it,* she thought. If she just pretended she was part of a Four, and that what was happening, happened every sleep cycle, what could go wrong? She was extraordinarily curious about marriage. In any event, she needed to bond Hoemei to her, if what Gaet said about him was true.

He sat beside her and touched her shoulder. She could feel the affection. He spoke. 'It takes time to know another. There's no hurry.'

She could love a man who created no pressure. 'I'll stay.' He was undressing, putting things away neatly, a compulsive man. 'Hoemei? Do you love Noe?'

'Of course.'

'Do you love your Liethe creature?'

'Now that you mention it.'

'Do you like me a little?'

'I was smitten at first sight.'

'Help me off with this lethal recessive of a dress, but remember I'm not ready for anything.' She knew she was both pushing him away and pulling him towards her. His hands came to her aid but she did most of the work herself with such haste that she tore a clasp. And so they lay beside each other, naked, not touching. It was curious. The flame made great leaps and flickers and died. The silence upset her in this city far from the comfort of any friend. She needed contact and she was afraid of touch. 'Hoemei, what is your price for helping us on the coast?' Words, even intellectual words of great moment, were touches – in a way.

'Do you know our form of government?'

'The Kaiel are the hereditary leaders. The usual. I don't

227

approve. I think other clans should have political duties too.'

'It is not as simple among us. When we go to the coast we won't be distributing food through the Stgal. We'll send in priests. Whoever of your people likes an individual priest pledges to him and the priest contracts to help him.'

'The Stgal will object.'

'The Stgal will have no say, having been bypassed. Suppose I sign up your people and supply them with food. Then they are no longer in the kalothi chain of the Stgal temples; they are in the kalothi chain of my temple.'

'And the price?'

'It is an exchange. We are problem-solvers. What is the solution of your problems worth to you?'

'I'll give you a problem to solve.'

'Women are good at that.' He brought his face close to hers in the dark until they could feel each other's breath.

'Cannibalism!' She bit his nose gently, just so he didn't get too close.

'Ouch. That's not the problem.'

'It is!'

'Meat is the *solution* to a problem and you don't like the solution. It is said that you are anti-tradition.'

'I *hate* ritual!'

'Tradition is a set of solutions for which we have forgotten the problems. Throw away the solution and you get the problem back. Sometimes the problem has mutated or disappeared. Often it is still there as strong as it ever was. Geta is a harsh planet. It kills us. We do better when ritual is in control of Death.'

'Rock in the Sky! I'm tired of hearing that!'

'The Kavidie priests were vegetarians.'

'You fling myth at me to prove your point!'

'The Kavidie are myth only because they are long dead. They lived among the Red Death Hills of the Far Side and

228

commanded twice as much territory as the Kaiel do today. I've seen their flaking books in the library. They were real.'

'We're just talking because we are afraid of each other. Why don't we just shut up and you can hug me and I'll hug you.' She put an arm across his neck, and shoved his head until their noses touched.

'Where did you learn to win arguments?' he asked.

'No last words!' And she was hugging him. 'You have such big ears. I could get lost in them. What does a wife whisper in a husband's ear?'

'Usually she tells him to shut up!'

She kissed him, wondering about the trace of restraint she felt from him. 'In case you didn't know, I'm ovaet,' she whispered to reassure him.

'Ah,' he said, reassured. The ovaet was a genetic trait possessed by four out of five Getan women that allowed a woman to self-abort if she did not wish a conception to take.

'When I'm on the pillows with a gentle man like you, being ovaet makes it easier to keep my vow never to be a mother again. I would have difficulty being celibate.' She rubbed her cheek against his. 'I can feel your concern. It's nice.'

'Aesoe never told me that they taught barbarians how to flatter a man.'

'Barbarian! We call you people The Hill Barbarians,' she retaliated. 'Do you want to hear a Kaiel joke?'

'I've heard it.'

'Why does a Kaiel take his sandals off before entering his house?'

'You got me.'

'So he won't get them dirty!'

He cuffed her. They were already lost in the pleasure of their lovemaking. She bet herself that Hoemei would go to sleep as soon as they peaked and he did while Oelita

229

stared at his dark image, wide-eyed, smiling, with her head in her hands and her elbows embedded in the pillows. She decided that she liked to play at being married. She had two men now who loved each other and were bonded to her. Two men in a strange and hostile city were always better than one. Under the quilt next to her body, the hot warmth of him was safety. *If he loves me, he'll save my people.*

She dreamed that her body was illustrated with shifting tattoos and that great scholars came to study her both by sunlight and by candlelight and went away shaking their heads in wonderment. She took her message to the catacombs, to evil cities on the other side of Geta, and through the temples and into the hells of the desert. The desert was hot, boiling her in her skin while the tattoos shifted. Moaning, she worked her way out of the quilt and let the breeze evaporate the sweat from her, then dozed back to sleep, holding Hoemei.

The dreams went on, mutating. Her body began to tell lighter stories, frivolous ones even, stories of casual love and humour. She snuggled up to her man. He was patting her buttocks affectionately, and she reached around to stop him, half awake now, and the hands were not Hoemei's hands. They were big and hairy. She was screaming before she was half awake, trying to drag herself against the wall away from the huge monster.

'Where did you get such a beautiful bum?' said the monster.

'Oelita!' said a tiny Teenae in the doorway, round-eyed.

Oelita didn't stop screaming. Hoemei had her in his arms by now, comforting her. 'It's only Joesai.' He was stunned. Teenae was hugging him and squeezing him. 'It's me! Remember me! I came back! And I love you and I am glad to see you!' The screams brought Gaet and Noe flying out of their bed to collide with Teenae, who had heard them coming. Teenae clamped her arms on Gaet's

230

neck while her feet crawled up around his hips to grab him vicelike in their embrace. 'My beloved lost lover!' she crooned. 'Aw, Teenae!' he said happily. Hoemei was bawling in relief. Joesai and Noe just stood grinning in the middle of the chaos. Oelita, backed against the wall in shock, holding the quilt to her breast, tried to understand the revelation that these people comprised a single family. In avoiding Joesai her terror had taken her straight to his co-husbands and here she was thrown into this room with him and there was no more safety.

31

In an open game like chess a player hides his moves behind complexity. In a covert game like five-card hunter a player hides his moves by withholding the face of three cards. But how does one play a game which is itself hidden? The opponent never speaks, is never seen, and never gloats. During that single unexpected moment when the magnitude of your loss is revealed, who has won?

The nas-Veda Who Sits on Bees, Judge of Judges

Humility was wrapped in the robes of the Miethi desert clan that inhabited the edge of the Swollen Tongue. Her face was veiled and her fingers clothed to the second joint. She poked in shops, wandering, sucking on flavoured mountain ice. For a while she watched a street funeral. Women of the Tunni, red flowers in their hair and naked children underfoot, flirted with their black-robed men who manned a spit that roasted the skinned corpse of some deceased elder. A cart brought musicians and bowls of food.

Nothing was as refreshing to Humility as their brief sun-heights of freedom from the men she obeyed, these moments away from the hive discipline, from purpose and thought. It was pleasant to amuse that secret person within herself, the Queen of Life-before-Death.

At the shop of a coppersmith she picked up some pieces she had ordered and, farther on, a thumb-sized jar of chemicals. She found a man-height of lace fabric she needed at a weaver's stall but did not buy it – tomorrow perhaps; today it was enough merely to imagine the lacy costume. Subvocally she hummed the piped tune of a dance and her ghost feet jigged while her real feet plodded an idle path down the street of Early Wings, now deserted as if she had planned to be alone. Such a street was seldom empty.

As she had been instructed. the jeweller-merchant was there, cooped in his narrow room that was hardly wider than his heavy door. Yes, the pale man was of the Weiseni, a merchant clan spread over half of Geta though rare in Kaiel-hontokae. He had the rectangular carvings in his skin and the nose ring. She was his only customer. He stared at her, not speaking, not thinking much of her, for the Miethi bought little except beads to weave into their robes.

She asked him shyly for beads, some rich green ones, and smiled at the man with her eyes, then readjusted her veil so he could see less of her. He brought the beads from a drawer. While he was stooping and she had her eyes cast demurely towards the door, she yanked a wire loop around his neck so quickly that he died without even surprise on his face. The body dropped behind the counter.

Why did the old crone want this particular Weiseni dead? She did not know. The old crones were too old for men so they played politics on a grand scale. A leisurely moment later Humility had closed and barred the door and drawn the shutters as if her victim were gone on some errand as jewellers were wont to do.

She listened. Then she returned and quickly cut the dead man's throat. For artistic completeness she slashed his arms as if he had defended himself from a clumsy knifing. She stabbed him viciously, as one would who knew no anatomy and bore the strength of a large man. After a careful review of the imaginary fight, she tumbled a counter to imitate a recoil against a stagger heavier than the counter could bear. For a moment she glanced at the jewellery. The emeralds pleased her, but she did not take them. She took the larger, flashier stones that were nearly worthless, and some gold. Even a fool would recognize gold.

Dusk was a pleasant time of day. She disposed of the jewellery while walking and sat washing her knife at the pool in the Bok of the Fountain of Two Women. Dead insects floated on the surface of the water. A hawker was selling hot spiced soybean curd to passers-by for copper coin. She felt delight that others were enjoying the dusk, too. A small o'Tghalie woman was strolling with two of her men, holding them one on each arm, smiling to her left and teasing with her hip to the right. Magicians, those o'Tghalie. They could tell you how the electron demons would fly along the shapes of metal that the coppersmith had made for her.

Humility's time to herself was over. She wandered back to the hive, gradually changing the appearance of her robe so that she would no longer be mistaken for a Miethi. The se-Tufi Who Possessed Honour met her in the hive briefing room where they tranced. Honour memorized Honey's latest exploits, donned Humility's clothes and left for the Palace. Humility spent a sun-height resting nude on the stone floor of her cell to drain from her mind the luxury of the Palace, and the feel of the hands of men, and the thoughts of pleasing. Then she took the copper pieces, the last pieces, and finished assembling the toy rayvoice that Hoemei had shown her how to build. She had seemed stupid but only because she was checking three ways everything that Hoemei said.

The only part she had been unable to make herself was the electron jar which she had had crafted for her at great expense in one of the market factories and seduced Hoemei into testing. The test she understood, but it was incredibly frustrating that she did not know how to make

234

the testing instruments. Magic always had its loose ends which made it hard to steal.

None of the Liethe knew what she was doing; even Honour had not been able to duplicate Humility's rayvoice experiences, and would need special training if she were to continue Honey's escapade as Hoemei's mistress. Humility needed to be able to give the hive a show. First she took Cocked Ear into her confidence, promising nothing, but sending her to a distant room with the voice box, while Humility retained the machine's ear. Sarcastically, she mimicked Aesoe's sweet talk into the ear, wondering if anything would happen.

The universe, according to Hoemei, was like a tuning fork. If you sang the right note at a tuning fork it vibrated. The whole world was many such tuning forks, conjoined, and if you calculated the linkages and built real ones to match the calculations, then you could have a musical instrument that would respond to your voice a hundred days' journey away. Humility didn't really expect her box to work even though she had been very careful with the calculations, checking them by hand as well as by o'Tghalie, but she hoped it would.

Cocked Ear burst into her cell, astonished. 'What is it? I heard Aesoe speaking! Was that really him?'

'Silly. That was me! You heard me?'

'I should have known,' Cocked Ear giggled. 'Aesoe is never that obscene!'

'I want to try it on the crone mother! Set her up for the game. As soon as she has the voice to her ear, wave a flag in the corridor.'

When the signal came, Humility said into her box, 'Your enemy sleeps!'

The crone mother was at her door almost immediately, huffing and trembling. 'What is this thing!' She held out the talking shell as one might the giant mutated head of a fei flower.

'It's a magic ear!'

'Did you steal it from the Palace?' the old crone asked almost in panic.

'I made it! Hoemei showed me how.'

Humility was received with disbelief. The ancient woman could not imagine herself learning how to build such a device. The se-Tufi had an illustrious place in the chronicles, but they were not magicians!

Humility smiled with engaging innocence. 'You never had Hoemei for a lover! He's adept at stuffing the best of himself into my head.'

But the old mind had retreated and was already testing the possibilities. 'How far can it reach?'

'Not far. This one is only a toy.'

'You've seen the fuller magic?'

'The magician's workshop in the Palace, yes.'

'How far does their magic reach?'

'You've heard the gossip. Anywhere on Geta. Sometimes noise demons cast counter magic.' Humility's eyes lit up proudly. 'I've *talked* to our Liethe sisters in Soebo.'

The crone's cane rose and jabbed the air. 'When?!'

'A mere few sunsets ago.'

'You chatted about the size of Manankrei dongs?' the crone asked sarcastically.

Humility bowed. 'No, honoured one. I have brought a special message for you. I knew you wished this information so I asked if it were obtainable. It is Winterstorm Master Nie t'Fosal who does genetic probings upon the lowly underjaw.'

'Ah, so it is true. Aesoe has made such speculations.'

'You didn't think you'd get an answer to that one for eons, did you?'

'You are immodestly aware of your abilities.'

'I have Hoemei tied to my hairs.' The slight flick of her hip was arrogant.

'Four rounds of penance tonight before you sleep!' the

crone commanded, whacking her with the cane for her pride.

Humility knelt to the floor and bowed her head, wiping the ground with it, 'I shall seek true humility in my penance, wise crone.'

The hive mother dismissed Cocked Ear. She waited until they were well alone. 'How went your afternoon?'

'I truly enjoyed it. I walked as far as the Bok of the Fountain of Two Women.'

'Frivolous.'

'To clean my knife.'

'Ah. The Jeweller. Did he suffer pains?' Hag eyes glowed like bone heaps in the cremation fire of a poisoned man.

'I do not dally to allow my opponent the choice of a response. He never knew.'

'Yes. I suppose,' she grumbled. 'Perhaps it is better that way.' The harridan did not sound convinced.

32

When a dobu of the kembri attacks a man, he uses the forces inherent in his opponent's defence to exact defeat. If a push is expected, the dobu pulls. If a pull is expected, the dobu pushes. In like manner we attack a man's mind. Do not use truth and reason to sway your enemy. Strike him down with cunning application of his own logic.

Dobu of the kembrei, Arimasie ban-Itraiel in *Combat*

In the year of the Moth, the week of the Horse began with a celebration dedicated to that mythical sidestepping insect, the Horse piece of chess who was commonly known as the Protector of Infants. Naked children wearing elaborate Horse heads had been prancing about the streets the moment Getasun was fully risen, begging favours and gifts from every passing adult. It was quite evident that none agreed either on the colour or shape a Horse's head should take.

'Watch out!' said Teenae, cautioning Oelita. 'There are more hiding in ambush in that alley.' A purple snout with bulbous hoiela eyes sprang upon them, holding the hand of a smaller grinning beast who was hideously hairy to her shoulders. They cajoled two glass marbles from Teenae and Oeilita who carried shoulder bags of goodies on this morning.

When the women reached the alley, they found more children. One was wearing a wooden mask with vaguely maelot mandibles and improbable floppy ears. Another youngster wore a long head with stripes while her companion appeared behind a huge checkered nose. The boy wanted candy. The girls wanted trinkets but fought over a tiny bean shooter.

Teenae had attached herself to Oelita since her return. She felt a fierce loyalty to this woman who had saved her nose, perhaps her life. They were bonded by that encounter and by the code which made the lover of more than one husband her personal charge. Nor could she forget her already once-failed vow to protect Oelita from Joesai. Gaet and Hoemei she trusted to behave circumspectly; Joesai she did not.

'Do you know this Kathein pnota-Kaiel?' asked Oelita.

'Very well.' Teenae was apprehensive about the meeting she had set up.

'I'm not sure I understand why she should be interested in my crystal. Is she a mystic?'

'Your crystal is a Frozen Voice of God.'

'That's why I thought she must be a mystic. She looks at it and hears things?'

Their chariot had arrived and they climbed in while Teenae gave instructions to the Ivieth porters. Now the two women were squeezed beside each other. 'It would be hard to explain to someone who has lived her life under Stgal rule just what Kathein does. She's a dobu. Think of how a dobu of kembri handles himself in a fight. The force in his opponent's body does his work for him. Kathein is a dobu of matter. There are forces within all-that-is-inert around us. It resists us with its passivity. If we wish a husband to got to market with us, he comes at the merest asking. If we wish a wagon to come to market with us, we must swear and push and sweat. Kathein is a dobu. She uses the lifeless forces against themselves to work her will. When she commands a wagon, it follows her. When she holds a crystal, it remembers God.'

Oelita shook her head at such quaint hill madness.

The chariot was stopped once by a hideous-headed child with clicking mandibles and a beard who demanded his tribute to the Horse. The Ivieth neglected his charges until he found something, Oelita and Teenae contributed a candy and a marble, and they were on their way again.

The old stone building by the Moietra aqueduct was Kathein's retreat. Oelita laughed, and lifted her skirts to avoid a patch of mud that leaked through the cobblestones. 'So this is the abode of the magician to whom wagons heed and stones talk? The sight of such a dark mansion so close at hand instils precaution. How will I greet her?'

'As one who has done her a Great Favour.'

'I will not reveal the location of my crystal until the deal is complete and widely known.'

Teenae felt a stab of pity. She did not comment. To negotiate with the Kaiel, the Gentle Heretic should not have come alone. Then she forgot Oelita as her curiosity surfaced. What had Kathein become?

A young bonded Kaiel from the creches greeted them and brought them to Kathein's presence in a tapestry-covered room of high ceiling. Kathein was standing. Her expression did not change. She wore trousers and a bodice that held her breasts but exposed them as was the tradition with a nursing woman.

'Kathein.'

'My Teenae.' The voice was warm, unlike the face. 'How happy I am that you are back with us. I had my fears.'

'We've heard little from *you*.'

'It is distracting, forging a new clan. Your wounds have healed?'

'You can't divide an o'Tghalie by zero,' said Teenae, trying for levity and finding none.

'Oelita,' said Kathein, taking up her duties as hostess, 'my house is yours. I am astonished at your possession of the crystal and grateful that you have brought it here to me.'

'I have not brought it as a gift.'

'You are refreshingly blunt,' The first wispy smile crossed Kathein's face. 'Soepei,' she spoke loudly to another room, 'bring the box.' She returned her eyes to Oelita. 'Teenae has told you of our fairness in dealings. I repeat that this is so.' She settled her guests on pillows and offered them hot spiced tea which had been warming on a low table. The box was brought to Kathein and she opened it to reveal a rectangular crystal on velvet, waiting silently for Oelita's response.

'Your Frozen Voice of God has the same pale blueness as mine.' Oelita used the name with only a hint of sarcasm. 'Teenae has told me how much you cherish it.'

'*This* Frozen Voice of God is the one that was formerly in your possession. It is not mine. You'll recognize the chipped end.'

Teenae swivelled her eyes to Oelita, examining her friend minutely for shock. She poised, ready to restrain her but Soepei was there, alert, strong, and Kathein sat, ready.

Oelita kept her game face, as if she had simply had a bad throw of the dice. 'And my man?'

'Detained at the Temple of Human Destiny. He has not been harmed. He will be free once you have spoken to him. He will receive a bounty from the Temple as reward for his fine care of the crystal.'

'You are gracious.' Oelita's voice revealed by its hollowness just how stunned she was.

'We are not gracious!' Kathein was irked. 'That bounty and that respect has been earned. We appreciate the deliverance of the sacred crystal by whatever means it came!'

'How did you find him?'

Kathein paused. 'Oelita, you do not understand this city. It is *our* city. Almost every human here has a personal contract with his own Kaiel and little goes on that is unreported to us. To hide from the Kaiel, you must hide from every eye.'

241

'I am at your mercy.'

'No, you are not at our mercy! We are profoundly grateful! We shall be negotiating with you as if you had retained possession of the crystal that God willed to you. That is the Kaiel way. You will not get all you wish because our resources are limited and our objectives different from yours, but when we cross hands on a deal it will not rankle with you in the future. You will not wake up some morning, knowing the true value of your crystal, and feel that you have been cheated.'

Teenae spoke. 'She is upset because of the Death Rite.'

'*She* is upset! You should see Aesoe's stormings! He called a full Council meeting. Joesai is to be banished!'

'No!' said Teenae, stricken.

Kathein turned to Oelita wearily. 'You have powerful friends here in the city. I do not know if Aesoe is angry with Joesai for his handling of you, or if it reaches his heart that my son is Joesai's son, but certainly the visitation of a Death Rite upon you is the excuse for his fury.'

'Where will he be sent?' asked Teenae in commotion.

'To the port of Kissiel on the Aramap Sea, probably.' Kathein was laughing without humour. Kissiel was on the opposite side of Geta at the other end of the diameter that touched Kaiel-hontokae. 'I could kill that man sometimes. I could roast him in burning dung and feed him to the orthoptera! I tried to intercede for him but it did no good. No, he won't be sent to Kissiel. Aesoe is shaking up a Gathering against the Mnankrei and will send him on the staff of Bendaein hosa-Kaiel to Soebo. Aesoe does not waste the talents of a man he intends to kill.'

'Does Aesoe wish Joesai dead?' asked Oelita.

'Yes!' Kathein answered her coastal rival, her almost hostile rage barely suppressed.

'He has no mercy,' replied Oelita thoughtfully.

'Of course he has no mercy! He'd send his own clone up for Ritual Suicide!'

242

'Joesai will object,' said Oelita.

'He won't object to going to Soebo. That's where his men are,' mused Teenae.

'The Gathering will kill many, Joesai among them.' Kathein was morose.

'I, for one, will bet on Joesai's kalothi,' Oelita stated calmly.

'He's foolishly impetuous!' stormed Teenae.

'He's stubborn beyond reason!' reviled Kathein.

'Nevertheless, he has rare kalothi,' insisted Oelita.

'Would *you* wish him dead?' Kathein was curious.

'As long as I live, I would make peace with him.'

Kathein closed her hand on Oelita's wrist. 'Aesoe is angry with Hoemei, too, for his part, but he needs Hoemei and cannot exile him. You will negotiate your deal with Hoemei. I will be custodian of the crystal. We have done preliminary work with it but our listeners are improper in their attitude and must be rebuilt' – she sighed – 'again. I'll show you our one conversation with God.' She gestured. 'Soepei, bring the silvergraph.'

The page was blurred, meaningless. 'It is not more genetic maps. It is writing. Teenae, it is God's writing. Three pages are superimposed and we cannot read through it, but see the alphabet? It is not our alphabet but it is close enough. It is like the carvings in the wall at Grief. See the "p" and at the side, that could be the inflected "t".'

'There's the under-edge of a line of writing at the bottom!' exclaimed Teenae in awe.

'We've puzzled it out. This is what it says.' She wrote for them:

SOMBRE HELICOPTER GUNGOD
FLEW BEYOND THE RANGE OF

'What does that mean?

'God knows. God's Silence comes in mysterious hushes. We need more silvergraphs. We must have better rituals. We need more reverence and better tools. We need more money.'

'You are deducing much from very little,' ventured Oelita.

'What? Did maelot excrete that crystal?' Kathein was impatient with barbarian speculations.

Oelita's mind was working, hunting for a place to fit their piece of data. The leaves in her teacup did not give her many clues.

'May I see Jokain?' asked Teenae sweetly.

Soepei took the box of the crystal and the silvergraph and Teenae followed Kathein, who warmed at the mention of her baby. 'He may be asleep. I never know. He hardly cries. Sometimes when he is awake and hungry he just stares about his world so intently, as if he really saw something. He's very patient. He only cries when he's been ignored outrageously.'

They found him in his basket, awake, cooing, fluttering an arm, not quite sure why one was free and the other pinned. Teenae lifted him, and he took that as the signal to attack her breast with his lips. Teenae squealed. Kathein laughed and put him to her breast.

'You do not visit us,' said Teenae reproachfully.

'It is forbidden.'

'Not everything can be seen by Aesoe.'

Kathein carried her child to the window. 'When you love people you cannot have, that is painful. When you see them, you inflict your pain on them though all you might ever wish for is to make them happy. Because of your pain they learn to hate you. I do not wish that to happen.'

'Kathein.' The younger woman could not get her attention. 'Kathein.' She took her beloved betrothed from behind, and held her while the baby nursed. 'You're full of nonsense for a mind so intelligent.'

'Oelita is very nice. I'm glad for you.'

'Oelita is the nicest person in the world,' whispered Teenae. 'But she is a barbarian. She is too different from us. She's unformed, uneducated. It will never work. A Six is a difficult creation. We need you, Kathein.'

'Now you have made my pain so much worse.' She patted Teenae's hand wrapped around her waist. 'We have to find a way to protect Joesai from Aesoe. I couldn't bear it if he died and I was mistress to Aesoe and could do nothing. Go. Please go. Our business is finished.'

Teenae brought out a bright ribbon with a bauble on the end. She pressed it into Kathein's hand. 'For Jokain. Homage to the Horse,' she said.

33

There is no way for the backward-facing mind to see what is spread before the forward-facing eyes. The eye is attached to the mind only across a chasm of time that falls from the here and now down to the turmoil of our conception. Every vision drops from the eye to the darkness of the womb and crawls up through a lifetime of ledges before it reaches the mind that watches now. The lower baby-who-was filters all sensation for line and form and colour, passing what remains up to the simple child who blocks out the sketch and perspective and sets the balance and passes what remains up to the convoluted adult who adds the detail and mutes the unnecessary and gives purpose to the image. Is it any wonder that two people seeing the same thing see such different shapes?

From *The Prime Compendium*

The Temple of Human Destiny was dominated by a circular window of blazing glasses that illustrated the backward-facing mind and the forward-facing eyes. It glowed like a lunar overlord in the dimness above the gaming dens where citizens played their wits against the priestly measures. Oelita thought the Kaiel temples obscene, profligate, grandiose compared with Stgal elegance. Noe, who had brought her here, showed a delight in overwhelming bigness that probably stemmed from an architect daughter's pride in the sheer ability to over-engineer. Still, the Temple was staggering.

Oelita released her man from his cell, comforting him. He was a guileless fellow who feared he had done her grievous wrong. She thanked him for not letting the crystal come to harm. She gave him money and told him where he could stay to await further word from her.

'Noe!'

A painted temple courtesan, roguish in his sensual outfit, rushed through the relaxed crowd and spoke to Noe with the gaiety of an out-of-touch friend. He had introduced Gaet to Noe when she was working here, consoling those who claimed Ritual Suicide and entertaining those who merely came to the Temple to practise their wits.

'How's the game?' she asked in the wry way she talked to people who never changed.

'The girls seem to prefer chess,' he lamented.

'You're not losing your ways?'

'I need new colours, new makeup.'

Noe took his hand and brought him with them to share cakes – for a moment. They talked of books Oelita had never read, and of Saeb's astonishing rendition of the Commandment Chant they were to hear tonight.

It was dizzying for a coastal villager to adjust to an exuberant people who were consciously building a city that they intended to be the dominant intellectual and ruling centre of Geta. The loose, almost revealing gown Noe had insisted that Oelita wear was stylish but she had never worn such a thing before in public. She found their religious pragmatism refreshing – but shocking to coastal ears – and it frightened her that she, who had always taken such a delight in shocking people, sounded conservative to herself when her conversation was interlaced with these people's easygoing disrespect for the temples they were totally committed to uphold.

Oelita was curious to visit the meat market. No such place existed in Sorrow. There the only meat was given away at the Temple when it was freshly available, or one waited to be invited to a funeral. Here it was sold by the temples at atrocious prices. Noe bought a small jar containing two pickled baby tongues. For a moment, remembering her own twins, Oelita hated Noe with a violent passion. Then she calmed herself. She had long ago learned that the way to tackle such widespread customs was to accept them utterly until she knew the very source of the thought patterns that created the custom. Only then did she have a chance of exorcizing it.

God's Will. That's what they would say. In the end she would have to destroy their God. He was at the root of all this evil. They thought: I am not killing and eating these children; God is eating them and I am merely the arms and mouth He lacks. She shuddered.

Oelita asked to see the back room where the meat was prepared. She spoke to the butchers gently, never showing her mind, searching theirs. They were jovial about their task as they prepared the carcass of a 'machine', the name the Kaiel seemed to have given the genetic monster-women who bore the babies for the creches.

'Ye covet a block o' that thigh? Cost ye an arm and a leg, it will.' He laughed.

'Was she very old?'

'This un, ye'll have t' boil. She mebe 30–40 chile down the road.'

These Kaiel machines matured sexually when a normal child was just learning to walk and hosted their first embryo immediately. Their second batch was always twins, and their third, when they were fully grown, triplets. Once they were as old as a normal woman would be at the first flowering weight of full breasts, the machines were worn out and ready for butchering. They were sterile, and reproduced by cloning.

Oelita left hurriedly and returned to the Temple where Noe was now engaged in a game of batra with an old gentleman, testing the quickness of her sight. The machines mainly supplied the creches but Noe, Oelita thought, would be the kind of woman who would use a surrogate mother to carry her own children. She'd have a batch of maybe six and keep the finest of the lot for herself after careful tests had sent the remaining five to a temple abattoir. How was it possible to reach a woman like that?

When Oelita expressed some curiosity about the 'machine' wombs, Noe took her out for more exploration. This wife of her lovers was inexhaustible. She walked Oelita halfway across the city to a small sacristy hidden behind iron gates. A friend of Gaet finally agreed to take them underground.

Pillowed and pampered, the sacred object looked like another superstition to Oelita. Its frame was crusted and bent. Had a colony of sea creatures been building their apartment around some piece of flotsam that had later been fished from the waves, then crushed, and burned?

'Another sacred rock,' she said, a touch of irony in her voice.

'You've heard of the Arant heresy?' asked Noe.

'Not the Arant side of the story.'

'They claimed they were created by machines.'

'As logical an origin as falling out of a star.'

'This is such a machine. It's old, old. It is a non-biological womb.'

Oelita only smiled.

Noe did not seem offended. She was well aware that the object was not impressive. 'Who knows what it was once like? It was recovered many generations later from a building burned and razed during the Judgment. Joesai wanted you to see it. He thinks your education is lacking.'

'Joesai is a superstitious man.'

'He accepts the word of many great priests. You've heard of Zenei?'

'No.'

'Zenei deduced the function of this machine from its remnants, no easy task. The carbon-based components have all been burned away.'

'Fortunately for Zenei.' Oelita was not hiding her scepticism.

'We learned how to duplicate the function of this machine.'

'No you didn't. Your machine is no more than a genetically modified woman.'

'The end result is the same,' replied Noe stiffly.

'Then you follow the Arant? You don't believe in the God of the Sky?'

The needling was successful. 'The Arant were wrong!' Noe blazed. 'They denied Original Conception. Even with such a machine, conception is necessary. We know God exists *because* this machine was part of Him.'

'Is She dead and Her parts scattered – a Finger here, a Womb there?' Oelita asked wryly.

Noe sighed. Was there no quick way to deal with ignorance?

They returned to the central hustle of Kaiel-hontokae, their conversation reduced to talk of men and sex. As the red twilight faded, dim alcohol torches were lit and Noe and friends decided it was time to wander towards the Chanting. They led Oelita past stalls where anything might be had. There were artists who showed their work and willingly carved into your flesh the design of your choice. A cabinet worker planed and polished while selling, potter joked with rugmaker, and og'Sieth waited to make you ornament or instrument out of metal. Oelita broke away to watch a craftsman building electron jars by ghoulish yellow electric light. Noe and her laughing male friend had to pull her away.

They arrived at the amphitheatre before the Chanting began and seated themselves beneath the stars on benches carved from bedrock. The crowd joked. Men flirted with women they had never met before, and women teased men. Children were hushed. Newcomers arrived to display their finery.

'Look. See where Saeb enters! He's here tonight!'
Saeb doffed his helmet and smiled for those who had
noticed him.

A party entered from below, taking honoured seats.
Instruments piped a welcome. 'Aesoe's group,' whispered Noe, pointing him out to Oelita. 'Your patron.
You could have no stronger ally! I have been commanded to introduce you to him tonight.'

Oelita craned her neck. He did not seem imposing at
this distance. 'Who are those women he is with?'

'Which ones?'

'They wear veils.'

'Those are only his Liethe whores. One of them has
her teeth into our Hoemei.'

The music began like a faint whistling storm, building
on piping reed instruments. The crowd hushed. Slowly
eight male and eight female Kaiel, carrying torches and
humming as does the wind blowing over the plains,
ascended from two narrow underground tunnels. The
procession moved by step and pause, step and pause.
They were dressed only in cape and headplumes but the
body designs that crawled in the flickering fire fully
clothed them. All threw their torches simultaneously into
the central pit, causing an explosion of igniting flames.
As if by signal, eighty children flowed onto the stage,
their bodies covered to hide their undecorated nakedness. Each wore a mask-piece which contained resonant
chambers and flaring beaks to distort and amplify the
voice.

Inexorably the Commandment Chant began its recita-
tion of the laws of genetics – but in an astonishingly
different form than anything Oelita had ever heard in
theatre. Throats swooped and boomed and danced in
alien harmony, sometimes to soft effect, sometimes
building on a rising timbre that shook the amphitheatre
with inhuman tone.

251

'What in the Sky?' asked Oelita so dumbfounded she willingly exposed her ignorance.

'Saeb has put God's Voice into the children.'

'But how does he do that!'

'Don't ask about it! Just listen!'

The celebrating went on all through the brief night. Noe moved her party to a temple that was nothing compared to the Temple of Human Destiny and only a third as large as the Stgal Temple at Sorrow. But it was intimate and quiet in its glory. Noe told Oelita that this was where Aesoe had commanded them to meet him.

He was already there. He waved his people away to allow Oelita access to his table and immediately set her up for a game of chess. Being senior to her he took God's side, white, and opened with a classic Farmer to Child's four. He smiled and waited. She moved. He followed her move instantly.

Noe settled down on cushions beside Oelita. Their male courtesan had been joined by a woman of the temples with shaved stripes along both sides of her head and platinum rings in the flesh of her right arm. Her eyes never left Aesoe. One of the Liethe appeared silently with juice for Oelita and disappeared. Aesoe's party watched. Of them all, Oelita knew only Kathein.

Every move was received with attention. There were horrified comments when Oelita let her Child run free without protection of Black Queen or Horse. She ate both of Aesoe's Priests and blocked him with a reach of her Smith. He counterplayed deftly. She had to hide her Child. It was the White God against the Black Queen. She was expecting to lose. Was this not the Prime Predictor who had the reputation for being able to see a hundred moves into the future? But she trapped him.

'Check,' she said, speaking her first word to Aesoe.

Aesoe laughed. It was checkmate. He waited for her to

252

eat the White Child as was the custom – but she would not. That was her custom.

'Come,' he said. 'I would speak to you.'

It was near dawn, and he insisted on taking her to the Room of Ritual Suicide to watch the vast red circle of rising Getasun transform the ovoids of the Kaiel Palace into molten iron. Oelita waited. It was not right for her to speak first, but she was content to observe.

'You will be dealing with Hoemei. That is my wish. Drive a hard bargain with him. Drive a ruthless bargain and I will back you.'

'I want Scowlmoon, polished to a bronze sheen, for my morning mirror.'

Aesoe laughed. 'You will not get it.'

'You only have a city with marvels of architecture, wealth, and land to give?'

'And very little of that is mine. I can't change the religion of my people, for instance.'

'What if your wealth is not great enough to buy me?'

'Then you must ask the Mnankrei for their wealth.'

So much for that. She changed the subject. 'It seems to me that you sent for me.'

'No. You came.'

'But you've been interested before I came.'

'And chose the wrong vessel to contact you! May Joesai die with no one to honour his flesh!'

'The first thing I will ask of you is that Joesai not be harmed.'

'So it is true what they say about you, that you collect the wretches of the world!' He laughed. 'I give you Joesai, in pieces or whole. That I can do. Joesai is not the moon. What next?'

'You could start by telling me what it is that I am to negotiate with Hoemei?'

'Why, the terms of the surrender of Sorrow to the rule of the Kaiel.'

'That is not mine to give.' This man was mad!

'Tell me then, to whom should I speak?'

'The Stgal are the priests of Sorrow.'

'Ah, the Stgal. I have made a study of whom they represent. They represent themselves. And who represents the people of Sorrow? There is only you, and while it is true that you are not a priest, little details like that have never bothered me overmuch. I'll make an honorary priest of you. Marry into one of my families and I'll make a genuine priest of you! You are Kaiel in your soul and don't know it.' He smiled gently.

'What makes me Kaiel?'

'You doubt my word?'

'Yes!'

'Ho! So it is true that I can see some of what you fail to see? After our chess game I was despairing for my vision!'

'You taunt me! Which of my ways are Kaiel-like?'

'Perhaps your need for flattery?' he teased.

'I would know how I am Kaiel-like so that I might cleanse my soul,' she retorted instantly.

'Then you must abandon the self-respect that makes you a political force,' he chuckled. 'The very first thing about a Kaiel is that he is not a hereditary ruler, he is a *hereditary representative*. Who knows how this came about? It did. Tae ran-Kaiel understood it and formalized our custom so that now we all understand why the Kaiel have had victory where all others have failed. Tell me, if one of your people had a problem, would you know?'

'I make that my business.'

'So my spies noticed. In Sorrow such behaviour is unheard of. It is your mission to work towards a mutual solution to the collective problems of those people who have sworn their loyalty to you. Who but a Kaiel thinks that way? A Kaiel is nothing in our councils until he represents somebody. It matters not where his genes come from, nor who his father was, nor who his mother was, nor the lineage of his teachers. You have a following. That is Kaiel. Why should I talk to a Stgal who rules because his father built a house on some hill? If the Stgal made a deal with me, would I have the loyalty of the people of Sorrow? No. If I make a deal with you, will I have the loyalty of your people? I believe that would be so.'

'I hardly speak for the most powerful in Sorrow. My people are mostly lowly in kalothi.'

'You speak with a misordered appreciation of kalothi. Does not a man who can bond himself to another for a mutual goal have greater kalothi than the fool who tries to carry a house upon his own back?'

'You're made of brass. I'm to sell you our land and our heritage and all the people in it, and with that piece of paper from me, you will march in and take everything!'

Aesoe roared amusement. 'Your attention span is short! How many heartbeats ago was I telling you to drive a hard bargain with Hoemei? I meant a bargain you will be satisfied with – now, tomorrow. I can deal with you because you represent more than yourself. *I* don't know your people. How would *I* know what they want? How should *I* know what they need? You do. And Hoemei knows what *we* can give.'

'The coast is not for sale.'

'Vomit of God! Once there was a fool who found a bar of gold in the desert that was too heavy for him to carry so he guarded it and left his bones guarding it! Is that your thought?'

'In Getan mythology wherever there is a fool, there is also a wise man.' She was asking him to continue his story.

'The wiser man found the bar and could not carry it, either. He selected a friend he could trust and offered him half the gold to help him carry it to the city. Is not the moral self-evident? For a *whole* bar of gold you can buy nothing. For *half* a bar you can buy even immortality for your genes! Is help so bad? Is a man who offers you help,

255

because you can help him, to be viewed as an enemy who will cheat you? Make a deal with me!'

'I'm cynical about deals. I've made contracts before.'

'Build all the guarantees you want into it! Of course some of the deal will fall through. A contract is a piece of paper made now. It has flaws. We can't foresee the future. Look into the Archives and see how often I've been wrong. But when the deal deviates from its stated purpose, you don't cry and feel cheated and rave about the dishonesty of your partner, you sit down and deal again until you are satisfied. You change the conditions to meet whatever happened up there in the future. What would I gain from cheating you? Position? A few pieces off the board in the early game? What is that worth to me if your children feel the necessity to cheat my children because you were cheated? Then the Kaiel would die! Then *I* would die! My sperm is on ice until the day when my dealings make their long-term payoff. How many priest clans are extinct because they didn't learn to live beyond immediate gain? The Stgal are surviving now by covert dealings – a smile to your face, and poison in your cup. How long will they last? How many drops of kalothi is there in the most flawless dishonesty? All I ask – make a deal with me that satisfies you.'

'It will have to satisfy you, too.' She was struggling with the force of his attack.

'Of course!'

'I think I understand you. You will outdo yourself to take half of my gold.'

'God's Eyeballs! Have I been raving in vain? You do *not* understand me. I want the privilege of being with a lovely woman while I get a hernia hassling her gold to market. I like the joy of planning how we're going to spend it. Now do you understand me!'

'Yes. You're a lecher.'

256

34

On the foothills of the Wailing Mountains above d'go-Vanieta Mi'Holoie spoke to the forepriests of the Gathering of Ache. 'Is it enough to be sharp? A merciful man may be sharp. Will the point of a needle that penetrates flesh pass through steel? Flesh is mastered by Metal and Metal is mastered by Cruelty. Our Love of God's Flesh has smelted us, the journey here has purified our Metal, and the Tourney of Extreme Trial has hardened our hearts to Cruel Temper. At dawn we pierce the metal of this heresy to its Arant flesh. Cruelty is not deflected. The Arant shall willingly offer us Feast by sunset.'

The Clei scribe Saneef in *Memories of a Gathering*

Bendaein Hosa-Kaiel was old enough to be wise yet young enough to be willing to partake in an arduous crusade. He had long been known as a man of action whose cautious strategy had extended Kaiel influence eastward around the Itraiel almost to the Sea of Tears. He was a scholar and a prime voice of the Expansionists. The full ten fingermen of his Hand Council argued with him in the den of his mansion, only Joesai remaining stoically silent.

Bendaein's face design was asymmetrical, built around knife wounds he had received during the gruesome subjugation of the lower Itraiel as a precocious youth. The marred face, layered with experience, gave this Event Mover authority in the eyes of his fellows but to Joesai it looked like the slashed face of a loser. The younger man had heard over mead that Bendaein had been skinned during the opening play of the Itraiel compaign and had been forced to borrow a coat to survive.

Joesai broke a toothpick with casual force. Bendaein

did have a reputation as a fast learner. However, from his pedantic words, Joesai suspected that he was not so much of a fast learner as he was a fast reader. He had even minted a name for their foolhardy venture: the Gathering of Outrage – useful if they should survive long enough to be written into history.

Bendaein planned to execute his Gathering with a meticulous respect for the formalities established by previous Gatherings. Such was Geta's meagre transworld law. Joesai found himself displeased with this sensible approach. A Gathering was by its nature an aberration, a response to something the Chants could not anticipate. Who would have predicted human genes in profane bugs? What could any past Gathering say about *that* crime?

Joesai grunted objections, mainly to himself, while others talked. Tradition was for the everyday: marriage and food and love and death. He felt in his ribcage the danger in patterning actions upon the rituals of past Gatherings. What did any of them have in common? If you really studied them you found that Gatherings had a predisposition to disperse in the desert from hunger and thirst. The underclans had a name for the phenomenon – a Gathering of Bones.

Joesai had contempt for the self-righteous indignation he was hearing. The Kaiel must know what a Gathering could become! They were a Gathering's wardens who had stayed to feel its consequences! When the whisky was flowing did not Kaiel jokes hint that Mi'Holoie's crusaders had sacked wealthy d'go-Vanieta – from whose ashes Kaiel-hontokae was to rise – more from the hunger of the trek than from piety?

His mind wandered to thoughts of Kathein as his eyes wandered from Bendaein to the wall tapestries. The weaving was of Orthei craftsmanship, a rich scene of mass Ritual Suicide, common enough as a theme, save

258

that Joesai could not locate its source. The rite was not as it was in these parts of the world. The man and the woman making their Contribution had slit their throats rather than their wrists and blood ran down their bodies in crimson dye, their eyes vacant. Temple courtesans and luxury abounded, the excuse for the tapestry. A particularly voluptuous courtesan, life-size, caught him with the enticing look of her threads.

She had forgotten the one she had just brought to the Last Pleasure and seemed to stare at Joesai intently, hoping for more. The woven carvings of her body were tight geometrical designs that flowed along her curves. She reminded him of Kathein and he smelled Kathein's perfume, his loins stirring while he half returned the courtesan's glance and would have faded into the tapestry to that couch and his dreams of Kathein had his startled ears not caught talk of a great land march.

Getans were a land-oriented people on a world of eleven disjoint seas. They tended to think in terms of mountain and plain, since every sea could be bypassed if necessary. No Gathering had ever had to challenge an island rule and that in itself made tradition worthless in the present case.

'Taking Soebo by land we're more liable to drown than set table for Judgment Feast,' Joesai lashed dryly, speaking for the first time.

Bendaein was not troubled by sarcasm. 'There is also land between here and Soebo. Would you have us row it or sail?'

Joesai grunted noncommittally. He was soured by the role he had been awarded. His mission was to set up an undefended Advance Inquest in the Plaza at Soebo. Such effrontery in Mnankrei territory would be Ritual Suicide without the trappings of temple decor. Prime Predictor Aesoe, acting through Bendaein, was brazenly asking him to make his Contribution to the Race, a sacrifice move in some larger strategy.

Of course there were advantages to heading the advance suicide party. He would be beyond Bendaein's communication lines. Then he could create his own campaign. What infuriated Joesai was knowing Aesoe knew he would disobey orders. Thus the master plan must call for a man to kill himself flouting clan discipline.

Aesoe can see my death and why such a death will be useful to him – may those who love him vomit at his funeral!

Joesai broke another toothpick and cleaned his nails. He was not listening to the Grand Strategy. *I'll need Noe,* he thought. One-wife was related to the sea-going peoples of the northern Njarae who were not pleased with Mnankrei rule. *She will have access to ships.* He thanked God for his family. They were loyal, come gain or sorrow.

A conference with brother-husbands Gaet and Hoemei was in order. He felt the old wild pressure in him, the need to strike without thinking – which was his asset in an emergency but which he, had learned was deadly if there was time for thought. The creche was closing in again. Gaet and Hoemei could calm him. There was a way out. There had always been a way out. Hoemei could think through any trap.

I wonder if Aesoe will ever turn on my shortest brother? I must be here if that happens. They need me. Now he needed them.

Joesai's fierce longing for action pulled at him. Dreaming about Kathein, he sneaked away from the lifeless meeting. It was because of her that he had been marked for death. The sweet mystery of that woman had driven him to oppose Aesoe's will with relentless abandon, until his persistent violation of official Kaiel strategy brought the final disfavour from a Council dominated by Aesoe's ambition. In opposing Aesoe's seduction of Kathein, he had opposed Aesoe's drive upon distant Sorrow. Now he was expendable. He would be used to blunt the Mnankrei who also had designs upon the coast.

He remembered a happy Kathein splashing nude in the pool of their central courtyard, wearing a crown of love vine, pink with the first buds of flower. Gaet had failed to herd her with the rest of his family to the Founding Day clan dinner with its mock Arant pudding made of beans. Kathein slipped away, not wanting to go, and he had slipped out of Gaet's clutches, unwilling to leave her. Love vine was not flowering now, but he bought some anyway in the half hope it would touch her memory. How could a Six-love of such intensity ever have failed at the bonds?

Beside her door he debated whether to whack the knocker or throw the arm of the silly electron bell she maintained to elevate hereself above the rest of humanity. Either way he would risk having the door shut in his face. It was easier to pick the lock and just enter.

'Joesai!' She found him on the second floor, staring at his baby.

'Ho! He's a big one!' Casually he handed her the green love vine. 'Remember when we made him?'

She threw the vine away. 'I do not! You carry your arse between your eyes! Aesoe will kill you when he finds you've been here!'

Joesai grinned at her and she trembled between reach and withdrawal.

'I made something for you,' she said as if she'd just cooked up a special batch of poison. 'Not because I like you, but because you'll need it, you fool. I have better things to do with my time!'

She tricked him into a room with four of her people. That was a disappointment; he'd wanted them to be alone. 'What is it?' he asked, looking at a box built into a packsack, cluttered with black knobs and a reel of wire.

'It's a portable rayvoice. It doesn't speak but it gives off powerful pulses that can be detected here in Kaiel-hontokae even if you are as far away as Soebo. Teenae helped me with the coding. It is slow but it is redundant. That means, stupid, that your message will have so much repetition in it that it can smash through heavy noise and still be decoded. Hoemei will have the code. You'll have to learn it.'

'What use would I have for such a cumbersome contraption?' He was really quite pleased. Hoemei's ability to locate his men in Soebo had made an immense impression. Better yet, Bandaein wouldn't know what to make of it and the Mnankrei might never suspect worse than a soup pot.

'You're a dunderhead. I don't even like you. Am I to receive no thanks?'

He put his arm around her shoulder and squeezed. 'Anytime. All you want.'

She stiffened under his arm. 'Not that kind!'

He held onto her body, refusing to be rejected. 'Kathein. We love you.'

She sneered. 'That's over. I have my own life and my own family, and my own lovers, if you please!'

Joesai was bewildered by her hostility. Few women had ever loved him. The ones who had still held him. He clenched his mind until the pain went away, then searched for some common ground. 'Teenae spoke of the wonders of the new Voice of God.'

'. . . that you nearly lost for us!'

He grinned contritely.

'More of God's words have appeared this high morning.' She sighed. 'Joesai, I'm truly sorry if I'm irascible. I'm terrified. God is speaking to us; He has broken His Silence, and it's not what I expected. I need your opinion. You. *Your* opinion. You're the only person I know who cares enough about the heavens to understand what it might mean. I'll show you the latest silvergraphs.'

There were only four clear pages of writings – in an alphabet that was almost familiar in a dialect that almost made sense. He puzzled over the script. 'I don't understand the key words. "Destroyer" sounds like a grain mill. Pulverizer? But "cruiser" and "battlegod"?'

'A god who plays games, I thought.'

'"Twelve-inch guns"?'

'There was a gungod in another fragment.'

'It is very obscure.'

'A form of the word "kill" is used eighteen times in those four pages.'

'I noticed that. This is an ancient language. It speaks of the world of the Heroic Solo Chant.' Joesai was awed to the point of religious revelation. 'He sets His tale in the World of the Sky.'

'What would "weapon" mean? Here' – she pointed – 'I thought it meant a knife because it is used to kill, but the other reference' – she pointed again – 'refers to a cart. A knife with wheels?'

'Let's make ritual to reveal more pages.'

'No. You have to go. Go now! Keep these pages. I have copies.'

'Kathein, I came to see you.'

'Out!' she flared. 'Or I'll have you thrown out! Can't you see I'm busy? And take your rayvoice. Hoemei will assign a man to you to care for it.'

He gazed at her morosely, unwilling to leave. Her craftsmen were watching him.

'I *know*,' she said, scorning his open love. 'You'd kill for me. Now get out!'

35

One cannot take a coward on dangerous missions or trust one's fortune to a fool. How then are cowards and fools to be employed? Fatten them while they entertain you. They are fodder for hard times.

From *The Prime Compendium*

Very carefully from behind the sand bags Joesai pulled the wire attached to the thumb that tripped the hammer. The air cracked! Then: deaf silence. Neither Joesai nor Gaet breathed for heartbeats. They ran over and examined the acrid-smelling tube. It wasn't split. A hole had appeared in the wooden target.

'God's Streak!' said Gaet, jumping up and down like a boy.

Joesai roared with laughter. 'By God! You just tell those og'Sieth to build something and they build it.'

Joesai opened the breach and put in another cartridge and screwed the breach closed. The cartridges had taken him a whole day to make. It was easy to use Shoemi's Method to calculate the structure of an organic compound that would break down into gases with a sudden release of energy – but cooking up the compound itself was scary. Such molecules are fragile. In the end he had used two explosives, one to detonate the other. God had said nothing to suggest an appropriate explosive and he wasn't sure that he had the right ones.

'This pressure tube has use in some ritual?' asked Gaet.

'God alone knows. It is used for putting holes in things.' The larger brother examined the hole in the wooden target with some care. A drill would have done much better. 'I think it is mainly used to punch holes in distant people. A knife for cowards.'

'A killing tool?' Gaet was not sure how it could be used in such a fashion. Perhaps the tube could be set up so that someone tripped over the trigger wire.

'It is held against the shoulder. You pull the metal thumb with your forefinger while you keep the tube lined up with whatever you wish to hole. Do you want to grasp it in your hands for the next explosion?' Joesai enjoyed teasing his brother.

'Do I look the fool?'

Joesai was cracking up with laughter. 'Not a fool. Perhaps a coward? You're not going to take God's word that such is safe?'

'Suddenly I hear Oelita's voice preaching atheism in my ear.'

'She has begun to talk to you?'

'Yes.'

'Same old bees in her robe?'

'She's not going to change. Why should we all believe the same thing?'

'Why should we believe lies? Go ahead, believe a stone is a potato – but you'll break your teeth! She signs contracts with Hoemei as if she were Kaiel. Ho. I grant you that she is as tough as the bi-wood that bends but cannot be carved. Still her mind is pudding.'

'She has a simple reverence for life that I respect.'

'She has a simpleminded reverence for falsehood. Before I leave I shall show her God. I vow that.'

'The Death Rite is ended!' said Gaet as a command.

Joesai smiled cunningly. 'You protect her from words?'

'Husband, she's had enough,' Gaet pleaded.

'You pity her,' Joesai exclaimed in astonishment. They were creche and they did not pity. To pity was to insult. 'She rots your mind with her sexy wiggle. How is it that you did not answer my question? If a Trial of Words destroys her, can she be Kaiel?'

'How will you show her the truth of God? How can you show the sky to a blind man?'

'And I ask you, how can she deny the revelations of God that appear from her own crystal? I'll show her this.' He shook his steel spitter-of-lead-pebbles. 'How could I have built this except at the command of God?' He mused, holding God's revealed weapon. 'What I hold is called a "rifle". Actually the description was enigmatic and I had to use my imagination. I had quite a discussion with your og'Sieth friend trying to reconstruct the fine details. Teenae verified my logic. The deduction demanded skill because there was no description of how the rifle worked. All I have is a few anecdotal recountings of its use. The World in the Sky is a weird world of killers. I'll show you a passage when we go back to the Palace that tells the story of hill people wandering around with rifles holing Russian priests who live inside mobile temples of steel four thumbs thick. That impressed me.'

'A God who preaches killing will not impress Oelita.'

Joesai lifted the rifle to his shoulder and aimed into the hill . . .

'No!' screamed Gaet.

. . . and pulled the metal thumb. There was another crack! a terrible impact against his shoulder, and a flying chip of stone. 'The logic that will destroy her mind if she is unwilling to change is this: God saved us from a world where they were breeding only for better killers. He did not speak to us of this until we had learned of ourselves to breed for better values. Now He tells us how to kill again through Oelita who has brought us His words. It is a test to see what we have learned. God is Oelita's partner. Can her mind survive knowing that? God abhors Death and through her gives us limitless new ways of Death. What Oelita cannot face today, and must face if she is to

266

survive, is that Death will stop neither for her nor for God. Death is senior to us all. We win only by tricking Death to our own purpose, which is the breeding of kalothi.'

The argument continued while they loaded and flung five lead pebbles. It slogged along intermittently as Geta-sun, at highnode, found the brothers concentrating their attention on a test of the portable rayvoice. They contacted the Palace and left a message for Hoemei that said simply, 'Creche reunion of the Wooden Triangle at sunset.' The argument continued more vigorously on Gaet's skrei-wheel, bumping back into the city, packsack loaded on the bars and rifle lashed to Joesai's shoulders. When Hoemei met them in his Palace apartment, its tables readied with cold feast, one of the Liethe playing softly as she sat by the window, legs crossed, the argument languished into an off trail and had to be reintroduced later.

The Liethe, unhurried, concluded her melodious piece before she rose, bowed, and helped them out of their clothes. She was temporarily waylaid in her gentle task by a fascination for the cold steel tube with its strange attachments. 'What is this?' Her fingers stroked the barrel.

'A device for quieting inquisitive women,' Joesai joked.

Receiving his joke as a command to be silent, she led them to their bath without even a rustle from her robe. Her delicate hands began to massage away their tiredness, with the dirt, running the warm water over their bodies in a relaxing glory.

Hoemei pulled up a cushion. 'I hear Kathein has found the title page.'

'Have you been reading the revelations?' asked Joesai.

'I haven't had a moment! God's Feet have been kicking me. Tonight I have a tryst with Teenae for the evening and she promises to read to me selections from the foul book if I properly satisfy her bodily hungers. I've missed the excitement. My God, on top of everything I now have duties to the Gathering.'

'Bendaein won't use you!' Joesai spat scornfully.

Hoemei sighed. 'I'm into the Gathering because of you. Some private organizing for your benefit. Bendaein knows nothing of my efforts.'

Joesai glared at Hoemei, telling him to shut up while they were in the same room with one of Aesoe's spies.

'She's loyal to me, Joesai.'

'You'd trust your own mother, if you had one.'

'It was Honey who found your men in Soebo.'

Without missing a knead of his muscles, she spoke. 'They are held underground at the Temple of Raging Seas. Some high sea priest thinks it will prove useful to keep them alive.'

'She is apprenticed to rayvoice work with me. Aesoe does not know and would not be pleased.'

Joesai turned to the woman with the smooth skin who had stripped herself to the waist so that she would not wet her robe. 'So it was you who set my heart at rest? I thank you.' He reached over and squeezed her wrist with a vice grip that was the custom when acknowledging a debt that would be paid whenever it was called, now or a generation from now.

'All I will ever need is to serve you well.' She dropped her eyes and concentrated on washing his knees.

Immediately he began to like this strange being regardless of his unwillingness to trust her. He thought for several more heartbeats about trusting her. Nevertheless he changed the subject to a non-sensitive topic. 'What does the title page say?'

'God is revealing to us the History of Man. Oelita's crystal is a fragment of Volume 1: *The Cradle Earth.*'

'Earth – the Riethe of the Heroic Solo Chant!' yelped

268

Joesai in an eruption of water that drowned Gaet and spattered the Liethe.

'Very possibly. There are eight major parts to the Cradle Volume. We have only Sequence 1: *The Forge of War.*'

'Those damn words that mean nothing!' stormed Joesai. 'I have fourteen pages from Kathein by now, and most of it doesn't make sense.'

Gaet had riffled through his neat memory for names and places and was smiling. '*Forge* would mean furnace or kiln or crematorium. There is a reference to a *fierj* in the Children's Chant. "Gowan gaien to *fierj* the shoes for Horse." Among the og-Sieth on the shores of the Aramap the word *foerj* means to work softened metal. It is sometimes used as a synonym for cremation as in the curse, "May your poisoned innards be *foerged* while your family starves."'

'I've crossed the word "war" in my readings,' Joesai recalled. 'It means nothing to me. It occurs in conjunction with the words "kill" and "peace". I speculate that it is a killing game and peace the opening move.'

'I have read none of it so I cannot guess,' said Hoemei. 'Kathein favours the translation "Furnace of Violence", others prefer "The Kiln of Åire" or simply "The Crematorium".'

'There are references to crematoriums,' continued Joesai. 'The People of the Sky are not nourished by the people they kill so it is logical to infer that poisoning is a widespread means of inducing Contribution. Or did they poison themselves to deny their enemy nourishment? I found one reference to factory crematoriums on a scale vaster than I would believe had I not seen God's word of its truth. The whole population of Kaiel-hontokae would be consumed in weeks by such a Black Temple. Then there was a reference to a city that flamed so fiercely in a firestorm that its whole population was burned or

269

asphyxiated. Many sentences contain messages by powerful priests implying a readiness to vaporize cities. Burning defenceless villages was a popular aspect of the game. The children danced as torches for the victors. But crematorium is not specific enough. What of the rifle? I like Gaet's og'Sieth word "foerj". Into what shape would such violence work a man's metal? We can thank God for our deliverance.'

'Praise God if such was the world of our conception,' said Gaet.

'Praise God,' said Hoemei with ritual fervour.

The Liethe girl said nothing. She dried their dripping bodies and brought them lounging robes dyed with red alizarin and went back to her tiny string instrument that permeated the conversation, listening.

'Do read about their clan interlockings, Hoemei. You'll be fascinated. They had priest clans as dedicated to random killing as we are to kalothi.'

Hoemei was devouring bread with globs of bean and nut spread in profane taimu sauce. 'Did they have a central government?'

'I don't think so. I'm confused. What can fourteen pages say of something as complex as an oz'Numae tapestry? I think the Marx priests formed a great government once but they had communication problems and broke up into Russians, Imperialists, Communists, Chinese, Socialists, Runindogs, Libyans, Fascists, Lackies, Trotskies, Gaulists, Revisionists, Kgbers, and Albanians. After that my memory runs out. The other side was simpler. There were the Amerikan priests and the Israeli priests, and their allies the Opeckers, the Capitalists, the Multinationals and the Degeneratburjwa.'

'Who won?' asked Hoemei with his mouth full.

'God has not revealed. I'm casting my bet towards the Imperialists. They always have an alliance at the right time and the right place. First the Russians are screaming insults at an Imperialist-Amerikan alliance, and then you turn the page and the Amerikans are off on a sacred Gathering against the Imperialist-Russian alliance.' Joesai was amused.

'Your story sounds like Getan history with the clan names altered,' grumbled Gaet.

'It sounds so because I've been skipping the details. Those Sky People have more ways of cutting your throat than you could dream. Conceive how popular a priest clan must be if its priests dare not visit another country except in mobile temples made of steel four thumbs thick.'

'Will you not need such an impregnable cart when you enter Soebo?' With that speech, Hoemei came to the purpose of the meeting. He spoke as he had at those intense discussions in the high tower of the creche or in the field or in a hastily found stairwell when one of them was in danger from the Trials. First there had been four maran brothers. Now there were three.

'She must leave.' Joesai was uncomfortable with the silken silent woman.

'She stays,' said Hoemei.

The Liethe put aside her instrument and caught Joesai with her liquid eyes. 'It is the code of my clan to take the secrets of our men to the grave. An Ivieth is vowed with his life to take you to your destination. An og'Sieth stands by the craftsmanship of his creations. An o'Tghalie will not take two and then two and give you back three. A Liethe is a priest's servant.'

'What say you, Gaet?' asked Joesai.

'She must make an oath.'

The Queen of Life-before-Death sank to her knees. 'Let God's Ears hear me. Nothing I sense in this chamber shall pass my mouth or fingers without permission from all of you. I serve your wishes.'

'The Death Oath,' said Joesai, unmoved.

Without objection she brought a needle. She pierced

271

her finger and, when one red drop rose upon the fingertip, touched Joesai's tongue so that he might taste her blood.

'I cannot tell you apart,' he said. 'The oath is upon your sisters also.'

She bowed and found her place again.

Hoemei spoke. 'I invited her here. She is more bound than you might think.' He brought out maps, unfolding them after pushing the food aside. 'Bendaein does not trust himself to my new powers. They are not part of the tradition. But with the rayvoice I can reach farther than Bendaein. And I have done so. I have the outposts. The Liethe' – he nodded to Honey – 'have been most helpful in transmissions of the call to Gathering. They know the priests who can act. I have decided not to demand action, or bargain, or offer alliance concessions. Instead, I have sent out the fastest Ivieth runner relays carrying the eggs of the tainted underjaw so that they might confirm this abomination for themselves. I'm appealing to their self-interest. Who will be willing to accept a biological attack upon our food supply? It is too dangerous, and added to drought and natural disaster, such threat is intolerable. I anticipate massive support.'

Joesai objected. 'Bendaein is himself certain of support. He is not certain that the Gathering will survive the route to bring Judgment upon the Mnankrei. He wishes to travel light with few but able men.'

'Such are the contradictions within Aesoe's inner circle,' replied Hoemei. 'He has visualized a planetary economy but he cannot handle the logistics of a large Gathering. I can, and I have done the preparation. The whole Gathering shall not converge upon Soebo. Nine or ten will work to maintain the supply depots.'

'All this while we feed the coast?' snarled Joesai.

'What is needed exists along the routes I have chosen. It is a matter of organization and coordination, not material.'

Joesai was unsatisfied with a solution that seemed to evade the central issue. 'My problem is not numbers. I would be happy to hit Soebo with a Gathering of Ten. I'd prefer it.'

'But such a Gathering would lack moral force. Since the other clans would not have participated, they would not abide by its decisions.'

Philosophy! 'Why is my death to be useful to Aesoe's ends?' That was what concerned Joesai. 'Perhaps *she* knows?'

The woman smiled faintly. Her liquid eyes sparkled like the sea. 'I am under Aesoe's oath. I cannot speak.'

Joesai grumbled. 'It is a setup. A successful Inquest in the Plaza at Soebo would require a verbal dancer, a man of great wit and irresistible charm, and a fast sidestepper. Even then, he would be murdered. I suggest you, Gaet. A much wiser choice! You take this mission, and welcome to it!'

'But a rock-fisted man who insults at the first opportunity is what Aesoe wants.'

'Because he needs a dead man!'

'Exactly,' said Gaet.

'And if I do it my way, swift, and without foot-kissing, I still get murdered.'

'Exactly,' said Gaet.

'Which is why you will do it *my* way.' Hoemei's manner was that of a surgeon at work. 'You will not enter Soebo with your advance party. You will stay a day's march from the town and *do nothing.*'

'God's Itch, you know I have not the mental capacity to do nothing!'

'You will *not* rescue your men. You will *not* make court. You will *not* fight. You will do nothing. I have my prediction registered in the Archives about the outcome of this affair. It is based on the assumption that you will do nothing. Aesoe has his prediction of the outcome of this event registered in the Archives. His outcome requires your death, perhaps to demonstrate Mnankrei unwillingness to host an Inquest. He does not think you capable of doing nothing. Thus that is what you *will* do to survive. My solution aids mankind, the Kaiel, and my brother.'

Joesai's whole inner body was rebelling. Do nothing in the middle of enemy territory? Impossible! 'And I just sit there while the Mnankrei skin me alive?'

'The Mnankrei will be poised to respond to your game, and you will have no game. Besides, God is on our side.' Hoemei grinned at the lethal rifle parked against the door. 'You will have one hundred of those with you. They will not approach you. You will not have to use them.'

Joesai calmed himself. Hoemei was faster of mind than anyone he knew. Survival meant listening to an unshakably loyal brother who had proven his worth. 'You know something I don't know.'

'We are looking at the same chess board.'

Joesai thought about that. His brother had just insulted his intelligence. 'If I move to a position one square from Soebo and sit there painting my nails, it is checkmate, eh?'

'In three moves.'

'He is marvellously brilliant,' said the Liethe creature proudly. She had been watching Hoemei. She saw that he was thirsty and rose to bring him a drink before he knew that himself.

Gaet smiled affectionately at Joesai. 'Don't look so bewildered, husband. Hoemei and I have done much feeling in the dark while you've been gone.'

Hoemei was cleaning up the meal so that the rubble would not be left for Honey. To keep her out of the way, he insisted she play a melody for them. 'And how is Kathein?' The timbre of his voice mixed concern and bitterness.

'Why?' asked Joesai sullenly.

'You've seen her more than we have of late.'

'She assaulted me!' exclaimed Joesai indignantly.

Gaet, who had been alerted by the mention of Kathein's name, rolled off his pillow, chuckling. 'She hit you?'

'With verbal fists! I bled internally!'

Gaet stamped his enthusiasm. 'She's learning! I didn't know she had it in her! That's a good sign.'

Hoemei, making quick work of the dishes, only smiled.

'And you insects pass for my brothers!' Thoughts of Kathein depressed Joesai.

'We'll talk more on the morrow. I don't want to be late for Teenae, and I have flowers to pick up on the way,' said Hoemei.

Gaet didn't like to see his brother brooding. 'Joesai, spend the night with me and Noe at the Great Cloister.'

'No,' rejoined Hoemei. 'He should stay here and study my file on Soebo. Honey will spice his time and make his rest a pleasure.'

So, thought Joesai, Hoemei offers the luxuries of the flesh to his uncouth brother who cannot inspire love. Wasn't that Gaet's role? He felt sarcastic until he remembered . . . Noe's warm teasing . . . the smile that always lit little Teenae's eyes under her lush eyebrows. 'Wait,' he said, 'I have messages.' He took paper and wrote two poems. For Teenae:

> The secret
> beneath dark eyebrows
> is a loyalty
> still there
> when a fool
> asks forgiveness
> for being a coward.

And for Noe:

You should never hit a man
my love
until he's down
or feed him salt
when he's not sure it's sugar
That way you prove
my love
that winter's snow is spring.

36

At the Conclave of Summer Heat, during the final rounds of the kalothi contest, Reeho'na, greatest living o'Tghalie, unveiled a theory of many participant games that tells us why the bargainer who seeks to optimize the gains of each member of a group can become richer than the opponent-mind who seeks to optimize his personal gain by minimizing the gains of others.

Foeti pno-Kaiel, creche teacher of the maran-Kaiel

The alliance document had come in from the printers. Oelita lay curled by the window of her room on the second floor of the maran-Kaiel mansion re-reading its lucid phrases, smelling the inked paper, and feeling smug. The prologue was all hers. She hadn't let them change a word of it. Some of the free poetry was hers – she liked images – but the contract was mostly the wordsmithing of Hoemei's students, edited by the iron hand of Hoemei himself.

How could Hoemei of the hairy chest and tender smiles love Joesai? They were so different!

The writing of the agreement had been an awesome experience unlike any group work she had ever undertaken. Her confrontations with the Stgal had taught her that priestly councils were ponderous affairs where hidden decisions were made in a guise to appease and lull opponents. Her own heretical group was scarcely better and many had been the times she had been forced to castigate and cajole. In contrast, the Kaiel mongered their wares with open enthusiasm and the precision of practised survivors.

The group assigned to bargain with Oelita consisted of

six men and five women, nine of them offspring of the creches. Three might take her for a game of kol at the temple, proposing, while they played, outrageous and often conflicting deals which they would bamboozle her into buying. The others would be off studying, creating new proposals, testing for flaws.

When she finally agreed to deal – she smiled, remembering her gullibility – they would start to bicker among themselves about why they thought she might later be unhappy with *that* deal. Sometimes some old teacher of Hoemei would sit with them mediating, teaching, guiding their efforts. They would be radiantly excited one day and dour the next after having dreamed upon the consequences. They were obsessed with consequences.

Oelita was familiar with Stgal organizational architecture which tried for no high structures. The Stgal governed by patchwork and emergency repairs. They were always having to redo what they had just done. Policies were reversed and amended. Failed policies were frequently reintroduced after the failures were forgotten.

With a lifetime of such experiences Oelita was amazed to discover these intense young Kaiel feverishly designing an edifice built on piles driven into the past, able to support whole future generations. Each paragraph was placed in the document like it was a foundation stone under a temple whose upper stories would give solid floor to an eyrie for beloved, if chimeric, grandchildren.

Of the eleven, Oelita became closest to Taimera, a studious hedonist, almost a child, taken only recently from her creche by Hoemei, her breasts, neck, shoulders as yet unscarred. She was a mischievous girl who had a sharp eye for which threads of the past a weaver must grasp to splice strength into any future design. She was the one who probed Oelita deepest for reservations, always sensitive to conflict between Kaiel ambition and heretic morality. One time when Oelita was giving Taimera a

278

lesson on coastal clan relationships, Taimera os-Kaiel explained why her co-workers were so thorough.

Those groupings of Kaiel who created *effective* laws gained power, money, influence – and the release of their genes to the breeding rooms of the creches. Predictions accurate over the immediate future were rewarded, but the big stake was in being able to control *distant* consequences.

The young group that Hoemei had assembled around Oelita knew that Kaiel auditors, armed with hindsight, would still be checking over the effects of this document when its authors were well into their political prime. If by then the coastal peoples were prospering in their relationship with the Kaiel, the votes of each author of such success would be enormously magnified, but if the document failed to do what they were predicting for it, then they would find themselves relegated to some petty job in the bureaucracy.

It was a matter of honour to Taimera, and some anxiety, to have the kind of record which spoke of continuous good judgment. She was ambitious. She had been driven to excellence to escape her creche, and was driven now to reach the top councils. As yet, she confessed to Oelita, she had managed a constituency of only five people, and so her voting weight was low, but she knew that the power of a Kaiel was not based on constituency size alone. In the end it was based on the craftsmanship of one's work.

The document had already been through the financial council to ensure that, if it became law, funds would be available for its implementation. There had been no trouble. It had been written with a full knowledge of the funding criteria it would have to meet. Now it was on the voting roll.

Any Kaiel in good standing was allowed to vote before the cutoff date, but few would because the Kaiel had a peculiar system. A mere yes or no was not sufficient. The Kaiel maintained that a yes/no vote did not require careful thought and so encouraged sloppy lawmaking. A Kaiel who voted, and they were constantly taking the trouble to vote on something, made a deposition in the Archives stating in detail what he believed to be the consequences of his choice. The archivist did not accept the vote unless the consequences were stated in measurable terms.

The voting on any issue was sparse, but indicated the decision of Kaiel who had taken the trouble to inform themselves and were willing to gamble their political future on their estimate of the outcome. There was no central lawmaking council. A Kaiel was trained from childhood to make laws in the areas where he felt a personal responsibility. He soon learned that, to get a law passed, he had to contact a representative number of Kaiel who were likely to vote on the issue and to work out a consensus with them before he put his suggestion on the voting roll.

Oelita was told by Taimera that there was an unwritten custom requiring twenty committed yes votes and a statistical analysis of the opposition before a bill would be accepted. Since every Kaiel prided himself on his ability to predict, little legislation was put forward that was not passed.

The nature of the attack upon the Stgal was to be a simple one. Copies of the alliance document would be distributed covertly among Oelita's supporters so that they would know she sought their support for a game play resembling the de-priesting play of kol.

Young Kaiel would begin to infiltrate towards the coast, recruiting constituencies. A Kaiel, taking on a member of some coastal clan, would assume a personal responsibility to protect that person and. if food became short, to bring in food for him or pull him out to the refugee camps that were being built along the road in the Valley of Ten

Thousand Graves. In return the represented one would transfer his name from the kalothi rolls of the Temple at Sorrow to the kalothi rolls of Kaiel-hontokae and swear to uphold the laws of the Kaiel.

Oelita felt guilty that the first people to be protected would be her own, but Hoemei only laughed and said that a Kaiel's first duty was to his own constituency – it was that obligation which gave Kaiel-ruled territories their vigour. When the people surrounding Sorrow found that the low in kalothi protected by the Kaiel were better off than the high in kalothi protected by the Stgal, the Stgal would find themselves deserted and suddenly powerless.

'Do you think many of my people will give Contribution in your Temple?' Oelita had been able to get no concessions about Ritual Suicide.

'We are better organized than you imagine. The first of our Kaiel to penetrate the coast will bring with them the deviant underjaw suppressor and it will first go to those farms who bond themselves to the Kaiel thus protecting their neighbours also. Taimera has herself decided to work with your Nonoep on the large scale processing of edible profane foodstuffs. It won't be much at first, but it will help take the edge off the famine and your people will get the first of the production. I can guarantee you nothing, only that they will be better off with us than with the Stgal.'

'What of the Mnankrei?' asked Oelita.

Hoemei smiled. 'It is convenient to be brother to a killer.'

'You're sending Joesai to Soebo?'

'Aesoe is sending him to Soebo.' Hoemei's smile broke into a grin. 'Even Aesoe makes mistakes and I'm ever willing to take advantage of them.'

'I'm still afraid of Joesai.'

'He has his gentle side. He does not dislike you. He is a child of the creches and all of us have been challenged by some form of Death Rite. It marks the soul. He would that you were his equal.'

'Wouldn't you like to abolish such cruelty?'

'Someday – when the land becomes water and the water, land.' Which meant never. 'The Death Rite is fair; it gives your kalothi a chance, and thus prepares you for Life, which is seldom fair.'

Aesoe dropped by the maran-Kaiel mansion and took Oelita for a walk. He brought her to the botanical gardens where profane plants were bred for beauty. Many of them had strange symbiotic relationships with the insects. The flowers that attracted bugs by shape and colour and smell had a similar effect on humans who bred them for ever more exotic show.

'Some bluenoses!' she exclaimed. They were darkly violet with the hugest flaring nostrils she had ever seen. Her mind drifted to the bluenose season when spots of violet covered the hills above the Njarae, thriving in the windy spray of sea.

Aesoe talked with her about the endlessly varied lives of the insects, a hobby of his, and he was genuinely glad to talk to someone as field-wise as she. He specialized in watching the eight-legged kaiel. He laughed when he told Oelita how lazy the kaiel were, how they always convinced the hogburrow to carve out their homes for them by stroking the backs of the hogburrow with scent that stimulated nesting behaviours.

There among the flowers he made her an honorary Kaiel. He bestowed an arbitrary voting weight of 200 on her and told her that she would be allowed to vote on any issues involving the coast. He was not going to require her to identify the members of her constituency until she felt sure that the Kaiel had not betrayed her trust.

Then he walked her back to the maran mansion, a long but interesting way over hills of stately homes. He flirted with her, patting her behind and telling her how voluptuous it was.

'You'll have to try kaiel smells,' she said, taking his arm, 'flattery doesn't seduce me.'

The Prime Predictor left her at the door, saying he had urgent business elsewhere, perhaps because he remembered that Joesai was home. When she entered the inner court of the maran household, feeling stronger than she ever had before in her life, she met Joesai standing alone in the high ritual garb of priest. Even that did not daunt her.

'Aesoe just made me an honorary Kaiel. I have a voting weight of 200,' she announced proudly.

'Ho! The madman is at it again, flaunting tradition. You think yourself worthy of such honour?'

'Yes!' she flung at his insult and felt gay. 'Will you be voting on the coastal treaty?'

'I'm voting yes. But with some reservations.'

Teenae had appeared on the balcony overlooking the inner court. 'You leave Oelita alone, you big bully!'

'What are you filing with the Archives?' Oelita persisted, watching Joesai for every flicker of his expression.

'I think the programme will be difficult to implement. It needs you, and I'm predicting that you won't be there.'

Teenae sensed Oelita's shock and vaulted off the balcony to attack Joesai with her fists. He simply reached out and snatched his wife by the wrist and jerked her up into the air, while his other hand lazily reached around and took her by the roundness of her buttocks, tossing her casually, clothes and all, into the central pool. She made a huge splash, accompanied by Joesai's laugh resonating from his massive bones.

Suddenly, Oelita was very afraid again.

37

And all who fell that day, both men and women, were twelve thousand, all the people of Ai. For Joshua did not draw back his hand, with which he stretched out the javelin, until he had utterly destroyed all the inhabitants of Ai. So Joshua burned Ai, and made it forever a heap of ruins, as it is to this day. And he hanged the king of Ai on a tree until evening; and at the going down of the sun Joshua commanded, and they took the body down from the tree, and cast it at the entrance of the gate of the city, and raised over it a great heap of stones, which stands there to this day.

Excerpt from *The Forge of War*

The rumours about Oelita's crystal ran through Kaiel-hontokae like quickfire through desert thorns.

It was an eye into God's Heart! It was an eye into Hell! The God of the Sky had broken His Silence! More sober talk simply puzzled upon a game called War.

Oelita had heard Teenae whispering to Hoemei about violence that consumed cities in flashes of light and thunder. She had heard voices in the streets talking excitedly of killer clans who faced each other by the thousands, in orderly rows, hacking at arms and legs and heads and bodies with heavy long knives while they hid behind shields.

No matter how she blocked off the rumours, they seeped through to Oelita like water through cracks in a retaining wall. She shrugged. For all their sophistication the Kaiel remained a superstitious clan.

Defiantly she took up Joesai's challenge on the eve of the great party. She was tired of his teasing her as if she were still a child believing in grumpmugs who lived in fei flowers and bit off thumbs. Thus she arrived at Kathein's physics shop in party finery. Teenae, insisting on being her bodyguard, was dressed in trousers stitched together out of radiant saloptera bellies and a wide belt of her grand-father's hide, a linear crown of jewels paving the shaved streak through her black hair. Behind her, Joesai loomed in ebony and silver and leather.

They entered. Joesai led them to a vaulted chamber of bulky magician's mysteries, tended by three sweating sorcerers. Oelita peered at shelves of tiny red insect eyes caught in glass cages. A fan whirled like the wings of a beetle migration. Kathein, moving as if she dared not generate shock with her feet, took Oelita to the Frozen Voice of God held by metal fingers that sprouted tentacles of wire. There were lights and glass lenses and the crystal was mounted in front of the great bellows of the silvergraph image maker.

Kathein hushed them while she fiddled with quick fingers. She waited and told them not to move, then pulled out a glass plate bound in black paper. 'Parts of your crystal contain visions as well as words,' she said to Oelita. 'Koienta!' she called to a servant, 'develop this silvergraph. I'll soon have to be leaving. I must dress for the party.'

Koienta bowed to Oelita. 'Our thanks for preserving the crystal,' he said as he passed her, squeezing by the shelves of bottled red eyes, his attention devoted to the black-wrapped glass. His was the ritual of one who has to believe every scrap of dogma he has been taught. It made her uncomfortable.

While Kathein gestured and touched, preparing a new glass plate, she politely explained her obsecrations-to-God. Oelita listened without trying to understand something that could have no logic. Joesai grinned, thinking she was being impressed. It was the ignorant men who were always so sure they were right!

Much later, when Koienta brought the printed silvergraph to Kathein, the physicist stared for long hearbeats, flickers of horror crossing her face from the reflected light of the paper. Silently she handed the silvergraph to Oelita, while Teenae craned her neck to see and Joesai watched faces.

'What is it? asked Teenae.

'God has been speaking to us this day!' exclaimed Kathein.

Oelita saw a still image of two rotting men hung up on thorned wire over mud. It was labelled at the bottom with readable numbers and almost readable words.

Two of l50,000 who died at Vimy Ridge, 1916.

Where could such a picture have come from? Oelita scanned her mind, her memories, her logic – and found nothing. It was like putting her foot on a familiar step in the darkness, ready for the pressure of the stone, and finding nothing. The fall was dizzying.

'There are a quarter of a billion words in your crystal and thousands of pictures. All like this,' said Kathein, leading them away. They waited while she dressed. Oelita did not speak. Joesai, smug, did not need to know what she thought. Teenae remained terrified by that one single peek through the Eyes of God. The silence broke only when the rustle of Kathein's gown descended the stairs. She appeared in brilliant silken blues, bare breasted, the platinum filigree of mask inlaid upon the noble cicatrice carved into her face.

Together they went to the Palace. The ballroom was filled by excited Kaiel scarfaces who loved parties with themes. *The Forge of War,* what little was known of it, provided an awesome theme.

Musicians were dressed in garb copied from the silvergraphs, resplendent in painted papier-mâché helmets, gaudy uniforms and breastplates of brass. Baron von Richthofen played oboe in red uniform, black cross full upon his chest, red goggles obscuring half his serrated face. Achilles, in great plumes of desert fire, tuned the strings of his ellipsoidal gourd. Hitler and Stalin, in black and yellow pinstriped pantaloons, thumped the organ drums.

Through the main entrance, blazing green and red Vatican Guards protected the arrival of the whisky kegs with proud halberds. Then across the ballroom strode the armoured and scowling samurai, Takeda Shingen, alias Aesoe, a dagger in his belt so comically long that its tip almost dragged upon the floor, carrying a yellow and pale blue banner atop a pole that read in vertical script: 'fast as wind; quiet as forest; fierce as fire; firm as mountain.'

In agitation, Oelita swept over to a table where a neat pile of silvergraphs had accumulated, each pinned to a tentative translation. Painfully she began to read a page, referring to the translation when it became incomprehensible. Once she had to ask one of the hovering linguists to help her guess at meanings and odd grammatical structures.

Thinking there was just one (killer clansman), he approached with the water. When he had penetrated the bushes, he saw there were about twenty men, and they were all in exactly the same (ghoulish) state: their faces were wholly burned, their eyesockets were hollow, the fluid from their melted eyes had run down their cheeks. They must have had their faces upturned when (the sunfire lit); perhaps they were (suppressor of engined-sailplane) personnel. *

She picked up another of the sheets.

They were ordered to lay down their (killing tools) and then were (butchered without intent to eat). Only the Caliph's life was preserved as a gift for (killer priest) Hulagu who made his

* From *Hiroshima* by John Hersey.

entrance to the city and palace on (fifteenth sleep cycle of second moon cycle of Riethe year). After the Caliph had revealed (by force of pain) to (the war game-winner) the hiding place of all his treasure, he too was put to death. Meanwhile (butchering without intent to eat) continued everywhere in the city. Those who surrendered quickly and those who fought on were alike (murdered). Women and children perished with their men. One Mongol found, in a side street, forty newborn babies whose mothers were dead. As an act of mercy he (killed) them, knowing that they would not survive without mothers to suckle them. In forty days some eighty thousand citizens of Baghdad were slain.

What was this? this geyser of paper from some demon world come to spray and scald them? Oelita didn't believe a word of it – but when she did, for just a moment, she was horror-struck by such unimaginable immorality.

How could anyone eat eighty thousand people in forty days? The bodies would rot; the leather would go brittle in the sun, untanned. To murder a man was horrible enough, but to murder a man and his relatives, too, so that there could be no Funeral Feast, that was unthinkable!

Her heart was pounding as she watched ten Chanters file into the room in mudbrown cloaks wearing their voice amplifier masks in strange goggled shapes with gross noses.

'Chlorine masks from the Great War,' said the linguist who had been helping her.

The Chants began, telling in thunderous sinusoidal rhythm of the God of the Sky delivering His Getans from some mystery too frightening to look upon. The wooden instruments faded in; the strings began to tell of warrior and fire while Hitler and Stalin beat upon their organ drums and the horns wailed. The Chants muted to moaning, one voice alone holding a delicate melody. Then out of nowhere three naked Liethe sprang through, their child-smooth bodies boneless in their leaps.

They attacked each other, circling, lungeing, stepping

288

aside, flying over one another like bodies being juggled. Six daggers appeared magically in their hands while they stalked enemies, making alliance and betrayal in deft moves. The blows began to sound as screams. Each touch pulled forth a streamer of red silk like spurting blood that attached to wrist or shoulder or hip or ankle, proliferating. They fought among streamers, and now the streamers lurched and shuddered as the weaving motions boiled the blood that enveloped the dancing bodies.

The crimson silk lost strength, fluttering, swirling, diving, dividing into three stained bodies now topped by silver skull-masks. A jerk. A lurch. A stagger. A final battle to wound the already dying, to use one's fading strength for destruction, then death throes among the mourning musicians. Only a glance of flesh did the audience get of Liethe slipping away, shucking their costumes in a convulsion that slowed and flowed down the steps into an empty red heap upon the floor.

Aesoe was stamping his feet. The Kaiel began to shake the building with their collective stamping until the naked girls, still in their skulls of silver metal, ran out from where they had disappeared, bowed, and ran away again.

Oelita turned from the spectacle. The pressure was building up within her to panic level. Her attempt to form an explanation for these impossible words was circling in failure. A hoax? Were the Kaiel building up a lie about Death to justify a coming bloody conquest of Geta?

But it was *her* crystal.

Who could write so small in visible-invisible ink? Who could conceive such stories where violence was the only means of transferring power? They could invent stories, but who could invent so many? Where was the Getan who would tell a story of mass murder without ending the story in a gluttonous Feast? Helplessly she moved through the crowd of feverish Kaiel, seeking Joesai. He was staring at silvergraph pictures.

He showed her one. A pair. To the right was a burning child running along a road beside a burning village with the title *Vietnam*. To the left was a burning child leaping off a road with a rocky mountain village in the background titled *Afghanistan*. The collective title was *The Superpowers and The Third World*. She remembered her twins roasting upon the spit.

'Have you found no love among all this?' she asked.

Silently he showed her another silvergraph. A woman was being stretched apart by a machine. *The Dominicans Save the Soul of a Heretic.* 'Or would you prefer a tale of the Christian clan exterminating the clan of Albigensians in the name of love?' He laughed and handed her some dried bees to munch on. 'While you are putting it all together think about why you can eat raw bees and why eating any other insect will sicken you unto death.'

'You think the only explanation for this is God, don't you?'

'I'll listen to a better one.'

She changed the subject. 'What's that?'

'The script underneath says it is a steel beetle big enough to carry five men in its belly across the desert. Its duty is to throw metal rocks at men.'

'How horrible!'

'I'm getting ideas.'

'Joesai!'

'This one I like especially. It is a giant intelligent candle that rides on the strength of its flame from one city to the other side of a world where it is cunning enough to find another city which it extinguishes in one blow by conjuring a bowl of sunfire.'

'Joesai!'

He smiled at her, glad to share his own horror with someone he knew could understand. 'I don't always think Death thoughts. Anything with jumping legs that strong

290

could jump up to God and talk to Him. I have some questions to ask.'

'Would you ever descend upon a city and kill more people than you could eat?' she asked.

'What a stink that would make. Kalothi can be overwhelmed. What is the point?'

'I'm confused. I don't know what anything means anymore.'

'It's obvious what it means.'

'For a simpleton like you, everything is obvious. You invoke God. God can be used to explain everything!' She was livid.

'Can't you tell what it means?' he asked gently. 'This Riethe is the world from whence we came! Don't the Chants say that God brought us across His Sky to save us? This is what He was saving us from.'

'You don't even know your Chants.' She was scornful. 'The Chants mention Riethe but they say we fell from the Star Yarieun.'

'There is no agreement on that. The same Chants vary from clan to clan and land to land. The Outpacing Chant that I am most familiar with mentions Yarieun, which we call Yarmieu, as the last resting place.'

'How can the Race be saved from itself by moving across a sky?' She was full of scorn. 'If I am poisoned and live in Sorrow, will moving myself to Kaiel-hontokae leave my poison behind? If I am afraid of my navel, will changing houses change that? If I chew my nails, will moving to the dark side of Geta give me long nails? You can't run from *here* because *here* is always where you are!'

Without letting Joesai reply, she lost herself in the crowd and left the Palace. She stood beneath the nested ovoids, her mind in chaos. Who were the Riethe and their Cult of Death? Her maelot theory of human evolution no longer made sense.

There was a God.

Her world reeled. It was madness. There was no God but God had revealed Himself. She turned back to the great door of the Palace, insanity striking her senses. Joesai was standing there. Joesai was God, and God was Death, and Death had found her, grinning.

She backed away. 'Don't come near me!' He took a step closer and she shifted two steps into the street. She was pregnant by Hoemei, and had been on the verge of creating the blood that would wash the child away, and now Joesai was coming after it with death, and she wasn't going to give anyone that child. Not again. Not ever again. 'Go away,' she said. He came closer and there was no one else about. 'I'll kill you!' she cried with deadly intent.

He paused. She was confused. How could she kill God? When God fell into the sea like a lost glowsting, He merely rose out of the mountains again to reclaim His Sky. Her fists were clenched in front of her. 'Go away!' He left and she turned and ran, stumbling in the mud somewhere, to lie against the cobblestones of a filthy gutter.

She thought of her defiance; she thought of the people she had turned from God, fomenting rebellion, and the horrors she had just seen that God had taken them from, that she had carried around with her all her life since she had been a child.

'Oh God, forgive me. I've blasphemed. I knew You and I rejected You, and my heart is full of sorrow.' She rubbed her face in the dirt. 'Oh God of Sky and Stars and Wandering, thank You for bringing us here from whatever misery You saved us from. I thank You again and again.' She rubbed her tears into the mud, her fingers clutching stone. 'Forgive me.'

38

No man can live in the future, but those who are not caught up by the struggle for some future find deadly surprises in their now!

    Inscription on the arch of the Kaiel Archives

A hard-earned gold coin can slip through a hole in a pocket. In this fashion Oelita vanished.

Aesoe, wearing only sandals with bath towel draped about his shoulders, raged and paced in his den, his genitals swinging to his wrath like gongs. He gestured quick motions that seemed to skin an invisible adversary. His Liethe, whichever one he had kept for the pillows – Hoemei remained unable to discriminate between them – lay sprawled on the cushions of the bed, a sheet between her legs, head buried from the ranting, tortured by a whisky hangover. She wore a tiny amulet on a single fine chain of gold about her neck.

Hoemei, unshaven and unslept and still in party dress, moved not a muscle. He carried a note from the Gentle Heretic, all they had been able to find of her. It said: 'Forgive me for being wrong. Please, please take good care of my people.' Nothing more.

Aesoe raved. 'See that Joesai banishes himself from Kaiel-hontokae by the first sunset of the Reaper or I will personally conduct services for his Ritual Suicide at the Temple of Human Destiny! He is a meddling nuisance, fouling the best plans of genius to soothe his woman-hating heart! And you meddle, too! Your sly hand is creeping everywhere. I told you and I tell you; that woman is vital. Find her! Will I graft the skin of you, still alive, to the wheels of wagons? Will I use your wired jawbone as a paper holder?'

The maran-Kaiel had already searched for her, of course, all during the remainder of the night, but had not found her. How does one find a woman who, as a youth, had wandered the desert plains with a shrewd father-teacher who lived to walk in the open world beneath the sky? Teenae was still out asking questions among the Ivieth. The task was hopeless.

Events disgruntled Hoemei. He had grown fond of Oelita. Her energy and intelligence pleased him, even to the point where he had been seriously dreaming of taking her as a replacement for Kathein. The family was far less sure of her suitability but he saw them beginning to meld with her, even Joesai in his churlish way. Gaet warmed to a woman easily, without agonizing debate. Teenae was outwardly friendly from the start, but was secretly threatened by another woman until she had a chance to know her well. Noe merely demanded that another woman be kind, affectionate, and easy to live with – and unquestioningly loyal to the family.

Now Hoemei was left with a breach in his plans. It was like having a route set to ascend a craggy mountain and finding the chosen path suddenly rendered impassable by landslide. He would have to send Gaet into Sorrow sooner than he had anticipated. Who else could convince Oelita's people that she had not been murdered in some treacherous deal? A delicate mission.

Shifts, shifts. Quickly he would have to find others to do Gaet's work here in the city. The inconvenience annoyed him. He cursed Joesai for the stubborn pressure he had kept on Oelita, then sighed. This was the price a Predictor paid. The future did not happen. People created the future with moment-to-moment action and decision, always adjusting to the unexpected. More than one route led to the same peak.

Hoemei bowed, dropping all the way to one knee. He had delivered his dreadful message. The Liethe creature stirred and stretched, smiling gaily at him behind Aesoe's naked haunches. Instantly he recognized Honey's special sweetness. *She* was here! The unnatural smoothness of her back launching itself into the summer hills of her buttocks sent a shiver through him more fearsome than Aesoe's anger.

'Come here,' she said.

He did not dare move lest he further provoke Aesoe. Nor could he find words.

Lazily she brought herself upright, amused at the silence, aware that her movements suspended even the Prime Predictor in mid-emotion. The chain with its tiny amulet swung between her breasts. 'My lover is afraid of my lover.' She was watching them both so that neither knew whom she meant. 'Come here.'

Hoemei remained frozen.

Her eyes, as blue and flecked as Assassin's Delight, remained fixed on him. 'Aesoe, tell him that you are not afraid to have him touch me, so that he will come here.'

'By God's Balls, Hoemei,' roared Aesoe, his mind completely distracted from its train of thought, 'don't just squat there on your knees playing her game! Crap and wipe yourself!' He nudged Hoemei impatiently with his foot, sending his councilman sprawling. 'They send me leftovers from the creche tables! I need men! Men!' he raved.

'My nice man,' said the Liethe called Honey, suddenly at Hoemei's side, 'I won't be with you before the first sunset of Reaper so you must give this to Joesai.' She slipped the golden amulet from around her neck and pressed its tiny eurythmic form into Hoemei's hand. 'I was pleased to serve your husband and brother. Give him this to wear. No man comes to harm wearing a Liethe charm.' She rose gracefully to face Aesoe while Hoemei quietly recovered his dignity. 'You see,' she said innocently, 'I protect your man upon his mission. I am with your Gathering. Liethe overcraft will guard him.'

'Nothing will save that imbecile!' snarled Aesoe, remembering what had moved him to anger.

Hoemei carried the amulet to Joesai with Aesoe's wrathful instructions. Joesai remained stoic about Oelita's disappearance in the face of all anger – as if she was merely a promising student of his who had gone bad. Teenae returned from her search and lambasted Joesai, out of worn frustration, blaming him. He took it all like the desert drinks a cloudburst. 'She did have kalothi,' he said, genuinely saddened, for he too had grown fond of Oelita.

Hoemei knew his brother's mind. Joesai suspected that Oelita had slit her wrists somewhere, and worse, slit them in hiding, denying even friends the nourishment of a Funeral Feast. She had found the Awesome God and been shattered by the magnitude of the concept. Those would be the silent thoughts of Joesai. He would pity her without ever being able to say so. What was a woman if she could not let awe run through her veins without being destroyed by the power of it?

Oelita had failed at the Sixth Trial. Hoemei remembered their brother Sanan. The eve of every victory, it seemed, was married to pain. Sanan would have loved Oelita in another time and another place. He dreamed of Sanan as a Roman senator and Oelita as a barbarian druid princess from Gaul.

39

Your enemy wins once you begin to take his strategy as your own strategy, and his means as your means – for then you have become your enemy. Do not be deceived that you use mellow words to describe your imitation and harsh words to describe your enemy. An infinity of words may be used to speak of the same action.

Dobu of the kembri, Arimasie ban-Itraiel in *Combat*

Noe watched Joesai leave the city with eighty men – only ten of them experienced – her heart filled with foreboding. She had climbed by herself to the tallest raceway of the Northern Aqueduct so that she could keep her husband in sight as long as possible. A climb she had not attempted since a distant day as an adventurous child. Its arches and levels had seemed easy then to a mind unused to assessing danger but had seemed deadly to two-father who whipped her with a cane for the climb. Now, the daring in her still unquenched, Noe held herself by the brickwork and looked out over the first column of the Gathering, ignoring the icy splashes of water that rippled by her hand.

Joesai was taking his column by the eastern route around the Wailing Mountains to avoid Mnankrei spies, planning to cut through to the coast at a point far north along the Barrier Pass. Hoemei's original scheme was a shambles. Aesoe had forced the departure of the Advance Court so prematurely that they carried only thirty rifles and were missing some supplies altogether. Maybe Aesoe had done that deliberately to derange Hoemei's plans since his prediction of the outcome was already registered with the Archives.

Noe was furious at Joesai for the trouble he had caused them, but she also remembered that the family had sent him to Sorrow with Death Rite in mind and only little Teenae by his side to restrain his hand. It was, in the end, a mutual decision that had caused the trouble. Even Oelita had contributed. One's life was not a dead chip on a roiling spring river. As a consequence, Joesai had been isolated, dressed for the spit fire, and banished from Kaiel-hontokae for the rest of his (short?) life. Was it for him alone to carry the ire of the Expansionists? Of the maran, he was the most vulnerable – and so her first duty was to him.

Noe waited impatiently the few days it took the og'Sieth to assemble twenty more tested rifles of the new quick reload design and then followed her husband with her own party at a forced pace, ruthlessly wearing out her Ivieth so that she might catch up with Joesai. Karval ngo-Ivieth, her lead porter, found fresh clansmen where he could and the pace never slackened. Sometimes when she was ready to drop, he carried her, without complaint, like a scarf about his neck.

'Karval,' she once asked him, 'what is your opinion of this Gathering?'

'It is a matter between the priests.'

'How are we to rule wisely if we know not the feelings of the underclans? Come! If your resistance hides disagreement, I must hear! The Kaiel do not fear dissent, nor do we harm dissenters.'

Karval considered. 'The Mnankrei interfere with our breeding rights,' was his only comment, but those words were weighted with disapproval.

Ah, so Hoemei may really have the scent! If Mnankrei fingers no longer touched the soul of the underclans of Soebo, then, given forbearance by Joesai, it might be possible, as Hoemei thought, for Joesai to inspire a revolt and to survive by taking its leadership. Aesoe anticipated no such resentment in Soebo. His plans were built around the death of a martyr. The Mnankrei were Noe's enemy, but Aesoe was also her enemy.

Noe's studies of *The Forge of War* had left her wondering that Getan clans had not invented the game of war themselves. The intrigue, the conflict, the hatred, the rivalry, the clash of ambition was there, the raw material of Riethian war. Perhaps her Ivieth's answer was the clue. On Riethe the clans were organized vertically. They had fierce up and down loyalty but only the weakest lateral loyalty. One priest clan of Riethe could set their underclansmen to killing fellow underclansmen of another priest realm, something inconceivable on Geta where horizontal loyalty was unbreakable and enforced by swift death.

She tried to imagine what would happen if the Ivieth of the Mnankrei, half of whom must have wandered in from another realm, were ordered to kill the Ivieth of the Kaiel. What would they do? Laugh? Grow red with rage? Gape at such foolishness? Politely ignore the order? Kill Mnankrei? No Ivieth would destroy the bridges and roads of another Ivieth, nor harm the travellers that their Geta-wide clan-vow protected. Noe smiled at a preposterous thought she could not have entertained a few weeks previous – how difficult was conflict when priest had to march against priest, and ethics forbade the killing of more enemies than one could eat!

Oh, those Riethe leaders were spoiled with their bowls of sunfire, their poison gases, and their specialized killer clans; the willingness of farmer to kill farmer, brother to kill brother, sister to kill sister, husband to kill wife, and right hand to stab left! *Here we priests have to do it all ourselves! And God's Wings, on foot!*

Karval called rest at a spring near grassy and bramble-filled foothills. Noe collapsed onto the ground beside the rifle wagon. She remembered that Gaet would touch these tools but not use them in his hands, pointed at something. Her coward husband!

She unpacked the topmost of the lethal tools while they rested, loaded it curiously, carefully, and lying prone on the ground, held it against her shoulder. After breathing deeply – twice – she squeezed the metal thumb, immediately forgetting where she had aimed in her surprise. She never saw the pebble strike. Five lead pebbles later, meticulously flung into the hide of an old tree, she felt ready to attack any man who might attack her husband. She was sad she was not going to Soebo with him. She would be stuck on the coast, working with her seagoing relatives, keeping open the sea-leg of the Gathering's supply line.

They found Joesai camped outside of the village of Tai. He was on a flat hill above the farmlands, teaching one of his fresh creche girls how to catch knives and throw them. Her hair was tied in a bun, her breasts shimmering with sweat and blood from a minor gash on her shoulder. The girl yelled and ran to Noe's wagons where she emerged waving a rifle in triumph, the hontokae carved into her face distorted by a smile.

Noe hurried her husband to his tent and fed him water, caressing him as she did so, eager for his body. 'A bloodthirsty pride of children I have here,' he glowed.

'We must forbid them to be Riethe,' she said. 'It is important.'

40

Who shall judge the priests? They are not monitored by our God of the Sky for He passes overhead in silence. The priests rule by the grace of the underclans.

> The nas-Veda Who Sits on Bees, Judge of Judges

So the crone mother had detected the rebellion Humility felt. The hag's speech had been a lash of fury. Humility's thoughts raged. *Why must I care why those who die are condemned? I'm young! I don't have to stay in a hive and think!*

Being young had its disadvantages. Youth was subject to the absolute will of the crones. And the crone mother saw fit to drill her on the Four Justices and the Lattice of Evidence and all the rest of it barring even time out for love. She was being readied for something. They always gave you the vessel before they filled it. The vessel was bisqued and then baked to stoneware hardness by the fire of their breathing. Methane-snorting witches!

Humility knew she would be nothing without the Endless Training. There would be no palaces, no mastery of grace, no adoring men, no power, and no pleasure of the hunt and kill. The Training was the price. One even learned to love its rigour. But why the sudden hurry? It was keeping her away from Hoemei!

The hive was grey; the floor of her cell was cold; her woven mat pricked her flesh with broken fibres: all minor tortures compared with the pain she was really suffering. She lay awake imagining the se-Tufi With Saucy Nipples giggling while riding Hoemei's rod during her stand-in at

301

being the Honey persona. *Why do I care?* Humility only knew that she desperately wanted to be in the Palace with Hoemei after being away from him only a week.

Would Saucy know to bring a nightslip petal for him to smell? *Why am I jealous of my own sister?* In all her intricately memorized knowledge of the se-Tufi, there was no hint of jealousy. Did a se-Tufi, who felt jealous, fear her shame so much that she kept the emotion a secret from all her sisters?

Once Humility had, on orders, smothered a Lineless Liethe for jealousy. The girl had slapped her lover's wife. It had been sombre to feast upon such loveliness. Weeks later there was nothing left of the beautiful body but the warm buskins worn by the crone mother. Jealousy was a foul emotion, lethal to the cause of the Liethe. The penalty was always death.

Dawn of the high day brought an early rising and a summons by the se-Tufi hag. They shared a bun and honey.

'Don't you ever relax?' asked Humility, trying to be offhand.

'When I travel.' A faraway look came into the ancient eyes. 'But I'm too old for the road. I shall die here in Kaiel-hontokae for my Feast. Keep a fingerbone for yourself. I have a special place for me in your belly. I envy you; you still have much journeying in front of you.'

Humility was quick to perceive that the reference to the road was not idle gossip. Her heart caught. 'Are you telling me that I'll be travelling for you?'

The hag grinned. 'I have been training you to be my ambassador to Soebo at the Crone's Court. In Soebo you will see how marvellously the Lattice of Evidence sifts for crime. You will know that I have taught you well.'

'But I don't want to go to Soebo!' Humility cried.

'Ah! You've changed.' The old woman first chuckled, then sighed. 'You must go. Serious scandal is afoot. The

Liethe watch all Gatherings. We participate in our own way. You will know what to do when you get there. Your youth is over. You are ready to decide for yourself who must die. Do not be impulsive. Remember always that you are acting for me and that I shall judge you. You leave tonight.'

'Shall I not see Hoemei again?'

'No.'

Only the White Mind seared away her tears. She bowed to duty. She bowed her head to the floor. She swore allegiance to mother and hive and clan.

And cheated. Saucy Nipples was her friend and sister. They arranged a brief switching tryst so that she might say goodbye to Hoemei who would never even know that she had left. She was crazy with excitement. She bathed twice and broke flower petals upon her skin. She read the love poems of the Sexing Chant to prepare her mind.

Hoemei was tired but she did not mind. She hugged him and enjoyed the caress, not clinging too long, for to him Honey had only been away for sun-heights. He was tired so she fed him; he was tired so she undressed him and laid him upon his back while she massaged the ploughings of his body; let him lie comfortably while she mounted him to feed him the pleasure of her hips. 'You're the love of my life,' she said, squeezing him with her lower self.

He only laughed because Liethe always spoke thusly to priests.

'Hoemei!' came a whisper at his door, a woman's voice, hurried, frightened, excited.

He held his Honey to keep her from moving. 'Yes? Who is it?'

'Me of course! Kathein! You're all alone – with Joesai and Noe up north, and Gaet and Teenae on the coast. I was feeling sorry for you all day, so I've come to see you.'

'God,' said Hoemei, rattled.

For the Queen of Life-before-Death, the moment was

pain. She had never before hated a woman, and what could be more painful than that? Slowly she lowered herself from her riding position until her breasts mingled with Hoemei's hairy chest. She gave him one last kiss, a quick one while she stuffed the feel of his body into her memory. 'She's an old love of yours, isn't she? Let her come. While I hide, she will be fascinated by you, and while you hold her with her back towards me, I will leave.' Humility dismounted, collected her things rapidly, and took herself behind the tapestry.

'Kathein, I'm not dressed,' he delayed.

'That's the way I want you!'

'I'll be right there.'

He got up and patted the tapestry, and of all the things he could have done, that pleased his Liethe the most.

'What's happening?' said Hoemei as Kathein slipped through the door.

'Silly, you've dressed yourself!' she admonished him.

'I'm in a state of shock. What are you doing here? Aesoe will have us for rugs!'

Behind the oz'Numae hangings, a dishevelled Humility snorted in her mind. *He hasn't learned how to handle Aesoe yet! When will he ever learn!*

'I'm tired of making love to Aesoe,' she said sulkily. 'He likes to sleep with his head on my breasts – and he snores!'

A sudden knowing smile erupted in hiding. Humility wondered why she was smiling while she was in such pain, and why she tolerated the agony when she could as easily go into White Mind and order any response she desired from her body. It was love. They told her it might happen someday. They told her it happened at least once to every Liethe and that if she were lucky she would be old before it did.

She felt a petulant exasperation. *They want me to know why I kill! And I get stuck with being in love!* She did not like growing up.

'How's the new clan going?' Hoemei asked.

'You're so the intellectual! How's my clan going,' Kathein mocked. 'You know how it is going! I'm surrounded by children who have to learn everything from me. I'm astonished by their speed! But I want people who have lived. I miss you all. I hate Aesoe for sending Joesai out to his death! God Above, what an astronomer he'd make!' She was crying and Hoemei took her in his arms.

Humility stuck her head out and motioned for him to pull Kathein to the cushions. He did so, holding her tightly, locking her into an embrace that generated passion from Kathein. Slowly, Humility tiptoed away, clothes in her arms. She wagged her tongue insolently, pausing just long enough to frighten him, waiting at leg's length from Kathein's shoeless toes, a nostalgic look on her face. If she were Hoemei's wife, she could join him on the pillows now.

Morality! she thought sullenly and was gone, silently crying, wetting her cheeks, anguished that her last meeting with Hoemei had crumbled into such a disaster. It was the first time in her life that she remembered tears she had not faked.

She took the route through the Valley of Ten Thousand Graves to the coast, an arduous journey that one did not make frivolously. She found a proliferation of the strange skrei-wheels and charmed rides from their pedallers in exchange for a hand at pushing on the difficult grades. There was evidence of new roadwork everywhere. A conqueror lays out roads. That was axiom.

Before reaching Sorrow she turned northward through the mountains because a signalman of the Moera clan, who was not a true Moera, worked the great tower atop the Peak of Blue Concern. No command ordered her to find him but he *did* live along her route to Soebo and there *was* a standing call for his execution.

Humility first encountered Anid toi-Moera at the inn

305

where he liked to eat, overlooking high cliffs above the sea. She waited and, after dinner, followed him into the wilderness fog. But at the perfect place for murder – a curving trail among huge trees that grew more than two man-heights tall – she hesitated.

Why did he have to die? The accursed Lattice of Evidence was prickling her mind.

The crone said he was a bearer of the foul underjaws to these parts and that he accepted coin for overhearing all messages that passed through his tower. Humility knew nothing more, not who had accused him or how his deeds had been catalogued, just that he was marked for death.

During her moment of introspection, he disappeared.

She slept in the woods to the crashing sound of waves below, stunned by her vacillation. See! It was *true* that no assassin should seek to understand her target! Orders were enough. The hunt and kill were enough. To be curious meant fatal irresolution.

Wearing modest robe and veil, she spent the next high day seeking Anid again, the empty Lattice of Evidence in her mind like a burr under the skin. Each branch of the Lattice had to be filled before a man was condemned. Who had filled it for Anid? Had some crone mother, at great distance, really satisfied those severe demands? What distortions and falsehood might have entered the judgment?

She found Anid on the road. Boldly she went to him and asked where she might have shoes repaired. He was curious that she would travel alone. She told him that she had a long ambition to see the sea, and truly she was awed by it. He smiled. He was a towerman, he said, and knew the best spots from which to view the ocean's beauty. For instance, there was a cliff where the moon laid a road of light across the night waters. Please show me, she replied, making him feel that she had long been without male company, and that, though she was modest, she might be seduced by kind attention.

So he led her to a nook above the cliffs where they could be alone. They talked. She probed to hear his view of Stgal and Kaiel and Mnankrei but learned nothing. He had no opinion about famine that would separate him from a thousand others. He did not seem to lust for power or reward. He seemed to be a towerman who took pleasure in seducing wandering women. Her Lattice framework remained empty, an unsatisfying hollowness.

The rustic hideaway he had chosen was grassy, at an awesome height above the beach below, hidden by rocky rises behind them. The slate was cracked and crumbling to grey age but was of a resistant nature that had held back the death attack of the waves like a great-grandfather watching over his clan.

'You must stay with me here to be enchanted by the moon's waxing increase as night unfolds,' he said.

'I have no time.' She let her voice express regret, lingering on the mysteries that might come with stolen heartbeats.

'Aw, stay with me a while.'

'Do you really want . . .'

'I'm dying of desire.'

'If you really want me, I might be convinced.'

'I'll be good to you.'

'I'm very inexperienced,' she said, dropping the eyelashes that peered from above the veil.

'There is no hurry. The early night after sunset covers much.'

'No. We have to do it now. Keep your back to me. Nothing looks more foolish than a woman undressing herself.'

He obeyed, careful now not to break her sudden mood.

'Promise to close your eyes?'

'They're closed.'

The stone smashed into his skull, crushing it. She tested his pulse to see if he were dead, surprised how he clung to life. A quick twist of his head broke his neck. Thoroughness was the mark of a superior assassin. Then she pushed him off the cliff. She had been careful to let her feet follow his tracks so that it would seem he came alone. She left no traces as she retreated, only traces upon a mind upset because it craved more than faith. She was slightly disappointed to find that, in the end, she was merely a creature of habit.

Gazing backwards, for the view pleased her, she saw a ship far at sea, its sails full. Mnankrei by the size of it. She could pick up a ship going north, probably as wench to a Mnankrei Storm Master. She did not relish more walking or those hideous wagon rides. Fast ships fascinated her and here was a new sea to explore.

41

Supreme excellence in warfare consists of breaking the enemy's resistance without fighting.

    Sun Tzu in *The Forge of War*

Six small boats were chartered from the Goei, a carpenters clan whose members often took up seafaring. Their double-masted ships were sturdy, the clinker-built strakes running along shallow sides, then rising in a rounded stem to hold a high bowsprit. The vessels were of necessity constructed with low draught to negotiate the inferior harbours since they were forbidden access to Mnankrei ports.

The Goei knew the foggy coast of the Island of Mnank as a sneak thief knows the windows of the nearest rich community. It was a week away in the best of sailing weather, two in the worst, and there was always a wind. In these northern waters, dominated by the Mnankrei, they either smuggled or stuck to cabinet-making.

The shoreline of Mnank twisted in such a cacophonous noise of bays that only the best were used by the trading fleets. No one could patrol them all. Smugglers thrived. Thus the swift and tiny craft of Joesai's party beached on a sandy inlet in the rosy twilight fog without mishap and began the trek south to Soebo through a land wondrously lush. In some places the ground was even moist and choked with flowering rushes! They traversed the eldritch woods that grew the sturdy timbers of the great Mnankrei ships until they broke into the cleared plains below where they began to meet their first farmers.

Joesai moved warily. Sometimes he took out the bound book Kathein had given him and pondered upon the difficulties of Hannibal, or re-read the obscure details of Sherman's march through Georgia. Sherman never manoeuvred in a direction which revealed his destination. The strategy pleased Joesai and he adopted it by striking across the Yearning Valley towards Ciern rather than directly over the central plains to Soebo. When camping he ordered the construction of a perimeter defence in the fashion of a Roman Legion advancing through hostile territory. All the while he made quiet contact with the people.

At each village they demonstrated the rifle by splatting a bag of water from afar with a lead pebble. Joesai demanded the obeisance due to priests but in turn offered respect. He and the ten fingermen of his Hand Council made it clear that they were the forepriests of a Gathering come to investigate the origins of the deviant underjaw. It frightened the farmers to hear that the strange underjaw carried human genes, obviously the meddling of some priest, though few of them believed the Mnankrei would do such a thing. Still, the tale loosened lips and Joesai learned the extent of Mnankrei unpopularity.

Besides his fascination for the pages of *The Forge of War*, which he carried in a waterproof sack of baby skin, he was reading Oelita's book in the edition published by Teenae in Kaiel-hontokae. The Gentle Heretic's forays into bio-logic enraged him, but she made good sense with her stories chiding priestly alienation from the underclans. It was interesting reading because his life now depended upon the good will of the surrounding underclans. The country folk they were meeting had been propitiative and overawed by Kaiel discipline – but if crossed could turn murderous.

Joesai's expedition lived off the land out of necessity, but his band had strict orders to make sure that the farmers were repaid in work and so they found their pace slowed by sun-heights of remortaring stone farmhouses or digging wells or repairing a weak bridge or cutting tipe pa-twine for a family short of stout labour. Such exchanges caused some amazement since these country clans had never seen priests doing manual labour. Joesai enjoyed working on thatched roofs and digging ditches. He was in no hurry to reach Soebo where Mnankrei strength outnumbered him hundreds to one.

What they learned while they toiled was shaping his whole strategy. The discontent voiced by every clan always stemmed from Mnankrei use of continuous Culling, which was seen as a threat to the established clan breeding rights. Joesai fanned the discontent whenever the subject was broached by using one of Oelita's favourite arguments modified slightly by his own prejudices. During times of plenty, Culling by the priesthood was a sacrilege and could not be justified as a pursuit of kalothi because kalothi did not demand the death of an inferior man, only that he spill his seed upon barren ground.

Joesai laughed when he found himself making converts to Oelita's heresy by campfire. It did not bother him at all that the Kaiel used continuous Culling within the creches of their own clan. That was different. That was an internal clan decision. Common law applied only to cross-clan affairs.

Once, to foment rebellion, he led a disciplined attack, eighty strong, on a local temple and freed a retarded woman, beloved by her father, who was being readied for Ritual Suicide. The only Mnankrei priest – there were a mere five of them – who was foolish enough to protest by drawing a knife was shot from a distance in the leg. While Eiemeni patched the wound of the old priest, sprawled in agony upon the ground, Joesai delivered his moralistic speech to the stunned farmers. He wasn't really listening himself. Already he could repeat Oelita's argument by rote. He was enjoying the impression he was making and dreaming of the look Oelita might have given him if only she had been here to watch his show.

Then the surgeon in Joesai demanded that he check Eiemeni's work. It was his first close look at a Mnankrei priest. The blood and the pain of a man made helpless by his own foolishness was not impressive. Even the flying-storm-wave cicatrice seemed out of place here among the rolling fields.

Reverie recalled sea priest Tonpa and how Teenae had coveted boots cobbled from his hide. Joesai knew her soul. She would never forgive Tonpa for hanging her upside down from the yardarms of his topsail. She carried vengeance to the grave with her, a concept he did not understand but one he respected. He daydreamed of a return from Soebo that defied Aesoe's silly banishment, wearing Tonpa's cured hide and giving it to the finest bootmaker in Kaiel-hontokae. That would please Teenae and perhaps make up a little for her loss of Oelita. Maybe then she would not be so angry at him. *I think she loved that woman, and never knew it.*

All thoughts led back to Oelita.

He lay by his campfire, without his family, alone, relaxing after reading, watching the brilliant stars Stgi and Toe rise like motes on the zephyr of Geta's swift rotation. They were the love stars in the Constellation of Six. The immensity of the white sands of the night sky contrasted the vast stellar universe of *The Forge of War* against Oelita's tiny planetary effort – a hot black iron skillet and a dancing drop of water. The People of the Sky would be out there killing.

God had seen fit to give His Race a history that told only of a beginning when the Race and the People were still one. Long ago, eons ago, the People of the Sky had sunfired the city of Hiroshima while they maintained laws against killing criminals. What would their power and

312

ferocity and inconsistency be now after millennia of practice among the stars? They would have their gods to carry them, too. Did not *The Forge of War* speak of battlegods?

By now they might be everywhere, singing their alien Passage Chants. What if they reached Getasun with their starwind sails? To what hideous level would they have perfected torture and killing-without-eating? Was Oelita's love powerful enough to shape a planet that could hold off even the People of the Sky?

Eiemeni dropped down beside Joesai near the fire, bringing with him his woman. Her name was Riea, and she was a fierce one. Perhaps that was why Eiemeni had come to cherish her and stumbled about attending her like a foolish boy.

'You are watching our love stars,' she said.

'The myth may be wrong. They may be death stars.' Joesai was sour.

'You read too much, old man,' she replied affectionately, adding a stick to the fire.

'Reading mellows me like mead in a burned cask.'

'You've been thinking of thirst that isn't slaked by mead,' said Eiemeni.

'I've been thinking of the ironies of life. You've been with me for a while now, Eiemeni. You saw me drive Oelita to madness. I forced her to believe in God, to see Him and to know Him. In the meantime I've become an athiest who slobbers over the philosophy of non-violence.'

'Joesai,' said Riea, 'cease such riddles. We are plain talk people.'

'There is no God of the Sky.'

Riea laughed. 'You've been without your wives too long.' And put her arms around him.

Gently he cuffed her.

She only snuggled closer. 'Keep your eyes to His Sky.

You do not see God? In a moment you will see His Streak overhead.'

'God is a rock.'

'Do you believe everything you read? Even God plays jokes.' Eiemeni laughed, whacking his bond master with the back of his hand.

'I've re-read my pages of *The Forge of War* so often by now I can almost think in the ancient language. They have strange words. There are battlegods and helicopter gungods and airgods and sailing gods and steamgods. Language sneaks through time like a miser on new adventures in old clothes. Our word for ship is their word for boat. Our word for God is their word for ship. Their word for sky is our word for highest. Their word for sun is our word for star. If we said "sky" to our ancestors they would think of the night sky, the stars. "God of the Sky" translates to "ship of the stars". Think about that for a while.'

'You're mad!'

'Yes.' And he laughed the great laugh, understanding completely Oelita's madness.

'God is intelligent!' admonished Riea.

'God reasons!' stated Eiemeni.

'God is silent,' said Joesai, 'and His Sky is full of pin-bright points of death-without-nourishment. Perhaps they cross the void even now with a cargo of sunfire for our cities. We may not be ready when they reach us.'

'*The Forge of War* drives you mad!'

'It has already driven me mad! I see dark visions among the futures. Kalothi can be overwhelmed. Poisoned. Trampled. Snuffed out. All of it.' He began to pile wood on the fire by fistfuls.

'Stop it!' said Eiemeni holding him. 'All of Mnank will see us!'

'Kalothi shall burn brightly! The beasts of Riethe are driven away by fire, so says their book. Tomorrow we turn course and march on Soebo. The pettiness of such as the

Mnankrei will not destroy us! The Kaiel shall rule! All power to the Kaiel!'

'Eighty of us shall burst upon Soebo and slaughter the lot of them?' chided Eimeni quietly.

'Ho! Do not think slaughter! Then you become as the Insect Lords of Riethe. Think of kalothi receiving its wood! The Last of the List, those Mnankrei who dare call themselves priests, shall die for the Race. Through their Contribution we shall bring Oelita's gentleness to our world. How can the brutality we saw at the granary fire in Sorrow survive the acid juices of our bellies?'

42

The priest who is a trader will do better than the priest who is a philosopher.

Prime Predictor Tae ran-Kaiel in *The Making of Mead*

Like the classic Nairn thrust of kolgame, they came out of the mountains through the Valley of Ten Thousand Graves to challenge the suzerainty of the Stgal. Teenae was astonished at the difference of style between one-husband and three-husband. Gaet was no Joesai hiding under covert masks and concealed action. He was Gaet maran-Kaiel in formal clanwear making use of conditions created by the Mnankrei before the Mnankrei were in a position to exploit them.

Even in the wilderness Gaet insisted on the life of wealth that Joesai discarded willingly. He ate with his wife in elegance off an inlaid table with stubby legs that was loaded with the best mead, flowers, and steaming food. They slept in a tent near a pot of coals to warm them. He was never too tired to court her, or to lift up the spirits of the lean hags they met with a little flattery that filled the heart if not the belly.

Teenae recalled a road long ago when she had been a sullen waif off the auction block and he had been wooing her with luxuries that had both tempted and frightened her. With Gaet along, this road did not seem as stark as the road she remembered trodding with Joesai on her first trip to Sorrow. Then their only luxury had been a palanquin.

They found that the foothill wheat crops were being devastated by the underjaw. The people were lead and in a hoarding, frugal mood. Food prices were high. As yet there was no starvation, but cases of profane poisoning were on the increase. The Stgal were calling up the Low on the List for their Contribution and meat was more available than usual. Events had created a perfect mood for Kaiel penetration – the desperate moment before hope metamorphosed into resignation. The Stgal offered the Discipline of the Famine, a martyrdom ingrained in the Getan soul because it had saved them so many times before, but the Kaiel offered food. Gaet came in all his riches to tempt them.

When Gaet negotiated he fed his guests. The welcome tent was a large one, erected wherever they moved, now sitting in a field of the foothills among the wildflowers. It was not a busy morning. Two curious farmers representing a local Nolar tribe had passed through the flaps and been given bean sauce on bread with a bowl of soup. Only after their plates were clean were they led to a young Kaiel clansman who squatted on a mat with them in the open air, exploring their goals.

Where had the Stgal failed the Nolar? How were the roads? Did an adequate supply of medicines reach the hills from the Stgal chemical cloisters? Did the Stgal pay well for the women they bought? How many of the Nolar clan members did they think they would lose to the underjaw famine by starvation? by Contribution?

The Nolar men clutched their robes about them and complained that the Stgal did not give back as much meat to the countryside as they took from it. The Kaiel youth nodded and made note. This gripe he had not heard before, though Stgal distribution irregularities were a constant complaint, so much so that Gaet had set up a special committee to overhaul goods distribution to the newly recruited.

Gaet was designing his support staffs along the Hoemei model. All of his administrative groups had to predict the effect of their efforts, and if their predictions failed to come true, the group was dissolved, inducing Gaet's followers, like this young man interviewing the Nolar, to make reliable promises. It was too soon for change to be noticed yet, but they all knew that Gaet would long remember the good predictors and would not fail to give latrine duty to his incompetent seers.

On this morning Gaet had dispatched the five fingermen of his Left Hand Council, with their groups, on a recruiting foray into the territory of a small hill temple that seemed undermanned. He was preparing for a major move downslope into well-defended Stgal territory. He sat on a carved wooden stool in his own tent in conference with his Right Hand Council and a local Ivieth chief who had come in from Sorrow under cover of night.

Oelita's general contract with the Kaiel was explained carefully to the giant by the pale light of a bioluminous globe hanging from the tent poles. Teenae fed the glowing bacteria of the globe and listened, learning.

Gaet was meeting representatives of each coastal clan and setting up committees, loyal to the underclans, to monitor the contract, to spot violations and inevitable flaws. First he had been concentrating on wooing the farmers near his lines of supply but was now swinging his attention to the Ivieth who were the most mobile clan of Geta and the people most accustomed to shifting loyalties. Ivieth from Kaiel-hontokae were to be brought in and Ivieth from Sorrow, first those who were Low on the List, were to be sent back along the newly refurbished road.

As a matter of tactics, Gaet was not signing up people faster than he could build the apparatus to serve them. Consequently Kaiel protection remained scarce and in demand, thus allowing him to negotiate conditions easier for the Kaiel to meet.

The Stgal were showing no real unity of command in their response. Later that day, rifle over her shoulder, Teenae brought in a delegation of four young Stgal to meet with Gaet. Obliquely they tried to bribe him. Without showing any expression, Gaet replied by offering a counter-bribe. He left the priests wondering whether he was serious or whether he was just roasting their legs.

In the evening, on the tent cushions, Teenae told Gaet of another Stgal group – she already had a network of spies in Sorrow – who argued in their councils for delaying actions that would suffice until the arrival of Mnankrei wheat and barley. Nevertheless, whatever internal dissent existed among the Stgal, they had agreed internally to postpone the Culling – which meant that they were feeding people from their reserves and thus alleviating present miseries by decreasing future options. They were gambling that the Mnankrei would come to their rescue.

Gaet laughed. He was enjoying this real-life kolgame. Teenae let him laugh but she busied herself cleaning her rifle, sitting by the brazier, deep in thought.

43

Whosoever insists on winning must play at trivial games; no interesting victory is ever assured.

Dobu of the kembri, Arimasie ban-Itraiel in *Rewards*

After a rolling journey in a small single-masted vessel that took her to three tiny harbour villages, the se-Tufi Who Walks in Humility found passage as High Deck Sensual on a large merchantman of the Mnankrei. It was not an ideal berth. The captain, whom she expected to be in charge, had been moved out of his cabin into the quarters of his mates by a certain Summerstorm Master Krak – a weighty official of Soebo on a tour of inspection – who was disinclined to share his appropriated luxuries with a mere woman.

Instead of being mistress of the High Room, as she had contracted, Humility found herself being shifted between two small bunks, three mates, and a captain who was in a foul mood for being ordered about at every change of tack by his finicky superior. Nor were all the seamen drafted from the Vlak or Geiniera clans as was usual. She had signed on to service the sea priests, unaware that the ship's crew contained fifteen virile Mnankrei doing their sailing apprenticeship.

Paraded before them along the deck she paled and somehow the youths noticed. They were in awe to have a Liethe at their disposal and, among themselves, overruled their captain, deciding that their collective lust would be too much for her. They fixed up a private bed among the oily smells of the dark rope room so that she might have a place of respite from the fetid mate's quarters. They gave her candles and smuggled special foods for which her smile was enough reward. Such unanimous gallantry warmed Humility and she responded by being free with her touches. Often she sang for them and once spent an evening by the light of Scowlmoon helping the crew mend ratlines.

One grey morning, while an easy rain was dropping upon the sea, a small ship hailed them and a wounded man was brought aboard. The patrol had tried to stop a boat smuggling the false judges of the Kaiel across to Mnank. Explosions had thrown pellets at them and one of the men had taken a lead ball into his stomach. Humility tended the man that she might hear him speak of this wonder. *The rifle!* How would these men of the sea respond to this awesome Kaiel magic?

'We couldna come close,' said the sailor in his pain. The wound was days old, but movement to the larger ship had opened the hole and his suffering was fresh.

'At what distance were you taken?' asked Krak.

'One hundred man-lengths.'

Krak was surprised and asked for more details to confirm the estimate. Finally he shrugged. 'Are you frightened?' he asked sarcastically of a young Mnankrei who seemed most awed by this report of metal flung through the air like seed popping from the ripened pod of a hurler.

'The game has changed,' came the reply, revealing neither fear nor foolhardiness.

'The sand is stirred but the beach remains,' quoted Krak, calling upon a common Mnankrei proverb. 'Let me instruct you. In the blood of this poor man's belly you see demonstrated a mastery of metal – a tinkerer's skill, worthy of the og'Sieth perhaps. But I ask you, why do the priests rule and not the og'Sieth? God gave the priestly clan no special privilege. Is it that we rule because priestly skills have proven their seniority? Knowledge of the sacred and the profane dominates all else. Lo! This lead ball flies across 100 man-lengths to attack us. Shall we tremble as we contemplate the vastness of 100 man-lengths? I tell you that the sacred skill of the Mnankrei can extend a Black Hand across 100 *thousand* man-lengths and clean a city bare. To what avail is a lead ball against the forces we command? Will not the Kaiel die even before they have seen as specks those they presume to judge? Will not they die while thinking they are safe because they are beyond the range of flying stones!' He laughed. 'The mite, on guard against the carnivorous flea, flies into the maw of the maelot.'

Krak dismissed the litter bearers, indicating that they should carry the wounded man below decks. He was happy with some secret knowledge. Humility, her assassin's mind alert to allusions of death, was left to wonder at a perishing over which riflemen could not prevail.

The ship rode out a storm with furled sails. Continuous heavy winds brought them into Soebo harbour, a long extension of the river. The sea's violence still grumbled as a cold drizzle but Humility braved the wetness to catch her first sight of the waterfront.

Ancient stone structures of the uniquely massive Mnankrei design reached into the bay, crusted at the waterline, some of them built on the ruins of older structures. Ships cluttered the wharves and canals. Flotsam floated and bobbed on the water, carrying with it the slight smell of sewage. Endlessly the city rose over the hills of the river valley.

Humility had never imagined that she would be so happy to see land again. One of the young Mnankrei, sensing her mood, pulled out a small flute and began to play to her from his seat on the wet ropes. She turned and listened. She picked up the melody. For a while she hummed along, then began to sing in her high voice of a city that waited for sailors to return from the sea. Soon she had an audience.

A tall Geiniera, stooped from the low ceilings of the ship, brought out a flask of whisky, brewed from the sombre barley of Mnank, and passed it around to the beardless Mnankrei he had been training in the lore of the sea. They drank. They clapped. The captain stepped from the warmth of the High Room onto the cold of the upper deck to watch. Soon she was dancing for these men who were her friends, Liethe in every movement and flirting gesture, thriving on their attention.

She had arrived at the greatest city on all of Geta, a city of rumour and fame and debauchery, that nurtured a Liethe settlement unequalled in size except for Hivehome on the islands of the Drowned Hope. This was civilization and she could dance to its glory on the deck of one of its magnificent vessels. Kaiel-hontokae was but a desert village grim in its determination, a waystation in her past. Kaiel-hontokae had only Hoemei, her lover, whom she still remembered a little, a man so deliciously arrogant that he was foretelling the imminent fall of this great city which would crumble, he said, on the day he chose to touch it.

She laughed. Did all lovers seem so foolish once they had been abandoned?

44

The Society will use all of its resources and energy towards increasing and intensifying the evils and miseries of the people until at last their patience is exhausted and they are driven to a general uprising.

Nechayev, teacher of Lenin in *The Forge of War*

Teenae took upon herself the duties of working in the forward organization, duties requiring her to slip in and out of Sorrow in her mediations with the people of the Gentle Heresy. Her best friend came to be an old weaver of the o'Maie who had grown enamoured of scholarship when he was crippled as a boy and could not work the looms or dye. He was poor, always in the same ragged trousers and sweat-soaked leather jerkin, always at home in his insect-ridden attic room, always smiling with his rotten teeth. His grasp of Getan history was great and he helped her translate portions of *The Forge of War* which she brought with her.

Teenae had become fascinated by a fanatic she found in that vile history who was plagued by the Riethe madness. His grandiose visions of an impending conquest of Riethe by the Worker clan were conjured in colour but proved, with the passage of time, to be delusional. By Kaiel measure his predictions were unimpressive. On the other hand, his ability to savage a wounded nation was awesome. The name was Lenin and he rode in a great steam-powered engine to take over the Russian socialist uprising so that he might destroy the embryonic Russian socialism with systematic Nechayevian terror to provide fertilizer for his own cardboard future.

The destruction of the very world he hoped to build began with the shooting of the demonstrators who were marching on the Tauride Palace in Petrograd in support of the first elected socialist Constituent Assembly. It was winter of the Riethe year 1918, full of cold snows. In the rage of Lenin's own words, brought to Teenae by God across the depths of His Unimaginable Sky, she felt that mean man's deathly fear of all power other than his own. She pitied him the loneliness it implied. To wield total power requires the destruction, everywhere, of all free wills. To need total power is to be totally insecure.

By the end of 1918 Lenin was calling for mass exterminations on a daily basis. 'You must mobilize all forces, establish a troika of dictators, introduce immediately mass terror, shoot and deport hundreds of prostitutes who ply soldiers and officers with vodka. Do not hesitate for a moment . . .' He never watched an execution squad at work and never saw the effects of the terror he created. Thus to Teenae he was a coward. He killed more people than he could eat. Thus he was a fool.

In the isolation of his Kremlin office the fury of his decrees escalated. Chekist leaders and political commissars vied with one another in rounding up hostages and shooting them without trial. Fellow socialists were murdered. The peasants who had fought with Lenin against the hated landlord clan were themselves exterminated when they discovered, too late, that the land had passed, not from the landlords to them, but to the state. In Tambov province there was a massacre of 200,000 peasants . . .

Death to the old Tsar! Death to the Tsar who sold himself to the capitalists and quailed before the socialists! Long live the new Tsar! Long live the Worker's Hero who destroys capitalist and socialist alike, who returns all land to the state, who cows the liberated peasantry back into slavery! Death to the old aristocracy, corrupted and weak! Hail to the new aristocracy, corrupted and strong!

It was a Kaiel maxim that terrible consequences inevitably arose when a priest brought simple solutions to complex problems of government. Teenae judged Lenin lacking in kalothi. When his solutions did not work he was content to let terror impose his visions upon reality, having neither the courage nor the intelligence to re-think his position. In the end, Lenin had nothing to offer but Restoration. He destroyed the Tsar by becoming Tsar.

The Bolshevik terror, she read with fascination, bred more terror, giving birth to the son of Lenin, Tsar Stalin, who mercilessly eliminated every remaining socialist in Russia. The nation was left so bereft of conscience that for five generations it puzzled over the simplest of ethical questions without finding answers, stubbornly seeking to dominate Riethe with no more than Lenin's unimproved vision.

These People of the Sky had a strange definition of help. They forced you into helplessness so that you might be in a position to receive their help which was the only True Help. They lied to serve the Truth. They made themselves Right by killing all who disagreed with them. She thought of the Mnankrei. God's History made it easier for her to understand such priests.

Gaet was not yet ready to understand. He had never met the Mnankrei, never faced death in combat with their ambition, never hung in terror from a yardarm of one of their ships. For a moment Teenae worshipped her contact with Joesai. His strength had become her strength. The plague of Lenin's life gave her a resolve that frightened her.

She would see that Sorrow was ready to resist the Mnankrei when they sailed into the harbour in alliance with the Stgal. Gaet could not help her. The Stgal would not. She shrugged. A priest clan like the Stgal, foolish enough to try surviving by playing one great clan off against another, was dreaming its way to an ugly fate.

In her fragments of *The Forge of War* Teenae found descriptions of naval conflict. She played with the ideas like the kolgame master that she was. All warfare, she had discovered, was based on deception. A military commander had to have a bag of surprises and the ability to use them quickly. Every army had to have a disciplined set of rules – and know how to break one every time it wanted a victory.

She spoke to Hoemei over the rayvoice and he encouraged her. A day later she got a call that told her three ships had left Soebo for Sorrow under the command of Storm Master Tonpa. And Hoemei gave her news of Joesai. He was safe. He had halted a day's march outside of Soebo and dug in and laid minefields waiting for the rest of the Gathering to reinforce him. He was receiving delegates from many clans. The Mnankrei's only response had been to construct an impenetrable defence around Soebo.

'Teenae!' Hoemei shouted through the static.

'I hear you clearly!'

'The danger with war seems to be that too much force is used.'

'I understand the min-max concept perfectly!' There were many points where different levels of force could be applied to achieve victory, but only one point where *minimum* force worked to the same end.

'The value of the victory, so far as I can tell, is in inverse proportion to the applied force. Minimum force assures the longest victory and fades into bargaining which is always our first choice of conflict resolution.'

'But that doesn't tell me what to do!' complained Teenae.

'You're the one who delights in kol. What can I say? Train for an attack that is mild, quick, and decisive.'

For heartbeats after the exchange, the woman stared at the wooden box which brought her husband's voice across the mountains. It was too plain. It needed decoration and polishing with fine oils. Few tools came that way anymore. She liked her rifle.

The Kaiel children under her command had given it to her shyly, the stock carved and inlaid in their spare time. No one else had a rifle so beautiful. They had fitted o'Tghalie and Kaiel symbols together perfectly. Touching that stock she had felt wholly Kaiel for the first time since she had been adopted. Her charges believed in her. They obeyed her. They supported her when she suggested that Gaet was not ready to meet Mnankrei violence, even to the point of stealing supplies for her and training with her when they could get away.

That evening she visited the old o'Maie weaver so that she might have someone to help her puzzle over the life of Lenin and draw morals from it. She brought whisky for him and a new coat.

'You worry that because you've learned to sling a lead pebble through a man's eye, you've become like Lenin,' he said when the dawn stars were rising. 'Lenin was a coward who hired men to murder for him.'

'There is violence in me. I talk of minimal force – but I'm not gentle.'

'"Minimal force" is not "no force". Pacifism is for an idealist like Oelita. The concept of minimal force would appeal to a pragmatist like you, where maximal force would appeal to a megalomaniac like Lenin.'

'I'll have to kill them,' Teenae said. 'Three ships. I see no other way.' She began to cry.

His heart went out to this woman who had befriended him. 'Killing a man puts a heavy burden on one's back.'

She laughed through her tears. 'That's not why I cry. I'm afraid they'll kill me first.'

45

The covert man who plots your doom in secret cellars of the
night while by the light of day does lavish all sweet service upon
your self, mistrusts reflected love.

 The Hermit Ki from *Notes in a Bottle*

Surely Soebo was the most magnificent city on all of Geta!
Casual sightseeing soon bewildered Humility. There were
canals, cut at angles through what had once been a river
delta, distorting her sense of direction. By unfortunate
choice she picked as landmarks two look-alike temples
whose alternating appearance turned her around. Finally
she worked her way down stone stairs, and hired a guide
with a waiting flat-bottomed boat.

'Can we reach the Temple of the Wind from here?'

'It is at the junction of all the canals,' replied the tall
female Ivieth while she poled her blue boat out towards
the centre of the waterway. 'The Plaza of the Wind is the
node for all Soebian gossip.'

Humility paid her fee and took her padded seat and
would have cooled her hands in the diluted brine except
for the drifting garbage. 'I'm starved for gossip. I've been
at sea.'

'All talk is of the Gathering. We hear only that the
pretenders have camped well beyond the robe-hem of the
city and seem loath to come closer where there might be
danger to their skins.'

'I think the Kaiel will be soundly chastized,' Humility
said, casting for nibbles.

'I don't think they'll come close enough to get scratched,' the woman replied scornfully.

'I once listened to Ivieth songs about the bravery of the Kaiel,' teased the passenger.

'We have songs about the bravery of everyone. We sing them when flattery is appropriate. We even have songs to warn our children about idle conversation within ear's range of the Liethe who wear the ears of our Masters for necklaces.'

Sunset found Humility in the Plaza of the Temple of the Wind soaking up the gossiping and the chess and the excited antics of a group of iron-ball players. She ate fruit at a table above the crowds, careful to leave untouched the poisonous yellow peel. She chatted, provoked, probed. The sea clan was thought to be invincible, yet there was an undercurrent of hatred; even the Ivieth female had been wary of her, thinking her to be a tool of the Mnankrei.

Against the Plaza and the seething power of this city, Hoemei seemed like such a village priest. Because Humility was bewildered by her feelings of love – alternately rejecting them and rediscovering them – she wanted Hoemei to be wrong so that she could laugh at him and right so that she could love him all the more fiercely. He was probably wrong. Soebo was too solid.

She spotted a Liethe holding the arm of a white-haired Storm Master as he led her across the Plaza. Now there was a powerful man! The slight girl hurried to keep up, and once touched her head to his arm affectionately. Would *she* want *him* to be right? Would she connive ruthlessly to *make* her man right? or would she drift with whomever was strongest?

Humility's baggage arrived at the Liethe hive long before she did. The hive in Soebo was an old building that had been in Liethe hands since before the first of the se-Tufi line had ever died. Even then it had been old, a stately derelict of the bawdy entertainment district. Now the whores and the theatres and the gaming houses were gone, washed away by shiftings of money that had not left even the hive untouched. Prospering Liethe had built onto their ancient mansion a wing of high towers around a walled garden where once had passed a street alive with drunken sailors. Perhaps the ghosts of Vlak seamen still bought orphaned women at auction in the brick theatre-of-the-round that was itself a ghost, having been replaced by a public fountain.

Humility was given a tiny tower room and a mat. Three crones questioned her at length. One, a high mother of the nas-Veda line which had been discontinued because of immunological irregularities that appeared in old age, took her down to a sealed, sterile room of the hive's genetic workshop where she met the se-Tufi Who Pats Flesh, a youth older than herself but who did not look older. They bowed slightly, giving their recognition gestures.

'You will be sharing Flesh's two men. She carries the persona of the schemer Comfort, who is consort to High Wave Ogar tu'Ama, and the servile persona of Radiance for Winterstorm Master Nie t'Fosal's use. She will be drilling you through the Nine Tier Matrix of Understanding immediately so that you will be ready as her back-up in either role by sunrise of the Knave's Oneday. Please strip and don these sterile clothes. The mask, too.'

The nas-Veda guided her charges through sealed doors to a hall adjoining a small resin-coated room which she did not let them enter. There were windows. Inside, a young o'Tghalie woman sat, seemingly without control of her eyes or neck or hands.

'Is she mindless, too?' asked Humility sharply.

'Quite. Mnankrei records show she has died and been cremated. We collected her covertly out of curiosity. We have been wondering what the Mnankrei have been doing with these *women*. They do not use men for this kind of experiment.' The nas-Veda crone turned her face towards Flesh. 'Now perhaps you can understand why we have assigned you to Winterstorm Master Nie t'Fosal?'

Humility's memory tripped a file. 'He is the designer of the deviant underjaw!'

The se-Tufi Who Pats Flesh was pondering the movements of the idiot o'Tghalie girl. They fitted nowhere in the intricate map of political intrigue she had been trained to perceive. 'Will she recover?'

'No.'

'That's horrible. Fosal creates such monsters?' This would be the reason that High Wave Ogar tu'Ama had opposed Fosal at such great cost to himself.

'Fosal is gifted. The horror is not that such men exist, it is that others have allowed such men to rise to power.'

Flesh had become intense. 'I am consumed with curiosity. How can the o'Tghalie have allowed their women to be used thusly? A sale is not an open contract.'

'They know nothing of what has happened to her, and you will tell them nothing. We have determined in our quiet way that she was sold in faraway Osairin and her clan believes her to be perished of a desert dust storm while she was being carried to the Njarae.' The old woman added ominously, 'Fosal has used Liethe, too!'

'Mother! And you've given me to him!' exclaimed Flesh.

A hundred thousand wrinkles chuckled. 'Humility will share your burden.'

Black pupils, embedded in blue and flecked irises, probed each other over the whites of the sterile masks.

'How has she been harmed?' asked Humility.

'You have been taught of the micro-life that sometimes rages in stinging scourge of death among the profane? Nie t'Fosal has found ways to bring such profane ills into the sacred world.'

'She is *diseased*!' Both se-Tufi spoke with astonishment.

'We are not able to decode the mechanism. We have sampled this girl's brain and all appears normal except that axionic and dendritic neural growth is unusually prolific. We believe a double process is involved. Viral constructs, hosted in free invading cells, have been used to play with genetic controllers. Mouth contact can transmit the disease.'

Suddenly Humility found herself in the middle of a huge attack of loyalty for the Kaiel. How could she have pretended to forget Hoemei! She was his abject servant! 'The Kaiel are *right* to call a Gathering!'

The crone swivelled in contempt, gesturing at the demented o'Tghalie. 'The Kaiel will be destroyed before they reach Soebo – by that!'

'We must warn them!' cried Humility. 'We have our rayvoice contacts!'

'We will *not* warn them,' retorted the nas-Veda crone angrily. 'With such a frightening thing loose do you think they will spare us? They will deliver a holocaust of flame to this city to roast us all – all of us – in a purifying total fire. All clans will be consumed to char as were the people destroyed when the Kaiel chastized the Arant! Would they see a way to mercy? Would you be merciful if you were they and knew of this horror that might spread from here like poison spores on the wind to every man-inhabited region of Geta? No, Liethe child, you will not warn the Kaiel. I bind you under penalty of death!'

46

Lay a man at your back to listen to the whispering of the wind.

Private poem of Noe maran-Kaiel

The reeking smell of drying weed drifted down from the racks on the cliffs across the beach. The simple docks were busy. A boatload of refugees from Soebo – perhaps eight all told – had arrived this morning, the third such group Noe had heard of, fearful ones who were afraid of the Gathering and rich enough to flee. They haggled with traders and she watched them from afar, wondering how she might question them. She coveted every bit of information she could glean, but was suspicious of spies.

How much did the enemy know? She expected an imminent Mnankrei sweep of the coast to clean out these carefully placed supply nodes of hers which were putting boats across the upper Njarae to Mnank loaded with goods and, now, with priests from distant clans.

The rumours that disturbed her proved nothing. Such hints were no stronger than the flicker across a game player's face, the slight holding of cards closer to the chest. It was Joesai's vulnerability that cast sinister reflections upon every rumour. There stood Joesai, fretting amidst the enemy, barely beyond the outer reaches of their city, and he was allowed to do nothing while the Mnankrei day by day readied whatever counterstrike they intended. The sea priests were not ones to test and probe. They struck.

The prescience of the Kaiel mind told her what it

meant. Joesai was doomed, however this adventure might turn out for the Kaiel. Joesai had always carried the aura of death with him. He dared it, lived with it, mocked it, because he could not escape it. He was born to be a tragic hero; his time was now but Noe did not want to lose him. Of all her husbands only he shared her thrill at the touch of danger.

Noe remembered, almost tearfully, that she had once thought of him as the husband she did not like, who coldly had taken her in hand, when the first paling of her love for Gaet had left her depressed, to teach her the best of the Kaiel tricks of genetic surgery because he had been disappointed by her ignorance, and resentful of Gaet that he should pick for them so soft a wife. A full orbit of Geta she had hated him, wanting to play and despising hard work, and then one day she had wandered among the hills above Kaiel-hontokae, searching out Joesai she knew not why, to find him glooming over a wrecked sailplane.

He put wings on her and risked her life above the valleys, and she had discovered from Joesai that she loved danger and could not live without it. Gliding had bonded them, and for some reason after that his faults had never bothered her. Strange that once she had wished him dead so that she might have Gaet and Hoemei to herself.

After Noe questioned the refugees – and learned nothing except that fears and speculation raged in the city – she was approached by a sturdy man while she was eating bread and honey pudding in the plaza of the village.

'He's Geiniera,' whispered her second companion.

'You know for sure?'

'Yes. He's been sulking around the village for days, keeping to himself, asking few questions.'

The man bowed to Noe. He was ragged but well washed. His eyes shifted suspiciously yet without fear. Deferentially he waited for Noe to speak first.

'May I help you?'

'Now tha' would be pleasant but no' likely. You be Kaiel?'

'We're all Kaiel, guests of the Twbuni who rule Tai.'

'You Gather t'shake Soebo?'

'Only that we may know the truth,' she replied formally.

'I see the dune, but each grain o' sand is truth.' His reply was the gentle rebuff of a practical man who did not believe in such nonsense as truth. Shoulders shrugged that had lifted sails and fought the lashings of the sea. 'You question th' folk wha' flee? Did they carry tales as woeful as th' tale on this heart?'

'Are your woes of your own making or cast upon you by the evil deeds of others?'

The Geiniera laughed and slapped his rags. 'No' a question I could answer!'

'Share our bread.'

'Thank 'e, kind priest. You Gather t'shake Soebo. Go with God's blessing and avenge me my daughter.'

Thereupon he told a story that fitted his mad state. He had shared a wife with his brother. They were poor but perhaps could have afforded another woman if they had been able to find her. The wife bore her sailors a daughter and died, leaving the baby to neighbours, while they were both at sea. That tragedy changed their lives. One would go forth on a Mnankrei merchantman and the other would stay home to care for the daughter, and perhaps to pick up work in the shipyards or mending sails. The daughter grew to be beautiful and proud, a soul to scorn her Geiniera roots and to love the wealth of her betters. She set her mind to becoming Mnankrei and in time found her man who took her as a lover but, when she was with child, abandoned her to her grief and poverty.

The agitated girl had taken her baby to the Temple of the Raging Seas, into the presence of the father, and murdered his child for him to watch. She had been seized, and no one had ever seen her again. The story told to the Geiniera fathers had been of her invitation to Ritual Suicide and one father believed and one father did not, for should not their daughter have been delivered to them for their rightful Funeral Feast?

He was a persistent man. Made wild by the loss of his daughter, never believing that she had died – for had he known her death by eating her? – he sought to find her fate and found memories of things his daughter had said about her man and dark rumours instead. No wall or door kept him out for he was a ship's smith, and one day, sure that he had found her, he came across a room sealed by glass that he could not enter. Beyond the glass were mindless women whose husks alone had been spared the bliss of death.

Afraid of being found, he retreated. Enraged and broken and deranged by grief he had gone to the house of his daughter's lover to kill him and had found instead a woman of the Liethe who had soothed him and taken his story from him like hair that falls against the smooth run of a honed blade. She asked him urgently to take her to see the husk women and yet when he was there at the appointed meeting place, ready for such risky venture, he had been betrayed to her lover who had also been his daughter's lover. The man had taken him to the deepest cells of the Temple, laughing at him that he could have trusted a Liethe. Walls did not keep him and he escaped but watched the low side entrances for weeks, seeing coffins being brought forth and carried away secretly to be burned. He saw Liethe at work there too.

His madness subsided and when he heard of the Gathering he set across the sea to bring vengeance for his daughter. He believed the stories told of Kaiel ruthlessness, but such stories did not make him cling to the master he knew, as was intended, instead they gave him courage that here were priests violent enough to bring death to the Mnankrei.

Noe pondered the story between all her errands up the coast in their small lugger. Usually she enjoyed the sea, commanding it, for her youth had been spent on the sea. She alone of the maran-Kaiel looked with pleasure to being stationed at Sorrow. She was not a mountain woman, or a desert woman. But now the flapping of the sails and the spray did not reach the storm in her mind.

It had been Kathein, with her sure knack of ferreting out the rule and law of nature from odd happenings, who had taught Noe the secret of a good intelligence procedure. Never meld the incoming data into a general overall summary. Always maintain two lines of report, the optimistic and the pessimistic. One report should weigh the data in terms of the best possible meaning, and the other report should squeeze out of the data the worst possible interpretation. If both reports agreed, the probability of error in the conclusion was small, but if both reports diverged wildly, then careful attention had to be given to the negative nuances that would have been lost in any general summary.

Pieces seemed to fit together, each piece so small that separately they should have been ignored. The Geiniera might be a spy planted here to mislead but then what about that other one-line story of masked Mnankrei burning coffins? It fitted. And Noe, who had worked long days on the genetic makeup of the deviant underjaw, had the final piece that made sense of it all. If the Mnankrei had spent so much time developing one deadly genetic weapon – she used that non-Getan word from *The Forge of War* – then it was possible that they had developed many such weapons.

Noe's home base was a farmhouse rented from a family on pilgrimage to their ancestor's Itraiel domain. Conveniently located near the sea, it was dug into the leeward side of a grassy hill, protected from Njarae storms and hidden from coastal scouts. It ran in three tiers down the slope, built over centuries, its thick walls moulded of hillside fieldstone cemented with burned mortar carried in from the kilns of a local quarry. The roofs were of wood overlain by the thick sod of saw grass. On top of the hill was their rayvoice antenna.

She waited until the stars were out. The rayvoice worked best under such conditions. 'Raise Joesai for me,' she told her operator. Should she tell Hoemei first? No. He was committed to a fixed plan and would try to hold fast. It was Joesai's life which was on the blade.

They spoke in code. Dots and dashes and warbles because she owned only a portable rayvoice. The code wiped out the personal urgency she felt.

You must act now.

Are you . . . cackle, splat. *Hoemei will kill me.*

Evidence of sacred disease.

??? Repeat.

Genetically engineered micro-life that moves from man to man, killing.

Verified?

No. No time. Attack. Your whole camp may be destroyed overnight.

Not enough data.

This may be deadly. You may have no choice but to sack Soebo.

??? Repeat.

Burn the place! Raze it! Sterilize it!

Drastic.

Your choice. Concentrate on the Temple of the Raging Seas. Attack.

Who is involved?

Any member of the Swift Wind. The Liethe are suspect.

Who?

Your cuddly friends. I have three sources of information pointing to Liethe involvement.

339

How much time do I have?
Attack yesterday!
May God be with us.
May God be with you.

47

A man who has been afraid all his life thinks that fear is the only winning strategy because he has been conquered by fear. Thus when an oppressed mind strikes in rebellion, he becomes the oppressor.

Prime Predictor Tae ran-Kaiel in *Government*

The light-hearted se-Tufi Who Walks in Humility had been too long independent during the easy life of her lengthy journey between hives, The crones of Soebo were well aware of her loose behaviour. They put her on a rigorous schedule to rebuild her discipline.

Mind Control occupied her attention after waking – the Resting Power Positions rebalanced her body and the Oina Thought Frameworks rebalanced her mind. Then, after morning meal, whenever the se-Tufi Who Pats Flesh was available, Humility was drilled in the ways of High Wave Ogar tu'Ama so that she might know the persona of Comfort, a sympathetic woman sensitively aware of the peculiar nature of a widower who had loved only one woman for two-thirds of his life and still grieved.

But Flesh was not always available to train Humility. Flesh specialized in political intrigue and she had lucked onto a bigger game than Ama, who was, after all, only a spokesman for the Mnankrei who did not follow the Swiftness Faction. Winterstorm Master Nie t'Fosal, of the Central Watch of the Swift Wind, was demanding. She could no longer afford to give Ama the attention the Liethe clan thought desirable but, simultaneously, much as she needed an alter ego, she had little time to be a tutor. Thus Humility caught her when she could, and tu'Ama pined away for a woman who could seldom meet him.

To keep their young assassin under strict crone control, Humility was given other assignments than her Comfort role.

Many of the crones were fascinated by the rayvoice. Their link with Kaiel-hontokae still astonished them. Such magic was arcane and seemingly beyond the powers of the most able seducer of men, but they were not unaware of their extrordinary fortune in having a woman among them who had some small skill with the mysteries of the voice that was everywhere.

Humility was granted a team of ten Liethe, some of them still too young to be apprenticed as courtesans and concubines, but quick and dexterous and patient and accustomed to ruthless discipline, some older and wise in the ways of logic. Two had high jeweller skills, as full in their knowledge of metals and gems as Humility was in her knowledge of death. One of the Liethe knew the working of tungsten, a rare metal which was malleable in its ultra-pure form and a metal more resistant to the depredations of heat than any other substance known to Getan chemistry.

When she was not with Flesh, Humility guided the rayvoice team until the dusk of high sunset dimmed the tower rooms. The darkness was used for Body Control, building again the supple performance of the dancer (and fighter). At low dawn she assumed various house duties – garbage disposal, cleaning, cooking, weaving – then again went to work with the rayvoice until the thankful arrival of low sunset, a sparse meal, and finally the surcease of the mat on her stone floor.

She had no trouble teaching the winding of coils and rolling of electron absorbers and the making of the copper maps. She could explain the formulae by which the

342

numbers on the maps were changed so that the devices might stay within the realm of magic, but the electron jars were beyond her abilities. She knew when a jar was moral and when one was stubbornly useless; she even had pictures of their assembly – but she did not know how to make them.

And so it was with some wonder that she watched a woman who could spin the finest gold filigree sit down at the table and fashion nets from silver. Small jeweller's tools built the docks and posts while, as a group, the women debated the tiny dimensions and gaps. Delicate blowing with a torch produced the glass house. Still it was not enough. The electrons needed their vacuum. This obstacle was overcome when a Liethe sister borrowed a clever mercury pump from one of the Mnankrei's dormant gene-synthesis programmes.

Their first four jars were totally immoral. With the fifth they learned how to precipitate out the final oxygen by oxidation inside the jar. But their real success only came with the twelfth jar. By the eighteenth jar they could consistently duplicate their efforts.

Soon after the first triumphant demonstration to the crone mothers, the entire rayvoice programme was abruptly terminated. Humility's teammates, all long residents of Soebo, some emotionally committed to their lovers, were shipped off one night by the new crone mother. They were angry, and yet obedient in the haste with which they prepared themselves. More and more of the established residents of the hive had been leaving. There was a heavy influx of newcomers – like herself – who had been imported for a purpose. She wondered what it meant.

Unexpectedly, Humility met t'Fosal in her Radiance persona before she met tu'Ama in her role as Comfort.

The One Who Pats Flesh had been putting too much sureness in the Radiance she was creating for Fosal. It

343

made him uneasy. He was a man who believed that women who were not afraid of men were dangerous. He beat her for no other reason than to restore the dominance-submissive balance. He did not stop. His rage at her wilfulness subsided and still he beat her for pleasure. She had never witnessed such behaviour. To have it directed against her was terrifying.

The crone mother who was in charge of investigating Nie t'Fosal was a se-Tufi, the se-Tufi Who Rings the Soul's Bell, and so she thought she could convince this young sister to continue her affair with Fosal. Flesh refused. The crone argued with guile and cunning. Flesh begged for another assignment, anything, a task no matter how demeaning, anything except to be touched by Fosal again. Soul's Bell finally laughed and called Humility.

'You are to see him tonight.'

'But I have not been fitted to the mask of Radiance.'

'Flesh will drill you until the highnode sun.'

'That is not enough time.'

Flesh made a noise of contempt. 'He cannot perceive even the grossest differences. I could train you during the fall of a pebble from my toe to the ground! He'll *beat* you; that's what you have to know!'

Part of Humility's training had been Kontaing, the art of being beaten without being injured. There were ways to absorb blows harmlessly. 'I will not know what to say to him.'

Soul's Bell folded her hands. Her face was inscrutable. 'You will have a sharp change in personality due to the beating. You will be afraid, unsure of yourself, desperate to please. You will have found the man you could be willing to die for if he would but ask of you such sacrifice.'

'Is he so insensitive he would believe that?' asked Humility.

'Yes,' said the crone.

'How can you bear to be with such an insect!' Flesh

stormed with scorn, directed not at her sister but at the man.

'It is my vocation.'

'Do not harm him!' warned the old one severely.

'No.' The Queen of Life-before-Death bowed submissively. 'You have instructions?'

'Yes. Obey him.'

A call came from the Temple of the Wind for five dancers to entertain at a feast. They were taken by masked Mnankrei boys to the upper terrace where the walls had been shaped with many slits that spoke in eerie tune with the wind. Humility found that she would be dancing only for males. The Mnankrei women, invisible in the world of pleasure, did not seem to attend their men when they were drinking heavily and speaking loudly.

A veiled crone mother chaperoned her children. She was still almost too young to be a hag, and she was the least of the hive mothers, but she was used to authority, and used to being silent, and to sparing her efforts. Only once did she slow Humility, indicating with the lightest hand a tall Mnankrei. 'Winterstorm Master Nie t'Fosal,' whispered her wise voice almost teasingly.

The wizard creator of the deviant underjaw. The man who experiments with the bodies of unwilling women. The man who has beaten the mask known as Radiance. The man I now fear and love for I am Radiance.

She pretended shock to see him here, the smallest gasp, a hair's breadth widening of eyes, a toe-length withdrawal. She stared at him for a moment of confused love so that she might have time to fix his face in her mind's file. She saw a broadly muscled giant whose eyebrows were so thick that they were braided into the design of his hair. His beard hid his face like seaweed growth upon a drowned corpse. He said nothing. She bowed, then propelled herself along the terrace into the friendly arm of another Mnankrei who saw her to the stage where the opening dance was to begin.

345

Her eyes returned to the Winterstorm Master all through the dances. He was a centre of power. Soebo would not fall until he fell. Hoemei was a fool to expect a man like that to crumble without taking the world with him. It was self-deluded wishing to believe that such a ruthless tyrant was primed to destroy himself! *Hoemei is only a man, a beloved man, groping in the dark like us all.* Such a thought shook her, made her feel alone, almost as if God had failed to cross His Sky.

When their chaperone led them away from the celebration, Fosal appeared and stood between the frightened Radiance and the others. The older Liethe tried to protect her but the Storm Master furled her sails. Radiance, still frightened of him, but wanting to be with him, aided his kidnapping and the crone was left helpless. How easy it was to manipulate this leader of men.

He took her to some male den deep in the Temple and ordered her to bring them all drinks in great crystalline mugs while he played chess with a friend, discussing the Gathering, sometimes seriously, sometimes as a joke. She watched him attack across the board recklessly with his White God and his Priests, penetrating deep into his opponent's squares, leaving his Child exposed. *He's foolish,* she thought, seeing how he could be annihilated.

'I shouldn't have done that,' he growled. 'Radiance. You've been watching. How do I get out of this scrape?'

You can't. She put an arm around him. 'You'll find a way.'

His opponent, an older priest with a face which had been half burned away by a fire he had survived, moved his Horse for the kill, covering with the Black Queen, destroying the line of White Farmers. Fosal simply continued his wild attack, having never lost control, and made checkmate in five more moves. It sobered Humility.

He set up the board again. When one of his sons arrived, Fosal ordered Radiance into a pillowed room adjoining the game room so that she might take his son in sex. He had promised her to him.

'But I want *you.*'

'Later. If you please my Beil.'

He pushed out a Farmer in the opening move of the second game. But he did not finish his attack because he was losing and that bored him. He wandered for a while, muttering to himself of plans and strategy, finally pushing through the curtains to stand over his son while he invented bawdy jokes about the helpless humpings of inexperienced youth. Eventually his joking turned into impatience and he threw his son out and took her himself. Humility was ready for violence but a gentle mood overtook him once he was relaxed on the pillows.

'Are you still mad at me?' she asked with a tremble in her voice.

He laughed the universal Getan laugh. 'You've been a good girl today. Why should I be angry?'

'I *want* to be a good girl.' She ran a finger along his nose, then withdrew in fear. He pulled her back to his body and took her. She had expected him to be impotent. He was not known as a womanizer. He had children but no wives, no permanent female companionship. The Liethe had tried to reach him many times before and had never broken through his aloofness, his lack of interest, his active dislike of women. But he was not impotent. His power was prolonged and stable and he even seemed to enjoy his clumsily unselfconscious thrusting.

'I like your dancing,' he said to make conversation.

'Thank you.'

When he was through with her he would not let her go but set her upon a pillow where he could touch and watch her. 'I don't understand why you like me,' he said.

'I don't like you; I *love* you.'

Impulsively he carried her through the curtains into the

game room and ordered all the games to stop. He ordered some music, which was quick to arrive, and then ordered her to dance, which she did. He stared at her, smiling, clapping his hands, drinking whisky when he wasn't clapping. He was too big ever to get drunk. Still, his mind began to wander.

She waved the musicians into a subsiding quietness, a sea calming after a storm. She stopped dancing. He was lost in some aspect of his own world.

'I have to go now,' she said quietly.

That roused him. 'No, no. You're coming with me. I'm not through with you.'

For a while they simply walked in the city streets, bundled against the wind. Then he led her to a tower apartment where Radiance had never been. 'I work here. The thinking work. It's lonely overseeing a city, planning a clan's next move in a wild game for our rightful place. I cook for myself. I do everything myself here,' he said proudly, showing her. He took out bread and carved off two big slices and laid a brown spread over them, giving one slice to Humility. That, she supposed, was probably what he meant by 'cooking'.

'I could move up here. I could help you.'

'It's no place for a woman. I don't even have men here. I like to work alone.'

'Am I here because you like me?'

'Very much.'

'May I stay here?'

He ate his slice of bread in one bite. That prevented him from answering her immediately. 'You can stay for one more sexing; then you have to go. I have too many worries. I have to be alone.'

'Couldn't I help?'

'What could you do for me!' he protested, and she knew he had a favour to ask. He was being too mild. She could almost see his muscles tense while he held in his abrasive-

348

ness, pleased at her love for it gave him control, but unwilling to test it with further brutality.

'I can do anything you want. I'm that kind of woman. I can at least try.'

'There are things a woman *can't* do.'

'What?' she challenged.

'Chase the Kaiel away.'

'You're worried about the Gathering, aren't you?'

'No, but I'm thinking about it. They're coming here to burn us all alive.'

'That's horrible. I'm frightened. I hear they've been murdering folk all across northern Mnank.'

He had undressed and was pouring whisky from a cut glass bottle by a hexagonal window that beamed reddish sunlight over his illustrated body. 'The Liethe are priest's women. Am I correct?' It was a statement, not a question.

'Yes,'

'Kaiel?'

'We've always avoided the Kaiel,' she said truthfully. She paused just long enough for him to tense. She watched the pressure on his whisky glass. 'But yes. Our code would allow us to service the Kaiel.'

'They must be bored to starvation after such walking and their seasick journey across the Njarae. A spice of entertainment might cheer them. They could use a roll on the ground with an affectionate wench.'

'I wouldn't want to do that.'

He laughed. 'For me you would. If *I* wanted it.'

'They're the enemy,' she said with revulsion.

Absently he went to his evaporation cooler and lifted out a small vial, sturdily blown from blue cobalt glass, padded in a basket wrap. 'If this was secretly added to the common meal, they'd all die. It is a poison that grows and can be transmitted from man to man. They'd all die. They'd take it from each other and die.'

'That's not my work.' She was masking her refusal with

349

tones of irresolution while she spoke but, at the same time, was thinking, *My God, the crones have told me to obey this man.*

'The Kaiel will not admit me to their camp,' he continued. 'They will welcome you.'

She reached for the vial curiously, holding it by the tips of her fingernails.

'You'll save us all,' he insisted. 'A whiff of my power turns a man into an idiot.'

Joesai would be out there, beyond the city, waiting impatiently but only because of Hoemei's orders. *I'll see him again.* It was a disturbing thought.

'I'll give your Liethe the Palace of Morning as a reward. It's beautiful. Have you ever been in the cupola at dawn?' He knew the Liethe were for hire.

She smiled wistfully.

'You're a delightful woman today.'

'A thrashing mellows me.'

'Will you do it?'

So that was what he wanted and why he had been almost solicitous. 'Let me think.'

Joesai! Humility remembered how Hoemei had given her to Joisai for the evening, not like t'Fosal had given her to his son, but like a man shares a wife with his beloved husband. She remembered Hoemei's trust. She remembered Joesai's suspicion. He had been funny to love, unused to affection from women and so easily pleased, easily bamboozled, but never wholly willing to forget his mistrust. He told her that his mistrust kept him alive in those few times when trust was fatal. He had known nothing about the transient pleasures of life. He was not used to courtesans. He treated her like a wife, like some beloved. Of all the men she had ever known, that experience had been the most painful. Even Hoemei, who held her in great respect, saw her as a sybarite. Perhaps she had been so touched by Joesai only because she had been so in love with his brother-husband.

'I'll go,' she said. 'I'm afraid.'

'Just be what you are. I'll show you how to use the vial and how to protect yourself.'

It was a naked grin that he fixed upon her.

48

My dreams were the colour of my family quilt washed in the mountain stream until it was as faded as the dawn of the late morning, smelling of rock and tree spore, moist as the hand of fear. Yet children's eyes remember the colours my grandmother wove like laughter stained by slippery grass. Today I finger that quilt, imagining the sudden reds of the mountain's ember flower, and the boiled blue dye of pfeina bark in the buckets. So are dreams remended into worn fabric that once warmed my sisters from the snowing flakes.

The hermit Ki from *Notes in a Bottle*

It is said that the hermits arose before God stopped speaking. Geta is a vast land populated by fewer than 200 million people and there are valleys and corners and mountaintops and whole deserts where men never go. Along the borders of these lands a wayward traveller might find the ruins of a hermit's stone hut, his altar to God, and perhaps even a stairway.

A conical stairway is the sure signature that a hermit once lived among the surrounding barrens. Sometimes they are very tall. Sometimes a later hermit will repair the work of a long-dead hermit's hand and begin to add to the spiral hill built cone by layered cone, stone by stone for a purpose without reason. Why a hermit's invariable goal was to build stairways, no one knew. A hermit worked alone, never bothering to train an acolyte to carry on his ritual. It did not matter.

How did the stairway tradition continue? Perhaps it was the wonder these bizarre objects caused, the whispers of puzzlement which, reaching mad ears, inspired the next generation of hermits who then went forth. They were all mad. It was known that they were mad.

Was that not Joesai among the shadows?

Oelita's father had shown her this ravine when she was adult enough to follow him into the desert. He noted such places carefully because they always meant water, never easy water, but a cup or two at the bottom of a sand-clogged well or a trickle from some stone's crack.

Her boy from Sorrow, whom she brought with her from Kaiel-hontokae, helped her at first. They cleaned out the pulpy stalks of the man-high Godstorch and fitted them together, thin top into thick base, to make a pipe that led dripping water from the fault-cave to the hermit's hut. Once the water was in and the roof rebuilt, she drove the boy away. He did not want to leave her alone but she raved and beat him with a broken Godstorch stalk, forcing his retreat to a ridge. From there he watched her until the second setting of the red arched sun beyond the badlands – reluctantly fading into the west as the sun faded, vowing he would be back some time with supplies and messages from those who loved her.

She rationed her motions on a pattern of cyclic flow that was unconscious of weeks or time, content to mark the passage of sun, then stars; day, then night. Food and water had priority. She always spent some effort ranging over the desert wilderness, gathering. Few knew that job as well as she did – what part of the seeds to cast aside, how to boil and then sun-dry the pith of the running cactus, how to eat the tiny orange and magenta-striped fruits of the low beiera tree.

It was sneaky how she moved so that Joesai would never see her.

Profane food would not be enough, or even satisfying to the secret hungers. Every day she worked a little on her sacred garden. She knew where the wheat would grow and how to set the squash and how to keep the beans alive.

She often spent the night in the well cleaning it out, cutting it down another layer. The spring gave her enough water for herself but not for her garden.

Other nights were set aside to prepare cloth or to hammer fibre for mats. While she broke soft stems into pieces for soaking so that the fibre might be pounded free, images of God came to her, thrust up from her childhood where they had been left in dungeon by her righteous atheism. A suddenly emergent girl rose from her place, superstitious, to set a glowing coal on the holy stone altar lest when God passed overhead, looking down, watching His people, He might miss her for the lack of a red glow upon her face.

She settled back on her haunches and began to chat to Hoemei about her pregnancy. She knew he was behind her, motionless in one of his silent moods. In the old days when man was new to Geta's refuge, and the planet had been killing them all so ruthlessly, she explained, twin-bearing had been a premium survival trait looked upon favourably by God. Many women still bore twins. She would probably have twins again, she assured Hoemei. She wanted to be well stocked before her twins came so they might never suffer.

'It's all right,' he said clearly in a voice that resonated in her mind, and she felt comfortable with his concern.

Her memories of Kaiel-hontokae still frightened her. It was a city of ten thousand Joesais, immense beyond anything she had imagined a city could be in all her dreaming – streets, buildings, richly gardened temple after temple fed by ethereal aqueducts that passed over the city like multiple Streaks of God, bare-breasted women, fine cloth, shops where you could haggle over the price of the flesh of a child who had failed some creche trial. And machines whose overpowering presence whispered of the distant strength of God.

Here in the desert the red and orange and ochre plateaus rolled away, eroded where sparse vegetation could not hold back the rare flash rains and God was almost invisible unless one looked for His passage at night, believing. He was quiet like the stars, but in more of a hurry.

'Teenae!' she cried, suddenly rigid, alert. She had seen the city beyond the cliffs of the ravine.

There, in the city, God was no Invisible Abstraction. God stood in front of you sternly with the face of Joesai, holding your wrist in iron shackles, arguing, and all your return arguments were met with bulbous glass insects, glowing from an internal red hue, who molested your crystal-from-the-sea and laughed out the resonant words of God telling of the Terror He has saved you from, saved us all from, until there was nowhere to turn but to believe. God had made her ashamed through Joesai. God had appeared to her through Joesai in all the personality of that man's violence let loose with sunfire devouring great Hiroshima in a moment which charred her own beliefs like a bug zapped in a temple's night row of torches.

Only Teenae understood her.

Could God, who came from a world of Terror, ever love a gentle woman? She hid from Him in the desert, yet left coals on the hermit-carved altar so that He might find her in His passage. Was this Saviour God also the God of the temples who took the weaker children so that His mankind might become strong enough to face the horrors of the Sky? How could He do that and be a Saviour, too?

Oelita's pregnancy dominated her. Nothing had been more unshakable than her refusal to bear children after her genetically crippled twins had been condemned to death for lack of kalothi. But when a woman loses her purpose, does she not hark back to an older purpose? The pregnancy had been premeditated. The city of Kaiel-hontokae was within her womb now, growing with arrogant power, its men the fathers of her second brood. The maran-Kaiel were formidable in her memory, worthy fathers, but also slaves of God. Men seeded their women but they did God's bidding and not the mother's.

Gaet still warmed her dreams. She had to be half asleep, in a pleasant mood, perhaps leaning against the wall before he could come and joke with her and play his noble charm. Hoemei was more reliable. He came to her while she was awake. Gaet had an emotional gentleness that attracted her, stirred her very genes; Hoemei was of the mind's gentleness – once he had shown her how to clarify a thought of hers with which she knew he strongly disagreed. How easy he was to reach.

'Hoemei? Are you there?'

'I'm reading,' he said from the shadows at her back.

'You don't remember the pillow play when you gave me child,' she laughed. Her one clear memory of tender infatuation for Hoemei came from that afternoon. She was using his chest as pillow and he had an arm on her far shoulder and the other hand in her forest while she stared somewhat obliviously at his chin knowing that she had made him a father. Why would she remember that moment so clearly? She had intended, then, to wash away the pregnancy with her blood.

Sleepily she put away her work, gestured a final benediction before the altar, and crawled to her mat. She put her hand out for Hoemei. 'Hoemei!' He was gone. *He works too hard,* she thought sadly.

Joesai was with her always. He was the dream man behind the bush or door who would appear in costume and shatter any plot. Awake, she often startled to see him as a speck on a distant ridge or he would be the shadow that had sneaked into her hut at twilight. In dreams he never ran after her when she fled but he always caught her and she would wake up gasping at the memory of his strength as he tied her into yet another death puzzle.

He tracked her in her dreams. He waited. If her leg was

356

sore, he attacked her physically. If she grieved, he smiled and attacked her emotionally. She would turn a corner and find him reading from some prized handwritten manuscript with a sarcastic sneer on his face. She would brace herself and then he would look up – and deliver a one-sentence riposte that would undercut the very substance of her words. Sometimes Oelita would waken in her hut sure that a faint outside noise was the prowling of Joesai.

Once she had a dream about Noe buying lifeless twins at a temple butchery.

Days passed. Oelita made an uneasy peace with God, praying ever more frequently on her knees at the altar. While she worked, while she rested, she had been scanning every Chant she knew for hidden wisdom. It was like her that she discovered a God of the Sky who differed from the God of the temples. The orange sun rose and fell. Her belly became filled with kickings and so she came to know for sure that she was with twins. Long-range foraging became impossible. She began to spend whole days inside the hut preparing the profane foods to rid them of the poisons.

She enjoyed her conversations with Nonoep who sometimes came to visit when she was deep in thought.

It rained. The shower lasted only during the twilight but days later a glory of flowers had popped up all over the barren hills, seducing the insects into mad excess. She could not resist a long waddle down the ravine, picking blue desert-lips for her hair. The restless wandering did not tire her. There were rocks she had removed from her garden and she began to carry them over to the stairway, a few at a time, placing them in the stairway so that they were solidly secured against weather, against age, against the force of roots. The previous hermit, dead before her father was born, had placed his rocks with exquisite care. She honoured him with as much care.

357

Nightfall caught her at the apex of her stairway to the stars. Flowers had folded while insects began a nocturnal chatter, seeking mates. It was a clear desert solitude for star watching. The Mist River flowed above the horizon bringing with it the constellations of the Moth and the Knave.

I am alone with beauty.

Darkness and distance hid whatever treachery might roil beyond that doomed excellence. *In a way, we are all hermits,* she thought. *God is a recluse like me.* What gods had driven Him to this secluded edge of space to meditate while others destroyed? She felt a sudden kinship with Him, and, as if in sympathetic response, He began His rise above the ragged black horizon to steer across the starfield.

Is it true that kindness is only the first symptom of a weak will? Did gentle people have to retreat into total isolation to survive? Perhaps God was no fierce protector; perhaps He was only a kind soul who had run from stellar warriors as Oelita had run from Joesai. Such ideas stimulated anger. She would not believe such heresy! Gentleness was the noblest of virtues! Kindness would make the world whole! Caring for the weak took a deeper strength!

Vicious images out of *The Forge of War* flooded her vision from every blazing star. Atop her stairway she began to curse this collage of armies with all the might of her raging lungs. Her acrimony shattered the darkened desert, reflecting from every arroyo, amplifying up the cliffs to throw its wrath at the sky of twinkling hiroshimas and bagdad-massacres and subtle tortures and avenging hordes of red armour that tracked over the stars, explosively punishing peasants and old women, selecting the occasional child for target practice.

'*STOP!*' she screamed at the avalanche of image.

A nefarious universe turned evil eyes her way – curiously. The combined assault of that attention hit like a clap of silence. Insects chirped to their mates in tiny voices. Oelita stood frozen on her cairn, searching, ears alert, aware that she was bathed in starlight. Had Joesai heard? She shrank down out of sight, listening for breathing, the crack of a twig. She dared not go back to the hut. She spent the night alone, trembling, hidden in the brush on the ledge above her wheat.

49

He who judges shall be judged in kind, but whosoever fails to judge for fear of being judged himself shall suffer tyranny.

Prologue to the *Lattice of Evidence*

The cobalt blue vial was cradled by a miniature cushion in a brass goblet that squatted upon the room's side table. The se-Tufi Who Rings the Soul's Bell was smiling at the tiny coal on the end of an incense stick she had just ignited. Humility stood stiffly, formally before her. 'You have done well,' the old crone said, turning to finger the vial. 'This is a poison to delight an assassin's soul.'

'It does not give the subtle unobtrusiveness that is desirable. It is not clean – for when does the blow stop throbbing?'

'You are reluctant to deliver this death to the Kaiel?'

'I kill one at a time,' said Humility frigidly.

Soul's Bell peeled a fruit, carefully cutting away the poisonous parts, and offered a slice to her guest. 'You may relax. Please recite the Lattice of Evidence.'

Humility did so, by now flawlessly.

'Good. It means nothing to you, of course, but it is like a seed crystal and you will find that much will grow around it in the years that follow. The pressure of events forces us to hurry you. Every Liethe lives out the Code of her stage. For you it is not the Time of Changes, but nevertheless we need you. The hoiela larva pretends to fly before it builds its cocoon. For the day that follows you shall be a crone. Please undress.'

Humility obeyed, not understanding the order, her arms and body moving to remove her garments with their usual grace.

Soul's Bell watched critically. 'That is not good enough. Move as if you were old. Move as if the mere act of walking were a Trial of the Spirit.' She noted Humility's hesitation without impatience. 'Walk as you will during the twilight of your life.'

Humility remembered her mentor of the Kaiel-honto-kae hive. She became like the se-Tufi Who Finds Pebbles, slow, dignified, every movement painful but each too proud to ask for help. Soul's Bell watched her, then gave her a platinum-headed cane. 'You are a crone now.' She took a thin pencil and other tools and began to draw lines upon Humility's face, shading her jowls, peppering her hair, shading her breasts so that they seemed to sag, aging her as if these flying fingers were the abrasive sands of some time-storm.

Then she dressed Humility in the eccentric luxury of an elder Liethe. 'Be as the crones are. Think as we do. Every action must be seen first in ghost thought that reverberates through the future until it rebounds off its own peculiar distant consequence. Only then make your action real. You are slow. You are deliberate. Your mind is cunning and never in a hurry. You have forgotten nothing of a full life.'

And so it was that this young girl, in the mask of wisdom, hobbled into the Deliberation Chamber of the Liethe hive at Soebo in her first initiation to the world of the crone. An old woman, jewelled in nose ring, chanted the nodes of the Lattice of Evidence. Humility first knew then that Winterstorm Master Nie t'Fosal was up against the knife. Each monotonous invocation of a question from the Lattice prompted one or another of eight crones to answer with an accusation and a line of evidence, coded in poetic metre so that every detail of the judgment might be

361

remembered with error-correcting exactness. Question and poem were repeated, flowing back and forth among the crones, fixing the memory of an event no Liethe dared commit to paper.

The details of the judgment impressed themselves upon Humility, passing through her mind and finally across her lips until the poetry of t'Fosal's guilt was tied to the Lattice cues like the flowers that give meaning to the trellis.

There were questions upon which no poem budded. Then the discussion ceased to be formal and debate raged. It was said that no clear poem could be composed unless the evidence itself was clear. However long it took, the crones were faithful to the Lattice which methodically exposed the world of sin, event at a time, through the multi-faceted eye of the squat Night Seer, the insect who had become the Getan symbol of justice.

Humility contributed her knowledge of the Kaiel analysis of the underjaw. She told of the blue vial and connected it to the o'Tghalie idiot being studied by the Liethe biologists. The flow of words became formalized, condensed, blunt, then slowly, in a back and forth ritual, were forged into poetry.

His crime was against kalothi, the worst of all crimes. He had taken Death as a slave to feed him power but should not Death serve only the rituals of kalothi? Who can safely keep Death as his personal slave? Thus the Liethe poem ended. The most omnipotent of Storm Masters was condemned to death by execution.

The beams of sunlight from the high windows of the Deliberation Chamber had turned through many angles and hues before the decision was composed. There had been a sunset and lanterns and the pastels of dawn and the direct rays of highnode and another sunset. Humility felt aged with tiredness, stumbling from the chamber with her platinum-headed cane.

She could be old, she could think and move with the cunning slowness of age, for she was a trained actress, but the process of the deliberation itself had aged her. She alone had had flashes of impatient need to pass through the tedious process. The Winterstorm Master's crimes were monstrous. The decision could be made in the time it took for a nod of a head, and yet none of the crones had shown impatience. Only later was she thankful for their stern example.

It was easy to kill on command. A hand was only an instrument. A hand made no life and death decisions, weighed no moral issues, deliberated no consequences. She had once felt superior to the crones who ordered her to kill, and now the killing seemed the simplest of it.

The se-Tufi Who Rings the Soul's Bell guided her with an arm around her shoulders to the crones' quarters. 'First a bath for you. Then you can be young again.'

Humility said nothing until she was in the tub, waited on by giggling Liethe children, each naked but for a belt and bead skirt, who poured pitchers of warm water over her and ran for more. Soul's Bell was scrubbing her. Sometimes the crones were harsh, and sometimes they were kind to their charges. 'Am I to assassinate t'Fosal?'

'If you wish. There is no hurry. Whoever will do it, will do it. You would do it best.'

'I don't think I could.' She shuddered. 'Knowing why he dies, having condemned him, could I strike? Yes I could strike – but swiftly and cleanly?'

'Bear this in mind, little One-Who-Sometimes-Has-Humility: the Storm Master's death will be no ordinary execution. He is the foundation stone of a large building, and does not a building fall when its foundation stone is removed? Perhaps on us. There is an art to such things so that the building falls into a heap and not out into the street. Knowing the nature of the building he supports will guide you. Remember that we do not wish to destroy ourselves.'

'Am I to have no help?'

'No. Should you fail we will mourn you at your Ritual Suicide in the Temple of Raging Seas.'

'I thank you for your confidence!' She flicked some water from her fingers at the smiling crone mother. It was impossible to be formal with a woman who was washing your body with a servant's circumspection.

'You will succeed. Who else at your age has carried traceless justice to twenty men?'

'What happens to old assassins?'

Soul's Bell rang with laughter. 'They become judges. You know that now.'

'The nas-Veda Who Sits on Bees was at the Deliberation today. I'm sure of it.'

'Such is not for me to say.'

'I know her. She trained me. The red veil did not deceive my eyes.'

'The woman with the red veil is our Liethe Judge of Judges.'

'Here in Soebo?'

'We are having our own private Gathering.'

'Why do we do this?'

'We are aligned with the priests. We rise or fall as they rise and fall. If they become corrupt, will we not be destroyed with them? The priests must have their checks.'

The arrogance of that statement triggered a fury in the young assassin. 'And what if *we* become corrupt?' she erupted, raising a tidal wave in her tub.

'Have you not noticed that one in every three Liethe has been replaced in Soebo? I am new here and was not ready for the hasty journey from Hivehome, I assure you. Thank God for the strength of the Ivieth! You are among the newcomers. Why do you think Fosal trusts a Liethe to murder at his command? Are we not the slaves of the Mnankrei?'

Humility was horrified. 'I cannot believe the Liethe have lost their centre!'

'Love is a thief too long and you become a thief, it is said.' She motioned to one of the girls to bring a large towel. 'Here. Let me mop you. I have a daub of perfume and we shall do your hair. Tonight you sleep with High Wave tu'Ama.'

'He is Flesh's man, not mine. I have my own business to attend to!' Standing in the wooden tub, she glistened by torchlight.

'The High Wave should be the ruler of Soebo. A weakness in the councils, in Ama himself, allowed control to pass to the Swift Wind. When Fosal dies, others of the Swift Wind will replace him but Ama will fight them and you must know him well so that your calculations are exact. You will meet him as Comfort and you will like him. He is a weak man; again he will lose his fight, but he is sensible and just. He has his following. It may be possible to pass command to him and in that case we can dispense with our Kaiel option.'

'I should be meeting Fosal, not Ama. He has requested it.'

'He will wait.'

'He will wait in hot wrath and beat me when I arrive.'

'My child, t'Fosal expects you to deliver his blue vial to the camp of the Gathering. He will be patient with you this once.'

Humility felt the gentle towelling of the old crone. She, too, was being patient this once. *She, too, depends on me.* The nakedness of her wet body chilled the Queen of Life-before-Death to the verge of shivers. They were all depending on her to save their skins from both the Mnankrei and the Kaiel. Clans! Did a clan never think beyond itself! The burden was like a padded overcoat of the north, but there was no warmth to it. Was life to be like this, so serious?

Ah, she sighed, while the two breastless Liethe slipped a fluffy cloak around her shoulders. Life had once been as warm as this bathrobe. Reverie recalled the simple pleasure of the pillow and the table and the wit of a flirtation and even the thrill of a cunning murder stripped of its overwhelming consequences.

Youth was passing so quickly!

50

You ask why the kolgame allows the violation of its rules? But are not rules subservient to strategy? and plans subservient to rules? and contracts subservient to plans? The player who fixates upon the rules has replaced his strategy with a lower strategy. He may be defeated by creating a condition under which an application of his own rules will abort his basic goal. The player who fixates upon plans has replaced his strategy with motions. He will find himself walking at the bottom of a river because his plans called for a bridge that was not there. The player who fixates upon contracts has replaced his strategy by a faith in the omnipotence of someone else, and will fail whenever that other man fails. Once strategy is set, rules, plans, and contracts become variables to be optimized continuously. Such is the way of victory.

From the Temple of Human Destiny's *Games Manual*

A multi-jawed vice was closing on Joesai. During his reluctant idleness, the Mnankrei had slowly been building trenches and check points in strategic places. The whole camp might find itself isolated any day now. He sat fuming in the farmhouse attic, confirming the rayvoice message from Bendaein hosa-Kaiel. There was to be a delay in the forward deployment of the main strength of the Gathering. Deliberately? Joesai strolled to the window, examining his self-made trap with an expert eye. A hill. Good stone fences. An excellent defensive position but little else. By the hairs of God's Nose what was Bendaein doing?

Via rayvoice Teenae had given Joesai an analysis of Bendaein's main kolgame strategy. He relied heavily on the sacrifice. *I'll kill him!* And now Noe's message that the Mnankrei were ready with a new biological terror to which he *had* to respond . . . except that he was under sacred contract to Hoemei to sit and do nothing. *Just what I need.* He clomped down the attic ladder so furiously that one boot shot through a rung, dropping him with a bone-shaking jolt.

The contract with Hoemei exasperated him and though he might honour it first with his wits and finally with his life he was also willing to break that contract – and allow negative assessments to enter Hoemei's Archive files – if the success of the Gathering was at stake. His personal goal was to make his family transcendent above all others, but the clan goal was to take Soebo and place it under Kaiel rule, the means of victory to be governed *only* by the Over Strategy of Tae ran-Kaiel. To honour at the same time, Hoemei maran-Kaiel, his brother, and Tae ran-Kaiel, his father, and yet to face a situation which neither had predicted, that was Joesai's dilemma.

His training taught him first to review his Over Strategy when confronted with the unpredictable lest he find himself detoured by an undergoal. *All power to the Kaiel through bargaining!* That was the Over Strategy. Bargain with whom?

Grumbling, he left the farmhouse to examine his trap on foot. While he paced impatiently in meditation along the ramparts his men had raised upon the farmer's field, wisdom sang to him a thousand cautionary verses. A strong man must move lightly. Each verse he listened to – unconvinced. Another, sweeter, melody rose from his inner soul in counterpoint to the warning dirge. Throw everything into a devastating thrust straight at Soebo and damn the consequences!

Drums marched over the counterpoint. 'Power is not safely abused,' boomed Tae in Joesai's memory, his scarred face grinning at his young children, 'anymore than a sharp knife is safely abused, or fire abused, or a sailplane abused. Misapplied power turns on you and consumes you and leaves your ashes floating in the wind. Abuse it and it *may* kill you instantly or it *may* play with you first, torturing you slowly while it decides what death to inflict upon your children's children.'

Returning, the melody of temptation sneaked through the feet of Tae's mighty drumming. As a child listening to Tae he had wondered just how far you could push your power before it turned on you – how fast the knife? how big the fire? how steep the climb?

The Tae from Joesai's memory had gifts for his children and he distributed them, still speaking resonantly. 'You are Kaiel. Our job is power. Expect to be hurt. Power does not forgive those who are ignorant of its limits, yet who has kalothi enough to know well that maze of limits? But, as Kaiel, also expect to do great things with the sharp knife you have cared to learn to control.'

Each of Tae's gifts had been a tool. Joesai was given an axe which his father whimsically named 'Four Toes' as he put it into Joesai's hands. In that one rare moment of contact, Joesai had asked him who set the limits. 'The ones who die,' smiled Tae.

In another of Joesai's ears, an ironic song replied to temptation, reciting vast French victories on the way to Moscow. The power wielded by Napoleon was absolute, so absolute that it forever deprived France of Glory. Until the very edge of the last impossible page of *The Forge of War*, Frenchmen were to be seen in hell pursuing a buxom Glory who flirted with taller lovers.

A battle song told of Greek destroying Trojan – but who among the blazing stars could still pronounce the names of those jealous warriors whose power had brought them only death?

Joesai's eyes raked the horizon, a band of haze that blended into the blue sky. He was restless to move on

369

Soebo and yet restrained. Victory was essential but could one bargain with the rubble his forces would create? Power was not to be had through transient victory.

Tae had endlessly reminded his clan that the Gathering of Ache achieved dominion over the Arant by terror, then created the Kaiel to oversee the terror but that, strong as terror gripped, it was a transient glue. Had not the Arant, decimated and scattered – cowed – nevertheless subdued the Kaiel through the backdoor of remorse, so that the Kaiel body now walked with a double soul?

Joesai knew that he could strike immediately while his group was still alive. A small band could take Soebo. Who else but he – and perhaps his crazy two-wife – understood the uses of the madness in *The Forge of War*? The Mnankrei would be *able* to defend themselves but they would not be able to *comprehend* the battle tactics in time. The victory would be stunning, complete, even awesome, its reward a cowering populace who anticipated every need of the conquering Kaiel.

The victors would be bathed, fed, carried, served, charmed. Every order would be obeyed. Yet the children would be hidden, and who would ever know the thoughts behind the smiling faces trying so anxiously to please? His Arant mind told him how cities responded to fear, and his Kaiel mind showed him the future: a Kaiel body thrown to the stones of a Soebian back alley, stomped, its throat slit, blood flowing between the stones to the gutter; a Kaiel body floating in a canal; a Kaiel body hastily butchered and roasted, its skin destroyed; his body; Teenae's body; his grandson's body. He shrugged, dismissing his main battle plan. There could be no victory unless the children came to greet you. No children cheered the German troops across the steppes of Russia. No children cheered the Russian butchers in Afghanistan. No children cheered the Amerikan troops at My Lai.

Whenever Joesai was perplexed he chose direct confrontation. He knew he did not know enough to make a decision that would honour the Over Strategy. *Find out.* He took ten youths he had observed all the way from Kaiel-hontokae. They melted through the Mnankrei watch stations unnoticed, first invisibly by night, then later in full view. Forethought had long ago provided safe houses in Soebo.

Cautiously Joesai contacted Hoemei's spies. He did not know who they were, or where their rayvoice tower was located – such was the way Hoemei operated – but communication channels were open. Puzzlement met his requests. They knew nothing of sacred microlife that could kill a host and then move to a new body. Joesai pondered his next move.

He set up an escape route over rooftops and into a canal barge, stationed men, and in broad orange daylight entered the Soebo hive of the Liethe. He waited in a room of tapestries, idle, amused. A startled girl found him. They were not used to receiving men. 'I am Joesai maran-Kaiel, High Face of the Advance Court of the Gathering of Outrage.' He took a breath. The girl became even more surprised. She fled and was replaced by an old woman.

He was alert for signs of deceit, for the small flicker of wrinkled face that would tell him these women were holding him until they could inform the Mnankrei. 'I am the se-Tufi Who Rings the Soul's Bell. You must tell me the purpose of your visit.' This one had an iron calmness which could hold either fidelity or treachery.

'Bell of Supreme Excellence, from Kaiel-hontokae we once contacted you regarding those Kaiel captured at sea by the Mnankrei. We were informed that they languished in the Temple of Raging Seas.'

'Ah, and you are here to free them. A difficult task.'

Such was not his task. He was using the suggestion of an escape attempt as a probe of Liethe intentions. Joesai noted that he was being offered no help. 'I realize you are allied with the Mnankrei and that makes your position delicate. Should the Mnankrei win this game and determine that the Liethe helped us in our failure, then it would go badly for your presence here.'

The witch smiled. 'You are telling me with your Kaiel tongue that if *the Kaiel* win the game and we do not help you, then events will begin to go badly for us.'

With great formality, Joesai countered her thrust. 'You are too familar with the ways of the Mnankrei. Do not compare us. In all ways we are more generous. I make no threats. I cannot ask you to violate the ancient customs of Soebo established when the Kaiel were but worms. I promise only that no word of any help the Liethe give us shall ever be revealed by us.'

'The Death Oath?'

Joesai took his knife and opened a small wound in his finger. 'The Death Oath is upon my whole clan.' That was as strong as he could make his contract. No Getan would lightly commit the gene pool of his entire clan. Treachery masked in honest words was never forgiven in the harsh courts of kalothi. He touched his blood to the crone's tongue.

'Then I have a girl for you. The fee will be dismissed since this is a matter between priests. You will like her. The wench's name is Comfort and she is mistress of High Wave Ogar tu'Ama who leads the opposition to the Central Watch of the Swift Wind.' The crone clapped her hands and a child Liethe appeared, listened and then slipped away.

Ho, already she has the grace, Joesai thought, remembering Hoemei's Honey moving through the Palace as the hoiela moved upon the breeze.

'Please be corrected,' said the old one who could still ring the bell in a man's soul. 'We are not allied with the Mnankrei. We are allied with all priests who come from God's Womb. We serve those who serve Geta.' She smiled and touched the small amulet he wore around his neck. 'You have earned the heart of one Liethe. Who was she?'

'A dancer of the Prime Predictor.'

'She gave that to you when she knew your life was in danger.'

'My life has always been in the shadow of Death,' he grinned.

'You did not come here alone. Your friends will be hidden outside, watching.'

'If two lovely women leave the hive holding hands, one wearing a hat with hoiela wings, they will be assured of my safety and will await a second signal from me in twenty sun-heights.'

'It will be done. But you have a bizarre idea of the finery we possess!' Soul's Bell escorted Joesai along a corridor with a hand that well knew how to hold a man's arm. They met a tiny Liethe child, fortified by the beginnings of a large vocabulary, who was outraged at the presence of a male and hit at his knees with clenched fists. Other eyes watched them from hiding.

He was led to a room that was meant for no man. Its luxury was eccentric. Satin pillows, lit by an eerie mixture of sunlight and bioluminous glow, spilled on the floor overlooking the garden. A platinum globe-swing hung from the ceiling beside a torch rack and a bookcase. Dominating the corner was a great wardrobe made of pressed woven iron-reed, inlaid with a lustrous stone. The tapestries were of the finest oz-Numae weave depicting the faery world of the mythical forests of Scowlmoon.

Then Comfort emerged from across the garden, carrying a tray of o'ca porcelain. The snouts of the centrepiece steamed with the aroma of herb tea. There were sipping cups for warming the hands and spice cake. She set the tray on a small table and sank to her knees before him.

'How may I serve you,' she said to his feet.

Instead of asking her to rise he lowered himself onto a pillow beside her. The crone disappeared. *Damn fool Liethe*, he thought while he poured them both some tea, *they never think a man can take care of himself.* She let him serve her, gracefully accepting the unexpected. The face, the delicate body, was se-Tufi, like Honey, and that disturbed him. She wore a pink robe of knotty texture tied beneath her breasts, casually, and tiny red jewels in the corner of her eyes. She was dressed for seduction, not talk. Did that mean they were afraid of him?

'Good tea,' he said gruffly.

Humility broke a piece of cake and offered the morsel to his mouth.

'You look like someone I know,' he said.

Her blue eyes sparkled, black pupils and ruby jewels. 'Did you love my sister?'

'For a moment.'

'The city is afraid,' she said, reverting to her serious manner.

'Of what?'

'Of you.'

'The Advance Court has done nothing.'

'That's what makes you so frightening.'

'Then you, little one, must be the bravest of all the cowards of Soebo.' Some of Noe's teasing ways had rubbed off on Joesai.

'Not yet as brave as you, for my actions still fall short of the foolhardy.'

'How might I reduce this fear?'

'Go away.'

He laughed the great laugh. 'I would rather stroll down the Avenue of Temples and have children rush to bring me flowers and climb upon my shoulders.'

'With a face like yours?'

'I shall have to be content to terrorize the Temple of Raging Seas.'

374

She sighed. 'You wish to free your men from the Temple. That is nearly impossible.'

'Ho! Notice that word *nearly*. It savours well upon the tongue. I will need maps of the Temple and of the surrounding buildings.'

'You will need more than that,' she replied scaldingly.

'The Mnankrei guard that evil place well, I hear.' He readied his surprise question. Noe had told him of the vile research into spreading death taking place in the Temple of Raging Seas and that the Liethe knew about it. How did one read an undecorated face? It was as innocent as a child's. He finished his tea – and began. 'What do you know of micro-life that visits the body's house and kills the soul?'

'You speak of profane diseases such as pass among the insects?'

'Sacred disease,' he pressed.

'There have been rumours.'

He gave her no pause to orient. 'Rumours?'

But she paused anyway. 'I know nothing. I will go now and ask those who might.'

'Stay. I'm not sure I trust any other Liethe besides you.' He sensed he would get nothing from her.

'Then I won't ask, but I know nothing. You suspect such abominations are being created in Soebo?'

'Yes.'

'You think great evil of the Mnankrei.'

'We are here to judge them fairly. First I plan to attack the Temple of Raging Seas.'

'It will have to be a job done in the dark as the burrowers eat wood. I need time to think and prepare. I will have a good plan for you by morning for your review. I am competent. Do you have two men, flexible in an emergency, quick to act?'

'Of course.'

'I cannot go with you. You may fail and die.'

'Do your schemes work?'

'Always. When executed by a woman.'

He liked the way she laughed at him. 'Why should you be so helpful? Who is fed when the Kaiel are given charity?'

'I am the companion of the tu'Ama who has long fought the evil of the Swift Wind. They must be broken on the reefs. But Ama, just and steadfast as he is, lacks cunning as a leader. He may be broken if *he* does not receive help.'

'I'm a dangerous ally for this lover of yours.'

She delivered the o'ca cup to the small table with both fury and sadness. 'You don't even understand what I'm talking about! What can tu'Ama do? We know that! The Liethe are between crushing forces – the Kaiel and the Swift Wind. I am being thrown at you, at your feet, a gift, so that should you win your game there will be a Liethe with you to mellow your revenge. You surprised us by coming here. There has been much preparation to send me to your camp.'

'It is not likely that you would have been admitted.'

'But if I help you now?'

'No.'

'Then I will not risk my life to send you into the Temple for your friends!' she flared, rising.

'Ho! This is a bargain you are suggesting!' He laughed. 'That is more like it! I shall have to reconsider. Let me sort this into boxes; in return for your aid you get to serve and flatter me.'

'And love you.'

'How can I refuse?'

51

A wise man acts before God crosses the Constellation of the Knife. When the Knife sets, is it being buried in the earth or in a man's ribs?

From *The Cynic's Compendium*

Like a golden shape, the Temple of Raging Seas lay atop an ancient volcanic upthrust that had defied the relentless smashing of the Njarae. The huge structure was one of the oldest of the Great Temples on Geta. As such it lacked elegance and height. The masonry was thick, crudely hewn. Built by the chattel children of the early slave-trading Mnankrei, half the awesome beauty of this Adoration of God seemed to belong to the rough tumble of sea-slimed stones crouching in obeisance at its feet.

Joesai did not wholly trust his efficient Comfort, who had put together an interesting plan he could not fault. It was either very workable or it was a trap. In case it was a trap he had constructed a careful contingency tactic. No one would expect them to retreat over the massive north wall. Explosive charges, laid with a quarryman's skill that night, were in place for a sacrilegious exit. Riflemen, not a part of Comfort's modest exercise, had been artfully stationed to cover such an emergency withdrawal.

In the early morning of the next high day, through the rose-tinted fog that drifted off the sea from the red mouth of an enormous Getasun, four impostors, wearing the ochre and purple-striped robes of Mnankrei Time Wizards, shared the stairway of God's Ascension with scurrying temple priests who clattered past them in wooden-soled shoes. Joesai brazenly stopped a boy bringing nectar up the steps and bought a gourd from him while a tradesman, encumbered by a packsack of honey, paused on the stairs followed by an impatient Chanter in full headdress and painted face.

The bronze doors were done in the theme of a tempest that flung water towards God's Sky. All Getan myths echoed the struggle of kalothi against the levelling forces. Inside the doors Joesai took a moment to admire the simple interior excellence of a vast room that predated the Kaiel. His seemingly casual glance oriented him, relating the structure to maps quickly memorized the previous evening.

A functionary was already waiting for them. The necessary paperwork, an ever-present part of Mnankrei life, had been done, presumably by an excellent forger who had access to secret Swift Wind marks, and they were ushered to a small room on the lower levels which was unlocked for them. Presently unsuspecting acolytes of the Time Wizards began to arrive – to be subdued by a silencing hold and drugged into paralysis by potions provided by Comfort.

Joesai and Eiemeni then exchanged Wizard costumes for the dark brown robes of a High Priest of the Inquisition and arrogantly descended into the depths, where again the proper paperwork had been done. One by one the Kaiel prisoners were brought out for 'intensive' questioning and returned to their cells on stretchers in a state of unconsciousness. Eventually the 'acolytes' left the Temple with their Time Wizard Masters. Watching them emerge, the forward rifleman relaxed at his hidden post, passing to his rear the sign of the unwon, but conceded, game.

Robe changes and rehearsed trickery dissolved the group one by one, later allowing the fugitives to assemble undetected at a prearranged canal-front warehouse. Once inside the wooden-beamed hideout, tension broke both among the liberators and those who had expected to make their Contribution as soup bones. The men hugged each other. They grinned their triumph silently, and cuffed Joesai. They loved him. Tears wet their eyes. They kissed the walls and swung upon the log beams.

Unobtrusively Comfort busied herself filling mugs from a keg of mead. She hurried to spread sauce over fresh whole wheat buns as fast as they were devoured, her eyes seldom leaving Joesai. She was wrapped in sturdy travelling clothes, her sleeping mat and essential belongings already tied together in a waiting backpack.

Still wearing his Mnankrei robes for the sheer humour of it, Joesai began to brief his men, exploiting their euphoric sense of immediate loyalty. His attack plan on Soebo was now clear in his mind. Passionately he explained the strategy behind the plan, developing action modules and assigning roles as he went along.

'What dries the resistance against us in Soebo? It is fear of Kaiel ferocity!' He struck the Post of Lurking Death, then spoke again. 'It is old memories of the fate of the Arant!' He tossed his hand and demons sprang from his palm. 'It is the remembrance of the fate of the clans who served the Arant!' His hand sliced to his wrist in the symbol of execution.

He continued his oration to an alert audience. 'The main strategic thrust of the Advance Court has to be to establish trust among the underclans. We cannot simply try to convince them that it is the Mnankrei who are the ferocious fei flowers of the sea and we the bees who make honey through a steadfast policy of bargaining. Would they believe strangers?'

'No!' roared the unanimous answer to his rhetorical question.

For a moment Joesai moved about the warehouse, mimicking the alienness of the stranger – his slight unsureness, eyes that noticed what was too common to be noteworthy, a queer walk. 'Nothing a man lives with daily is ferocious to him. It is the *stranger* who seems ferocious. We will not be able to convince these people that there will be no overnight change of laws with the coming of a Kaiel government, no confusion, no retroactive Contribution for laws invented today. They will think we lie to gain their favour so that we may have their skins. All logic reaches one conclusion: without trust, no argument is effective. Trust must be the key word of our strategy.

'What then is trust? Trust is the emotional residue of contracts entered upon and fulfilled. We have no time to make elaborate contracts that must persist weeks or seasons before completion. But we *can* do *one* thing. Human beings inately understand the nature of bargaining and they trust the *bargaining process* wherever it appears, whether from little children or from old enemies. All of you here know how to bargain. That is the Kaiel tradition. So that is what we will use.

'Selected underclan spokesmen have already been contacted. You will meet them covertly. Begin bargaining immediately. Establish the needs of your assigned clan in *detail* by means of the opening move of the Tae Bargaining Ritual:

'"What desired event has failed to happen?"

'"What has happened that should not have happened?"

'The mere act of delineating the differences between their ideal world and the real world will generate the crucial preliminary trust. You will then know their most pressing needs. Match Kaiel strengths against these needs and make your offer. Do it formally. The first offer is to contain no lies, no fantasy, no promises you know the Kaiel cannot keep. Write down their first offer. Then haggle.'

He smiled. 'Within six sunrises I want the main clans of Soebo to be in awe of Kaiel skill at the bargaining game.

380

They will be impressed. The Mnankrei do not make social contracts by bargain. Do as much as you can before I come again. Do not stop talking! Build a constituency!'

For the first time Joesai introduced the odd phrase 'Will of the People' into his exhortations. He had picked it out of *The Forge of War*, thinking that it perfectly expressed Kaiel notions of obtaining the loyalty of the underclans. Was not the function of a hereditary ruling clan to sense the thousand conflicting wills of its people and artfully shape that force into a single Will?

Joesai had found himself bemused by the context in which the People of the Sky had used the phrase. But they never spoke words in simple ways. The Amerikans wrote 'Will of the People' into their Constitution to justify slavery as if the Black clan itself had devised slavery to promote the Greater Will.

Even more peculiar was the use of the phrase by the Russian Tsar, Lenin the Terrible. Joesai had been intrigued by certain passages in *The Forge of War* suggested to him by Teenae. Lenin, dismayed by past losses of Tsarist property to the expanding Capitalist clan and outraged by Socialist calls for land reform in which former state slaves would be awarded the farmland they had tilled for generations, had, immediately after his coronation, begun the extermination of the Capitalists by mass terror while, simultaneously, conniving from within the Socialist clan to restore all property to the Tsar by systematic liquidation of every Socialist within his realm. In retaking the land for the state he justified the mass murder of peasants as the Will of the People because it was the peasants who had given the Tsardom to Lenin and therefore was it not their Will when he ordered them destroyed rather than relinquishing to them the land which historically was his?

Joesai said it another way. 'Let bargaining forge from the will of the clans the Will of the People. Then when I return to Soebo shall we not have a new city?'

381

The Liethe woman followed him out of the old Soebo. She was a brown shadow, indistinguishable from any other traveller. For a while they walked boldly by road in a direction too westerly to be connected with the Gathering. He was impressed by Comfort's strength. She was too small, tiny even, but if he slowed out of sympathy she was soon ahead of him, cautioning him about branches, picking their path.

She wilted first, though. Fondly, he took her packsack, and then she was holding onto him. She never complained. He was not sure if she was really tired, or whether she simply wanted an evening alone with him. He would have continued all night but, pleased with an excuse, he found a campsite.

'We'll have Scowlmoon to ourselves,' she said, building a small fire. She had brought water from a brook and was making broth.

He let her – why fight her need to serve a man? – but to busy himself, unrolled their mats. Her essential things amused him. A comb; a blue glass bottle, probably perfume; eye shadow; the leaves of the olinar, a powerful contraceptive. 'Your clan knows the Mnankrei like few others. They are hardly real to me except for a priest who once hung my smallest wife from a yardarm. I was angry for a while.'

'Did she survive?'

'Yes, but *he* will not! She never forgives. To this day she reproaches me for acts I cannot remember committing.'

'Do you miss her?'

'Yes. She's small like you.'

'Tonight you shall have me at halfmoon. You'll forget her for a moment. What will I get in exchange?'

'Ho! I see I spoke too much about bargaining!' He tried to read her smile in the darkness. 'I'll carry your packsack,' he said to make her offer seem casual.

'I want your nose for an amulet,' she said to tell him that she was priceless.

Idle fingers picked up a rust red stone, flecked by copper green. 'How about a jewel instead?'

She brought him his bowl of broth and kissed his nose. 'How about Soebo's Palace of Morning? The cupola at dawn is enough to break a girl's heart.'

'And a man's purse!'

'If you promise me the Palace of Morning I'll massage your back.'

'Give me a sample to see if you're worth it.'

'Hug me first. You have to be tender, or we won't let you into the city with your ridiculous Court.'

The desire was on him. He tugged at her sashes, and found buttons, and lifted her body so that he could get her clothes off. Then he laid her on the mat, head in his lap, and whimsically put his stone in her God's Eye, which was what Getans called their navel. For a moment he was content to look at her. 'I've slowed down,' he said. 'Nothing seems to be such a hurry anymore.'

'It's better that way.'

'Are you tired?' he asked.

'I sleep better when I've ridden a man who loves me. You've been kind to me. I'll dance for you all when we reach camp.'

He shook his head and lifted her body so that they were coupled in an upright position. 'No dancing. When we reach camp, we break camp and blister feet towards Soebo.'

'There's *always* time for celebration,' she replied petulantly. 'The world seems less cruel when we have been laughing and dancing.'

He held back his thrusts – remembering Noe's patient lessons on how to arouse a woman. He wanted to be better than any Mnankrei lover she had ever known. He listened to her breathing.

'Is marriage like this?' she asked. 'Holding a stone in your Eye out in the wilderness while you hold a man you never want to leave?'

'You must be crazy! Marriage is more like your wife stealing coin from you to pay a forgotten debt while she's humping your co-husband.'

He felt her breath on his cheek, a sacred human perfume unlike any other smell of the red sun's world. Slowly her rhythm built, slowly her fist tightened around the Liethe amulet he wore.

There *was* a celebration when they reached camp with the news of the moves on Soebo. The young Kaiel were restless. They were not used to idleness but to the Trials, to winning, to cunning escapes from death and so the celebration came spontaneously. His strange Liethe taught the Kaiel girls a simple dance that their quick bodies perfected while the boys provided vocal music and enthusiastic clapping.

These youths were too fresh from the creches for Joesai to think of them yet as men and women. He watched the gaiety with affection. Even if they were inept at sea, they were lethal on land. He was proud of them. They called themselves judges. In another age, among the stars, they would have called themselves warriors. Joesai found himself clapping along with the throbbing voices of the choir.

Comfort insisted on providing the recipe for the celebration feast. The camp was being taken down around them but eating was a constant of life. She rushed between the wagons, serving the Kaiel, seeing that everyone was well fed, making sure that there were no leftovers. Joesai she found busy in the old farmhouse organizing the march and she had to sit beside him and feed him or he would not have bothered.

Much later, when the camp was already asleep, the watchers stationed, Comfort returned to the farmhouse, waiting to sweeten his mat. When he felt his way down the ladder, tired, ready for oblivion, she massaged him, relaxing the cramps that came from stooping over a torch to do his papers, working his muscles with experienced hands, limbering them.

'What's it like to be married?' she asked, returning to her favourite subject.

'Hectic.'

'That doesn't tell me anything. Life is hectic.'

'Try a few husbands someday and find out.'

'No,' she said. 'I've taken my vows. Who's your favourite wife?'

'The one who is on my pillows.'

'Will I do as a substitute?'

'I'm not complaining. You take better care of me than Teenae or Noe ever did.'

'Thank you.'

'You have a magic about you.'

'Why do you stay married? Why don't you just wander from woman to woman? That would make life more interesting.'

'Why should beginnings be more interesting than middles or ends? I *know* my wives and husbands. We're the kind of team it takes a lifetime to build. Without them there would *be* no other women; I would be dead. Beginnings tell you very little. I didn't even like Noe when I first met her. I thought she was altogether too flighty for us. I wanted a serious girl from the creches, not one of those soft Kaiel who come from a family. So beginnings aren't always where the fun is. I didn't really get to like Noe until we started to go sailplane gliding together.'

'And Teenae?'

'How can you resist a child who worships the very ground you walk on? I was rough and uncouth with her and laid her without much thought to her own pleasure. It was a long time before her fierceness and brilliance tamed me. I found strength in her. She planted tolerance in me and ruthlessly tore at the inconsistencies I was so prone to have. All these things take time. They are not for beginnings.'

Comfort sighed with faraway eyes. 'I feel so lonely with you. I suppose that's because I haven't known you long enough. I'm not at the middle yet.'

He pulled her to him, pleased with the warmth of her small body, feeling less lonely than he had for all the time he had been on Mnank. He caressed her. There was nothing he could say that was really appropriate. 'A man should not talk to a Liethe of his wives.'

'Nonsense,' she replied sadly. 'I have to know everything.'

Joesai wondered why, on the eve of every great event, the talk was so trivial – of gossip, of past events, of the shape of breasts, of how much whisky a man could hold before he fell over, of love and loneliness. She had lapsed into silence, words gone from her.

'Hi there,' he said.

'I don't want you ever to forget me.' She took him then.

It was still dark when fever woke him. He tried to move and couldn't. He could hardly open his eyes. The pale face of Comfort was staring at him. She was fully dressed in her brown travelling robe.

'You're sick,' she said.

He tried to move his tongue and it was like moving a mouthful of dough.

'The paralysis isn't part of the sickness. I've poisoned you with the juice of ei-cactus so that you won't be able to kill me for having given all your judges the sickness.'

He tried to lunge at her by sheer will and managed only to fall on his own arm and pin it. Ponderous grunting noises came from his mouth.

She rolled him into a more comfortable position. 'I'm sorry. I didn't want to do it. You were not wise to trust me. I arranged the escape of your friends with Nie t'Fosal. So that you would not question me.' And she was gone.

He could still think. Thoughts came with an unfamiliar despair. *I've made the one mistake I've never been allowed to make.* He was dead and the Advance Court was dead and Joesai maran-Kaiel was an idiot. Aesoe had won, as usual. Joesai had been a foil to bring out the most deadly counterthrust of the Mnankrei and now they had made it and Bendaein would know what he was up against and respond to that, Bendaein the Cautious. *I've disgraced my family.* He could still cry though he could not wipe the tears from his eyes.

Hoemei had trusted him to wait, and he had grown impatient and gone to the city and brought back the pestilence as a lover. Noe had warned him. Teenae would have shot Comfort at a hundred man-lengths. Gaet would mourn him as he had Sanan – and then go find another husband. Fever began to take the coherence from his mind. Kathein's child, bearing his genes, would give whatever kalothi he possessed one more risky chance but Kathein's face faded into Joesai's last image of Oelita – mad with her sudden belief in God. He had driven her to her death and now the Liethe were returning the favour.

Joesai's most horrible loss was that there could be no Funeral Feast. No one would share his flesh. He would be cremated, unclean.

52

Why should a government which is doing what it believes is right allow itself to be criticized? It would not allow opposition by lethal weapons.

Vladimir Ilyich Lenin from *The Forge of War*

The storm gale lashed in from the sea, driving the spume off the wave tops. Teenae's spies ducked into the hut and told her that the Mnankrei vessels had arrived. There hadn't been enough warning because of the fog. Cursing, she scampered to the observation station just in time to see the three ships breaking into the relative quiet of the bay. She shouted orders in her first moment of confusion and then relaxed. Tonpa would have to delay unloading until the storm had subsided. She had plenty of time. The surprise would be hers. She waited.

A full day it took for the two smaller double-masted ships to dock and begin disgorging their wheat and casks of famous Mnankrei whisky. A flat barge shuttled loads of grain from the bigger three-masted vessel, Tonpa's command. Curious boats surrounded the flagship. One of them was Teenae's. Through a lens she watched the Stgal greet their saviours who would have the Stgal for snacks once their usefulness was done.

She gave orders for her rifles to take up position. Each of Tonpa's men was assigned a double tail – an inconspicuous heretic and a Kaiel rifleman. Poor Gaet was probably hiding somewhere. He would not touch a rifle and he was not fond of violence. She had three portable rayvoices in operation and a whole system of rooftop flag stations, except she was using people and coded costumes instead of flags.

The first important message she received was that her bomb had been attached to the bottom of the flagship. It had two fuses, one a clock, already set and ticking, the other a sonically activated switch. The Mnankrei knew nothing of war.

The second important message she received was that the fire bombs for the smaller docked ships were in place. The Mnankrei knew nothing about the fate of the Spanish Armada.

The third important message she received, from a horrified runner, was that Gaet had taken it upon himself to negotiate with the Mnankrei and had been forcibly removed to the Temple and was now a prisoner of the sea priests and the Stgal.

She left her command post in a towering rage with four Kaiel riflemen who had to listen to the brunt of her cursing. 'That husband of mine! A smile! A caress! A little flattery! A little haggling! He thinks himself able to trade with any man! What did I do to deserve a husband like that! I'll have his hide for a duffel bag! He eats with his anus and pisses with his mouth! God! God above!'

Her rifle was swinging in the fierce grip of her hand, her black hair flowing and flapping about the bald streak down the centre of her head that needed a shave, her breasts bobbing inside her light blouse with every angry pace that took her closer to the Temple.

She met the slyly smiling Stgal who presented her with their demand that the Kaiel return whence they had come. Her mind was a winter's storm. She had to think quickly or Gaet would die. She wasn't ready yet. They had captured Gaet too soon. The ships weren't fully unloaded and the people of Sorrow needed that wheat. She pretended to pace, to consider the Stgal's demand. Instead she passed to high ground and gave the signal.

A ripple of gaily coloured gowns paraded upon the rooftops of Sorrow.

Distant *whoomps* broke the silence. There was a pause while the expression on the face of the Stgal changed. Then two great shafts of fire rose into the sky. 'I shall write you a reply,' she said, turning to the Stgal. She could hear rifle cracks. There would be feasting tonight but her mind could only think of her beloved Gaet who had bought her in the child market. She fought back the tears, at a loss for words. Somehow the words that came to the paper she was preparing were Leninesque in their heartlessness.

'Your message received. It is necessary that Gaet maran-Kaiel be released *immediately*.' Immediately was Lenin's favourite word. 'All Stgal who do not comply will be pebbled without mercy by sunfall.' She paused to cross out 'pebbled' – they would not know what that meant. She substituted instead a Leninist word they would understand, 'liquefied', and continued. 'The Mnankrei fleet no longer exists. The sea priests occupying the town have been eliminated. Conduct yourselves accordingly.'

She triggered her rifle to fire into the air under the nose of the young priest, shattering his nerves, and sent him to deliver *her* demand.

Stgal lookouts in the Temple tower saw the destruction of the Mnankrei fleet before the sea priest guests were aware of the disaster. There was whispering. Then Teenae's message arrived, stated in a language so blunt, and promising consequences so bizarre, that they immediately switched sides without telling the Mnankrei until they were in irons and Gaet freed.

'You are emotional and not logical,' she raged when she was escorted into Gaet's presence. The sight of him whole, with his skin still on, quieted her trembling. 'Oh Gaet!'

'I've been signing up my captors for my constituency,' said Gaet, smiling.

'You machine! I don't think you were a bit worried while I was out there scared to death for your life!'

'You've created problems for us!'

'I captured the whole town!'

'I was in the middle of negotiating with the Storm Master for a pair of boots when we were so rudely interrupted.'

'You have him?' Teenae questioned, a glint of hatred in her eyes.

'He's in the tower.'

'I get him! Tonpa is mine! I want to conduct the Last Rites! I'm a priest. You made me a Kaiel when you married me.'

'There is no pleasure in revenge,' Gaet said sadly.

'There is! I want my boots! Nobody else has boots with such a pretty storm-wave design!'

Later that evening, Kaiel priest Teenae, Symbol Master, sat in a carved chair in an opulent room of the Temple that had yesterday belonged to the House of Stgal. Her long black hair was washed and curled, the strip along the top of her head freshly shaved, her face flushed with its furrows that emphasized her cheekbones and the sensual turn of a mouth practised at smiling. She wore the formal black robe of the Kaiel, stiffly, unused to its folds.

Tonpa was brought in naked, wrists manacled in brass chain, holding his head high, long hair braided into his beard, his emotions hidden behind the flying-storm-wave cicatrice. He was guarded by two erect children of the creche.

She felt a cold hatred. She was going to put him through the terror she had never forgotten. Instead she laughed. The words of Oelita were speaking to her of mercy but she felt no mercy.

'We arrive here,' she mocked his long-remembered speech, 'after building a road to bring in relief supplies for a Mnankrei-induced famine. This village lies across difficult mountains, but we think it is our sacred obligation to alleviate the famine of these valued members of the Race. And what do we find? A scheme of conquest based on the rule of misery. You ally yourself to those who create abominable life forms wickedly designed to destroy sacred food. You burn silos.'

She waited for his reply. Tonpa remained rigid.

'You do not reply? Tonpa, you have overestimated our gullibility and now we have set a Gathering upon your clan. Speak! Defend yourself!'

'Your mind is made up. I offer no defence.'

'Because you *cannot* defend yourself!' And the hatred was there again. 'I am not in a merciful mood!'

'*I* granted *you* mercy.'

'That was not mercy! That was part of your plan to spread lies about the Kaiel among the people of Sorrow. You were fatally stupid to construct a lie that would not convince us also. I would be noseless or dead had I needed your mercy.'

'I will work for you.'

She laughed. 'Indeed you will! As my boots! I offer you an honourable death. You have violated the Code of Survival. The Race must work as one, not against itself. To atone, you will make your Contribution to the Race so that it may be rid of the elements of the gene pattern that came together as such a vile individual.'

He seemed to study her, testing her implacable feelings for an opening, but finding none, he accepted his fate stoically. He might resist, even try to escape. Then he would die by a stab in the back, a dishonourable death.

Teenae rose. 'I have been reading the Gentle Heretic. She is a woman of mercy and very convincing.' She let her expression flow to softness; she touched his arm – to torture him with hope. She wanted to torture him. But when she escorted him to the great tower room, he knew there was no hope.

The high Stgal were there in crimson, stripped of their priestly insignia, watching with terrified unease to see black-clad foreign priests so casually asking for the life of another foreign priest. Gaet stood by, inscrutable. A choir of young Kaiel were there to Chant . . . and to guard. A young temple courtesan smiled lazily in her gaudy half-nakedness, ready to administer the last pleasures. The tower's view was awesome: sprawling village blending into sea that reflected a giant moon, and in the other direction, the purple mountains.

Teenae erased her hatred. Gaet said she could not conduct the Last Rite unless she had prepared a clear soul. She was willing to make that sacrifice. Storm Master Tonpa remained pale. He stumbled. Had he ever been fearsome? Had he ever hung her cruelly from the yardarm of his topsail? Had he ever played with her, half drowning her? She seated the large man of the sea before the blood bowl, shackling him there, and began her Rite.

'We did not have kalothi. We died of the Unknown Danger. And God in His mercy took pity and carried us from the Unknown Place across His Sky so that we might find kalothi. We wept when He gave us Geta. We moaned when He cast us out. But God's Heart was stone to our tears . . .'

Teenae was barely listening to the monotony of the memorized words. She had a recipe in mind for roast with potatoes and sauce that she would serve to Gaet back in the hills where they could be alone. She knew a tanner and a wonderful cobbler here in town. The boots would be thigh high and flaring at the calf. There would be enough leather left over for a new vest. Perhaps she could wear it with her green blouse and fawn trousers.

She stretched out her arms in salutation, holding the

priest's wooden talismen, the Black Hand and the White Hand. 'Two Hands build kalothi. Life is the Test. Death is the Change. Life gives us the Strength. Death takes from us the Weakness. For the Race to find kalothi the Foot of Life takes the Road of Death.'

She forgot her unfamiliar lines for a moment and smiled at Tonpa, then glanced shyly at Gaet. Something giggled inside her at the dour expressions of the Stgal. 'All of us contribute to God's Purpose . . .'

She was eager to reach the Giving of the Last Delights. The temple woman was beautiful. There would be Chanting and moonlight. Would Tonpa's fear, visible now, seeping through his pores, be enough to make him impotent?

'. . . the greatest honour is to contribute Death for we all love Life.' God, the view up here was staggering! 'It is with awe that I accept the offering of your defective genes . . .'

Tonpa was staring at her with rancour. He could not resist a parting snarl. 'All of you will die a death of horror!'

53

When masters play, treachery is their least valued tactic, not because the ways of deceit are ineffective but because of long-term consequences. Is not the treacherous player isolated by mistrust during the end game?

Tae ran-Kaiel at the Funeral Feast for Seir on-Biel

Her killing mood as invisible as her secret name, the Queen of Life-before-Death stalked slowly through the Swift Wind's victory party in the se-Tufi persona of Sugarpie, a woman who wore gaudy clothes of her own design, flirted without much interest in sex, and was an avid gourmet of gossip. Sugarpie's smile was quick to say hello and as quick as her eyes to wander in search of people more worthy of her smile. This evening she was spreading colourful rumours of the violent end of Radiance who had turned traitor for the sake of the hairy Kaiel.

There were no Mnankrei wives present. This was Nie t'Fosal's victory party, a celebration of male prowess. Everywhere the talk gave the greatest Winterstorm Master of the Mnankrei credit for destroying the Gathering of Outrage as easily as the Red Death tree poisons the swarming gei. The tales were of Fosal's invincibility. No enemy stood against him! no friend dared betray him! no woman dominated him! He had promised his followers that in time he would snuff out the Gathering as if it had never been. And he had been right! The final fevered agonies of the Advance Court embellished the tales like decoration upon cake.

Humility finally targeted the ideal carrier of her lie. From a distance she saw t'Fosal at the gaming tables being served by a naked courtesan whose scarifications had been outlined with blue and red paint. This garish beauty left her master for a moment to fetch him a drink and Humility caught her just long enough to tell her of the grim death of her Liethe rival, knowing that the story would go directly to the ears of the Winterstorm Master.

The antidote t'Fosal had treacherously instructed Radiance to take after she had infected the food of the Kaiel was no antidote, but a poison violent enough to rip the muscles from her bone. He was not a grateful man. Tonight he would be keyed to hear about that death. Let him feel the elation of total success. An enemy with his belly full was a dead enemy.

As she drifted back through the party, Humility wondered at this madman's perception of people. He despised women and so he perceived the Liethe as incompetent to perform a simple chemical analysis. Humility herself had done the preliminary toxicity study of his 'antidote' as a normal precaution and had been appalled by the crudity of his chemicals as well as his tactics. Only a man who longed to be vastly superior to others needed to see his enemy as a fool who might be persuaded to eat strychnine like candy. Nie was a brilliant biologist lacking understanding of people. He did not even know that to murder a Liethe and leave the slightest trail was an act of suicide.

Moments later Humility was inside the cabin of a small canal boat with an adolescent se-Tufi, changing from the guise of Sugarpie to the black robes of the night assassin. They chatted about romantic love. The young girl was disdainful and sure that it would never catch her. She was trying to say that she was in love with her brave older sister.

Humility thought only of Hoemei. Scowlmoon, trailing a ruddy scarf upon the canal, was all she had to remember him by. His room in the round ovoids of the Kaiel Palace had looked upon Scowlmoon, night and day, and all the changing moods of that moon had watched the loving of their bodies. Why should she still feel the touch of his hand above all others?　.

The two identical women, one smaller and less breasted than the other, poled the boat to the buildings of Nie t'Fosal's residence where Radiance had been but once. Humility kissed her young sister and disappeared into the shadows, and, from the cover of a silent alley, climbed the walls until she gained one of the slate rooftops that led to the tower lair of her prey. A rope trick and a swift flying fall took her to a parapet of the tower. Another climb found the hexagonal window. Nie had never noticed how Radiance had spent one pensive interlude beside the window. Now the lock broke easily and she entered this place where the leader of the Swift Wind did most of his lonely thinking and some of his chemical trickery. Once inside she reclosed the hexagon.

The joy of killing was on her.

Carefully she folded away the black robe and its contents, keeping only the ring that t'Fosal had given to Radiance, which she wore on her index finger, and a perfumed garter for her right leg where she could reach it with one touch of her fingers. She rememorized the room, checking over possible emergencies, and then crawled into bed and went to sleep, setting her mind so that she would be suddenly wide awake when her victim returned from his party.

She dreamed she was a courtesan in some exotic Tower of Contribution set in a black city on the outer reaches of the Sky where the stars were dim, tendering a man who would die tomorrow.

Alertness. It was already light. Fosal must have stayed for the dawn display at the Palace of Morning. She watched him lock his massive door, waiting for him to notice her. He was already half way to the bed before the shock of her appearance registered. She chose exactly that moment to emerge from the covers.

'My lover.' The toes of her gartered leg reached over the pillows and a happy breath moved her body as she held her ring hand towards him, telling him with her smile that no other man on Geta was as powerful as her master. She watched Nie struggle with this vibrant image of a dead woman.

'I didn't invite you here!' he said coldly.

She bowed her head contritely. 'I had *such* a headache after that antidote. What was in it? Liethe bodies are immune to just about everything.' She watched his amazement as he calculated the number of grains of poison she must have survived. Was she killable? She let him think about that, then apologized with a voice that evoked forgiveness. 'I'm sorry I missed your party. It was all I could do to drag myself up here. But you're pleased that I destroyed your enemies? Have I done something wrong?'

'How did you get in?'

She smiled coyly. 'I don't remember. I had a headache. Liethe can walk through walls when they really want to be with their lovers. We're a magical clan.'

'It's my private place!'

The better for killing you, thought the Queen. 'Oh,' Radiance cried pitiably. 'I've angered you and all I wanted to do was please you. Punish me! But don't make me go! I don't mind when you punish me because you are so just. There's a cane over there,' she said, pointing with her ring finger to a rod heavy enough to kill her, tempting him. She crawled from the bed and began to grovel towards him on her hands and knees. 'Punish me. I want you to feel better. Beat me till you feel better!'

At the moment he reached for the rod, she was close enough to spring with her dancer's legs. He reacted instantly to the shock of hitting the floor by rolling away from her but she was already disconnecting the motor nerves between his brain and body with a tiny syringe she had pulled from her garter. A heartbeat later she whacked him in the throat to stifle his scream. With a stabbing thrust, her thin knife cut his vocal cords. She disconnected his tongue next, and with other quick probes eliminated all sensation from his body. He still breathed. His heart beat rapidly.

'Look at me and see my hate!' she sneered as she slipped a tool behind his eyeball and destroyed the vision in one eye. She turned his good eye towards her. 'I am the face of hatred!' And he saw a valley of black hair that led to eyes of blue cremating fire. 'I am the vengeance of Geta come for you. I am the sibyl of the Silent God!' It astonished her to be talking to a man while she was killing him. The force of her hatred was overwhelming. Her hand started to shake and she stared at it while the helpless one-eyed man stared back.

Was it because she knew why he had to die that her hate was like fire? *My God, I'm ruined as an assassin!* Nevertheless she disconnected his other eye.

'Die, knowing that you have failed,' she raved in a whisper to two hearing ears. 'The Kaiel could never have destroyed you. But when the clans of Soebo desert you, your priest will become a mind severed from its body. I've seen one of the women in whose body you grow your disease. Does that make me, a woman, loyal to you? You have stupidly thought to poison a Liethe who knows poisons, and the whole clan rises against you. Are we the only clan so offended? Winning command of a ship is not the same as sailing her!' Humility's rage was building; she wanted to hoard this pair of captive ears and berate them with the contempt that Radiance could never show.

An old discipline watched her lack of control with dismay. What was served by striking at a victim's ego? Would he then jump away from his crimes? Was this need to hurt him a defiance of someone seen to be stronger? *Boasting gives an opponent time to react,* echoed the voices of her teachers. *Boasting tells your opponent that you fear him.*

Humility breathed. The White Mind took over. Then, silently, she destroyed his hearing. Whoever might come now would be unable to communicate with Nie to discover what had happened and whom to blame. She rose from the once most powerful man of Soebo to redress in her black robe. She coiled the rope about her waist while she checked escape routes.

The se-Tufi Who Finds Pebbles, her crone mother in Kaiel-hontokae, had said that the Liethe ruled Geta. Perhaps it was true. She looked down at the priest she had forcibly imprisoned in his own skull, her killer instincts still at full alert for he was not the only danger. How alone it was to have power. She could never share this triumph even with Hoemei who understood power.

Quietly she set up an apparatus to drip poison into t'Fosal through a tube connected to the blood vessels of his wrist. She had given much thought to the choice of the poison. It was temperature-resistant and not affected by roasting. It was slow-acting even in huge doses but still lethal in minute quantity. And it was known only to the Liethe who had developed it accidentally while trying to eliminate some of the common side-effects of a drug used to retard senility.

Afterwards, she lifted Nie to the bed, laying him out in a pillowed comfort he could not feel. All day he marinated in the poison, but before it killed him she slashed his wrists and let him bleed to death. She left a knife in his hand in the normal position for Ritual Suicide, though the simplest autopsy would discover that he had been murdered. No routine autopsy known to the Mnankrei would indicate that he was poisoned bait.

The long shadows across the room faded into the

dimness of twilight while Humility cleaned out every clue to her presence. When the nocturnal stars opened their eyes she left by the window whose lock had been repaired. It clicked shut and she became a rooftop shadow again.

54

If a man has been tamed,
The woman is never blamed.

From the Liethe *Veil of Chants*

In the days that followed her execution of Nie t'Fosal,
Humility stayed with moody High Wave Ogar tu'Ama,
feeding him what little he could eat, listening to his self-
recriminations, his foreboding, his wild plans. Her quiet
sister, Flesh, who did not like to be beaten, loved this
gentle man but Humility pitied him. She had been the
companion of Aesoe the Prime Predictor and Hoemei the
Thinker Who Could Act. She longed to teach white-
haired Ogar of the slashed face the art of leadership, but
he was too old. He could make fiery speeches and
pinpoint moral issues but he could not delegate authority
and somehow in his long life, with only one wife and no
husbands to help him, he had never been simultaneously
in all the places he had needed to be to block the Swift
Wind.

The murder of the Winterstorm Master had shaken
him. At first he was elated and gave his Comfort a rousing
speech on the new glories that now awaited the Mnankrei
while he broke out a special bottle of whisky. Then drunk,
he became obsessed that he would be blamed for the
murder. Finally, with the empty bottle hugged in both
hands, he gloomed that the murder meant nothing, that
the young ones of the Swift Wind would simply take over
and run a more ruthless ship.

He snored away his stupor until sunrise, then contritely helped her fix the meal though Mnankrei men traditionally found kitchen work demeaning. They played game after game of chess. She could not beat him; he was a chess dobu. He refused a game of kol. Its strategy was too real.

'I'm going for a stroll. You nap,' she said.

Humility chose a direction down the Grand Avenue and then over along the Blue Canal where there were few people. When the orange furnace of Getasun became a distorted red oval at sunset, the great gongs began to sound over Soebo in a dirge for t'Fosal. She listened quietly. The rollings of the bass vibrations were the echo of her deed reflected off the mountainous grief of hundreds of the Mnankrei who had allied themselves with his vision. She returned home to find Ogar dressing for the Funeral Feast.

He had decided to drop overboard the grudges of the past. Death meant a new beginning. If he showed good will and partook of the body of their leader, perhaps they would show good will, too, and begin a programme of reform.

'You will not go to that man's Feast!' Humility was astonished by this new tack. 'Where is your morality? How could you face your people with his flesh as part of you?' She knew of no other way to handle Ogar's sudden rationalization than rage, but her rage was real enough.

She had to argue. She had to threaten to leave him. She called in his friends and juggled the chaos of their conflicting positions until she won. She made them write down a manifesto. Those who disapproved of the policies of t'Fosal would absent themselves from the Feast as a declaration of what they stood for. It was dangerous to make a public show of opposition to the Swift Wind, and they debated the dangers interminably as they composed their manifesto, muting *this* phrase, and padding *that* one with double meanings. They were accepting the danger, with prodding, but Humility was internally enraged that they did not make the gesture spontaneously.

Thus it went.

Ogar was an old man but his vacillations carried with them the energy of the sea, sometimes calm, sometimes cresting and troughing with sickening speed. She was appalled. This was the man that crones would place as the Master of the Mnankrei? Controlling him was exhausting and she called for Flesh to spell her while she took an earned rest walking the heart of Soebo as Sugarpie.

It was as Sugarpie that she first heard the rumours telling of the sickness and death of the powerful men of the Swift Wind who had attended the sombre Funeral Feast. A relieved and then gleeful Queen of Life-before-Death skipped over a puddle and began to play Miss the Crack on the cobblestones and managed twenty-seven hops before she slipped. Sugarpie wandered from bakery to n'Orap skin shop to stall to bazaar to park, her curiosity aflame, listening and provoking response and adding her own black comment now and then to the wild rumours.

Her wagging tongue was of the opinion that the virulent disease the Mnankrei priests had launched against the Gathering had got loose and been caught by the creators and it served them right for mixing the sacred and profane in ways God had never intended and God only knew but that this horrible disease which made your eyes bulge and your head wobble might break out all over the city soon enough.

Soebo was terrified by nightfall.

In the morning the rumours were even worse. Over one hundred Mnankrei had died in the night and they were being *cremated* in secret! It was horrifying! They had become unclean! The best of the Swift Wind were unfit to eat! And the Kaiel! The *ghosts* of the defeated Kaiel were

404

advancing on the city and they were coming with the vengeful fury of the sinister winterstorm, piling the waves before them like a wall moved by the wind.

Humility had spent the night as Comfort describing to Ogar in rich detail the dying agonies of those who had been foolish enough to pay homage to the great t'Fosal at his final Feast. A long night it had been, and the rumours were well into their late morning form before she heard them. Unbelievable! The judges were coming! She rushed from tu'Ama's residence to the hive, striding, sometimes running.

'Is it Bendaein or Joesai?' she asked, breathless.

'It is Joesai the Scythe,' said the crone.

Humility turned her face because tears had burst upon her cheeks. Without dressing for the journey, she hired an Ivieth palanquin to carry her towards the Gathering as far as those giants would take her and then continued impatiently on foot, still wearing Comfort's flighty morning dress which had been chosen to please the High Wave to make up for her teasing.

She saw them before they saw her. They were hardly the storm wave that the morning gossip described. She recognized them because each of the distant figures carried a rifle. They moved with no great speed. A small group would take some high point, whether it be hill or roof, from which to cover the flow of their fellow judges. Behind that point she assumed was the main body of Kaiel youth. She pressed on, cursing herself for not bringing walking shoes. She was captured by one of the girls she had taught to dance.

The three female riflemen handled her more roughly than any men would have. They tied her hands behind her back so tightly her fingers went numb and they dragged her along the road through the Gathering on a long leash about her neck that nearly choked the breath from her. Those they met gave her a wide detour. Even Joesai, walking with the two-wheeled supply wagons, would not come closer to her than several man-lengths.

She bowed to him, kneeling and touching her head to the ground, graceful even though her hands were tied.

'Just the woman I want to skin alive.' He was scowling.

'Why? Have I committed some crime?' She spoke up to Joesai, from her knees, defiantly.

'To some, I won't say who, the murder of a Kaiel is no crime.'

'You are a ghost then, as the rumours in Soebo say?'

'Ho! You tease me. But three of my judges died.'

She bowed her head. 'For that I am sorry. Eight Liethe also died, and more horribly.'

'The Liethe die, too? For that I am sorry,' he mocked.

'I have come for my reward,' she said brazenly.

He grunted. 'I am willing to reward you with a knife to your wrists.'

'I would prefer that you transfer into the name of the Liethe the deeds to the Soebo Palace of Morning. That was to have been my present from t'Fosal and I want it! You, too, promised that if I helped you, the Palace of the Morning would be my gift!'

Joesai laughed a genuine laugh of amazement. 'Is it usual in Soebo to reward treachery so lavishly?'

'Are you not all alive? Most of you? For that you may kiss my feet.' Her voice trembled. 'I was afraid that I had miscalculated and you were all dead. But you are more than alive! You have become invulnerable! Liethe gifts are not given freely. I have earned my reward!'

He went to his haunches so that their conversation might be less awkward. 'You speak like a madwoman.' He loosened her collar. 'Perhaps your brain has been deprived of oxygen? I am to reward you for bringing t'Fosal's sacred disease to my camp?'

Humility smiled insolently. 'I did not bring the disease. I brought the antidote developed at great expense in life

406

by the Liethe of Soebo. If I had brought you the disease you would all be mindless. The Liethe antidote mocks the disease and grants immunity but the micro-life carrier does not contain the genes that cripple.'

'What?'

'You have been immunized. We call the potion you received a tocaein.'

'The honoured tocaeins of our temples are the teachers of games – not the givers of pain.'

She mocked Joesai's seriousness. 'The tocaein is indeed a teacher of games. But does he play to win? Does not the tocaein deliberately handicap his moves so that the novice grows strong by winning? So it is with our potion. It attacks you only to challenge your body to great efforts so that when the real attack comes, you are ready. Your body has matched wits with a tocaein who has taught you how to resist the deadliest of Mnankrei ploys.'

Joesai softened as one of his major worries evaporated. 'You could have told us,' he said gruffly.

She watched him with a mischievous glint. 'And would you have permitted me to poison your entire camp? What if I had told you that you would be vomiting and shaking in your weakness and also delirious with sunfever? You did not even trust me!'

'I trusted you because you helped me free my men from the Temple of Raging Seas.'

'You shouldn't have. Besides I didn't even know if the Liethe antidote would work. It was very hastily concocted.'

Joesai yowled as if stung by an angry bee. 'Women like you make bitter soup.'

'Untie me, please.'

He cut her bonds. 'And what news from the city?'

'The greatest minds of the Swift Wind have been murdered. Mobs are already out, shouting, gaining courage from the visible reassurance of other like minds.'

407

'Murdered? By who?'

'It is not known.'

'And those I left behind?'

'I know that one of your Kaiel will be leading a mob to the Temple of Raging Seas. They will find the mindless women in whom t'Fosal's disease is grown and that will feed the rage and fear. The city is headless. It is yours.'

'It is not my hope to frighten the city.'

'I will introduce you to the High Wave tu'Ama. He is a just man. If you deal with him and no others, he will become leader of the Mnankrei and salvage what is left of that clan.' She paused. Studying Joesai's mood, she took his arm affectionately as if she were about to ask for another Palace of the Morning. 'Take from them their priesthood, but leave them their ships and the city will be soothed by your mercy.'

'It is a strange scene you paint. I will send men forward to confirm. If true we will move in today.'

'Strike today,' she said.

He kicked a stone. 'Will the children bring me flowers?'

'Of course. And tu'Ama, the coward, will offer me to you as a present and pay the coin I cost from his vaults.'

Joesai stepped aside and gave orders. He walked for a long while beside Humility, deep in thought, absorbing some surprise. He laughed and spoke. 'My brother Hoemei has vision. I would not have believed it. He told me that if I waited patiently enough, I would walk into the city unopposed.'

'A man only has vision into the future if he has friends who care enough to share his vision and make it real for him.' *Hoemei taught me that,* she thought, wishing she could say it. 'May I ride on your shoulders?' she cajoled.

He laughed and three riflemen who had been keeping their ears cocked also laughed. 'I'm the tired one,' complained Joesai. He lifted his leg and climbed onto *her*

408

shoulders so that she buckled and he had to walk along on tiptoes with her head between his legs.

'You're mean!' She was outraged.

'All right, little undecorated child.' He picked her up and threw her legs around his neck. She grabbed his hair and stooped to whisper in his ear. 'When do I get my Palace?'

55

It is recorded that Bendaein hosa-Kaiel took the Gathering of Outrage to the island of Mnank on an awesome strategy of evasion, moving to those places where he was least expected. Only when Soebo had been completely demoralized by his unpredictability did he send his Second Judge in a lightning thrust at the heart of the city to restore order. Even then he continued to confound all Kaiel detractors by prolonging the Judgment of Outrage to one thousand sunsets and sending to Feast only one-sixth of the surviving male Mnankrei. Bendaein's creation of the Matrix of Evidence to meet the needs of his Gathering and to avoid the excesses of previous Gatherings established the Kaiel forever as the unhurried defenders of true kalothi. Let God's Will be done! All power to the Kaiel!

Coieda mahos-Kaiel, first son of Bendaein, in *Honour for the Outraged*

Time sweeps away all things, and though the annexation of Mnank by the Kaiel had fascinated the whole Race, that was part of the past. Now the clans of Geta were concerned with more important matters such as the rayvoice, the revelations from *The Forge of War*, steam engines, rockets, kalothi among the stars. The millennium of the Saviour Who Speaks to God was at hand. In the Era of Silence, how had the Great Danger evolved?

A cool wind was blowing in over the beaches near Sorrow at the back of a hardy native girl who ran towards the tall Kaiel priest through the sand that retarded her by sinking under her feet. 'I want to ride on your shoulders! You gave Saiepa one last time and you didn't give me one!'

She came up to about the height of his hips and her nakedness was undecorated except for scarred stripes that ran from her knees to her ankles, the universal symbol of the money-lending Barrash clan. 'Ho!' glowered the giant called Joesai, 'and who says priests are fair?'

'You *have* to be fair or they'll send a Gathering after you to make themselves some shoes!'

'In that case, since you *insist* that I ride on your shoulders . . .' And he swung a foot over her head and pretended to ride her, marching along on tiptoes in the sand.

'I didn't say that! You have sand in the wax in your ears! I said: give *me* a ride on *your* shoulders!' She tried to squirm her head out from between his legs.

He squeezed his legs.

'Hey, you're pushing my ears into my brains!'

He reached down an arm and pulled her out from between his legs by the feet, hanging her upside down, one large hand around each ankle, her long hair sweeping the sand. 'And now what, little beetle?'

'Put me on your shoulders or I'll get a nosebleed,' she threatened.

He flipped her up and placed her carefully around his neck.

'That's better! Run! I like it when you run!'

And Joesai, in lucent folds cut like the chitin cover of an insect, the hontokae emblazoned in blue on its front, was suddenly thrown back to that immortal day long ago when he had entered Soebo with his Advance Court. He smiled at the ridiculous image of himself staggering into the city at the height of the insurrection like a common Ivieth with a Liethe whore riding his shoulders, having just bought Soebo with a palace he did not own.

Those had been strange days compared with his exile now. He had been in control, not because he could have done anything with the mobs, but because the mobs did

411

not want the power they had usurped – they were traditional folk, shocked by their own rage and fear. It had been a time of rushed juggling, marathon talks with every clan leader he could find, speeches at the flaming cremation for the diseased host women taken from the Temple of Raging Seas, and the consecration of 170 Ritual Suicides. The city came back to normal after six sunsets. Two weeks later Bendaein hosa-Kaiel arrived and took over. The life of the exile was very different.

Joesai often wondered about Comfort. Rumour said she had been given to Bendaein. If so he kept her out of sight at some country estate. She never wrote. The last he had ever seen of her was a surprise visit on the docks when he and Noe were leaving for Sorrow.

'Why do you live alone in that big house?' asked the girl on his back.

Joesai laughed. 'I don't live alone. You haven't known me long enough. Two-wife comes tonight from Kaielhontokae to stay for the birth of her second child. And you can be our three-wife if you learn to bake cakes.'

'I'm not Kaiel; I'm Barrash. But you can be my eleven-grandfather.'

'I'm not old enough to be a grandfather.'

'You have grey hairs.' She pulled one out and showed it to Joesai.

'That's because I owe your three-father so much coin.'

'One-mother says you are in prison. Are you a debtor?'

'My family visits me but I do not visit them in Kaielhontokae because I am in exile. Exile is not prison and my nose is firmly on my face.'

'How did you get to be a bad man?'

'I kidnap and eat little girls.'

There was a long pause from above. 'That was a *bad* joke. You even scared me. *Really* why are you bad? I'm bad, too – sometimes – so don't feel left out.'

'I fell in love with a woman who was also loved by a very

412

powerful man. She had my child, and he does not want me around so he never forgives me.'

'That's sad. A man who keeps a woman for himself is not polite. Do you miss her?'

He laughed. 'But she comes into my life. We see each other to share our son, meeting at the sky-eye in the mountains. I brought some lens grinders back with me from Soebo. Did you know that Getasun is a double star? We share space with a distant midget sun that is red and hardly bigger than Nika. It was discovered by a Mnankrei girl not much older than you. I made shoes out of her fathers and she tried to kill me so I adopted her. She has great kalothi. She always wanted to be a navigator but Mnankrei women are not allowed on ships so I'm training her as an astronomer. If she passes her Trials I will make a Kaiel of her.'

'Did you kill her fathers?'

'No. They slit their own wrists.'

'I wouldn't want to be a priest. They're always killing people. You won't kill my fathers, will you?'

'No, not unless they want their money back too soon.'

'There was a priest who was chasing the Gentle Heretic. He killed her.'

'No, he didn't. I used to think he had, but today I bought a book that she wrote after she last saw him.'

'Are you a Follower? My mothers say it is all foolishness.'

'Oelita the Clanless One is human like us all. She is foolish and wise at the same time. She has passed the Sixth Trial of the Kaiel Death Rite and that means she has great kalothi which is better than wisdom.' Six out of seven.

'You sound like a Follower. They are all over.'

'No, I'm not a Follower. I'm the priest.'

'You're *him*?' She squirmed and slipped off Joesai's back. She turned and stopped at a distance of four man-

413

lengths. 'I'm not a Follower, either,' she said. Then she fled.

Joesai carried the title of Coastal Predictor. The de-priested Stgal had built his residence overlooking a curving beach that pointed out towards three rocks rising from the Njarae that, since olden times, had been called the Old Man, the Mother, and the Child of Death. Joesai loved his family's new mansion and, though it was far from finished, it had the beauty of Life Incomplete. (Perhaps he didn't like the wirevoice pole.) The Stgal spent at least one lifetime on a building they cared about, feeling how it was lived in before they added the next organic layer. When the Stgal had been broken as priests Teenae logically decreed their new role as architects. They were clumsy with chemistry and rule but, ah, the miracles they made with stone and wood and mortar!

He toured the rooms, seeing that all was ready for Teenae, his anticipation stirring his dormant loins. The cactus flower was blooming and he moved it to a prominent position in the light from the tall leaded window. The lustre of the wooden table disappointed him and he found oil for a rubdown. The fruits and breads that Teenae liked were in stock.

He took special care with his room for that was where they would sleep. It was a kind of formalism they had developed over their marriage. When he arrived from a journey, he would spend his first evening in the bed chamber of one of his wives and when a wife had journeyed she became a guest of her husbands.

He poured his best whisky into a better bottle and washed the shot glasses a second time until they sparkled, remembering how Teenae hated to drink from spotted glass. He bathed and perfumed his underarms and put on his cleanest undergarments.

The wirevoice chimed. When he answered, disembodied male words from Sorrow's switchery told him

414

Teenae was on the way. *God help us if the copper line ever reaches Kaiel-hontokae,* he thought grumpily, but quickened the pace of his preparations.

From a balcony in the sloping roof he watched her arrive by four-wheeled skrei-wheel powered by a male and female Ivieth couple. He let them unload her iron-reed basket, then set off two rifle-powder bangers whose crack! crack! made the three of them look up in time to see his rocket rise on sparking tail to explode in a blue flash that spread across the sky while it burned to a dazzling white.

'Joesai!' Teenae screamed up at him, 'you'll scare the neighbours out of their skins!'

'This lonely exile welcomes you home, beloved!'

He rushed downstairs to meet her. Teenae was directing the placement of her basket and flashed him the open smile that had addicted him to her. She waited until the basket was safe before she hugged him. 'Your bathwater is hot,' he said.

'Don't you ever think of anything besides giving me a bath! The world is falling apart and all you can think of is having a wife on your pillows who doesn't smell! Oh Joesai, I'm too exhausted for even a bath! To think I once *walked* over the mountains!'

'With a little help from our tall friends.'

'I'm heading straight for the whisky and I know where you hide it!'

He followed her to his room, where she poured herself an amber gulp, downed it, undressed, and began to sponge her body with cold water. He tried to help. She pushed him away.'Keep your hands off me,' she said almost angrily. 'You know how I am when I haven't been with you for a long time. I have to get used to you again. You're so big!' Her pregnancy was showing, her belly just beginning to swell with child. Hoemei's this time.

'Where's Gatee?' Gatee was her baby daughter by Gaet.

'I left her in the mountains with relatives. Noe or Gaet

will pick her up when they come out. I thought I'd have you all to myself for a while before Noe arrives to distract you. Hoemei is coming, too. I hope. I practically had to put a ring in his dong and haul him here by chain. There's trouble in Kaiel-hontokae and I want him away from it.'

'I've heard nothing.'

'Because nothing is blabbered over the rayvoice. I'm too tired to talk about it.' She sank onto the pillows, her profile outlined like stitching in a quilt, her last bit of energy used up. He smiled warmly, just happy to have her with him again, relishing every ridge of the cicatrice design that flowed down her back and up over the hills of her rump. The best of the artistry was the wheat stalk of the Heresy that she had put there to fill the last gap on her body to defy him, to tell him that she was a finished woman and no longer a child bride who had to listen to him, a decision which led to her swinging upside down from the yardarm of a Mnankrei ship for a whole night.

He touched Oelita's slim book that he had bought from a man who did not know Joesai as the priest who had cast the Death Rite upon his prophetess. It was a present for Teenae. She had a special place in her heart for Oelita. But he took his hand away from the cloth binding. Tomorrow, when she was rested.

Teenae shifted her legs and looked up at Joesai. 'I'm not asleep yet. Hug me a little. Don't be shy. You know I'll be madly in love with you again by about the time Scowlmoon goes into eclipse, which isn't too long to wait. Lover.'

Much later they made love with a sleepy passion. Her half-awake sighs faded back to unconsciousness but when he tried to leave, she held him. So he waited for a while, enjoying the warmth of her, before he brought some simple food to their bed. He sat on the pillows while she ate and with his lather and knife shaved the centreline over her skull from forehead to the nape of her neck. He rubbed his nose in her hair, smelling the black silkiness of it. They chatted.

'Gatee has teeth and she has decided to bite everything!'

'Did anyone ever restore the masonry on the north face?' He was referring to their mansion in Kaiel-hontokae.

'Long ago.'

'I miss the city.'

'I, for one, am glad to be away. Hoemei has finally split with the Expansionists and you can't believe the uproar that caused! Aesoe is after his hide and when two-husband goes to the Palace he avoids Aesoe. He's furious at the blindness of the Expansionists. He's pulled in a whole group to support him. Aesoe calls their proposals and predictions Stomach Thinking because Hoemei's basic policy is Digest first, Eat Later. The conflict is dangerous because the split is basically along creche and non-creche lines.'

'That's been coming for a long time.'

'You Who Were Born of the Machines are in the minority.'

'That won't last.'

Teenae frowned. 'It is not logical. The Expansionists want to move out rapidly and the only ready source of the priests they must have is the creches and that means they must sharply curtail the mortality rate of the Trials, but if they do that for long the creche children will be in the majority.'

'Aesoe will be dead by then and won't care. And remember, his children will mainly come from the creches.'

Teenae gestured impatiently. 'I don't even think that is the real issue. Kathein is seeing Hoemei, more and more openly – she moons over him publicly, and makes no secret of her sexual interest in him. That drives Aesoe 'wild and he is about to exile Hoemei, too, or worse. I sent Gaet to talk to her, and she was her usual sweet self, but distant and uncommunicative. Hoemei thinks he is reaching her and will bring her back to us, but I think she is using him in some way I cannot compute.'

'She loves and hates Aesoe,' said Joesai. 'I caught the breath of it when last at the mountain observatory. We were discussing finances. I carried a gold bar as gift from the Mnankrei for the new sky-eye.' He paused. 'I was telling her of my policy of supporting and adopting Mnankrei children who have shown an aptitude for the priesthood and how that was paying off in good will. And she was telling me how she gets coin, bags of it, from Aesoe.'

Joesai threw his hands up in despair. 'Aesoe is mad. He is so possessed by her that he strains all projects to please her whims. Thank God her whims are in line with the goals of Geta. I've come to see her as a religious fanatic. She is determined that in her lifetime our son will rise to meet God in a rocket. Everything to that end. It drives her. She hates Aesoe but he is the centre of power so she loves him in order to get what she wants. I no longer know her myself. I've tried to seduce her but she won't have me. What am I to her? An exile who wanders the beaches.' He smiled. 'Remember how shy she used to be? And how the least encouragement would bring the kalothi power welling out of her?'

'She has placed Hoemei in great danger.'

Joesai laughed. 'I see that Kaiel-hontokae hasn't changed a bit since I was last there.'

'Kathein knows that Hoemei will be the next Prime Predictor and she is damming the mountain waters at both ends.'

'You think Hoemei has even a chance at that exalted position? He is creche. The non-creche would never permit it.'

Teenae rose to a straight sitting position with a fury that made her breasts point like fists. 'The succession is not an issue of votes! It is a matter of an audit of the predictions! Such is in Tae's constitution!'

'And have the Kaiel ever hesitated to break the rules?'

'I've called a family council. We'll all be here, in one spot, for once. I don't know what we'll talk about. I did it to get Hoemei out of the city.'

Joesai laughed the great laugh and threw Teenae around his neck like a shawl. 'The world is one big creche.' And he took her to her room to see her new furniture.

'It's here!' exclaimed a delighted Teenae.

The wood was the finest desert Okkai, planed and oiled to show a black grain. The surfaces were inlaid with polished Mnankrei leather, lead pebble holes and all, and was bordered with carved squares from the skull of Tonpa.

'Sorrow's craftsmen are good,' he said.

She wiggled in delight. 'The next low night we spend here! I'm so pleased! When I make your child it will be in this room!'

He chose that moment to present her with Oelita's bound book, done in the crude print of a secret print shop. 'She's alive.'

Teenae's eyes widened and he could see her heart begin to pound. 'How do you know?'

'They keep knowledge of her from me. This book was kept from me. If she is dead, why would they protect her? But that's not the reason I am confident of her health – in this book she speaks of God. She has worked Him into the weft of her warp. That means that she has recovered from the shock of discovering that God exists and so has passed safely through the Sixth Trial.'

Teenae burst into tears. 'I've hoped so to hear that she was all right. So she believes in God now, does she? Do we?'

'Four weeks ago when I was last at the observatory there

was a perturbation in His Orbit that can't be accounted for by gravity. Whoever He is, He is not passive; He stirs in His Sleep.'

'We should have married Oelita. Our antagonism was immature.'

'I know where she is,' he said.

When a startled Teenae looked up at her husband she saw an old glint in his eyes. He was older, more cunning, and less stubborn than he had ever been. 'No!' she said. 'I forbid it! Leave her alone. That's over! Six is enough!'

He smiled gently. 'I only meant that she revealed her location in her book. There's a touch of the hermit philosophy in the images she uses. She can't be far from Kaiel-hontokae. There are records of the old hermit haunts.'

'Leave her be, Joesai. For God's Sake!'

He would not answer his wife. He showed her the new clothes he had bought for her and dressed her and took her down to the tall leaded windows where he read to her from Oelita's book.

56

Once there was a poor girl of the clan of oe'San whose family lived beside the river Toer making their way by pounding clothes on the rocks to free them of dirt and stiffness. Her riches were long eyelashes and a flirting smile and a body carved in the most intricate cicatrice forms by her father. She owned one ragged gown that often embarrassed her when it tore. She dreamed of mansions with pink glass and coloured tapestries and cloud-like pillows in the bedchambers. She dreamed of travelling by carved palanquin with four mighty Ivieth as her servants. In her dreams she rode ships to the lands of hoiela cloth where tailors fitted her for weddings and tall men took her to the games in the high temple rooms. Her dream words spilled like poems from her mouth. She reddened the whitest pillow cloth with her love. Casually heaped food steamed on golden plates. There was no poverty anywhere in her dreams.

But when she pounded those robes in the Toer and wrung them dry for her basket, she knew that it was coin which bought such dreams. With every whack she vowed that she would never remain poor like her family. She would find the gold and platinum and the silver to live her dreams.

I passed an old woman of the clan of oe'San living by the river Toer. Her riches were long eyelashes and golden teeth and a body carved in the most intricate cicatrice forms. She owned one ragged gown held together by heavy thread that passed through pierced coins that weighted her every move and jingled. I showed her one silver coin and she reached for it with a flirting smile, but I held back, asking for her dreams. 'I dream of money,' she said, and stitched the coin into her rags.

The Hermit Ki from *Notes in a Bottle*

Once Kathein had thought she could subdue Aesoe by draining his wealth to feed each of her vast projects, but he had always found more coin. She discovered to her horror that she could never break Aesoe; she could only bankrupt the Kaiel. In a desperate walk along the Hai aqueduct she was trying to figure out a way to leave him.

She could not deny that he had pleased her. He was good-natured and carried brilliance enough to match her own. She loved his parties. She loved the casual way he wielded power, bending rules, doing whatever had to be done. But she *hated* him.

God's Mind, that man is awesome! Because of him, she had a clan of her own, destined she thought, to be so dynamic that it would rule beside the Kaiel. Because of him she had been able to snap her fingers and create an instant family – in which she did not belong.

She had everything. She had a son she adored. Nobody believed her but he would be the Saviour Who Speaks to God. She could feel it. He had Joesai's strength and her mind. But his father was far away in exile.

She had intellectual adventure. The breaking of the code that had led to the revelations of *The Forge of War* was enough excitement for one lifetime. But more had followed. Hints from descriptions of military weapons had propelled her simultaneously into subatomic theory and cosmology and all the land between, from rayvoice instruments that could be etched into a thumbnail of silicon to rockets that could reach God.

And yet she was alone.

The happiest time of her life had been that brief courtship with the maran family. It seemed so long ago. When she first met Gaet, showing him one of the first primitive rayvoices, there had not been a wirevoice in all of Kaiel-hontokae; now they were everywhere, weaving their copper webs like an insect species gone wild at the discovery of a new prey. Men had walked; now they rode their skrei-wheels. The Kaiel had been a clan confined to the mountain steppes; now they ranged over half the

Njarae and in the northeast were pressing against the Itraiel. Life had become a maelstrom.

How does one refuse a man of power?

Sometimes, at the height of her hatred for Aesoe, in those rare times when she had taken Hoemei to the pillows out of a kind of nostalgia for lost love, the tenderness she met was almost too much to bear. Gaet still courted her but with the genteel formality of the compulsive flirt. It was a duty he felt towards all women. Joesai's love had turned to anger and that puzzled her. She kept track of them all. Noe had been to Soebo, a logistics coordinator for the Gathering. Teenae was still trying to organize the world into logical categories — contracts were to be met, secrets were to be kept, and betrayal was to be answered with a lead pebble between the eyes.

An Ivieth found Kathein on the road. He gave her water and watched her sceptically when she told him she was all right. He made the decision that she should come back with him to the city. The Ivieth were keepers of the road and none defied them there, not even priests.

So she arrived at the Kaiel Palace anyway, her revolt short-lived. She was half a day late and Aesoe was distraught. He was not pleased with her leggings or the dust in her hair or the dirt clogging her toenails. He sent her with his servant, one of his budding creche daughters, to be bathed and dressed. After an interval of sufficient length to have allowed a woman to wash off the first layer of grime, he arrived in the bathhouse himself to hold court as was the custom among the Kaiel when they had lost time and matters were pressing. Such was Aesoe's way of telling Kathein that he was displeased with her tardiness.

He brought with him two priests of the Itraiel, both formally attired in headdresses of iridescent insect wings and in black suits fronted by scarf-like collars of brass mail. Each wore large brass buckles inlaid with erotic platinum figures that hooked down to protect the genitals. Black leggings of iron cloth hugged the skin, their interwoven platinum tracery describing the same lethal flower that scarred the faces of the priests.

They bowed to her in the tub, and if they were astonished by Kaiel custom, they did not show it. They did not bathe in water and bathhouses were not within the stricture of their rules. Kathein coldly extended her dripping hand and each man kissed it in turn.

'Kaesim of the kembri-Itraiel,' said one.

'Suesar of the kembri-Itraiel,' said the other.

Aesoe brought his mistress a bowl of rinse water. 'Our honoured friends travelled with the Gathering to Soebo and served as administrators there and are now returning home. They offer us a proposition we must take seriously. I wish you to discuss with them the weapons of *The Forge of War.*'

Kathein wiped the foaming suds from her hair with several backstrokes of her hands. The weapons of the Riethe madmen were not her favourite subject. 'Why?'

'Kaesim and Suesar have been observing our rule in Soebo and have decided that there are advantages to ceding their land to the Kaiel. This is, of course, a bargain, and our end of the bargain must have substance.'

Kathein poured the warm rinse water over her head. Her reply was sarcastic. 'In exchange we give them weapons to fry whole towns, cities even, and machine rifles to murder more women and children than can be eaten before they rot?'

Suesar bowed. He was not insulted. 'You impugn our morality,' he said formally.

Kathein laughed. 'No. I was questioning the sanity of my bedmate.'

'Sanity!' Aesoe snorted. 'Even Hoemei believes that the Sky is full of enemies and that we survive only because we have not been found. God's Sky is also full of other gods, and where one god has gone, so can another bring himself. And what is our defence? Shall we sit and beat these Sky Demons at kol? Shall we take them through the desert and covertly scratch their legs so that they sicken and pass away? Shall we pompously declare them of low kalothi and offer them the knife and a pretty courtesan in some temple tower? Who is to defend us, Kathein? The Race is not alone!'

'The fire that burns the son, burns the daughter!' Water cascaded from Kathein as she stood and stepped into the towel held by Aesoe's daughter-servant.

'Geta needs a "military" clan.' Aesoe used the word from *The Forge of War* for there was no such word in the Getan language. 'They must know the game of the enemy so that when we meet him we can define the play. Such a role I propose for the Itraiel. We rule; they defend. It is a role that requires study, foresight, dedication, bravery, great game minds and great kalothi. I think the Itraiel are worthy of this trust and will be challenged by it.'

'Perhaps.' She considered.

'We think we are well suited to the role,' said Kaesim.

Kathein cut him short. 'I know the Itraiel.'

They were fierce desert rovers, rulers of a nomadic domain. They had no knowledge of genetic manipulation and she doubted that they had a single genetics work-room. Their temples were tents. They were known for their strange gentleness. What clan made less fuss over physical handicaps? It was said of the Itraiel that they would hold up a legless man with their right hand while lopping off the legs of an enemy with their left. It was said that no man could attack a kembri-Itraiel with a dagger and live. It was said that none played games like the Itraiel. Their kalothi rituals were almost purely game-determined. At their annual competitions the big losers were expected to organize the joyful Dispersion Feast and by their Ritual Suicide provide sustenance for the long journey home. They demanded no less of the underclans who used their land.

Aesoe brought out several gowns he had ordered for Kathein, some in dubious taste. Politeness demanded that he offer the privilege of dressing her to his guests who were requested, after much bowing between the three men, to adorn her in such a way as to most please themselves. Kathein was amused. Suesar wanted no part of the ritual and stepped back a pace – a pace long enough to put Kaesim in command but short enough not to insult Kathein.

Kaesim examined the robes, absorbing yet another strange Kaiel custom with complete ease. Each perusal was accompanied by an unobtrusive glance at Kathein. Thus he was able to dress her in the attire which most pleased *her*. Kathein was willing to bet a gold piece that Kaesim was the finest diplomat of the kembri-Itraiel.

For one heartbeat she saw an image of him riding turret on a Second World War tank through the North African night with five Gurkhas hitching a ride behind him. Her soul was chilled.

She took this desert priest by the hand and led him through the Palace maze towards the aroma of Aesoe's private dining quarters. Suesar and Aesoe followed to the feast which she knew had been kept waiting and warm past its time. She seated them and served Kaesim first in repayment for his service to her. Last she carved the tiny carcass and heaped their plates with meat and gravy. The foreign priests made some sign over their food and began to eat heartily while Kathein began her stories of war, emphasizing atrocity so that she might make these men so loathe the horror of it that they would reconsider the role of warrior clan.

She told of the total extermination of the Jews in Britain on orders of the Pope so that the British people never thereafter had a Jewish problem. She told of the massacre

426

of the Persians at Thermopylae. She told of the mountain of skulls in India. She told the story of the Turks forever cursed with the blood of the Armenians. She told of the inefficiencies of Belsen and the efficiencies of Hiroshima. She told of the post First World War invasion of Poland by Russia, and the retaliatory invasion of Russia by Poland, and of the final solution to the Polish problem when the Russians, a generation later and allied with the Nazis, overran Poland and executed 15,000 members of the Polish military clan and buried them in a mass grave at Katyn.

She told of the great Amerikan Peace Movement whose theory of justice was that the brutal Amerikan Army should move out of Southeast Asia so that the Cambodians could fertilize their fields with the bodies of Cambodians so that the Vietnamese could prey on the corpse of a decimated nation so that the Chinese could punish the Vietnamese so that the Vietnamese could drown their own Chinese in the sea. She told of the sack of Rome.

The priests of Itraiel listened to her as one listens to an Ivieth chew the leg of a traveller with tales of distant places. They began to ask her questions about strategy, purpose, gain. She answered the difficult problems they posed as best she could. They tried to make sense of Hitler at Stalingrad and the perplexities so gripped them that, for a moment, they forgot their meat. They came to the tentative conclusion that the Riethe were not mad, just stupid.

'They understood weapons,' said Kaesim.

'But they did not understand strategy,' said Suesar.

Both began to question Kathein about weapons. She told them of the axe and sword and crossbow and rifle and canon and tank and fighter aircraft and helicopter gungods and long-range bombers and ICBMs and spy satellites.

Kaesim grinned through the fei flower scars upon his face. 'Maybe God is a spy satellite for the Riethe.' He laughed. They all laughed the great laugh until the tears came to their eyes, for that was too terrifying a joke to take seriously.

Kathein told of the weapons cycles that passed through Riethe history. First the bows and arrows and the staffs and slings made the individual supreme. Then the invention of the two-wheeled cart was taken over by nomads who lightened and perfected the design for rapid control of their herds. (Herds, Kathein explained, were small clans of people kept for their meat and hides and milk). The chariot was pulled by a Horse.

'The Horse piece of chess?'

'The Horse is historical? Not mythical?'

'The Horse of *The Forge of War*,' explained Aesoe, 'is a very large humanoid creature with a long face and four legs and no arms.'

The Itraiel priests grinned hugely and clinked shot glasses of whisky to this image of a four-footed Ivieth trying to pull a wagon.

'Horses were expensive and hard to train. Chariots were costly, so a select military clan grew up around them and swept down over Mesopotamia and India and as far east as China, killing all the priests who were not afraid of them.' She smiled at Aesoe.

'The confusion of weapon with strategy,' commented Kaesim.

Kathein told of the next wave of weapons: long daggers of cheap iron, wielded like staffs, that made the individual soldier supreme again. An untrained man with an iron sword was a match for a highly trained and wealthy aristocrat in his chariot. So aristocracies died.

Then came the light Horse mounted by an archer. The foot soldier with iron sword and spear and shield was no longer effective. The only defence was an armoured Horse and an armoured rider who took years to train and the wealth of a village to support. Central government collapsed. The man whose sword no longer defended his family lost power to the armoured warrior of his village who became a hereditary priest.

But the exploding powder of char and sulphur and nitrate was invented. A man with no training and a musket became the equal of the armoured lord. The lords were swept away in revolutions that gave power to the common man.

Weapons grew more sophisticated. Machine rifles, aircraft, tanks, artillery, seagoing battlegods. Clans with industrial power learned to sweep away the riflemen. ICBMs that held ransom over cities were manned by an elite corps trained at great expense. The common man ceased to be a soldier. He refused to be drafted. Professional armies rose to power. Democracies crumbled. Socialist aristocracies took their place, exploiting the now impotent common man.

Then in the everlasting search for more sophisticated weapons the insect-sized machine-mind came as cheap iron had come at the end of the bronze age. With a basket of wheat any man could buy a demon missile that would fell a huge aeroplane or roast a tank or peel open an armoured car. Industrial peoples could no longer control poor peoples. The new socialist aristocracies, no longer able to frighten the common man, withered away.

And the message was always the same. When the priest clans of Riethe dominated with their expensive weapons, their world was ruled by massacre, and when the underclans dominated with their cheap weapons, Riethe turned red with blood.

Kathein finished her analysis with an accusing glance at Aesoe as if to say: you would inflict that on us?

'The military lords of the Riethe would nourish us at our Dispersion Feast,' boasted Kaesim, unimpressed.

'The Riethe pose no absolute threat,' mused Suesar. 'They have no sense of strategy. But we will need the weapons. Even a genius is flattened by the mindless boulder rolling down the mountain.'

She was furious at them for the casual way they had taken her stories. 'You would want the responsibility of holding in your hands a machine that would make sunfire to devour a whole city?'

'We would welcome it.'

Aesoe called for entertainment. His Liethe woman entered. Honey played her instrument while Cairnem and Sieen danced. The dark guests shouted their encouragement and pleasure, and clapped their hands for it was that type of fast light dance. Then the priests begged to demonstrate their own skill.

They stripped so that they were only wearing their brass belts and genital protectors. Cries erupted from their lips as they began to circle each other on the dance floor, hissing. Suesar snarled and attacked and through the magic of swiftness and leverage was thrown high where it appeared he would crash onto the floor. But he pulled and twisted in mid air and landed on his feet.

Of the three Liethe only the Queen of Life-before-Death stayed to watch the combat, rapt with fascination, wearing the persona of Cairnem.

The play of kembri wills continued, where a gesture might rescue one from a smashed skull, or an attack might seem to pass right through an opponent. They bowed to Aesoe's foot stamping. Cairnem grinned.

Before they had finished their bows, she was hissing a challenge. The priests turned in astonishment because she had used the kembri form of major insult. While they stared, she repeated her insult and stripped to her belt, a tiny belt with a wooden buckle that matched her tiny size. The priests burst out laughing.

A flash of flesh moved at them and they had to react quickly to stop her. They made kembri noises and she hissed back. There was a rapid exchange of words and then she attacked again, first one, then the other. Kathein gripped her chair. She expected the girl to be killed, for she was often thrown, once with a cracking thud, but she always rolled and flipped to a standing position. Finally she stopped, exhausted, the sweat rolling off her unscarred body, still grinning happily. The men were grinning, too.

'Cairnem uses the kembri form "otaimi",' Suesar explained, 'which can be executed by small women but not by men as large as us. She is good.'

'But I lost three to one. And they gave me handicaps.'

'Two against one is hardly fair,' bowed Kaesim, 'but your form of insult gave us no choice.' His grin had not left his face.

'My dance teacher was trained in the kembri arts by Niel of the kembri-Itraiel.'

'Ah, yes? Niel!'

Cairnem was all Liethe grace now and she had an arm for each of them. 'I'm part of the hospitality. You may have me this evening.' She turned to Aesoe. 'I lost to them after insulting their genitals and it is obligatory that I pleasure their egos. So give me permission.' She looked Aesoe straight in the eyes.

'And if they had been defeated?' Aesoe queried.

'Why, then they would have had to pleasure me.'

'I see that I have lost my warriors for the evening. The bargaining will continue tomorrow.'

Tonight I will tell him, thought Kathein.

But when they were alone in his bedchamber, she hesitated and found other things to talk about. He was light and witty, having chosen to forget her tardiness, and she found it easier to joke than to confront him. *I'll undress him* – like she had seen Sieen do so many times – *and when he is warmed by my fingers, then I will tell him*. But she couldn't go near him.

'I've made a major decision,' she said. She was huddled by the window.

431

'Yes, you want to start building that proton accelerator, or is it something less grandiose?'

'The maran-Kaiel are all in Sorrow.' She stopped. She couldn't go on.

'I gave them the Valley of Ten Thousand Graves. Sorrow is where they should be.'

'I'm going to Sorrow.' She took a deep breath.

'I know you are fond of them. Is it necessary to keep telling me?'

'I'm going there to . . . marry them.'

He didn't even react. It drove her crazy, the calmness of that man, except when it was something trivial. Then he would rage.

He pulled out a hair from his nose. 'You are already married.'

'I intend to divorce.'

'Ah, so. Divorce,' he repeated. He flicked the hair onto the floor. 'You are sure that the maran even like you anymore?'

The tears were streaming down her cheeks because she wasn't sure.

'You're leaving for Sorrow?'

'Yes.'

'I will stop you.'

'You can't.'

'But I can.' His voice told her that he would say no more. He switched off the electric torch.

She began to imagine the things he could do because he wasn't going to tell her what he would do. He could have them all killed and she would be to blame. 'Aesoe,' she pleaded to the darkness with its phantoms.

'Come to the pillows,' he said.

He could cut off the money. He could destroy her fledgling clan. She went to the bed, ran a finger down his chest, played with the hairs, gently. 'I want you to love me,' she said.

He pulled her to him, misunderstanding what she meant. She let him. What was the use. He took her. Such drive for an old man! Hoemei. She saw Hoemei with his throat cut, lying there, his arm flopped lifelessly, dripping blood from the fingers. The thrusting began. She let it happen. Joesai. Joesai had gone to Soebo. Aesoe had intended for him to die. And the Mnankrei had reached out to kill him, and when they touched him, the electron river flowed back from him and lit all of Soebo by the spit fires of roasting Mnankrei. If Aesoe tried to kill Joesai, would it be the same? would the electrons flow back from the torch and crisp Aesoe? She rode his thrusts. He was *alive*. She was dreaming. Life did not have happy endings. She saw Joesai with a lead pebble in his skull sinking to the floor. Teenae. Teenae's glazed eyes stared at a pool of her own blood. Gaet and Noe. Gaet was dead where he had tried to shield Noe and failed. Would these knifelike thrusts never stop? She moaned and her tears came in little sobs. *How I hate you,* she thought and clung to him.

She didn't believe his stories about danger from God's Sky. That was an excuse for his ambition. The armies of the kembri-Itraiel would march over Geta with their weapons, uniting the planet for the Kaiel – and Aesoe would say that it was for the best. There was danger from the stars and we must unite now, not tomorrow. Hoemei was going to try and stop him and Hoemei would dissolve in the flash of sunfire.

'My honeycomb,' murmured Aesoe.

57

Be wary of the Death Rite for you become bonded forever to the one you challenge – whether death or survival is the outcome.

From *The Kaiel Book of Ritual*

Once he knew she was alive, he had been able to find her. That was the legend of Joesai. The clues were minor and unrelated but indicated that the Gentle Heretic was re-establishing tenuous contact with the coast.

A group of trackers followed one of her messengers over the hills to the south and east into a land that grew progressively more desolate, the grey and red rock surfaces harsher, bolder. Scrub retreated to shelter, then fought desperately to defend the shabby havens that chance provided. So much of Geta was like this, so much was far worse, yet who dared the really uninhabitable regions? Even the hermits stopped short of total barrenness. The messenger was taken prisoner just before he reached Oelita.

Joesai sat rooted behind a boulder, caught between the dried branches of a dead bush, watching her through the hand spy-eye made for him by his students at the observatory. He had her. The joy welled in him.

'She seems healthy,' he said to Eiemeni and the woman Riea.

'We observed children yesterday before you came up.'

'There can't be children here!' Joesai exclaimed.

'Two of them. Very young.'

Joesai continued to watch patiently. She was bringing

water to her garden patch. Where did she get it? Presently two little figures joined her. 'My God, you're right! Two! Wait until this evening. Kidnap them when it is darkest. She won't know you are here. I'll take care of her.'

He moved in silently, avoiding the line of sight. He was standing by her well, admiring it, before she noticed him. When he turned to look at her, she was frozen.

'You found me.' A stricken anguish filled her voice. He remembered that he had felt like that the moment he saw the dead body of his brother Sanan.

'I persist in my goals,' he said.

'*Stay in the hut!*' she shouted at the twins who were rushing to her for protection.

'The children will not be harmed,' he said.

'Are you going to kill me?'

'The Death Rite is a test, not an execution.'

'You have two more chances at me. That's an execution,' she replied bitterly.

'*One* more chance. I read your last book. You believe in God now. You handled the challenge to your mind quite well. I admire you, Oelita.'

'What will happen to my children?' She was crying.

'Who is the father?'

'Hoemei.'

'My brother-husband's children are safe.' He said that sharply.

'No they aren't. You'll take them to a butchery after you've killed me. They have Ainokie's Curse.'

'No they don't. I've seen them.'

'As a recessive.'

He shrugged. 'That hardly bothers their kalothi. There's a half and half chance that they don't even carry it. When they are grown and wish children, if they have their children at a creche, that gene can be eliminated. The procedure is becoming standard among the Kaiel.'

435

He glanced at the hut. 'Go reassure them. They are frightened. They feel your fear.'

She went and he wandered through the small garden, marvelling.

When she returned the twins were quiet. Children who are afraid whine, but once they have felt the strength of their mother they can understand the necessity of silence. 'Are you going to destroy my garden and see if we can survive that?'

'No,' he said.

'Tell me why you are here!'

He ignored her. 'I'd forget how to talk if I lived in such a bleached place.'

'You learn its beauties. I've seen it when there were flowers.'

'Show me the cone. I've never climbed one of those.'

'So you can throw me off and see if I bounce?'

'Peace,' he said softly. 'Peace, for now.' He found a stone and carried it with him to the hermit's stairway. She followed him. He fitted it tightly into the new layer among the other stones and mounted to the top. She climbed behind him but stayed out of pushing range.

'It's quite a domain you have here.' His eyes swept the desolate hills and the distant mountains and the high whiffs of cloud. Scowlmoon was a broken orange rock on the horizon and Getasun blazed harshly. 'I wouldn't have lasted out here. I would have jumped into the well head first to drown myself.'

'You'd stick before you reached bottom,' she commented acidly. 'Your hair wouldn't even get wet.'

'If I lived out here, I'd be skinny.'

'My children are very good company. I don't mind this desert. I love it.'

'How long do you plan to stay?'

'I don't want my girl and boy ever to go near a temple.'

He worked his way down the spiral of the cone. 'Do you

think your children will ever have any trouble with the temples? With you as a mother and Hoemei as a father? Kalothi is hereditary, more or less.'

'How long are *you* going to stay? I want you to leave. This is my place.'

'I'm leaving when you come with me.'

'I'm not crazy!'

He laughed. 'Yes, you are.'

'Crazy people are sent to the temples for their Contribution.'

'We humour them first.' Joesai let himself smile.

He walked to the hut that was built out from a tiny cave. She followed him, agitated because he was going towards the twins, but he made no move to get close and the little boy and little girl latched onto Oelita's legs silently. He noticed a weakness in the roof and went to his backpack for materials and repaired the roof so that it might last another generation, barring an earthquake.

'Are you planning to stay?'

'We build for those who come after us so it is wise to build well,' he replied formally.

Joesai offered her his food but she refused, recalling Kaiel wizardry at drugs and potions. Oelita offered him flat cakes but he refused, politely noting the abundance of poisons in the surrounding vegetation. They laughed.

He noticed eyes watching his smile and directed it to the boy who buried his head in Oelita's arms. The girl began to compete with her brother. Her gestures were wild and she set up a chatter which her mother seemed to understand – but when she succeeded in attracting Joesai away from her small rival, she, too, fell silent and held her hands over her eyes. Only when he ignored her, did she begin to flirt again.

Oelita saw to their urination and put them on their mats for sleeping. They found all manner of excuses to stay awake to observe the stranger but lost the battle with exhaustion and cried themselves to sleep.

As Joesai prepared to leave, he turned, attacking for the first time. 'Your children are not as healthy as you think they are. It is a harsh life here. One day it will kill them quickly. Even if you broke a leg, they would die.'

She followed him out of the hut. 'I will not allow you to go unwatched,' she said.

'I intend to make camp far enough away so that you can sleep peacefully.'

'You think I'm going to sleep with you here!'

He stood silently, bulking against the starry desert sky. God began to pass overhead. God's Streak was always a spectacular sight, a pinsized glow of sun-orange light visibly moving across the void, brighter than any star. Oelita folded to her knees and with the traditional gesture of supplication, arms raised and crossed, head lifted back, made one fervent prayer: 'Let this man be gone!'

Joesai ambled away across the ravine. She followed. He kept his promise to make camp far from her abode. She hunched down to watch him, something panicky in the glow of her eyes. 'You'll need some sleep,' he said.

'I'm not going to let you sleep,' she replied.

He curled up on his mat. She poked a stick at him. He played the game, stoically ignoring her. At intervals she poked him or threw a rock. When he heard the faintest insect signal from Eiemeni, Joesai decided it was time to be annoyed. He sat up and began to curse her the way a man desperate for sleep might curse his torturer. She hurled his invective back at him, and he learned the subtleties of Sorrow's gutter language that had defended the Clanless One long ago. He shifted tactics and began to plead for her to be reasonable.

She never heard the cries when her children were being silenced. He gave up the argument and tried to go back to sleep again. She prodded him with irregular mercilessness. Only when the sudden distant wailing of babies caught her ear, to the west of her hut, did she startle and

438

pass into terror. She began to run. He followed her. She flew out of the hut, wild murder in her eyes. 'Have you killed them?'

'They are very safe, and probably very frightened because you are not with them.'

'You machine-made bastard!'

He could see her wavering. Should she stagger towards the west into the impossible night? She'd never find them. She'd have to be equipped to survive out there, and that would take time. Should she plead with Joesai? Should she risk everything and try to kill him so that he wouldn't follow her?

'I will take you to them,' he said.

She slumped in anguish. 'So you've laid your trap.'

'No. I'm taking you out of this Death's Jaw. The Seventh Trial is over. You survived it and I'm impressed.'

'You didn't cause me to come here!' Contempt and wild hope and suspicion were all in her voice.

'Who knows the workings of the Death Rite? It seems to affect the challenger as much as the one on trial. I've changed.'

'You haven't changed! What you've done now just demonstrates that! You're taking me away from my home to kill me and I have to go in blind hope for my children. You deceive me that my little haven here is the Seventh Trial. It has cherished me, protected me! My well, the abode of Death? I love this place. You will lead me from here in chains to the Seventh Trial and *that* will kill me.'

'The Seventh Trial, though the most difficult of the trials, cannot be a death but *by law* must be a measure of your kalothi. This ravine could be harsher, yes, but then it would be a simple assassin. What would it tell us of your kalothi? To have settled in *this* place and lived is possible but not probable. You have great kalothi, Oelita, and I am bonded to you by my own foolishness in casting such a Rite of Trial upon you. I owe you a Great Favour.'

439

'Then you must return my children and leave me here in peace,' she said bitterly.

'The bond of kalothi does not require me to humour my friend's madness.' He loaded her packsack. 'Your twins are waiting. They have never before been separated from you. They will be suffering.'

She had no choice but to follow him. For the most part she did so silently, but sometimes she would stab invective at his back. 'You're the same long-tailed monster I've always known!'

'I'm a mellowed monster.'

'To sip you is to quaff the burning taste of raw whisky!'

He led her over a bridge that showed them the whole dome of the stars under the desert night. 'Every life is a whisky cask with a man inside,' he said, 'and the man struggles to break through the charcoal barrier of his prison but never gets out. He only grows mellower.'

'Don't compare my life with that wooden barrel you wear for a head!'

A long pause mediated the altercation as they negotiated a razor-back outcropping. On the other side he spoke to the stones in front of his feet. 'I remember when I started this thing. I was going to deliver to God an inferior upstart. One of my wives asked me how we might be reconciled if, at the conclusion, you were to prove pleasing to God. I said this was no concern of mine because the only way you could survive was to kill me first – there was room in this world for only one of us. Thus I have created a problem for myself. Such is the way of life.' He chuckled.

'And I remember that you were enjoying yourself! I remember drowning in the Njarae while you watched as you might have delighted in watching a pinned spider in a carnivorous feiri hive!'

'Ho! You accuse me of enjoying your pain? It is true that every time I set a trap the grins were upon me, but every time you survived I found within myself this cancer-ous traitor growing in happiness. You ran from me, but in the end I, too, ran from you. I have never felt such joy as when I first saw you in my spy-eye tending your hermit's garden.'

Oelita cried when her children were brought to her from Joesai's tent. At her reappearance, the twins were too stunned to speak but clung to her. The three slept huddled together in the tent. When Oelita woke, she found Joesai stretched beside her, watching her, one young guard outside, and the noises of the eight-man camp. The sense of danger was gone. 'What are you going to do with me?'

'I have carefully considered that. I am bonded to you.'

'That could be a nuisance to me!'

'We will be married.'

She rose to her elbows, waking sleeping infants. She breathed. 'We will not!'

'Don't say I wasn't generous,' he said with Noe's straight face. 'I gave you seven chances to decline the offer.'

She stared at him, amazed. He was teasing her! She groped for words, intrigued by the game. How did one tickle a friendly monster who was known to have a bad temper? 'Is *this* your Seventh Trial: marriage? I think I've been very good at avoiding that one.' Suddenly she laughed.

'There was an ominous ring of *no* in that laugh,' he said.

'Joesai, you're mad! Of course I shall say no!'

'The Kaiel are bargainers. I will suggest a bargain. You wish kalothi for your children. Some of that mighty stuff is beyond bargain, for part of your children's kalothi is your own. Some of it comes from their father, and with Hoemei you have made a wise choice, for who is greater? Some of a child's kalothi comes from within and that, too, is beyond the help of a family or clan. But some of this elixir of life is the gift of strength grown under wise protection and that we *can* give. You saw how vulnerable you were alone? The maran-Kaiel are not alone. And we need a three-wife. Your children will thrive.'

'What of Kathein?'

'She has sold her body and her soul to Aesoe,' he said blackly.

'I was not wanted.'

'Mine was the greatest objection. We maran have a free will. We revolted at imposition from above. Aesoe's order soured us. But Teenae always loved you, first with calm logic and then with her heart, And Gaet was at least willing to try you out on the pillows.'

'My little ones will piss all over me if I do not take them out to water the flowers.'

At the tent flap, she paused, her backside to Joesai. 'I have grown old in the wilderness. I have wrinkles.'

'I have grown old waiting for you.'

'My will crumbles before your words. Have you become so used to seducing women?'

'I have been introduced to women, and women have seduced me, but I think it can be said that I have borne the brunt of this courtship. I have been clumsy.'

'Yes,' she said and was gone. He wondered if she meant yes-I-will-marry-you or yes-you-are-clumsy.

She let Reia play with the twins and returned to Joesai. 'It is nice to have a giant slave. I'm already enjoying it. Will you do anything for me?'

'Within reason.'

Her desert-etched lines wrinkled into a smile. 'Already you are trying to back out! Cut your nose off for me!'

'I like my nose.'

'Something a little less drastic, then. Kiss me.'

He reached for her and she countered. 'Not now!' In fending him off the fingers of her nearest hand closed with his fingers. Male and female hand held the other tightly,

'Once when I was a little girl I was at an engagement ruckus in the hills, I had to stand in my father's lap to see the drunks. I still remember one of the songs. The famine was over and the crops were in. A skinny boy and girl had decided to risk leaving their families. It was an excuse for people to be happy again – to laugh, to make fools of themselves.'

> At the rising of Stgi and Toe
> We sing what songs we know.
> If the underfoot is rocky slope
> We dance the dance of hope.

'I use it as a lullaby for my babies.'

'I brought you along a bag of whisky,' said Joesai.

She sneaked a glance at the face of the man whose fingers she wouldn't let go. 'Could we have a ruckus and make fools of ourselves? There are ten of us and two babies. *Then* I'll kiss you!'

58

To ride on a man's back, you must have a tight grip on his ears.

A proverb of the Liethe

The new Liethe hive in the city of Kaiel-hontokae was the old Temple of God's Praises, a mere stroll from the whisky warehouse of the old hive which was kept as a cell block for budding Liethe. In the tower of God's Praises the notorious crone known as the se-Tufi Who Finds Pebbles poured her tea into a pale blue o'ca cup that sat on top of the oiled goldwood box that was her private wirevoice. 'You wish my advice,' she stated blandly.

A woman stood in front of her with the peculiar poise that comes before the discovery of age and after the loss of innocence. 'It is more than I can handle,' pleaded Humility.

'It is always more than any of us can handle.'

'I need to make a wise decision.'

'We will live with whatever decision you make.'

'Why are you doing this to me?'

'You have been well trained, and if you fail it is our failure also. Time passes. In the same storm the river that displaces a grain of sand, replaces that grain of sand. The old die and the young grow older. When we were young, the crones did not make for us the critical decision of our lives. Thus we learned to rule before our teachers died. Before I die, I wish to see who you are when you work alone.'

'I've always worked alone,' said Humility rebelliously.

'You have obeyed our orders,' said the crone sternly.

Humility changed tactics. 'Aesoe is in violation of Kaiel law. The predictions are to be audited and the man with the best record automatically becomes Prime Predictor regardless of his political beliefs or his alliances.'

'It is not so simple. One principle that the Liethe have learned in our parasitic role is that the law is never clear no matter how many noses are grafted onto the public face. The o'Tghalie say that the law is a map and, by theorem, that every map fails to locate at least one stone.'

Humility insisted. 'I have done a major gaming of the audit myself with the help of young girls in my class who I am training in Kaiel politics. Hoemei should have been declared Prime Predictor and the policies of Aesoe should be void.'

'"Should" is a word with volume enough to paint infinity. A point in case: Tae ran-Kaiel wrote the present constitution of the Kaiel. He refined the unwritten traditions of succession that were no longer working. Indeed, he specified that audits of the Archives must take place and that the best predictor must be elevated to Prime Predictor. But no man challenged Tae in his lifetime. Even Aesoe, Tae's best student, never came close. Aesoe was declared Prime Predictor only *after* the audit following the Immortal Funeral Feast. Thus the tradition is not clear in the minds of men, however clear it is upon paper. Does the audit that determines the new Prime Predictor come before or after the death of the old Prime Predictor? May a Prime Predictor be replaced by a rival or must the rival wait on Death?'

'The law is clear,' said Humility.

'And you are in love with Hoemei. Others are not. The law is what is read, not what is written.'

'I beg you, crone mother, this matter is of some importance. Aesoe's policies have drastic consequences for the Liethe and for all of Geta, and Hoemei's policies a very different consequence.'

'Doubtless in a thousand-thousand revolutions of Geta about Getasun it shall seem as the differences between the red and blue flecks of the sandstone of the Dry Bones.'

Humility flared. 'It is against the Word of God as revealed in *The Forge of War*! Shall we be only another star among all stars? Aesoe has succumbed to wicked temptation! He would follow the policies of the Riethe devils and call it defence! Only a week ago as Cairnem I mussed the pillows of two priests of the kembri-Itraiel who have come here to negotiate with Aesoe's Expansionists, hoping to relinquish their priest status, before they are conquered, in exchange for the role of warrior clan. They would ally themselves with the Kaiel as a fighting arm and with their force unite all of Geta in one generation. We talked all night and they lusted for more than my body. They lusted for all of Geta, they lusted to walk upon Scowlmoon, they lusted for the stars and I felt their passion to the depths of me.'

'Power will always be with us. It is the way of the human.'

'But this is the very way that God has warned us against! There are many ways! I would take God's way. I need your help!'

'The decision is yours.'

'Aesoe outreaches Hoemei three to one in the number of his Kaiel allies and two to one by voting strength. Kathein sneaked away from Aesoe for Sorrow under cover of night to take the maran in marriage in open defiance of the law. The maran will be destroyed. I do not have time to make a wise decision!'

'But you contemplate a decision you consider to be unwise and expect me to save you by countermanding it. You would deny the Itraiel their warrior march among the stars in exchange for a gift to Hoemei of one cactus bloom picked at the full fragrance of highnode.'

'Yes. I would do that.'

The eyes of the crone glinted. 'The right decision is always best no matter how painful.'

'The *right* decision!' exploded Humility. 'Yours or mine!'

'Neither. This is a test of your kalothi. I give you one week of power over the destiny of Geta for the next thousand generations. See what you come up with. I repeat, the decision is yours.'

'You and your illusions that we dong-kissers rule Geta!' stormed Humility in open rebellion, jerking her finger upward at the tower. 'Our rayvoice doesn't even speak today! At the library I tried to find out the numbers of the Itraiel and no one knows. And you want me to make a decision in the flutter of a heartbeat that God has pondered silently since you were born!'

'It was ever thus.'

'The crones will accept the *consequences* of my decision, whatever that decision?'

'Of course.'

'Good!' she snapped and left, the fabric upon her small body fluttering in agitation behind her.

59

The eyes of the audience must be upon the assistant when the magician's hands are distorting reality.

A proverb of the Liethe

Humility paused on the ladder of the tower, watching the sunset's reds flash off the windows of Kaiel-hontokae, before she continued up the ladder to the tower rooms of her young friend, the ru-Paie Who Catches Redflies, an adept of the rayvoice quite capable of designing devices that even the Palace Kaiel did not have. Her line was young – as yet only six units of the ru-Paie had been cloned – and Redflies was the first of them to leave Hivehome, still concubine to the crone who had brought her across the Njarae. She was teased about her virginal innocence more than most girls. Recently her peers at the whisky warehouse had served her a mock male genital in her soup when the crones weren't looking. Humility watched over her.

'You're my one friend who isn't afraid of that ladder!' greeted Redflies.

'Did you ever find out from anyone the population of the Itraiel plains?'

The girl smiled in a way that was going to bewitch many male bodies. 'I don't think we ever will. We don't even have a rayvoice in the Itraiel. I'll keep trying.'

'No,' Humility decided, 'you have better ways to discipline your time.'

'My table is a mess, isn't it?'

Humility smiled in wonder. 'I used to understand rayvoices.'

'This is a web I think will give better sensitivity for less antenna length. I think.'

'Can it wait on a party at the Palace tonight?'

Redflies turned with anxious grace. 'I'll have to ask permission of my crone.'

'I have permission to take you whenever I need you. Your crone tells me you are ready.'

'But men are different!'

'In a week you'll be making as good dong soup as the rest of us.' They both laughed.

'Do I get to serve drinks and make witty sayings?'

'You are very good at the Fire Dance. I had that in mind.'

Redflies turned her head in modesty. 'I have only been practising. The Fire Dance is for a woman of great passion.'

'Or a girl whose passion is just igniting. You will be dancing for an audience of two hundred but your eyes will be for one man.'

'Two hundred! I'll be embarrassed!'

'The White Mind will banish all trepidation and the Circling Focus of Seduction will pull Kasi mon-Kaiel to you like he was iron from sand.'

'Does it really work that well?'

'Yes, but to make sure, I'll pass by at just the right time and whisper to him that you are a virgin. He is a middle-aged romantic. See that his foolishness is not in vain. I want his nose in the pocket of a woman I trust.'

'A girl,' she corrected.

'Not after you meet him.'

Redflies turned, stricken, to her component-scattered table. 'What of my web?'

Humility grinned. 'Think about its copper and glass intricacies while you make soup between his crotch and he will be awed by the intensity of your interest in him.'

'You're not very romantic.'

'Sometimes I am.' A wistful smile.

'Is he like Hoemei?' asked Redflies coyly.

Stabs of sadness passed through Humility. Hoemei's affair with Honey had languished while Humility had been in Soebo and had never recovered. The other Honeys hadn't cared. With Noe gone and Teenae on the coast, he had concentrated on the hopeless courtship of Kathein the Slut. Damn the pain of the soul! Unrequited love could dismember one's sanity. 'There are few such as Hoemei.'

'I'd like to sleep with *him.*'

Standing, Humility wrapped her arms, from behind, around her sitting friend. 'You would, would you!'

'When you're a crone, of course.'

'You'll make fewer mistakes on an older man. They're good for practice. Kasi is handsome and so gentle that he imagines only a virgin girl could appreciate his tenderness.'

'My crone says all Kaiel men are handsome. That's what makes them so arrogant. What does he look like naked? With his girdle off?'

'Like the stars thrown into the firmament, like stones thrown into a lake. Maybe to you he would look like a dozen transmitting rayvoice stations.'

'In less flowing language that means his body is scarred in spirals or circles.'

'Circles.'

'Why do you want to use me in such a hurry? I always thought that it would come slowly. First a man would see me nude and I would not look at him. The second time I would undress and lock eyes with his. He would not be allowed to touch me until the third time and only after he had dreamed about me for weeks and was wild with desire would our bodies join.'

'With such cynical crones to raise us, where do girls like you come from?' wondered Humility.

'I was born for love.'

'Then listen to the romance of politics. Kasi is the Auditor of Predictions. He has been lax in his duties. There is a sudden necessity for him to meet a pure love, unsullied by a lifetime of crass bargaining, who has such high ideals that she could not love a man who has not demonstrated his integrity. Kasi is the man who will make Hoemei maran-Kaiel the new Prime Predictor.'

'I'm frightened. Just a little bit. Have you ever been in the pay of Kasi mon-Kaiel?'

'Once Aesoe gave me to Kasi as his reward for cleverly delaying the audits.'

'That's why you are so cynical! Aesoe *knows* and he's trying to block the full play of kalothi!'

'Come. Your crone will dress you for the evening. She will cry to lose one so sweet as you.' Humility kissed the girl who was to become her sacrificial card.

60

At the time of the destruction of the Arant, the cynic Miosoenes spoke of the rulers of men as the candles we blame for causing our stumbling in the dark.

From *The Cynic's Compendium*

The party flowed from Aesoe's seething energy, pulsing with his pulse, beating at the skull's temples to the music of God. And Aesoe took the stage of his celebration to reveal in compact speech his newest Racial Future, every word arranged for the cymbals of oratory so that Vision seemed to blend with the dancing.

At his side was the faithful Liethe woman known to the Palace as Sieen. His friends were glad she was there to fill the void of Kathein's abandonment. Sieen was the symbol of the continuity of loyalty. She praised her man. She defended him. She advised him. Tonight when the whisky was poured, she added colour to his Vision by describing troop carriers, longer than planets, stuffed with loyal kembri scarred-men as they slipped across nebulae to bar the reaching Riethe. Aesoe smiled at this dream, vaster than any thoughts of Hoemei.

The Fire Dance came late in the evening when the party was building to a sensual throb and enough barrels of whisky had been emptied so that even a sky lit up by the stellar explosion of Getan seed did not seem preposterous. Redflies, under the persona of Star, modified her dance to the constraints of the Circling Focus of Seduction. The elemental flame of her motion darted through the audience or warmed the fire watchers with licking undulations but always her eyes found a moment's heart-beat to settle upon the radiating cicatrice of Kasi, to flit away, to be pulled again into his aura. He drifted closer like a convection current drawn to a temple torch.

Her arm rose, her head flashed and stilled while her hair continued its sweeping caress of her shoulders. One smile flew from her face and did not return. Humility, as Sieen, was in place and on tiptoes whispering, 'She is a virgin,' to the ears of a heart caught admiring the smile, now disappearing on downcast eyelashes as the fire burnt to ash.

Kasi turned to Sieen urgently. 'Introduce me to her.'

'She makes you feel young again, does she?' said Sieen, pulling him off to the dressing rooms. 'Star, this is a friend of mine. I think he liked your dancing.'

The dancer, in a clever reversal of her own dream of seduction, would not look at her guest at all, but dressed slowly so that he could be warmed by the ember glow of her body. 'I'm pleased that you like me. I'm new in Kaiel-hontokae. I have no friends here.'

Later, much later, he would be allowed to touch her body and then Kaiel and Liethe would slip out for a long walk in the park or maybe along the raceway of the aqueduct where there was danger and he could protect her. Only when the dawn was red on the clouds and his desire properly fanned would she let him enter her body.

Humility, pleased with an underhanded job well done, made the sign of the Chopped Nose as she left the dressing room. *That wanton will go far.* She met the ghost image of her own first man. He had loved her as a farmer loves his fields and she had murdered him. Orders. Love had been the only way to get to him through his wall of guards. But where was Aesoe?

A hand was laid on her shoulder from behind. 'Let's depart before the brawl begins,' Aesoe said. 'I was watching Kasi. Is he growing the lecher's tumour?'

Alone, Aesoe's gaiety vanished into morose depression. Sieen undressed him, massaged him, oiled him. She chattered to fill his silence. 'You were great tonight. I saw! As you talked every Kaiel grew by a full thumb-height!'

'Did their breasts stop sagging?' he grumbled, half reviving.

'Mine were tingling.'

'I'll have to work on Xoniep's report tomorrow. God's Nose, and early, too.'

'I have it memorized. I can tick off the essentials whenever you wish.'

He laughed. 'I need a hundred more like you.' But a secret thought caused the relapse of depression. He stopped Sieen's hands, got up, went to his study.

She knew he had chosen to stand and stare at the portrait of Kathein and think his thoughts. It was not a true likeness, but clever paint that put into her face the strength of character that Aesoe wished she really had. The artist was a floor-kisser who had never seen more than the feet of his patrons.

Humility left for the bedchamber, calculating the necessities, here the pillows fluffed, there the curtains parted to make best use of the dawn light he would never see again. She undressed and chose to wear only the golden ankle chains with their dangle of jewels, gifted to Sieen by Aesoe and worn now by a dozen se-Tufi Sieens, that faithful myth who loved him so much he could do no wrong, so much she took his love when he gave it and called in her replacement when he didn't. He often chided her for her tolerance of his foibles.

She recited the cue mnemonic of the Attributes of the Male as keyed to Aesoe, checking out every detail that might facilitate his pleasure. She arranged the candles. She brought down the delicate goblet that Kathein had given him, cold with the soft blue of fine glass. Her other fingers took hold of a tiny cut monstrosity, a gift from the

454

Prime Predictor that had brought tears to the eyes of some Sieen long ago when Aesoe had been a more thoughtful man. It was one of his cues. The Liethe who drank from that glass was Sieen. She found a bottle of common Oza, a liquid as pale blue as Kathein's goblet, pale as the dew on the flowers of Assassin's Delight. How he loved this common Oza that was brewed in a thousand cellars!

She fluffed her hair and styled it with silver combs in fantastic shapes that would not keep by themselves. All to be beautiful for him. She chose a position on the pillows from the Bewitchments of Form, plucking her instrument with a calling sound to seduce him from Kathein's portrait as the green bower of a desert well calls the stricken traveller.

'God's Sweet Smile but you're ravishing. I'm the wrong man for you. Tell your crone to demand more coin.' He stood by the door, the riot of his fierce cicatrice somehow muted.

'I adore you. I am happy. There will be happiness for you, too. Kathein will come back.' Her words triggered the rage to the forefront of his eyes. Protected by the White Mind, she did not react as she read those eyes. *The decision to destroy has been made. Hoemei, my love! Hide! Hide!*

'Kathein return to me? I see no such vision.'

'You do not know women. Hoemei is a fantasy to her. She's in love with a sinewed man who can reach as far as the stars. I know. Hoemei will disillusion her. She will be back. She will cry and the tears will yet wet your feet and roll between your toes because she will be sorry and you will forgive her because you love her. This time when she comes to you she will appreciate you as she never has.' Sieen changed the tone of her voice from hope to doom. 'But if you destroy Hoemei, her fantasy will stay intact and her emotion will set like lava cooling to stone. I caution patience. Wait. Calm yourself.'

Humility's anguish was great at the telling of these lies.

'It will take too long.' He made the gesture of impatience. 'Disillusionment will come to an old woman when I am long-used soup stock. I cannot wait. I am too old.'

'One week. It will take no longer.'

'You dream!'

Sieen smiled as the prophetess smiles. 'I promise you.'

She could see the tension drain from him before he spoke. 'I will give him one more week to live.'

She abandoned her stringed instrument. Arms about his neck, smiling, she reached up to kiss him, not as a prophetess but as a lover. 'In the meantime, I'm glad to have you all to myself. For the whole of a week!'

He laughed and lifted her feet off the rug by the crotch so that the kissing might be easier for her. He carried her body to the pillows. She squirmed away.

'Some Oza first!'

'Oza! When I have you?'

'It clears your head. It cleans your bile. Besides, it sweetens your mouth so that you are all the more kissable!' While she spoke, she was pouring the Oza on top of a single dew drop of the essence of the blue petals of her Assassin's Delight. This poison did not survive in the body and so could not contaminate the Funeral Feast. She handed him Kathein's goblet. Liethe fingers took her own.

'To love,' she said. 'May we live long enough to taste all of its pleasures!'

He drank. She drank. He flirted with the jewels at her ankle. She took him in love, knowing exactly how much time she had. Every motion was Liethe perfect, the touches, the pauses, the rhythm, the sighs. Clumsy Kathein had never honoured him like this. She straddled him, her hands tender on his carved face, her arms compressing her breasts. 'Remember me my love. Remember this heartbeat of time, for in the end it is all we have.'

'My little friend,' he said and pulled her to him, giving

her his semen. The union was so complete that in her shudders she felt the very poison in his blood. The tears came and he kissed her eyes.

She was holding his head in her lap, tousling his hair, whispering endless nothings while the fuzziness that he thought was alcohol came upon him. His hands jerked. 'Sieen. My heart!'

She found no last words. He died. She bawled. Of what use is the White Mind when you are alone with a dead lover? For a moment she calmed herself enough to remove all evidence of the crime. Then she went back to the pillows and hugged the corpse and did not stop crying.

'Oh Aesoe! Why did you break the rules so often?' Sobs caught her again. She pulled her voice into a half choking, half lecturing tone. 'You can break the rules but there are consequences. Didn't your teacher ever tell you that? Silly man.' She talked to his body, to herself, affectionately patting Aesoe from time to time, pulling the covers over him so he would not get cold, kissing him.

'I'm sorry. I wanted to figure out another way. But no one helped. I didn't know how. Why do we always use the solutions of our training? You too!' she scolded. 'I don't want to kill people. I want to love them!' She touched her lips to the still-warm lips. 'You were a great man and I loved you and I'm mad at you!' She tried to surround his cooling body with her body to give him warmth.

But in the morning she woke beside a statue of Aesoe done in alabaster, a low relief of symbols carved on its surface. She ran her fingers along the cold stone and there were no more tears.

61

Brilliant by night, bright enough to be seen by day, God passed seven times between sunset and sunset for two hundred days to watch my Trial, to guide me across the roadless Kalamani for I had no maps. The Kalamani is no place for man. I slaked my thirst by distilling the juices of insects. My comrades died and there was no one to honour their flesh but me. Life was chewing the sun-dried strips of their life. All honour to my comrades!

Harar ram-Ivieth from his *Following God*

Most of Kaiel-hontokae seemed to be at the Funeral Feast. The tables of food at the Temple of Human Destiny would have ended a famine. The great gongs never stopped sounding. Aesoe was the steaming centrepiece, below the stained glass, skinned, dressed, decorated, roasted, no longer human. The entertainment that whirled around him never ended. His three Liethe danced for him a mourning song that crawled from the blacks and browns of a dirge to the ebullient roses and reds and pinks of birth. Aesoe's little children fluttered about being important, serving the food, keeping order.

Men gave speeches and men wept, cooks rolled in carts of food, choirs sang, whisky flowed, robed Kaiel flowed about their temple like trapped floodwaters from a sudden melt.

The Queen of Life-before-Death found herself huddled under a table to avoid the crush, savouring her own small strip of Aesoe, dreaming dreams, feeling his strength. She saw a black and purple robe pass by and grabbed at its legs. The wearer of the robe looked down. She peered out smiling.

'I'm Honey – just in case you didn't recognize me.'

'Who but Honey would be hiding under a table?' grinned Gaet.

'That's a *hat* you're wearing?' she exclaimed. 'What are you doing here?' she asked breathlessly.

'I thought polite form required my presence. Travelled my bum off non-stop by skrei-wheel. God's Laugh if I won't be bowlegged for weeks! Wasn't sure it was safe for Hoemei to come. Joesai is in the bush somewhere chasing his tail and Teenae didn't even want *me* to come.'

'Did Kathein reach Sorrow safely? Aesoe was so upset!'

'If it didn't give him heart failure! Kathein's arrival was a surprise! There will be a wedding when Joesai and I get back. This unfortunate Feast makes it easier.'

Honey pulled Gaet's head down to her ear level. 'You're such a hypocrite,' she whispered. 'Why do you say "unfortunate" when you mean "fortunate"!'

'Not "hypocrite"; the word is "diplomat",' he corrected. 'Let's get out of here. They've run out of meat. Funerals are a pain when there are more than twenty people. Never get enough to eat.'

'May I just go with you? Just like that?'

'I give shelter to the unemployed. Or shall I be your private escort to the hive?'

'Not there!'

'My humble home?'

'God yes. Is it still standing?' she teased. 'I thought the Expansionists might have burned it down by now.'

Halfway there she couldn't resist the question that was dominating her mind. 'Do you think they'll make Hoemei Prime Predictor?' She was clinging to Gaet's arm.

He grinned and bumped her hip affectionately. 'I think you like my brother.' He was teasing.

'I want to know!'

'Yes. It is checkmate. Hoemei was blocked every way by Aesoe. Aesoe was the key piece. So the Black Queen took him off the board and now it is a new game and I believe Hoemei has control.'

Gaet escorted her through the maran's darkened city mansion, straight to his room. He brought out gold coin and gave it to her without any preliminaries in repayment for the sexual favours he was obviously expecting. She stiffened. Suddenly their camaraderie was gone and she felt alone in the whole universe. 'That's not the way it is done,' she said coldly. 'All money matters are handled by the crones. A gift as bonus might be welcome if I were to please you enough.'

He laughed while he undressed. 'I offer my apologies,' he said without being the least contrite. 'I'm used to the way wives handle their husbands.'

'I'm not your wife.' She was surprised at her anger.

He was staring at her as if she was a child on the auction block. 'You could have been. Hoemei really loved you. He wanted me and Joesai to love you, too. We were very short of a woman then. It is hard for two women to keep up with three men.'

He was making her more angry. 'The Liethe never marry.'

'I know. So does Hoemei. He's a family man and not an old reprobate like me.'

She pushed his money back across the table.

'I was just cutting out the middleman. The crones will never know. Keep it. Consider it an advance. You're coming out to Sorrow to dance at our wedding. My invitation. I know you want to see him.'

The anguish was there again, and indecision. She knew she would do anything to see Hoemei again, just to pass him in the halls of Sorrow's Temple, anything. She'd walk across the world to spend an evening with him.

Gaet threw up his hands. 'I can't argue with you. Not now. I'm dead on my feet. I didn't think I'd make the Feast.' He turned around and fell like a collapsing building onto the pillows and was sound asleep, still half dressed.

She stared at him, no longer angry. *Perhaps he thought I was out of a job and needed help.* He would not comprehend the ethic of the hive. She wasn't used to friends. She moved the gold coins with her fingers. Impulsively she tidied the room. Gently she finished undressing him so that he would not wake. She put his things away. She put her own gown away, and the money with it. By the time she found courage to sleep with him, he had the pillows well toasted. It was cosy under the covers. It was good to sleep with a warm body again.

62

The multiple apparitions of futures fight their spectral game on the deadly field of the present, destroying one another, until, heartbeat by heartbeat, the victor comes alive, takes on substance, mass inertia, the glory of a summer form or the cancerous monster of some mad being, the very warmth of his solid body dissipating the wraiths of the lost futures – to reign in ephemeral glory for a day before twilight makes of him the corpse upon which the next phantom battle begins to rage.

From the essay 'Futures' by Hoemei maran-Kaiel

Fog had been crawling through the cracks between the hills so that there was no sea to be seen, only the pale cleaver of Scowlmoon hanging in the whiteness. Noe found them beside the road and parked her skrei-wheel next to theirs where they had been resting and eating bread. She crossed her arms to warm herself against the flowing fog.

'I'm sorry I wasn't home when your wirevoice message came through.'

She was glancing at Honey. Gaet could sense her distress. He rose. 'You forgot your cloak. You're cold.'

She shrugged, a shiver warming her. 'I thought you were alone.'

'I brought Honey to dance at our wedding. She's been a good friend to Hoemei, more loyal to us than to Aesoe. Somehow with his death it seemed appropriate to bring her.'

'You have a flair for complicating matters.' Noe's voice was the sting of a bee.

Listening, Honey pulled her black scarf around her face, like the sheathing of a beekeeper, but imperturbable eyes watched Noe. She did not rise. The Liethe woman's demeanour chastized Noe for her bad manners.

With a flicking gesture of impatience at Gaet, Noe turned to sit beside the woman who had been the mistress of her husbands, reaching into her pack for bread to feed both travellers. 'I'm not myself. I welcome any guest of Gaet.' Her voice was briefly warm again. 'You may have come in vain. There may be no wedding.'

'Eh?' Gaet queried.

'You,' Noe turned savagely to one-husband, 'may not even find a family to greet you!'

Gaet was diplomatically inserting himself between the two women. 'I see I'm behind on the gossip. Has Kathein changed her mind again?' He laughed.

'Sometimes I despise you!'

Gaet caught her bitter mood for the first time, and the fog clutched his heart. 'Someone has died?'

She took his hand and kissed him on the cheek, then compulsively put spread on a slab of bread for the silent Honey. 'Joesai is home.'

Gaet grunted. 'Since when is that bad news?'

'He brought Oelita with him. He found her in the desert, mothering twins by Hoemei.'

'Ah,' said Gaet. 'She'll be welcome in Sorrow.' There was more to the story. He waited.

'Joesai expects us to marry his Heretic.'

Gaet laughed the great laugh. He could not restrain himself, even to match Noe's mood. 'Did Joesai bring her in tied to a pole and drugged?'

The answer carried deep puzzlement. 'She loves him. There is a bond between them. I don't understand it.'

'God's Sky!' said Gaet.

'Joesai and Hoemei have been fighting. I've never seen rage like that. They're brothers! I was frightened. Teenae

463

was terrified. She and Oelita ran away to the village and left me and Kathein holding the pot. Kathein wants to return to Kaiel-hontokae and I've had to use persuasion to keep her here until you arrived.' Noe was crying.

'Shall I speak to Hoemei?' said Honey with great concern. She reached across Gaet to comfort the sobbing woman. 'I have certain catalytic powers.'

'You stay out of this! You'd steal him from us!'

Gaet slipped his arm around one-wife. 'Your foul mood staggers without reason. Our Liethe friend will steal no one. They are a gentle clan, and Honey is the gentlest of them. Their place is to serve. The man who thinks to abandon his family and elevate his Liethe always fails. The Liethe are known to be incorruptible in the purpose they have set for themselves.'

'Speaking to Hoemei would do no good.' said Noe, disconsolate. 'My husbands have lost their reason.'

Gaet laughed. 'Such is the price we pay for having women in our lives. I'd best end my rest and begin the peacemaking process.'

'There will be no peace! Don't you think we've tried?'

Gaet was staring at the wind-shaped trees in the gulley beside the road, trees older than any man alive, short trees which had fought off the violence of the sea a thousand times and stayed rooted. 'I think it was Hoemei who taught me when we were still in the creches that when a problem is insoluble, then it is essential to change the problem.' He rose. 'Noe, I'd best go on alone. Take care of Honey for me, and remember, she's a little afraid of Kaiel women. Make her your friend.'

Honey rose, too. 'I could go with you. I won't get in the way.'

'No.'

'We could all go together,' Honey pleaded.

'No.'

'It is all right,' said Noe. 'We'll go back to the village

464

and visit Teenae and Oelita. Gaet knows what he's doing. If he'd been here none of this would have happened.'

Gaet pushed his way through the trail to the maran's coastal mansion, cursing the bump that had put a wobble in his wheel. Another job, retensioning the spokes! For a moment he stopped to examine the damage, but also to give himself time to think out his attack on his brothers. He turned the skrei-wheel upside down.

The maran were a strange group, viable because of the different substance of their individual abilities. Gaet knew that most of the world saw him as the easygoing lackey of his family. If Noe wanted to go to the theatre he would go. If Hoemei had a political deal to make, Gaet would negotiate a resolution of the conflicts. He was known for his pleasures. He was too pliable to be seen as a strong man. And yet this family was his creation and he valued it above all other things in his life.

He spun the damaged wheel and watched it wobble. That was his skill – retensioning the spokes.

Some of his weakness was an illusion of his magic. As a child he had learned to appear to be giving way while he was leading. He retreated into carefully constructed traps. It had been no easy job to weld together the bonds between Hoemei and Joesai. It had taken trickery. They still clashed. They were still rivals, Joesai envying Hoemei's analytical skill and Hoemei envying Joesai his game with danger. From time to time they had to be played off against each other.

He could already surmise the forces behind this clash. Neither Joesai nor Hoemei had been particularly adept in their handling of women. Joesai had been clumsy and Hoemei had been shy. Yet it had been Hoemei who had persisted in the pursuit of Kathein, the only dangerous game he had ever deliberately dealt himself. And Joesai had plunged into his conflict with Oelita, sure that he did not want her, sure of the soundness of the tradition from which he worked — only to find himself in play with a woman who could manipulate the nuances of wisdom that could never be embedded in tradition. Oelita had forced him to be rational.

How could Hoemei ever give up the danger that he had survived without the aid of Joesai's defending fist? He would be fundamentally attached to Kathein. How could Joesai ever give up the feeling for philosophy that he had found far from Hoemei's mind? He would be fundamentally attached to Oelita.

When Gaet finally arrived at the Coastal Predictor's mansion, and quietly hung up his skrei-wheel before slipping upstairs, he found Joesai reading in the upper room overlooking the Njarae. Of the three rocky islands that rose from the sea only the ghost of the Child of Death peered through the fog at them. Joesai inserted a cloth marker in the book and turned down the wick of the lamp, until the pallor of the room's bioluminous globe provided the dominant light.

'I'm pleased that you located Oelita,' said Gaet.

His largest brother let the book sag and stared at Gaet, unspeaking. The design of his face looked like the carvings from a death urn.

Gaet began again. 'I hear of troubles.'

'Hoemei pulled a knife on me.'

Like the squabbles of little boys accusing one another. 'And to get even, no doubt, you whacked him over the head with the latest philosophy.'

Joesai smiled wanly, turning his head to the invisible horizon. Gaet wondered if his brother was remembering how accusations were handled at the creche — a boy was punished for whatever crime he had loudly thrown upon another.

'So the old reprobate is dead,' said Joesai, changing the subject.

466

'That's good for you. Your exile will be lifted by the new Prime Predictor.'

Joesai laughed, half in amusement and half cynically. 'Maybe not!'

'God's Eyes, brother, don't look so glum. We haven't run out of alternatives yet. The plan is not the strategy.'

'Oelita is a good woman. I think Kathein has betrayed us.'

Gaet became cold. 'I don't want to hear what you have to say about that right now. I want you to think about compromises. I've never yet seen a compromise between two adversaries that didn't give them both more than each would have taken from his original plan.'

Joesai wasn't listening. The rug and the stone tiles of the floor had captured his restless eyes. 'I'm paralysed. Fighting my own brother . . .'

Gaet did not let him finish. 'I'll be busy in the next few days. You'll be doing some baby watching for me.' He began to leave.

Joesai grabbed his arm and took it in the wrist-to-wrist grip. 'You old compromiser.' He squeezed. 'Say hello to Oelita for me. I mucked that up again.'

For a while Gaet spent time in the kitchen with the servants, working the accounts and discussing the fight. The story they told was different from Noe's story. Then he walked along the balcony and stopped beside the green glass of Hoemei's window. He stared at the poignant love scene. They were still on the pillows together in a sleeping embrace. That was dangerous. If Kathein felt too unwanted, she would return to Kaiel-hontokae and take Hoemei with her. Such a schism could grow into divorce.

One-husband ducked inside and found the room of Jokain, first-son. They always thought of him as first-son even though they had never married Kathein. He was awake and busy building houses. The rug was the sea and blocks were on the sea, dredging for iron-reed. He did not speak but held up a hand so that Gaet would know not to walk all over the landscape and create ship-smashing waves with his feet.

Gaet smiled. Here was the saviour of mankind. Kathein, for all her ruthless reason, was a religious fanatic, and yet . . . maybe she was right. This boy had a better chance of discovering the true nature of God than his flawed parents. 'What are you building?'

'Those are boats. These are big houses, and those are little houses and that is a house for the sky-eye.'

'I need your help, Jokain. Your gene-father is building a real sky-eye on the roof and I want you to see that he does it right so that you can look at the stars with him. You are in charge of making sure that he gets up in the morning on time and dresses and eats all of his feed.'

Jokain carefully placed another block. 'Jo and Kath fight,' he said, and with the back of his hand knocked down his building with one sweep.

Gaet dropped to his haunches and wrapped his arms around the boy. 'You know what families are for? We take care of each other when bad things happen like fights. You take care of Jo and I take care of Kath.'

'Who takes care of Ho?'

'Maybe I'll send the twins to make him smile.'

Jokain thought it over. 'What stars do I get to see?'

'Nika is bright these days. Nika is a planet like Geta with moons. You can look at the mountains of Scowl-moon. Maybe you can catch God.'

'Will Jo smile?'

'Sure. He likes you a lot.'

When Gaet arrived at Sorrow's inn he was amused to find Honey wrapped up in the children. Gatee and the twins were down on the docks and Honey had them playing chasing games. That woman-shy creature had found a perfect way to avoid his wives.

First and foremost he gave Oelita his warmest greetings. If she couldn't think of him as her husband, he wanted her to feel very strongly that she was his friend. There were no real obstacles between them. Gaet had been primarily responsible for seeing that the Kaiel contract with her people was kept and he knew there was no reasonable way she could fault him.

She hesitated but when she felt his warmth, she hugged him. 'I'm glad to be back,' she said.

'What's happening at the house?' asked Teenae, anxiously.

'I have my brothers on a stake. I did my creche father's pre-butchery script on Joesai and Hoemei and spent the morning with Kathein. I was going to bring her into Sorrow with me, but the thought of handling five women at once weakened my nerve.'

'A likely story,' chided Noe.

He looked down at the docks. 'How's Honey?'

'She loves my children,' said Oelita.

'She's shy,' said Noe. 'She reminds me of Joesai's se-Tufi in Soebo, always finding a way out of a conversation.'

'Is it safe to leave those maniac husbands alone?' Teenae was still worried.

'Everything is under control. Jokain has Joesai by the nose. And I'm going to leave the twins with Hoemei.' He watched Oelita while he said that.

'No!' The Gentle Heretic was suddenly frightened.

'With your consent.' He took her hand and gestured for Honey to bring the children.

They put together two tables near the windows of the inn. Honey found high chairs for the children and retreated to the kitchen.

'Honey!' said Teenae, trying to recall her.

Gaet held out a negative hand. 'Let her serve us if she so wishes. That's the way she is.'

'Hoemei doesn't like me!' pleaded Oelita. 'I'm sorry I've caused your family so much trouble. Joesai had me wrapped up in his dreams. The changes in him gave me faith in mankind again.'

'Hoemei doesn't dislike you,' Gaet explained patiently. 'He was just defending Kathein. Marriage is like juggling. Anybody with any kalothi at all can handle two balls. Anything after three is complicated. Hoemei was up to six and doing well, and then somebody slipped in a seventh ball and he dropped everything. Oelita, you are no ordinary seventh!'

The twins started to kick each other. Their mother turned to quiet them and Honey arrived with sweetsticks for them to suck.

'There's a reason I want him to take care of your twins,' said Gaet.

'Hoemei is gentle,' interjected Honey. 'More than you know.' She ran her fingers shyly through Oelita's hair, along the scalp, communicating gentleness. 'He'll love your children because they are his, too. He'll see that they are raised in the desert and that way know your strength.'

'What good will that do!' cried Oelita morosely.

Gaet used one of his oldest tricks in reply. He reached into Oelita's philosophy and picked out one of her dearest maxims. 'You have told us that love changes us away from violence. That's what I'm doing. While your children are with their father, you will be with Kathein.'

'No. I can't do that! It's too painful. I lived on struggle, not willing to die, not willing to hope. Joesai brought me a dream and now that dream is ashes. Either Kathein or I shall lose, and if one of us loses, we both lose.'

Gaet began a story. 'Two men each dreamed a house and woke up at dawn intending to make real the house of their minds. They both planned to use the same tree as a

470

centre beam, each unaware of the dream of the other. How is such a problem resolved? They can fight and destroy each other's foundations. They can fight and one can win. Or one can arbitrarily give up his dream. But that assumes there is but one tree on all of Geta and only one way of building a house. What if these two talked, bargained, explored? Maybe there is a second tree that two men can carry. Maybe a single conversation will suggest a whole new architecture. That's why you must talk to Kathein.'

'Do that,' said Honey quietly. 'Gaet is known as the best arbitrator in all of Kaiel-hontokae.'

Oelita looked at Teenae for support. 'Kathein is a good woman,' said her friend.

Noe was waiting for her to say yes.

She turned away from them all. The dining room was gay with its oiled wooden tables and aroma of spices from the kitchen. Getasun had banished the fog. Sorrow was alive. 'I'll try.'

'We took the White Wound together. Remember? It wasn't easy, either.'

63

(1) Without help from others, any being's future contains only lean alternatives.

(2) Help can be:

    (a) mutual as in cooperation,

    (b) enforced as by the use of slaves.

(3) An individualist – a man who has no intention of ever exploring the goals of others because he has no intention of compromising with his own – may become:

    (a) a hermit of limited goals,

    (b) a tyrant surrounded by slaves with rebellion in his future and covert hostility in his present.

(4) A being may choose the route of mutual help, having no fixed goals because he is constantly exploring the goals of others and so modifying his own. Such a wandering road leads to loss of individuality, but such a person always finds a land where there is a rich choice of futures and so his gains are greater than his losses.

Prime Predictor Tae ran-Kaiel in *Bargaining*

Gaet rented a sailboat to take Oelita and her boy and girl up the coast to the bay of the Old Man, the Mother, and the Child of Death. He had little knowledge of sailing and gave command to Oelita who remembered her sailor motions as if she had never left the sea. They beached beneath the maran mansion. Gaet left a bewildered Hoemei to manage as best he could with two squalling infants. Kathein gave him instructions and then apprehensively followed Gaet back to the beach.

'I've never been in a boat before,' said Kathein, 'not even to cross a river.'

'You'll like it!' Oelita said with a smile. as she helped her rival aboard, glad that she was in command.

'Tell me what to do,' said Kathein.

Gaet was shoving the boat out into the waves again. 'You should know all about the forces of tacking.'

'The boom adds and subtracts on its fingers faster than I do!'

'Where to?' asked Oelita.

Gaet was aboard, dripping, helping Oelita hoist the sail. 'You once told me long ago that you found the Frozen Voice of God along the shore near here when you were a child.'

'I know exactly where.'

'I thought it might be a place to picnic. *The Forge of War* is the common meeting ground between you and Kathein.'

Kathein's eyes brightened. 'Do you really remember where you picked it up? That's very exciting!' The boat was gathering speed, splashing a fine spray into her face when they crossed a wave. That was exciting, too. 'We've never found more than the one we had and yours.'

'The cove has a sandy bottom. A lot could be buried there.'

'Maybe God will nudge your hand again.'

'We'll try. It is a wonderful place to swim.'

'Is swimming in the sea different from swimming in a pool?'

'Oh yes. I'll show you how.'

The cove was isolated and protected from the storms and, because of that, sheltered peculiar kinds of insect life. Oelita remembered why her father had been here, and found a green-backed digger for Kathein and then a whole colony of tunnelling insects with peculiar clawed eyes.

'What are these?' Kathein was holding blades of an underwater grass in which grew a delicate band of silver flowers all the way up each spine.

'They are delicious when rotted for a week – and quite

poisonous. A nerve poison. Long ago when the Stgal first took over Sorrow from the Nowee priests they gave a great feast in honour of the new pact between the Nowee and the Stgal and fed the Nowee a salad laced with such grasses. A tale among other tales – and the Stgal wonder why they have a devious reputation!'

The two women shed their sailing clothes and began a diving exploration of the shore bottom. Gaet built a fire on the sand and roasted a lunch in bundles of leaf packs. He watched the swimmers, pleased with the emotional smoothness of his venture. He could relax now and worry about trivial details like the penetration of the leaf aroma into the food.

Women were beautiful in different ways, he thought, watching them. The artists of the coast had used simple designs over Oelita's flesh, leaving sweeping areas of plain or lightly etched skin for contrast. Kathein was decorated more in the high fashion of the Kaiel, delicate work, lavish detail, symbols, intricate dye work overlaying the scars so that not a patch of child's flesh remained, showing her to be a true Master of Pain.

He spread mats on the sand. With the sun at highnode and the fire to dry them, they did not bother to dress when they returned. 'Did you find anything?'

'No,' said Oelita. 'There's growth down there, more than when I was a child.'

Kathein laid up her wet hair on a lattice of fingers. 'Sea life entrances me. I learned to swim with my eyes open! I'll have to bring a dredge up here sometime. It's a shame. I wonder how *The Forge of War* got into the sea? There is no sign of ruins or an old boat, or anything at all down there.'

'I'm glad you brought us,' said Oelita. 'The problems of our men seem very remote out here. We've been talking about that.'

'Between mouthfuls of sea!' laughed Kathein.

Gaet unwrapped a leafy fist cake and let them smell its steamy fragrance. 'I'm working on a compromise that will satisfy us all. I need new information. You two will have to be my source.'

'Do you want to know how Joesai feels?' asked Oelita.

'No. I know Joesai. I'm not sure I know what drives a Gentle Heretic.'

'You know *me*,' said Kathein.

'You're positive?' asked Gaet. 'You've been with Aesoe a long time.'

Kathein dropped her eyes and Oelita took her hand and confronted Gaet for the both of them. 'What do you want to know about us? Just ask.'

'Let me go over some history first. We've had a Five that works well. I didn't really understand it when I started it. A family was a misty dream, something to do as I climbed the ladder of Kaiel tradition. I was told that the bonds of a family created abilities that no single man could aspire to by himself, and I wanted to do everything – and be everything – and so a family was just a natural extension of myself.'

'Do you think of your family as beginning the day you met Noe?' asked Kathein.

'The day I met Noe was a disaster. Whatever happened began the day I met Joesai.'

Joesai was a studious child, intolerant of the flaws in both his peers and masters. He was larger than his peers and used his strength to bully. Whoever crossed him ran the risk of dying at the next Trial. Joesai never exacted revenge through an intermediary but if the offender could stay out of Joesai's way for at least a week, the slight was forgotten. He had no friends. He was a thief but no master ever caught him.

He knew his father was Tae ran-Kaiel, the Prime Predictor, and that gave him an arrogant hope that he might survive the creche. But he didn't know who his mother was and that made him unsure of his worth.

He pestered his genetics teacher for his record. Then he learned why no one had told him about his mother. They thought he wouldn't understand. It was puzzling. His mother was both a woman and a man and two people and the same person.

Tae ran-Kaiel had authorized an experiment in an attempt to create a predictor as powerful as himself. He had bred himself with one of the early successful predictors, a Gaieri ma-Kaiel, whose sperm had been frozen in liquid nitrogen yet never used because he was a known carrier of multiple lethal recessives.

In a technique developed by Tae's own study group, hundreds of 23-chromosome sets from Gaieri sperm cells were infused into chromosomeless ova and triggered to yield a cell of 23 chromosomes in the dyad form – each with two chromatids and one joining centromere, similar to the stable secondary oocytes carried by women prior to ovulation. Tae's group developed a process by which the final meiosis was inhibited, the centromeres broken and a fully homozygous 46-chromosome cell formed that when transferred to the womb of a machine mother began to grow into an embryo.

Four million homozygous *female* individuals – subclones – can be formed from one heterozygous male. One hundred and eighty pregnancies were started. One hundred and fifty-three of these aborted before coming to term because of doubled y-chromosomes and doubled lethal recessives. Twenty-one of the surviving twenty-seven babies were judged to be substandard and were used for medical experimentation, teaching purposes, or sold to the abattoir.

The best specimen of the final six, Joesai's mother, was artificially matured, butchered, and her ovaries used for further experimentation. She became, in this indirect fashion, the genetic mother of nine of Tae's children. At the time Joesai read the records, four of that batch were still alive: Sanan, Gaet, Hoemei and Joesai. Unilaterally, he began to protect his Gaieri-derived brothers for no more reason than he felt their kalothi was somehow tied to his own.

'We didn't even like him,' mused Gaet to Kathein and Oelita there on the beach. 'We made fun of him. We taunted him.'

'You made fun of him? And he was helping you!' said a saddened Oelita.

'Poor little boy,' said Kathein.

Gaet grinned.

At their first Trial of Strength Joesai bullied Hoemei through his failures, saving his life and teaching him the value of an alliance, but Hoemei, instead of joining forces with Joesai, made a blood oath with Gaet and Sanan. Joesai remained on the periphery of the alliance, bullying them, goading them, tormenting them – and protecting them. They reacted with scorn.

It was only later, after the death of Sanan when he saw Joesai crying, that Gaet understood the folly of their petty bickering and made the conscious decision to forge a team from the three of them. He began to mediate the disputes between his brothers. When Hoemei was trapped, he actively sought Joesai's help and when Joesai was up for soup stock he worked out an aid programme with Hoemei. It wasn't long before they were impressed by their alliance. Gaet negotiated them out of trouble, Hoemei anticipated trouble, and Joesai fought them clear.

'What I'm trying to say,' said Gaet, 'is that the ugly fight you've witnessed is nothing new. I know how it is going to turn out and so do my brothers. Noe and Teenae are a little frightened because the worst of our brotherly conflicts were over before women came into our lives and so our wives still don't understand the roots of our fights.

You two aren't used to them at all. My brothers take a fight as far as it will go, and then they turn round and compromise. Probably, I don't even need to be there anymore. I'm more worried about you two charmers.'

Kathein was watching sand slip through her fingers. 'Don't be. I'm used to heartaches.'

'Don't say that!' said Oelita, all empathy with Kathein. She was afraid of heartache herself. 'We're in this together!'

'Yes,' said Kathein wisely, 'but can we stand it?'

Gaet put on his smoothest manners. 'Is it such a tragedy that life doesn't fit the pictures we have of what life should be? That's what makes physics exciting – when the reality-trials don't fit the theory.'

'I'm a romantic,' said Kathein. 'I worship Stgi and Toe. Love is not like physics.'

'Did I ever tell you how we came to marry a madwoman like Noe?' Gaet laughed. 'What is the Kaiel picture of a courtship? Doesn't a single man seek a woman? Doesn't a woman keep her eye out for that special man? The man and woman love and marry. Then don't they look around for another man or woman or couple that they can love and, finding such, court them and marry again to increase their kalothi? So it goes.

'But we were three *men*. There weren't any women we met who knew what to do with *that*. Noe married us for all the wrong reasons. She hated responsibility. She started something new every week and finished nothing. Her temple work gave her contact with men without any long-term responsibilities.

'I met her the night she first noticed that she was unhappy. She thought with the three of us she'd have all the advantages of marriage and none of the disadvantages.' Gaet's amusement warmed his voice. 'It was a disaster. She was a spoiled brat. She knew everything about holding a man for the first week and nothing beyond

478

that. She was the terror of her family; very sober people. And we knew nothing about women beyond the basics of getting our wicks dipped.

'She was so impossible that Joesai beat her from time to time and Hoemei and I would sit around in the next room listening to the screams, biting our nails and saying Thank God someone is doing something about her. Then when it was over, we would ostracize Joesai and comfort and cuddle her.

'Money was never a problem. We were very successful with the coins – we had our mansion already – but our Four got worse and worse. And worse. Finally she left us.'

'She never told me that!' said Kathein.

'Of course not.'

'Did you miss her?' Oelita asked with sentimental curiosity.

'Miss her! I was never so happy in my life that she was gone. Hoemei was wiped out. It was sexual withdrawal. He moped around not saying anything. Joesai was our moralist. He always has been. He didn't even like her but he hunted her down and brought her home against her will. I've never found out what happened then. I couldn't get rid of her afterwards. I was pissing from my nose, I was so mad at Joesai for bringing her home. He remembers being very firm and gentle. But she acted like she thought he was going to kill her if she didn't behave, that there was no escape from him. I don't think he ever threatened her, but when you are fresh from the creche you have a certain cavalier attitude towards death that the non-creche never really want to test.'

'I think I know the man,' said Oelita.

Kathein was wistful. 'I'm sure Noe returned because after she'd been away she knew she couldn't live without you all. She was probably happy that Joesai came for her.'

'That's when I found Teenae. I was up in the mountains and happened to pass through one of the o'Tghalie estates when they had a child auction. My maran prescience, which we all have from Tae, could see the woman she was to become and I was smitten even though she had shaved her head to make herself ugly so that no one would want to buy her.

'Mostly, though, I was thinking how nice it would be to have a child bride around who could be trained properly in the ways of serving a man and wouldn't be spoiled like Noe. It never struck me that the reason the o'Tghalie were selling her was that she was unmanageable. So I finished my trip in the mountains with this girl-child terror who would follow me because I owned her, but who wouldn't do the tiniest thing I asked.'

'She loves you now,' said Oelita.

'Of course.' He smiled. 'I'm telling you these stories because marriage isn't an easy thing, and when we look back we never see the thing we saw then. Some marriages that look perfect, don't work. And some marriages that are the despair of all rational people somehow have the basics that make them work.'

'How did you win her?' asked Kathein.

'I was trying to resell her for half-price to an og'Sieth steelsmith who was interested in her because of the reputation of the o'Tghalie women as superior servants for their men. He asked her about her ambitions and she jinxed the sale by telling him she wanted to be a mathematician. Back on the trail I muttered and told her I'd teach her some mathematics if she'd fix the food. She looked at me sceptically and told me that if I taught her the mathematics *first* then she would fix our food. So I taught her some algebra that I'd learned painfully and that she learned as fast as I could remember what I knew. She smiled for the first time.'

'Did she fix your meal?'

'The best road meal I ever had! Joesai was the one who really got to her, though. He had her number from the start. He came on with total assurance and would teach her some manipulation that was *always* flawed. She'd catch him and then he'd grab anyone who'd listen and tell them in amazement how smart she was. When he didn't know what she wanted to know, he'd hire an o'Tghalie male to teach him and then smuggle what he'd learned home to her. She became our slave. We could get her to do anything provided we were consistent. If we weren't logical, then she'd fight us tooth and dagger. It would have been a good life, but Noe took pity on her and taught her some of the fine points about bamboozling men.'

'When I met your Five you were very happy,' said Kathein. 'I loved your happiness.'

'A baby learns to walk. Every other step was a disaster no matter how hard we concentrated – and then suddenly we were running and we were such a good team that our services came to be in high demand.'

'I thought you were the smoothest people I knew,' Kathein said, laughing.

'So did we. That's the danger signal. As soon as you learn to walk so well that you can run over rough ground, then you want to fly and you break your bones in your first sailplane crash. We hadn't counted on Aesoe.'

Oelita broke her silence. 'Joesai told me that one day Aesoe just ordered you to marry me.'

'That's the way it was. We were outraged.'

'He wanted me,' said Kathein contritely.

Gaet grinned. 'He gave us a fair trade. Aesoe had excellent taste in women!'

The women stared at Gaet and he knew the question that each was asking him with her eyes but was unwilling to speak. *Which of us do you prefer?*

Gaet paused solemnly. 'We have arrived at a conflict of futures. The five of us learned to love you, Kathein, and I think it was mutual – and then you left us and we still loved you but we began to look at alternatives. The five of us didn't want you, Oelita, not because we didn't love you when we met you, but because you had been imposed on us against our will.'

'And against mine,' she added.

'But wasn't Aesoe right? You could have become part of a functional Six. Still, Aesoe's vision went awry and so we have this situation in which two futures try to occupy the same present. The five of us cannot resolve this conflict. It's up to you two.'

'We're back where we started,' said Kathein, almost angrily.

'You cannot ask that of us,' said Oelita.

'We could flip a coin,' said Kathein bitterly.

Gaet was smiling. 'Do you like each other?'

'Of course we like each other!' flared Kathein.

Tears were running down the ridges of Oelita's facial cicatrice.

'Could you live with each other?'

A look of astonishment crossed Kathein's face. She turned to Oelita. 'Do you know what this man is proposing?'

'No.'

Kathein was on her feet. She was dressing. 'Poor Hoemei and Joesai are back at the mansion feeling miserable, and this lecher here has the audacity to think he can have both of us. I know this man very well. I know what he is thinking.'

'I don't believe it!' said Oelita staring at Gaet's face. She saw it was true and rose with Kathein to dress, too.

'It's one solution,' said Gaet. admiring two women he loved.

'But a Seven is illegal!' exclaimed a shocked Oelita.

'By custom, not by law. With Hoemei as the Prime Predictor it would hardly be a problem.'

'Where were you planning to take us? I know you!

There must be pillows around here somewhere.' Kathein was sarcastic.

'The Temple of the Grey Rocks. It's small, but it has a charming game room. What better place to spend the night?'

'See!' said Kathein indignantly. 'See how easily he betrays his brothers!'

Oelita was still staring at Gaet, remembering all the lonely nights, the suffering, the string of lovers who had been her fate because of her vow never to marry, the fear she carried with her which even the peace of the desert had never mollified. She began to speak firmly. 'Joesai and Hoemei have fought. Let them suffer. At the creches they would have a name for it: the Trial of Stupidity. Kathein and I have not been fighting. We've only committed ourselves to loving, and challenged our fear to find that. We deserve our pleasures. Gaet, I'll go with you.' She turned her eyes to Kathein defiantly. 'I love this man. And I can live with you – because I love you.'

64

Until her hair has gone to grey
   A woman will not know to say
That all of loving's painful play
   Was worth the joy of every lay.

   From a Liethe drinking song

A few window-framed globes added their green glow to the night sky. Then, like a black cloud across the stars, a shadow passed into the yard, examining the stairways and balconies and the footholds in the face of the wall. The Queen of Life-before-Death clutched the black shawl that made her invisible by night, waiting for the globes to be shrouded. Gaet had left her with women and she was resentful. She wanted to be with Hoemei. It was her duty to be with men. Her knees were like jelly knowing this was the most important night of her whole life. Someone inside the mansion covered the globes.

She heard sea noises. She was a wave rising as it ran towards shore at the very heartbeat before it crested, foaming, roaring, to lay itself on the beach.

As silently as God flowing across His Sky she moved up the stairs. With an assassin's stealth she stole through the window-door open to the night breeze. She knelt beside the figure on the pillows, coloured by the pale reflection of a waxing Scowlmoon across the sea. She longed to touch him but pulled her fingers back. Hoemei. This was the man she was raising to the highest position on Geta.

His sudden darting hands reached out to grab her by the arms, paralysing her.

'It's just me,' said her soft Liethe voice.

'What are you doing here?'

'I came to dance at your wedding.'

'You're early.'

'No I'm not. I'm your beloved Honey.'

'You gave me heart failure. I thought you were an assassin for the Expansionists.'

'They've hired me to enchant you and take you away with me to the North Axis where we can go around in circles together for the rest of our lives and not bother anyone.'

He dismissed the notion. 'Gaet must have sent you,' he sighed.

'I have a present for you.' She brought out a tiny strip of dried and salted Aesoe. 'Eat it. It will make you strong. I have a gut feeling that you're going to need all your strength.'

He looked at her, wondering at the symbolism and the smug smile on her starlit face. 'Are you thinking that they'll make me Prime Predictor? Have you been listening to gossip at the Archives?'

She stuffed the fragment of Aesoe into his mouth. 'That's not the kind of strength I mean. Silly. You're going to need all your strength to make love to me – now.'

He munched and laughed. 'Be a good woman and tell me what Gaet is cooking. I have a shortage of spies.'

'Ask Joesai.'

'I'm not speaking to him.'

'Gaet ran away with Kathein and Oelita. He was looking very hard-crotched. I think they are off to the South Axis for a cosy ice cave to be away from us mortals. I couldn't bear the idea of you being left alone – so I came to console you.'

'Hmmm. Do you still have your job at the Palace?'

'No, silly. Not unless you hire me after your triumphant

return to Kaiel-hontokae. If you love me, you'll hire me. Do you love me?'

'Only a besotted fool loves a Liethe.' He was undoing her black robe.

He wasn't shy anymore. He had changed. She liked his hands. 'Are you a besotted fool?'

'All kinds of a whiskied fool this week.'

'Do you have remorse?'

'Yes.'

'Let me make you feel better.'

She prolonged the loving of their bodies until the moon was three-quarters full. Then she couldn't hold her grief in any longer. She let her fingers run over the rough texture of his scars and sobbed. 'You forgot me! You left me all alone! You didn't care! You don't think about me because you know you'll always have me!' He rocked her and patted her and kissed her tears away and she liked that. Rocking her, he rocked himself to sleep. She watched him wide-eyed, loving him.

Happy now, she rose stealthily to her feet and unhooked a covered globe from the wall. In the corridor by the mirror she unwrapped it to fix her hair so that she might be less mussed in her beauty. The globe was dim enough for her to think to feed it and clean the scum from its filters.

Then she brought herself to Joesai's room where she smashed her toe on one of Jokain's wooden toys and, biting her tongue, found a place above the messy desk to hang the globe. She read some paragraphs of what Joesai had been writing. It was the sober list of attributes that a warrior clan would have to possess. She sat near him on the pillows. He was a sounder sleeper than Hoemei, and she had to pull his ears.

'Ho!' he started.

She rubbed his chest gently. 'I see you still wear the amulet I gave you.'

486

'It has brought me luck.'

'Not luck. It has magic Liethe power.'

'How did you get here?'

'You were dreaming about me and the amulet summoned me. It's a superior way of travelling.'

'What was I dreaming about?'

'You were dreaming about making love to me!' She kissed him.

'I don't believe you. I must have been dreaming about Comfort.'

She smiled in the swinging light like an apparition and touched the carved charm to her breast. 'I *am* Comfort. I told you when I gave you the amulet that it would protect you. All you had to do was need me and I would be there, pazam! just like I'm here now! I take on different names depending on my mood.' She straddled him.

'Ho! I've never heard a more unlikely story. How do you travel so fast?'

'I don't; I live in the amulet,' she said mischievously.

'So that's why you are such a small handful.'

She had not wanted to talk to Hoemei during their body loving, but she wanted to talk to Joesai with every thrust. 'You're beautiful,' she said.

'I'm ugly.'

'You're my master!'

'That's why I'm underneath.'

'I'd like to be your woman at your Ritual Suicide.'

'I'd rather be your man at *your* Ritual Suicide.'

'Do you like se-Tufi women?'

'I'll take three of them at the breaking of fast, slow-fried.'

'What was it like to make love to Comfort?'

'We did it with a stone in her God's Eye.'

'That's a romantic story.'

'For an encore she poisoned me!'

'I love you.'

'Now you're getting wax-mouthed.'

'But I do!'

He had to be silent while he held her in the final heaving embrace. He sighed. She kissed him, wet little kisses while the tension went out of their bodies.

'You can go back into your amulet now,' he said.

'No,' she teased.

'I was afraid of that.'

'You have to come with me.' She unhooked the bioluminous globe with one hand and pulled Joesai to his feet with the other. 'Every pleasure has its price!'

The smooth-skinned Liethe with the sapling legs and rounded hips and firm small breasts and laughing face dragged the fiercely symboled Kaiel giant down to Hoemei's quarters. The two naked brothers confronted one another guiltily.

'You have to hug each other!' she ordered. When they did, she made them hug her, too. She cried while she dressed – a wave finally smashing into the beach – and disappeared into the dawn.

65

Only a hermit can avoid talk of weddings and politics.

A saying of the Kaiel

'He's more of an Expansionist than you are!'

The Kaiel woman arguing in the tavern at Sorrow wore her finery, and silver cheek-inlay that fitted the curves of her facial cicatrice. Her two intense male friends were also Kaiel and were dressed in their formal black robes. All three of them had arrived from Kaiel-hontokae for the wedding. The men were unhappy. It had already been announced that Hoemei was to be the new Prime Predictor.

'His nose bows to his anus and asks permission to sneeze.'

'Why is it that you think he is so formal and cautious?'

'He forbade his brother to move on Soebo when that city was ripe for capture, fearing illusional Mnankrei terrors.'

The woman was exasperated. 'But Joesai reached the city before Bendaein arrived! He took the city within days with little murder and less disturbance than Aesoe predicted. Because of that easy transition the underclans there have long ago shifted their loyalty to us. Hoemei *is* an Expansionist. Of course he is! He was trained by Aesoe!'

'But he is afraid to *grow* however much his heart . . .'

The creche female interrupted with annoyance. '. . . which is why he is Prime Predictor and you are not. He is no Lenin, like you, with grandiose plans for immediate world domination and a bee brain to go with them. He is a complex conqueror with a complex mind.'

'You do not sense the simplicity of Aesoe's plan?'

'I *like* simple plans! I hate plans *so* simple they are inadequate for the task at hand! It is not enough to be able to lead men! Who cannot lead the underclans to their death by choosing to oil one's speech and to veneer one's lethal programme with slogans to impress the masses? Look how that fool Lenin became a butcher trying to extricate himself from the bizarre consequences of his simplistic solutions.'

'Aesoe was hardly as simplistic as you claim. You slight him. When did he ever fail? He had more success than Tae!'

'Aesoe knew small systems very well. He was like Napoleon in Europe. His disasters would have come in a larger theatre – like Russia. Hoemei predicted his coming failures!'

The older of the men scoffed and downed his mead; the younger man smiled at the creche-woman's fire and spoke. 'You underestimate Aesoe. He was a superb organizer.'

'How would *you* know? You know nothing about organization on anything larger than a city Bok level! You do not rule a world in the same fashion that you rule a Bok!'

The girl-woman, with her auburn locks shaved along two off-centrelines, was one of those who had worked within the loose but dedicated structures which had aligned themselves with Hoemei's organization – though she had remained so far-removed from him that he was unaware of her loyalty. Once she had stood next to him and he had accidentally bumped into her and excused himself and smiled. She remembered his smile to this day. She was one of the many people he attracted who somehow made his projects go easily when he wasn't even sure where the help was coming from. He would have appreciated her, had he known her, for he enjoyed people who could quickly duplicate his vision and who could create a role for themselves within it.

'I do not like Hoemei's opposition to our bargaining with the Itraiel,' said the older man darkly, filling up his mug from the mead pitcher and spilling some on the wooden table.

'Have you read *The Forge of War* or only skimmed it? A military clan is not to be founded casually to pursue the immediate goals of an Expansionist who wants more paperwork for his cluttered desk!'

Their serving girl came over for a moment to wipe the table and they changed the subject. 'What do you suppose they'll be wearing?' asked the young man.

The barmaid glowed at gossip which interested her intensely. 'I've seen the dress of Joesai at the tailor shop where it was made by my friend and splendid it is in blue and silver brocade with great insects woven in!'

'Will they be by soon?' she was asked.

'You'll know! We're closing up then!'

Once the happy girl was gone, the three resumed their quarrel. 'Expansion is God's goal!'

'But God deplores Racial Suicide! A military clan is the most dangerous idea that the Kaiel have ever played with! It is worthy of Hoemei's caution. Have you seen his military plans? I've read the report. It is still too tentative to commit it to the Archives. Half of it was written by his brother Joesai. Still, preliminary as it is, it is an awesome document. They show us ways we can safely build a military clan. Beside these maran thoughts, Aesoe is a Napoleon wading through the snows of Russia! Hoemei will take longer to build his clan. He will use it with more caution, more restraint, and not as soon. But he will not stop at Moscow! God has brought us here to mend our wounds and to meditate upon the harshness of human life.

When we pass into God's Sky the very stars will twinkle from the shakings of the Riethe. They will fear to touch us because they will never know where our dagger is. And those future Getans will thank Hoemei for his farsighted caution!'

The older man grumbled. 'It is useless to believe that we will ever be gaming the Riethe of *The Forge of War*. That was long ago. Did it not all happen before the Passage? They will have changed. Change is eternal. They will not be the fools who charged against the machine rifles at Vimy Ridge. Those French peasants so weak in kalothi will long have made their Contribution to be replaced by a more deadly breed.'

'Hoemei plans to breed for military talent like we Kaiel are bred for our ability to predict. Every soldier of the clan will be a military dobu.'

'Of what rank?'

'At least the rank of Alexander the Great or Guderian.'

'Then I will back him.'

'But he does not intend to breed for such talent recklessly as was Aesoe's aim. Such a talent must be balanced. We must predict, before such violence is unchained, what the balancing forces will be.'

They heard the noise of a crowd outside and the older Kaiel went to see. 'They're here,' he said, beckoning.

The three of them had chosen this tavern because the high steps leading to it would give them an excellent view of the wedding procession. All of Sorrow was dressed in its best and jockeying for position. People hung from windows and were crowded onto balconies. Two children had climbed a wirevoice pole. Other children ran on ahead, happier to lead the procession than to watch it.

'Seven!' said the older Kaiel in disgust as the maran came into sight.

Kathein and Oelita led. Kathein wore a robe of red, slit vertically, blue-dyed hoiela wings showing through the

492

slits, and a headdress of hoiela wings with silver inlay for her facial cicatrice. Oelita wore white Orthei lace with a tall crown of white lace and white paint along the ridges of her facial design.

Hoemei followed them in more subdued attire, a black and grey striped ankle-length skirt, and a billowing silky blouse of grey sheen, open at the front in a swoop that flowed under his stomach to show his scarred chest. The blouse was held in place by a decorated spring-clasp at his waist that did not close over his midriff. He wore the bronze helmet long linked to the high predictors with its polished wings that swept so low over his shoulders that he was restrained from tipping his head to either side.

The young Kaiel woman on the tavern balcony thought she saw him turning her way and threw him her bouquet of desert flowers. He was only signalling Oelita, and her heart sank, but Teenae was watching and caught the bee-loved blossoms with a smile, kissed them, and tossed her kiss to the balcony with her other arm.

Teenae wore an elaborate headdress that began with a green jewelled insect crawling down the shaved centreline of her skull on a hundred silver comb-like legs that wrapped her black hair in happy coils. Her neckpiece, in black and white lace, rose to her chin. Her blouse was white and close-fitting with sleeves slit from the back of the shoulder to the wrist and held at the elbow with silver chains. The valleys of her facial cicatrice were dyed black. Her pantaloons were black and flaring around her hips. They, too, were split at the back, from waist to ankle, to emphasize her feminine walk. Silver chains held the pantaloons together. The valleys of the designs on her buttocks and legs were painted in white.

'That giant with her must be Joesai,' said the older Kaiel to his youthful friend. 'He looks like he had an Ivieth for a mother and a fei flower for a father!'

Joesai was dressed in what he thought was the court

finery of an Imperial Chinese Warrior of the Han Dynasty. It was immaterial that the coloured insects embroidered into his blue coat were Getan and not Riethe.

Noe's hair was wound into a silver cage like a nest for the insect that sat there with lustrous blue-green wings and eight silver legs and four green eyes. The silver motif was repeated in the filigree of the wings. They reached down to rest on her shoulders and rebounded to stretch a hand's length beyond them, acting as the perch for two more grinning insects. A bolt of the finest white silk hung from the wings' framework and down between her legs and up along her back to leave her sides bare to show off the exquisite skin carvings along her ribs and hips. Metallic insects, holding hands across her waist and clinging to her legs, held the garment together. She gripped Gaet by the arm.

He wore top hat and tails, a costume he had copied from a picture of Abraham Lincoln. To enliven the effect he had added tassels to the top hat and wore a rubied platinum nose ring and platinum wire, set with tiny rubies, in the valleys of his facial scars. On the ridges of his cicatrice he had let the beard grow to fingernail length and dyed it green. He thought he made an elegant Amerikan groom, a Mormon perhaps.

Behind them came two male Ivieth in their finery, carrying a coloured palanquin with Jokain, who watched the crowds with every awareness of his destiny. Teenae's Gatee clutched the railing of another gaudy palanquin, wide-eyed at the pageantry. Another transported the twins. A tall female Ivieth, bare-breasted and in elaborate skirt, carried Teenae's new baby who ignored everything in her contentment with the milk of the bosom at which she suckled.

When the procession had passed, the young creche-Kaiel affectionately took the arm of her younge male companion. 'Let's get married so we'll have a broader range of topics to fight about!'

He gave her a hug. 'I think bachelor Aesoe had the right idea! Once you start this wedding business, where does it end?'

'Seven!' snorted the old man.

66

One is at the Centre;	Hoemei is our Centre;
Who but One creates?	Who but One creates?
Two are on the edges	Gaet is on the edges
Binding inbetweens.	Binding inbetweens.
Three, the vertices	Joesai's vertices
Holding plane intac.	Holding plane intact.
Four, a pyramid, makes	Teenae's pyramid makes
Solidarity.	Solidarity.
Five, the human senses	Noe whose woman senses
Fill us up with life.	Fill us up with life.
Six points of kalothi	'Lita is kalothi
Letting life persist.	Letting life persist.
Seven Godly forces	Kathein's Godly forces
Pass between the stars.	Pass between the stars.
Eight is not a number	Liethe is not a number
Spoken of by Death.	Spoken of by Death.
The Numbers Chant	Parody of Numbers Chant

Weddings had serious moments but mostly they were times for fun. Six tumblers, three men and three women, slipped into the great plaza of the Temple of Sorrow in mock wedding finery, one malevolently tripping another to be caught by a third, to be tripped himself and caught in a cycle of marital quarrel and assistance that accelerated into a dazzling display of body-throwing.

A rustle of attention fell over the audience as the

members of the real procession found their seats. Behind the maran and the new brides, the Chanters were grouped on the stairway with the wall behind them to reflect their voices into the crowd. They wore the resonant facemasks that changed the trained human voice into a vibrant instrument able to handle the deepest rumbles or highest trills. Now they sang for the tumbler-contortionists.

These buffoons never stopped their torrent of jokes. Three-husband would flirt with two-wife, and becoming lecherous, would back up to run at her for an embrace, only to crash into two-husband while two-wife stepped aside into the embrace of one-husband while two-husband had to throw three-husband at one-wife to save his robe from the intended fate of the robe of two-wife. Everything they tried ended as a miscalculation but miraculously every disaster landed them on their feet or in some astonished rescuing arms. Their lovemaking was a breathtaking vortex of contortion. Sweet flirtations ended in mayhem: A sly husband ran off with Teenae, followed by three irate wives who tumbled over each other in pursuit, not quite catching him before he managed to kiss her . . . and so it went, to the audience's delight.

With the tumblers gone, men with casks moved among the crowd pouring a free sweet punch touched by the flavour of whisky while the Chanters began a light melody that pranced through the party almost unheard above the laughter. The sun was setting.

A Liethe woman slipped out of the Temple unnoticed, shifting in happy steps, dressed in a luminous sun orange and white with a bridal crown. Hers was the hesitant motion of a blithe woman unused to such happiness. She ran and stopped. She skipped. She leaped – and had the full attention of the audience who wondered where she had come from.

Her suppleness was the merry frolic of a girl recalling

moments with the husbands she loved, a blush, a touch, a tryst. She bounced in a way that made her audience gasp, as if she were free of gravity. Gradually, she moved out among the people, dancing for an awed child, or she would take an old man for a partner and prance with him until he was young again, or climb mischievously to the shoulder of an Ivieth. All the while, as the twilight deepened, she spread her magical cheer over the wedding guests. Then, at the very moment God appeared in the purple sky at the horizon, she vanished.

This was the first ascension of God in the week of the Reaper in the year of the Spider. Weddings were always timed to begin with God on high so that He might witness the ceremony. The crowd began to hush as God rose into His Darkening Sky. The Chanters became silent. A few stars peeked through the cobalt-blue vault of the heavens. A woman pointed out Stgi and Toe to her young son. The insects clicked and rustled even here in the middle of the town. A baby cried and was hushed. An old woman coughed. God moved, His Tiny Beacon brighter than any star. All eyes were on the Streak. Suddenly, at the very moment of highnode, the Wedding Chant resonated from fifty masks.

> And the God of the Sky;
> The God of Life;
> The God of Silence
> Brought us to a harsh land
> That we might discover
> Loyalty!

Fifty right hands which had been raised beside the masks came down and drew the sign of loyalty between the Chanters and God.

The seven Kaiel who were making Union were now in the centre of the plaza and dropped their eyes from God to themselves. They were silent, motionless.

> And the God of the Sky;
> The God of Life;
> The God of Silence
> Waits in the quiet blue
> For your seven signs
> of Loyalty!

Each of the maran, and the maran to be, raised their right hands, fashioning the gesture of loyalty that bound them to each other. Teenae's eyes flicked to Oelita and Oelita looked from Kathein to every maran in turn. Noe thought about loyalty and thought she was beginning to understand it. Joesai was thirsty and his coat was uncomfortable. Gaet admired the beauty of his women. Hoemei was at one with God, at peace with himself, and in love with his family. Kathein wondered if she would make a good wife this time.

The masks resonated again.

> And the God of the Sky;
> The God of Life;
> The God of Silence
> Who returned our lives
> Asks your witness
> to Loyalty!

The crowd, as one, raised their right hands and made the sign of loyalty in the air before their scarred faces.

The chanting took on a new timbre, a moaning ecstasy.

> Across the Swollen Tongue
> Canarie marched and fell
> Within the Cruel Ravine
> Beside the poison bush.

> Across the Swollen Tongue
> O'Danie marched and gave
> Within the Cruel Ravine
> A shoulder for this girl.

Across the Swollen Tongue
Mieli stumbled twice
Upon their dried embrace;
Cool water for such thirst.

Across the Swollen Tongue
Jon saw six blinded eyes
Beside an empty cliff
And took their hands in his.

Beyond the Swollen Tongue
Marish fed starving souls
Four meals of sacred food
And jug of water, too.

In plains beyond the Tongue
Hoeri built a hut
And nursed five spouses sick
Till they were well again.

Across the Swollen Tongue
The unwed men still fall
Within the Cruel Ravine
To leave their bleaching skulls.

The moral message on the virtues of a large marriage done, the chanting changed again to the Call of the Bonds. Each of the brides and grooms were given a coloured twine and they began their stately weaving dance that let each of them touch and smile and bow at each other and twist and turn and jump and duck in such a way that they braided the Cord of Seven Strands that was the legal evidence of their marriage. They smiled and teased each other as they went through the elaborate manoeuvres. No one was quite sure that they knew how to weave a Seven Cord. 'It better not unravel!' whispered Kathein to Oelita.

It had become dark enough for the newly installed electron torches to be switched on. The people of Sorrow, who were not used to such marvels, gasped when the yellowish light turned the plaza into a cloudy day and left all else in shadow.

Next came the giving of the five Gifts. The already married maran each had a token gift for their newly wed wives. Oelita was given a platinum ring, an ebony spoon, a tiny carved spice box, a golden pen, and a comb. Kathein received a tiny mirror so curved that it showed her a miniature of her whole face, an anklet chain, a polished fossil, a bone of her grandmother carved into an ikon by one of Sorrow's best artists, and sapphire earrings.

The brides returned these favours with food, grall for the men, a kind of hard pastry built up in alternate sacred and profane layers and cooked the night before the wedding, and honeycake for the wives.

Joesai was grinning as he eyed Oelita's grall offering sceptically. 'I remember you threatening to poison my grall if we ever married!'

Oelita blushed. 'You would remember that! How can you remember things like that at a time like this!'

The Temple was opened up for the wedding feast. In concession to Oelita there was no meat. At Noe's wedding the three brothers had served roast leg of criminal and for Teenae's wedding a whole roast baby. Meat wasn't really practical for such a large crowd. There were tables of salads and baked beans, cakes and breads, honeycomb and pastes, and some very strange but aromatic stews concocted by Nonoep almost totally from a profane base.

The central floor of Sorrow's Temple was cleared for dancing as a string quartet arrived to play for the dancers. There were formal reels for ten, squares for eight, tricates for six, intricate weaves for four, and fast-paced yabas for two.

Humility stood by herself thinking that she might be bold enough to take Hoemei for the next yaba, but a bright young Kaiel woman took him instead, so she asked

Joesai to dance, but he only laughed at the idea of them whirling together, and picked her up by the waist and set her on a ledge where she was tall enough to talk to him. She had never really become used to his size. She remembered riding into Soebo on his shoulders.

Oelita took Joesai away. She wanted to go into the tower and see the room from which she had escaped the Stgal. 'Come with us,' she urged, but Humility declined.

She watched Kathein from across the dance floor.

Then Gaet started to invite her to dance but three pretty women from Sorrow stole him away for the complicated weave. He was enjoying himself gluttonously.

She moved over to eavesdrop on Teenae who was with a group of her o'Tghalie clan, laughing. Teenae puzzled Humility, for she had no convenient place to put two-wife in the Liethe spectrum of women – perhaps because Teenae wasn't really Kaiel and she wasn't really o'Tghalie. She was having fun insulting her male relatives. No matter what they said, she topped them with a grin. They couldn't even make a crack with a hidden mathematical meaning without her catching it. They seemed to like her – though this was the family that had sold her to Gaet.

Humility wondered why she was so melancholy on this gay night. She decided to forget the maran and just enjoy herself. She found a young Kaiel who did a superb yaba, and then joined him later in the Red Canyon Reel. People noticed her dancing and called for her to do a solo and she obliged, but only because Hoemei was watching. Then she found her way back to the food and ate ravenously and disappeared into an unused game room where she stared at the boards. For a while she moved a Black Queen on an empty chess board, talking to it. Then she went to sleep. But even sleep did not please her, could not quiet her, and she wandered out of the Temple to find a place alone where she could watch the dawn come over the mountains. Noe found her there.

'I've been looking for you!'

Noe did not like her, she knew. What did a rescued temple courtesan have to complain about anyway? 'I'm having a chat with Getasun.'

Noe sat beside her on the stairs. 'I've decided I like you.'

'No, you don't.'

'It is with apologies that I remember my rudeness to you.'

'It doesn't matter.'

'I was watching my marriage disintegrate and I was upset,' explained Noe.

'Sometimes we are too close to something to see what is really happening,' said Humility. 'Who would let the maran break apart? We'd skin you alive and boil you in oil if you dared!'

'My marriage is precious to me,' continued Noe simply. 'It wasn't always. There was a time when I wanted out, and hated Joesai for bringing me back, knowing that he, of the three, liked me least. That was long ago. I was immature.'

'You have no fears from me.'

'I didn't mean it that way. I really think you are loyal to us. That's why I like you. Loyalty is the most important thing a person can ever find.'

'It is one of the importances.'

'Honey, I'm going to intrude on your privacy. Another of your names is Comfort, isn't it?'

Humility went into White Mind and smiled, pausing long enough to think out the consequences of any answer. 'Comfort is my sister. I have a hard enough time telling the difference between my sisters myself; how could you?'

'There are chemical ways. I am an accomplished biochemist.'

Humility did not believe such ways existed. How could se-Tufi clones be differentiated by chemistry?

503

Noe took Humility's arm and showed her a small scratch. 'I brushed against you when you were taking care of the children. Remember? Without your permission I infected you with the anti-toxin of Fosal's Disease out of curiosity. The Kaiel did not trust the Liethe anti-toxin and we brought the disease home from Soebo and made our own. *I* brought it home. Ours has fewer side-effects than the Liethe variety, but still you should have had some swelling and a rash. Nothing. You are immune. Why should a Liethe from Kaiel-hontokae be immune to a disease that never left Soebo?'

'I wouldn't know. I'm not a biochemist.'

'I was with you a week in Soebo.'

'You were with my se-Tufi sister.'

'All right. I won't insist. But you won't change my mind. Comfort, whoever she was, saved Joesai's life in her own strange way and I love that man. She was somehow in harmony with Hoemei for she did much to promote his predictions. Such manipulation weakened Aesoe considerably and made Hoemei ascendant. I think you helped us at the Palace. Did Aesoe ever suspect?'

'I am fond of your family,' said Humility, moved.

'Where are you staying?'

'My room at the inn.'

'Come with me.'

'No,' said the Liethe.

'I'm looking for Hoemei,' Noe tempted.

'All right.'

The wedding revelry was dispersing. Noe found her family in a tub in one of the tower rooms, scrubbing off their make-up. There was water all over the floor and they were splashing each other and shrieking. They were slightly drunk. 'There she is!' shouted Gaet. 'Get in the tub!'

'Not on your life!' said a grinning Noe.

'Get her in the tub!' Gaet ordered his family. A great

naked Joesai and a little naked Teenae began to chase her.

She retreated down the hall, pulling her Liethe se-Tufi with her, and bolted the door of an apartment she had taken for herself. She was laughing. 'I'm sitting this one out! I know what comes next! I've been to maran weddings before! I married those maniacs when there was only one of me!'

'Shall I give you your bath?'

'I'm a woman,' said Noe, surprised that a Liethe would offer to bathe a woman.

'You're a priest, too.'

Noe lit the fire for the hot water and sank down on the pillows. Humility began to undo her priest friend's elaborate hairdo. Noe stared at her in the mirror. 'What a wife you'd make!'

'Would you like another wife?' Humility asked mischievously.

'God forbid!'

'What is it like to be married?'

'Well now,' mused Noe, 'if you are a single wife with three husbands. . .' She went into reverie. 'They were always bringing home a new woman for the pillows on the excuse that they were looking to fill the empty wife slots. I think they had a great time. It made me sulk. How can you bring a new man home when you already have three of them? Now that the numbers are reversed with four of us and only three men, I think the situation will be interesting. How do you suppose the brothers will react when I bring home a nubile youth without a brain in his head and tell them so casually that he is a candidate for four-husband and don't bother me tonight while I try him out.' She laughed. 'I can't wait!'

'You're naughty!'

'I always was a spoiled brat.'

Noe tried to draw out the real woman in her Liethe but

found Honey opaque. She could talk music and art and dance, speak of philosophy, writings, politics, even science – but she was never personal. What kind of a childhood had she lived? She never said. She was as evasive verbally as she was quick on her feet. Noe decided to try a new tack against the same soft breeze. When the tub water was warm and Honey was bathing her with massaging hands she got her chance.

'Do you like my touch?' Humility was asking, while she gentled Noe's neck to relax it.

'I'd give anything to be able to do what you are doing right now,' said Noe. 'Then my husbands would never leave me.'

'It's a secret. I can't tell you. Then they'd never need to come see me.'

'Let me offer you a Kaiel bargain. Teach me how to be a Liethe and I'll make you an honorary maran wife.'

Honey hugged her briefly. 'If you are a spoiled brat, you'd hate it. You have to be able to sleep on a hard floor. One night in my cell at the hive and you'd quit.'

'And if I didn't?'

'Then I'd teach you more – like how to sit all day without moving a muscle either in tension or relaxation.'

'That sounds like a fair exchange for giving you Hoemei when he comes home from a hard day at the Palace!' Noe laughed. She splashed out of the tub and wouldn't let Honey towel her. 'Now it's your turn. Get in the tub and I'll scrub you!'

'No. I'll do it myself. You're a priest and I'm a priest's servant.'

'Don't be ridiculous! I scrub Teenae all the time. Here; right now we'll do the ritual of making you an honorary wife and get it over with. Quick. Desert style.' Abruptly Noe made the sign of loyalty.

Humility timidly returned the sign.

Noe took one of her small silver combs. 'Here.'

'I haven't any honeycake for you,' said Humility, bewildered.

'I smuggled up some honeycomb. That will have to do.' She rummaged around in a bag and brought out a sticky piece and gave it to her honorary wife. She opened her mouth. Humility put the fragment of honeycomb on Noe's tongue.

Noe then took a few strands of her hair and a few strands of Liethe hair. 'You have to help me braid them.' When they were finished she fixed the ends with bee's wax from her mouth. '*Now* get in the tub!'

Humility obeyed. 'Do you tease your husbands, too?'

'All the time.' She soaped Honey. 'I've fulfilled my part of the bargain. We're married. What do I have to do to become a Liethe?'

'First you have to have a secret name.'

Noe thought while she was busy with her friend's breasts. *Wanderer* popped into her head. 'I've got one. Shall I tell you?'

'No. Then it wouldn't be a secret.'

'You sound like Teenae! What fun are secrets if you can't share them!'

'Your secret name tells everything there is to know about you. It would give me too much power if I knew.'

'And you have a secret name?'

'Yes.'

'And you won't tell me?'

'Even my sisters don't know it. Even my favourite crones don't know it. To be a Liethe you have to have a *secret* name.'

'You're *all* secret. I don't know anything about you. Why were you so sad during the wedding?'

'Nothing. I was thinking about growing old.'

'What happens to a Liethe when she grows old?'

'She gets to raise the young ones.' Humility laughed and looked sidewise at Noe with her seducing glance. 'Young

507

children – like me.' Then she added soberly, 'The crones aren't any different from old men. They play politics and get the young ones to do their dirty work.'

Ah, thought Noe, *she really said something.* That was somehow so important that she dared not speak again. Noe waited, mutely, until Honey was dry before pulling down the iron-reed blinds so that they might have some darkness to sleep by. Wordlessly she lay herself on the pillows, anticipating something, not knowing what she was expecting. Honey dropped close beside her, but did not let their bodies touch.

'Are you happy?' asked Noe.

'Why shouldn't I be happy? It's my first wedding night,' replied Humility whimsically.

'Night? It's dawn.'

'What are they doing in the other room?'

Noe punched her. 'You know what they're doing! And we'd better get some sleep in case they decide to visit us!'

'They really wouldn't do that, would they?'

'You hope. I'll be generous and give you Hoemei,' she teased.

They fell silent. Noe slept. Humility did not want Noe to sleep and touched her shoulder and woke her. 'I was reading one of Oelita's books. I felt very close to her. I like her. I don't like to see people die either.'

Noe took her strange Liethe in a comforting embrace. 'Some of us make our Contribution to the Race through Death, and others of us make our Contribution to the Race through Life. That's the way it has always been. Now go to sleep, little one.'

A Dedication

Some Words for Bill Kingsley

Those of us who never left the home planet Earth are endlessly curious about those who did. What happened to them and why? But a student of galactic history suffers an embarrassment of silver in his black ore. There are too many clusters, too many stars, too many suns, too many worlds, too many outposts, too many peoples who drift in their ship abodes independent of planet or sun, too many conflicts and dynasties and discoveries.

Some historians try to master this dilemma by removing themselves to such a distance that the silver worlds of man's galactic heritage merge into the Milky Way of a single fine-grained photograph, no world distinguishable from the next in the general pattern. But then, how is that different from standing in the dark desert night of Earth to gaze at the awesome heavenly smear of the Milky Way in unsatisfied wonder and curiosity?

It was people who went out there. What do we see when we have a 'telescope' so powerful that the individual grains become worlds and men and women and conflicts? What is the micro-texture below the general rules of the rise of dynasty and the flow of trade and the vorticular forces of change? And so I have become more of a story-teller than a historian. But it is not easy to make sense of gossip that flows slower along the starlanes than tales of China moved into Europe on the old sailing vessels.

I've long had fascinating files of information on the worlds of the obscure Finger, that wisp of stars pointing across the Noir Gulf towards Sol from so far away in the Sagittarian direction that few Earthmen have ever heard the name. From time to time I've tried to put the pieces together in various ways, but who needs the noise of facts? It is a story I've always wanted.

The Finger Pointing Solward is a trivial peninsula reaching out from the edge of the Sagittarian Arm towards our own Orion Arm, a logical trade route across the great emptiness between Arms. At the tip of the finger shines Akira. Where did the Akirani come from? How did their empire creep out from the Akiran System to Butsudo and then to red Rokakubutsu and in time to distant Iwa Katsura? Beyond even Iwa Katsura lies Enclad. Who stood on the icefields of Enclad and decided to make it a world? Why are orphans loved by the black men of nearby Talatus? And who are the Getans who appear from nowhere and disappear again and never trust the men they meet?

Geta of Getasun, the world of this book, is not really one of the Finger's Worlds. It lies somewhere Centreward from the Finger in the Remeden Drift. Those who know of such things, know that the Getans, today, are no longer human though they are flesh and blood and, like the chimpanzee, share 98 per cent of our genes. This is not so strange in a galaxy where men have gone their own biological ways, but the Getans are extreme in their differences. They keep recurring in the history of the Finger Pointing Solward and information about them is scarce. The mystery around them made me curious.

Why did they choose their peculiar path? What were they like long ago when they were still human? For years I poked for an answer. The pieces were tortuous to come by. I got them. I remember trying to fit it all into a story. The best that came out was a dry documentary.

Artists go into rages at times like that. I stormed into the home of my friend Bill Kingsley and threw down the manuscript. 'What's wrong with it!' When Bill isn't playing handball with our heads, he makes a lot of sense. I was sulking. Well, facts are facts but it is how they relate that

510

is important. When Bill had finished directing my mind, some kind of miracle had happened inside. I wasn't on the Earth with my notes and theories. I was on Geta at a pivotal time in its past.

I had tough leggings around my feet to protect me from the poison feelers, Getasun was huge and orange and harsh, the desert air sucked water from my skin, a stationary moon stood near the horizon, half lit, half dark, and the city of Kaiel-hontokae was laid out along the mountain foothills. An insect was trying to colonize my ear.

You've just read the story I lived. There will be others. Thanks Bill!

Donald Kingsbury
The Earth; Galactic Standard Kiloday 980

Appendix

The Getan Calendar

The *Ennead Cycle* (approximately 22 Terran months) consists of the nine Getan years:

1–Maelot	2–Mantis	3–Hoiela
4–Glowsting	5–Moth	6–Spider
7–Bee	8–Skrei	9–Night Seer

plus the Day of the Joker, a leap day devoted to celebrating the foolish plans of the last nine years, such a leap day being necessary because a year consists of 140.111 Getan days. The Joker is a minor constellation leading, and overwhelmed by, the ten major constellations of the Getan ecliptic plane.

The *Getan Year* (about 75 Terran days in length) consists of ten weeks:

1–Skull   2–Reaper 3–Loser   4–Vixen   5–Knave
6–Amorists 7–Ogre   8–Winner 9–Boatster 10–Horse

named after the constellations of the ecliptic plane.

The *Getan Week* (approximately 7.5 Terran days) consists of 14 days:

> 7 high days (for activity),
> 7 low days (for sleeping).

The *Getan Day* (46,203 seconds, 12.83 Terran hours) is broken into:

> 7 Orbits of God,
> 245 sun-heights,
> 49,000 heartbeats.

The *Orbit* (110 Terran minutes) is the time from one high passage of God to the next, and is broken into 35 sun-heights.

The *Sun-height* (approximately three Terran minutes) is the time it takes Getasun to move across its diameter in the sky of Geta and consists of 200 heartbeats.

The *Heartbeat* (0.9429 seconds) is a heartbeat.